A Novel Based on a True Story

DEVIL

IN THE

BASEMENT

White Supremacy, Satanic Ritual
and My Family

CHARLOTTE LAWS

For information about this title or to order other books and/or electronic media, contact the publisher: Stroud House Publishing, Offices in New York and Anaheim, CA

StroudHousePublishing.com

Contact@StroudHousePublishing.com

ISBNs:

978-0-9961335-3-1 (print)

978-0-9961335-4-8 (eBooks)

Printed in the United States of America

Dedicated with love...

To the Moroose Family

&

To victims of racism, anti-Semitism, speciesism,
sexism, and other forms of prejudice

"Magical, artful, and unflinchingly tragic. A living, breathing dragon of terror and surprise. Devil in the Basement is a sassy and haunting thriller that pits a bipolar Hannibal Lecter against a Mr. Smith goes to Washington and proves once and for all that fact can be stranger than fiction—and way more creepy."

– Pamelyn Ferdin, actress and author of upcoming memoir, *A Good Little Trouper*

"A fascinating, unflinching and entertaining read... The story simmers and bubbles. You will not be able to put this book down!"

– Kelly Wilson, best-selling author of *Caskets from Costco*

"Riveting. Powerful. Fast-paced. Delectable. Best writing of the year."

– Every Way Woman Show

"Devil in the Basement will make you think twice about evil and satanic cults. I highly recommend it."

– Dr. Bruce Goldberg, best-selling author of *Past Lives, Future Lives*

"It will inform you, shock you, and shake you up.

Filled with historical detail, *Devil in the Basement* is a beautifully written account of racism, hate, and justice."

– Greg Mongrain, best-selling
author of *To Kill a Sorcerer*

"A page-turner with plenty of twists, spellbinding turns, and complex characters. *Devil in the Basement* is a stirring cauldron of pure delight."

– Sue Jones, Hollywood Report TV

"There is ingenuity and soul in every character. There is authenticity in every scene spanning the roaring twenties through post-World War II. *Devil in the Basement* is a soup of passion, history, rich language, and complex immigrant experience, nestled against the backdrop of the KKK, Hangman Forest, and a basement where a life-sized, satanic doll conspires with its human monster. This book, based on incredible true events, was kept hidden in police blotters and FBI dossiers until now. It is more than a story; it is an experience. Enjoy!"

– Rohan Chaubey, columnist, author
of *Make People Want You*

"Charlotte Laws has taken her family and through copious research turned lore into legend. I couldn't put it down."

– Diana Wagman, best-selling and award-winning
author of six novels, including *Spontaneous*

"Reminiscent of Steinbeck's writing and cleverly crafted. This book is a gem not to be missed."

– Paulette Mahurin, best-selling
author of *The Seven Year Dress*

"If genre-straddling were an Olympic competition, Devil in the Basement would take the gold. This impassioned and riveting book combines historical detail with full characters, rich language, a poetic rhythm, and a spine-chilling true story that culminates in bloodshed, explosives, and mayhem—all on a gray and memorable Wednesday in 1948. It brings attention to the plight of Italian-Americans in the early twentieth century. The "devil in the basement" is much more than a real-life Satanist doing dastardly deeds in the cellar. It reveals the prejudice that resided in some Southerner's hearts. Charlotte Laws' compelling story captures the racism, poverty, struggle, horror, and difficulty of the era for an entire class of citizens who were locked in the basement of society—namely those of Italian descent. Get ready for a wild ride! I highly recommend Devil in the Basement."

- Laurelee Blanchard, author of *Finding
Paradise: Leilani Farm Sanctuary of Maui*

Contents

Introduction. xi
Chapter 1: The Klansman with Fancy Shoes 1
Chapter 2: The Back Barn 19
Chapter 3: The Locked Basement Door 29
Chapter 4: A New Name and an Old Mine 45
Chapter 5: Mines of Disaster 57
Chapter 6: The Bearcat and the Flapper 67
Chapter 7: Bessie Ain't No Putty Head 83
Chapter 8: Two Weddings and a Snitch 93
Chapter 9: The Kewpie Doll 113
Chapter 10: The Mouthpiece and the Pharmacy Buff 123
Chapter 11: Eat, Drink, and Be Jealous. 135
Chapter 12: The Devil Comes to All Who Wait. 143
Chapter 13: Strike While the Iron is Hot 155
Chapter 14: The Asylum for the Criminally Insane 169
Chapter 15: Scaring Off that Old Crate of Seaweed 185
Chapter 16: Run, Nellie, Run. 197
Chapter 17: Longing for a Leg Up 207
Chapter 18: Fate and the Phone Call 221
Chapter 19: The Devil Gets His Due 235
Chapter 20: Bodies, Bombs and Drano. 251
Chapter 21: Cut Off My Legs and Call Me Shorty 263
Chapter 22: The Wilted Rose. 271
Chapter 23: The Devil Bird of Revenge 283
Chapter 24: A Lemon Pie in the Sky. 295
Afterword: The Aftermath. 303
Photos. 309
Appendix 1: Note on Fictional Characters 319
Appendix 11: Author Biography. 321
Appendix 111: Why the Nonfiction Novel. 323
Glossary 329

Introduction

T HIS STORY MIGHT be called the bee's knees, the goat's whiskers, the clam's garter, the gnat's elbows, or all the berries, at least in the flapper language of the time. During the 1920s through the 1940s—the generation discussed in this book—a person might be described as a dollface (cutie), Hitler's work (ugly), a dead hoofer (a bad dancer), a pantywaist (wimp), a cake-eater (a ladies' man), or a chowderhead (idiot). The language of the period is rich, flirty, fun, wacky, descriptive, and playful, all at the very same time.

This is a tale about two brothers who fight poverty and prejudice until one devastating Wednesday in 1948 when Satanism worms its way into their lives, meting out murder and mayhem and leaving one brother to fight for his dreams alone.

Newspaper reporters have called the crimes embedded within this story "the most shocking in the history of West Virginia." The bare-bone facts made headlines across the nation, but no one has ever researched the slew of scandalous, simmering, and heart-wrenching details until now—until this book. Having worked as a private eye and even with the FBI, I used my skills to track down anybody who had knowledge of the murders, satanic rituals, explosives, mobster dealings, romantic relationships, wife-beatings, and familial ties which make this book a roller coaster of ecstasy and tragedy, of thrill and anger, of humor and passion.

I chose this story for one simple reason: it is about *my family*—my birth family. I was raised in Atlanta, Georgia as an adopted child and only learned the true identities of my natural parents in my late twenties. I met my half-siblings five years ago and was given a shadowy sketch of the sordid tale that involved my grandfather (Tucker), my great uncle (Jal) and some of my Italian kin in Fairmont, West Virginia. I flew to the area twice and met with a slew of cousins, as well as other witnesses to the mind-boggling events of the past. I toured the location of the eerie rituals and observed bomb-blast residue that has not been repaired to this day. I was shown a murder weapon, satanic carvings, and photos of a creepy, life-sized doll that, in the mind of one man, conspired with him to carry out his heinous deeds.

This book is written in the style of the "nonfiction novel"[1] because I cannot possibly know all of the conversations and actions that took place some eighty years ago. For the most part, I stuck with facts as they relate to the crimes, main characters, and the bulk of scenes. However, in order to fit with the events in a more concise way, the details of some characters have been altered (i.e., in relation to ages, addresses, or dates when conversations took place). Plus, I invented a few

---

1 See Appendix III for an explanation of the "nonfiction novel" (or "creative nonfiction" as it is sometimes called).

people who I believe existed in some form, although there are no living witnesses to the fact.

I hope you will enjoy this story about my family—a family with which I am quite proud to be linked. I love these folks and grieve that I failed to meet my amazing grandfather before his death, as well as some of his siblings (such as the always-colorful Rose) and my hard-working great-grandmother, Margaret.

Feel free to kick off your ground-grippers (shoes), pour yourself a glass of giggle juice (alcohol), and enjoy the roller coaster that was my family's life. I think this story is the ant's pants. I hope you will agree.

Chapter 1

THE KLANSMAN WITH FANCY SHOES

IRONING WAS WOMEN'S work—except when it came to his Klan garb. Mr. Ray Clark called it his "armor," although most of his brothers called it their "glory suit." It was starched, crisp white, and folded with precision. It was his private treasure, wrapped in smooth brown paper and stashed in the rear of his closet. Mr. Clark was no coward. His Ku Klux Klan clothes had nothing to do with hiding. It was protection from the radical Republican liberals, Negroes, Italians, and do-gooders who might have made his job harder, made it tougher for him and his buddies to keep the streets free from mayhem, criminality, and sin.

It was 1928. The world was a battleground, and Mr. Clark was a soldier, a soldier of God. He took his job seriously, marching into the night to promote truth, purity, and justice. The state could not be trusted. It had been corrupted decades ago by Union fanatics and darkie lovers. It was up to him and those like him. Prayers and hymns could not penetrate evil. Action was required. He liked to say, "Jesus was the first Klansman." Mr. Clark and other members were simply obedient and humble disciples carrying forth God's word.

There was one battle Mr. Clark had joined without armor. It was eight years prior in Minnesota when he was working as a sleuth for the Minneapolis police department. He caught wind of a lynching tooling up in the nearby town of Duluth, so he made tracks over there in his street clothes.

Dark skin was a crime—both to Mr. Clark and to the ten thousand other toughs and troublemakers who had taken to the streets outside the local jail. It was a massive mob. Some carried ropes. Others clenched crowbars or hammers. But all seemed to be keen on getting revenge on the Negro circus workers who were being held as suspects for the purported rape of a white girl. It was "purported" because the doctor who had examined the girl did not think she had been ravished. Plus, other folks suspected she was a liar.

The vigilantes wore no masks, but for all practical purposes, they were invisible due to their impressive number. They equaled a full one-third of the local population. The on-duty cops hoped to arrest some of the instigators and plunderers, but saw only a sheet of nondescript white faces stark against the backdrop of the Minnesota sky.

Mr. Clark joined five other rabble-rousers in the back of a green Ford pickup truck. The group rode down Superior Street and through the business district, riling up the crowd.

"Let's hang the black niggers," Mr. Clark yelled to passers-by. "Join the necktie party." Folks in the street flashed smiles or raised their fists in a show of support. An elderly fellow in Mr. Clark's truck had a pistol from the army surplus, while a younger man placed a noose around his own neck and pretended to be choking in a display of theatrics.

Around ten p.m., bricks were hurled through the police station's windows. Sledgehammers destroyed the front door, and water from a fire hose gushed into the building, creating ankle-deep pools. Dozens of agitators stormed into the prisoner holding area to find the coloreds in their cells. Mr. Clark did his part by sawing at the twisted steel bars while teams of others used railway iron rams to pound at the enclosures. There were sounds of banging, chiseling, hooting, and cursing mixed in with the whimpering and pleading by the colored boys. It was a regular cacophony. The police were dreadfully undermanned and beside themselves with distress. They knew they could not fend off the irate crowd or get outside assistance (such as from the state militia) in time to save the Negroes' lives.

An hour later, angry white men gained access to the scared black prisoners. Two Negroes were dragged out to a lamppost at the corner of Second Avenue East and First Street, where they were taunted by the turbulent crowd. They were socked and kneed. Their jackets and shirts were ripped from their bodies and nooses were placed around their necks.

"The less you kick, the less you'll hurt," Mr. Clark hollered at one of them.

"Lynch him!" Another man bellowed. "To hell with the law!"

The first Negro was strung up and killed. Then, the second was raised up the pole. He went into dying convulsions to plaudits from the crowd. Mr. Clark and a few other men went back into police headquarters for a third Negro, who was then toted out to the same lamppost. A rope was placed around his neck and his body was lifted into the air. The man squirmed and twitched. Then he was still.

Although there were more black prisoners in the jail, many in the crowd felt satisfied with their "catch" and headed home. Mr. Clark had also gotten his fill and calculated that he should scoot along before the militia's arrival. He did not want to get clipped and figured if the vigilantes grew too small in number, he would need his Klan garb or a mask. At two-thirty a.m., 130 troops and officers arrived in Duluth to get the situation under control, but by this time, Mr. Clark was half-way back to Minneapolis. He moved to West Virginia six months later and read in the newspaper that only two vigilantes had been convicted of "inciting to riot." Each served a little over two years in jail, and nobody was arrested for murder. One Negro was imprisoned for the rape of the white girl. But, after serving a meager four years, the parole board released him, probably because they thought he was innocent. By that time, most everybody thought the Negroes were innocent—that is, except for Mr. Clark.

Mr. Clark's thoughts returned to 1928, but he was still in reminiscing mood. He ran the iron over his Klan garb, remembering a close call with it a few months prior when the washer lady was sniffing around in the back of his closet. Luckily, he was present, grabbing the partly opened package from her hands and referring to it as a bundle of dress shirts.

"Gotta have spares. What if you get sick and can't come around for a week? You know I'd make a downright mess of the laundering."

She believed him. After all, a lovely man like Mr. Clark,

who tipped her well and kept her dutifully employed despite the rough economy, could not possibly have a secret. He had always been open and friendly, generous and considerate. And she liked that he was a retired police detective. She was a firm believer in law and order, the need for rules. She never called him "Ray." In fact, no one did. He was "Mr. Clark" to friends, strangers, and even his sister. Formality was required in a world that had become all too lax and rash.

"A man's name's important," Mr. Clark said. "Sit up straight, clear your throat, and say it proud." People usually did as he asked; he had a commanding presence.

It was the day of the big march. Mr. Clark had prayed for this moment, and it had become God's will. In fact, he figured there was a good possibility that the Almighty had created him for this very purpose, to fight for Anglo-Saxon blood. Thousands of brothers were gearing up to crisscross West Virginia, Maryland, Virginia, and Washington, D.C. in rows of four or five across. They would emerge from the dark corners of justice to make their cause known. They would spread over streets and sidewalks, carrying flags and KKK banners. They would be in the daylight and in the newspaper, maybe even on the front page. It was an accomplishment, a downright accomplishment. Mr. Clark could not subdue his bloated pride.

He finished ironing and laid his armor carefully on the bed. It swallowed up the rest of the room with its weightiness. He spoke to his image in the mirror: "This is your big day," and then turned his attention to footwear. He would show off his best: the brown calfskin Oxfords. They had cost $4.80 from the shoe shop on Adams Street. He'd bought them on special and regularly got compliments when he wore them around town. He plucked them from the closet and ran his stubby fingers over the square toes, wooden heels, and heavy stitching. They were snappy and sharp. His face would be masked, but his ground-grippers would be styling and deliver a melodious clippety-clop on the pavement.

Mr. Clark glanced at his pocket watch, alarmed. It was time. He hurriedly donned his armor and shoes. He wouldn't be late for the march. He couldn't be late for the march. He was never one to disappoint God or the brotherhood. He was not that sort of man.

Fairmont is a small, eight square mile town tucked away in the north part of West Virginia, only ninety miles from Pittsburgh and two hundred miles from Washington, D.C. It is where the Tygart Valley River and the West Fork River join to form the Monongahela River. Adams Street, where Mr. Clark had bought his shoes, was the center of business. The county is called "Marion," and it is situated on one of the largest and most important coal beds in North America. Mining was the default occupation for poor immigrants in the region. The industry employed over one fifth of the area's workforce.

1928 was a time of change, upheaval, and industrialization. There was a tremendous influx of Italian immigrants into the area; most had come through Ellis Island. The stock market was about to crash, there was a nationwide ban on alcoholic beverages (the Prohibition), and Christianity was the centerpiece of folks' lives. In fact, religion was seen as the proper remedy for social ills.

On that particular day, if one squinted in exactly the right way from the hill next to Nickel Bridge, it looked as though a thick, white spray was fanning over Fairmont. It was as if a crop-dusting plane had dropped toxins onto this garden-variety small town. But it was not pesticide or fertilizer; it was an oncoming wall of people in white. It was the Ku Klux Klan. They were on a march through the region, and there were thousands of them. Some have estimated forty thousand. How could there be so many? Of course, four to five million U.S. citizens were bona fide members of the Klan at the time. During the march, some people wore masks. Others didn't. Some carried flags or signs. Others didn't. It was a spectacle and would no doubt leave a lasting impression on observers for decades to come.

Handsome, twenty-year-old Tucker Amoruso and his nine-year-old brother, Jal, were leaving the Adams Street barbershop when they heard the commotion and saw the approaching rows of robed zealots. Tucker opened his eyes wide, but quickly realized it was just another racist display, another example of the hatred of foreigners. As an Italian, he was used to narrow-mindedness and bigoted remarks. He had grown up in Fairmont, and racism was a staple of existence. He figured it was no different in other parts of the South. He remembered a student at college saying, "You should be grateful. You're better off than the Negroes." He hadn't responded, even though the fellow had been right. Italians were considered one notch better than coloreds. But it was only one miserable notch. Tucker preferred to keep his head down and his tongue still. Why rile up folks, he thought. But his younger brother, Jal, was a whole different breed.

"Who are they?" Jal pointed.

"It's a group called the Ku Klux Klan." Tucker pursed his lips, hoping there wouldn't be any more questions. But, of course, he knew better.

"What do they want?"

"They don't like Italians, so don't get near them. You hear?" Tucker regretted the words as soon as they left his mouth. He was well-aware of his brother's headstrong nature. A warning to stay away would have an equal and opposite reaction. It was Sir Isaac Newton's law.

Jal was a fire truck on the way to an emergency—high gear was his only gear. He wore his emotions in his fists and relied on them more than his winter cap. He was a scrapper and sported a grimace at school so as to look like a toughie. He had decked at least half the boys in his fourth-grade class. Of course, they deserved it for calling him names: "Dago," "Guido," and "Wop"—and for picking on the weakling kids. He did not like rotters. So, after Bobby K. pulled Nancy G.'s pigtails and called her a "pug-ugly nigger," Jal pushed him to the ground. Bobby K. broke his toe, and Jal was sent to the principal's office. It was the thirteenth time in two years.

"Thirteen demerits." Principal Madge made a clicking sound with her mouth and shook her head. But she never did anything beyond taking a paddle to his butt. It was more like a light tap. She was afraid of hurting him. Jal bided his time during disciplinary sessions, staring at the scuffed wall and letting out pretend grunts of distress.

Jal was always fighting, stealing dime store treats, cheating on tests, showing off his sassy mouth, or causing some sort of mischief. "He's only nine." "He'll outgrow this sort of thing." "He didn't really mean it." Grownups had their excuses for little Jal, but Tucker took the lack of discipline seriously. He was uneasy about his brother's future, concerned that he would end up in jail (as a "Jal-bird") or dead.

"If they don't like us then why are they here?" Jal asked.

Tucker hesitated, trying to come up with the perfect answer, but Jal had no patience and took off toward the Klansmen.

"Wait." Tucker threw up his arms and followed.

Jal reached the first marcher—a curly-headed fellow with a russet face—and snarled at him. But the marcher did not react, so he galloped alongside the stream of Klansmen, fists raised as if hankering for a brawl.

Suddenly, Jal stopped. He couldn't believe it. He had spotted them. They were right there in all their leather-bound glory: Mr. Clark's movie-star shoes. He had spied them many times at the dime store and in the barbershop. Although the former police detective's face was covered, Jal knew it was him. The shoes told no lies.

"You can't hide from me. I know it's you, Mr. Clark." Jal kicked a powder storm of dirt onto his perfectly polished shoes. Jal felt a tinge of regret after, but that was always the way with him. Act first and have qualms later—sometimes serious qualms.

Mr. Clark was steaming when he stepped out of line. He raised his arms like a monster and plunged toward Jal as if ready to strike. But instead of snatching the boy, he shouted, "Boo," all sinister-like.

Jal was scared and stumbled backward, almost falling. Mr. Clark crowed with delight.

Seconds later, Jal was grabbed from behind. He screamed and tried to run, but couldn't. Someone had overpowered him. Jal slowly turned, thinking a Klansman had nabbed him.

But it was only Tucker who held onto his arm and shirt collar. "Jal, we need to get home. It's time for dinner."

Jal, still shaken, sprinted toward the alley next to the pharmacy, which served as a shortcut home.

"I'd control that little brother of yours, Tucker," Mr. Clark warned before rejoining the march.

Tucker did not think much of the threat. Threats were all too common, especially from those cross with his mischief-making brother. The grocer had said he would call the cops if Jal didn't stop thieving from the store. Principal Madge had said Jal would be expelled if he got another demerit. The police chief had said someone would have to pay "fixin' costs" after Jal accidentally hurled a baseball through the window of the plastics factory. There had been lots of threats. Thankfully, no one had made good on them.

Tucker noticed folks hiding from the Klan. There was the kindly Negro girl who handled "sweeping up" at Frances' dress shop. She was peering through the storefront all nervous-like. There was the elderly Italian gent who played chess in the park. He was tucked away behind the sugar maple tree. But there were also folks who stood in the open, mesmerized by the gaudy demonstration, including two waitresses from the diner. One was quite plain-looking, and he recognized her as Matilda. But the other immediately caught his eye. She was a beauty, a hotsy-totsy with chestnut-colored hair and an aris-tocratic demeanor. He'd never seen her before. Had she just moved into town? Was she visiting? He knew most of the folks in Fairmont. It was rare to stumble across a newcomer.

Suddenly, Tucker heard a verbal flap, which caused him to glance up at the open second-story window above the station-ary shop. The ten-year-old Jackson girl was tussling with her mama and waving what was clearly KKK regalia out of the window. "Looky here, everybody."

Mrs. Jackson tried to grab the garb. "Give me that. Right now." She made a second pass. "You're gonna be spanked, young lady." Her daughter giggled.

Finally, Mrs. Jackson prevailed, snatching the robe and hiding it out of plain view. She was flustered when she noticed Tucker below on the sidewalk. "Hi there, Tucker."

"Nice to see you, Mrs. Jackson."

"Looking forward to buying some of your mother's fine cucumbers tomorrow."

Tucker smiled. "I'll let her know you're coming by." Mrs. Jackson closed the drapes.

Tucker was surprised to learn the Jacksons were Klan. He wouldn't have thought it. They were upstanding members of the community and they bought produce regularly from his family. On the other hand, Tucker had been around the pumpkin patch a time or two and knew folks could be all hugs on the outside and dark thoughts on the inside. Character was not like the nose on one's face; it could be shrouded in lies. There was one consolation to his thinking: Mrs. Jackson had felt shame. That's something, he thought. It's certainly worth more than two whittled sticks and a slap on the back.

Tucker glanced back to where the pretty waitress had been standing, but she was gone. He headed home. Although the marchers still poured through town, they began dwindling down to lines of two or three across and to rows that were roughly one hundred paces apart. Plus, they increasingly lacked regimentation. Those before them had appeared as a well-tuned squadron of troops, but these stragglers were more relaxed, more like a meandering stream, chatting among themselves with happy-go-lucky expressions. Most of their faces were exposed. Some carried their hoods, fed up with the tiny eye-holes.

Walking near the Klan ahead of Tucker was Carlo, an awkward thirteen-year-old Italian who took odd jobs around town. He delivered flowers, washed cars, mowed lawns, and did virtually any chore for a dime. He was a Fairmont fixture. Carlo was struggling to balance a bag chock-full of groceries. His mother had sent him on an errand to get fixings for dinner. Three Klansmen became captivated with a cookie tin poking out from Carlo's sack. They abandoned the march to confront the teen.

"What's your name, son?" one asked.

"Carlo Lorenzo di Francesco."

The men laughed. "Your parents are setting you up for the poorhouse with a name like that."

"Cookies aren't good for boys your age." One of the men snatched the cookie tin, which threw Carlo off balance, causing him to drop his sack. The contents scattered. "Don't be clumsy. Pick 'em up."

"Hey, let's help the little guido." The second Klansman reached for a bundle of bananas in the dirt.

"We're gonna get left," the third one said, and the three marchers scrambled back into the procession, taking the cookies with them.

Tucker bolted in Carlo's direction when he heard the badgering, but got there too late to confront the thieves.

"Let me get these for you." Tucker stuffed items back into the bag.

"Mother's gonna be mad."

"Where do you live?" Tucker asked.

"Warren Street."

"I'm going that way. I can explain to her if you like."

"Thank you, sir."

Carlo started down the road with his re-stuffed sack, but Tucker lingered behind, frozen and contemplative. He watched the thieves in the distance, bantering with each other and offering cookies to other marchers.

This was the moment of the epiphany. Tucker realized for the first time that he and his family were slaves—slaves to their background, to their Italianness. Prejudice was the devil in the basement. Tucker and those like him were trapped in that basement. The walls were moldy and the lock was rusty. Hope was a faint light under the door. Tucker knew he had to escape. He needed a plan.

"Are you coming, mister?" Carlo shouted.

Tucker set aside his thoughts and hurried to catch up with the boy.

Everyone called it the farmhouse, even though it looked more like a white barn. It had a crescent-shaped overhang above the door and was smack-dab in the most treacherous spot of all: at the apex of the fork in the road. This meant that, if a driver was barreling down the busy street and forgot to turn, he'd plow straight into the structure. Actually, he would smash through the wall of the boys' bedroom and, God forbid, kill a child or two.

Each night before bed, Jal, Tucker, and their brothers would recite the prayer, "Now I Lay Me Down to Sleep." And each night when they got to the line, "If I die before I wake, I pray the Lord my soul to take," they thought about only one thing: that fork in the road.

Tucker figured the farmhouse's location was a metaphor for the on-the-edge existence of the Amoruso family. They were always one meal away from hunger and their rent was always one excuse away from paid. The produce they grew in their backyard was their lifeline. They sold it to grocers through-out Marion County. Plus, they relied on it for the dinner table. When store-bought provisions such as bread and rice grew low, Tucker would rummage around in the yard and conjure up an armful of green tomatoes, almost-ripe squash, or some other kind of patchy but edible produce. Then the family would cheer, "Everything's Jake," a phrase that meant "Everything's fine."

Margaret was the beefy Italian matriarch of the family and she had nine children, including Tucker and Jal. There would have been eleven, but a set of twins died at birth. She was industrious. As a youngster, she worked twelve hours a day as a shepherd in the mountains of Campobasso, Italy, which is located southeast of Rome. Her maiden name was Pollutro. At fourteen, she'd married Nick, who was eleven years her senior. Poverty and lack of employment forced the couple to immigrate to America. They departed from Naples and arrived at Ellis Island on the ship "*Adriatic.*" The boat was filthy, and the trip was a disgusting experience. They immediately took a bus to West Virginia, a popular destination for Italians due to coal mining opportunities.

For years, Nick worked in the mines, or as he called them, "the bat holes of hell." Then one day he just keeled over from a heart attack. There was no warning, no indication that he would leave the earth during his heyday.

"Nick had such a warm heart that it went and exploded on him," Margaret said after the funeral. Folks whispered. Her words were too matter-of-fact for most people's taste, plus she had not shed the appropriate number of tears. She did not bend to the tradition of mourning for a full month without leaving the house. She needed to stay strong. She could not get all sentimental—she had chores to do. There was too much work to be done. It would have been bad for the children.

Jal ran all the way home without stopping following the spat with Mr. Clark over his shoes. Now he was on his knees, backward, on the plaid couch, looking out the front window at the KKK marching down the street.

"Where's Tucker?" Margaret shouted from the kitchen in her usual garb: a dark gray, high-collar dress. Then, she peeped into the living room. "Jal, answer me, boy."

"Downtown, Ma," Jal said without turning. "I think he'll show soon."

"Get away from that window."

Jal did not obey. Margaret knew he wouldn't, and she didn't

mind. But she did mind that Philip, her oldest child of twenty-four, was shaking the dirt from his shoes all over her freshly cleaned rug.

"Stop that, Philip. And why can't you get a shower before dinner? You always look like a scarecrow."

"You think it's easy working in the mines?"

Despite the constant volley of harsh words and the shared appetite for faultfinding, there was much love in the Amoruso household. Plus, Margaret was a hugger.

"A mother who doesn't nitpick... she doesn't care about her young'uns. Don't forget that, Philip."

"Yeah, Mom." Philip rolled his eyes. He'd heard this before. To his mind, it was a flabby excuse for carping, and she was always carping at him. When Philip didn't feel like a leper, he felt like a nuisance. He was the sigh of Margaret's life. He figured she was thinking, "Philip won't amount to a hill of beans." To his mind, she had given up on him. He was a flop, partly because he never had a nickel to his name. She had a different sigh for Jal, which said, "If he doesn't stop with this nonsense, I'm gonna whoop his behind." He was not a leper. There was still hope for Jal. Philip figured the "flesh and blood thing" accounted for the difference. Jal was Margaret's real son. He wasn't. He was only linked by marriage. Philip's real mother—Nick's first wife—had died giving birth to him.

"Make yourself useful, Philip. Get your brothers and sisters. Dinner's almost ready."

Philip grumbled and headed upstairs to fetch his siblings.

Moments later, Tucker arrived home. He was shaken to find the Klan on his very own street. "They're spreading thick all over town." He removed his overcoat.

"Like oil on a driveway." Margaret folded napkins into triangles. "Did you bolt the door?"

Tucker nodded as he noticed papers jutting out from the

roll top desk. He found an overdue rent notice, an angry letter about an unpaid bill, and other invoices.

"Mom, you haven't paid these? This one's three months old."

Margaret shrugged and disappeared into the kitchen. She never flinched over money troubles because what was the point? Being stone broke for years had left her with a stone face. Plus, she was an ace at dodgeball. When a bill arrived, she knew how to duck here or sidestep there. She could stall a creditor, get a bill cut, or—if all else failed—lean on Tucker to chip in. This is not to say that Margaret did not pay what she could. But, when the money ran dry, it ran dry. That was it. Only God himself could squeeze water out of a flask of dry sand.

"I could help with these," Tucker shouted into the kitchen. "I've got a little extra this month." He imagined his mom smiling on the inside if not on the outside.

Seven of Margaret's children scooted downstairs and took their usual spots at the dinner table. There was James; Mary; Betty; Louis; Robert; Philip; and the sexy, fourteen-year-old Rose, who wore a low-cut dress. Margaret appeared with stew and ladled it into bowls.

Jal was still on the couch, staring out the window. But this was not an innocent stare; nothing was ever innocent with Jal. He was doing his best to stir up the KKK marchers by making faces at them. He was stretching his cheeks with his fingers, contorting his face into grotesque shapes. Deep inside, he felt pressure. It was like a faucet turned to high. He had a hankering to give ugliness a jab, to belt narrowmindedness in the whiffer. There were too many pantywaists who never fought back, too many jugheads who allowed bad men like the Klan to loll around in the light of day. Jal fashioned himself as a boomerang—a boomerang for justice.

Suddenly, a Klansman glanced over. He locked eyes with

Jal and pointed his finger as if it was a loaded gun. Then, he mouthed "Bang." Jal's eyes widened and he felt scared. Sweat trickled down his neck and welled in the crease of his clavicle. He backed away from the window but was suddenly yanked from behind. He screamed: "Ahhhhhhh!"

"Get away from there. You're going to get yourself killed." Tucker was holding his shirt sleeve.

"Stop sneaking up behind me. I can take care of myself."

"Listen to your brother," Margaret said. "He's the man of the house now that your father's gone."

"Why is he the man of the house?" Philip griped. "I'm older than he is."

Jal and Tucker took seats at the table. Rose ate as if every bite was a sex act just to annoy her mom.

Jal was full of grim thoughts. He could not shake the image of "finger-gun" man. Would he burst in? Would he have a real pistol? Would he bring his friends?

"Aren't you going to eat, son?"

Jal slowly raised his spoon to his mouth. He knew it was just a matter of minutes. He was sure he was done for. His whole family was done for. He stared at the brass door knob.

Chapter 2

THE BACK BARN

THE KLANSMAN NEVER showed, not at dinner and not during the wee hours of the night. Jal had lain awake for hours atop his bunk bed, listening to every dog howl, every car on the main roadway, and every eastern screech owl's "Whoo." He had been sure the man in ghastly white would hover over his bed with an insidious smile and a cocked double-barreled shotgun. But he was wrong. He never came. And when the morning sunlight hit Jal's face, he felt relief. It was like stepping out of a bathtub and feeling new. He could stop holding his breath.

Now, it was time to partake in some "well thinking." Jal liked to do this before breakfast. "Well" was his word for "deep." He used a pretend bucket to pump insights from his tummy and bring them up to his brain. Even though most people thought he was rash, he knew he was a bit of a thinker. He was not one to shuffle his thoughts aside. He closed his eyes. He wondered why he couldn't stop himself from bad behavior, from upsetting the grownups. He could not figure it out. He was sorry for trying to rile up the Klan and made a vow in his head: he would try to be more restrained like his mom and Tucker wanted. Next time he had angry thoughts, he would pretend there was a rope around his body, holding him back.

Jal hopped out of bed, landing on the hollow-sounding floorboards, and put on his overalls. But he was not done with his "well thinking." He thought about the thick black shadow inside of him. It would step out and do wicked things. There were so many times when Jal had tried with all his might to stop that shadow, but he had always failed. He would try again. He would try really hard. Plus, now he had a rope—a strong rope. Go away black shadow, he said to himself over and over as he ran downstairs.

There was no breakfast on the table. In fact, the kitchen was empty. He screamed "Ma!" at the top of his lungs, but no one answered. Then he yelled, "Tucker." Again, nothing. He looked in the yard but saw no one except the usual field hands. Where was everybody? Maybe his mother was in her secret place. Although this was hush-hush as far as Tucker and Jal's other siblings were concerned, it was not secret to him. This was because, two weeks earlier, he had been spying on his mom. He liked to spy on folks, pretending he worked for the Confederacy like Jack from the movie *Hands Up!* Jal had seen his mom sneak into the weathered old barn at the back of the property. He had crept closer and closer, eventually finding her surrounded by all sorts of copper and metal contraptions. She was stirring liquid in an old barrel. When she noticed him, she looked startled and made him promise to keep his mouth shut.

"Jal, you are not to tell anybody you saw me here."

"Why, Ma?"

"Because it's a surprise."

"A surprise?"

"Yep, like when you get new shoes on your birthday. You don't want to ruin the surprise."

"What are you stirring?"

"Lemonade. Very special lemonade, and if you tell anyone, you'll ruin the surprise."

Jal liked that he was the only one who knew about the secret. It made him feel special. He hadn't told a soul. When it came to ratting on folks, he had his black shadow under control.

But now Jal was alone in the house, and he suddenly felt scared. He knew his mom and siblings would not leave him unattended, and he remembered the Klansman. *Did the man with the "finger gun" kidnap my family?* He prayed everybody was in the secret place as he ran out the back door along the dry mud path toward the old barn. When he got to the structure, he peeked through a gap in the broken slats and immediately felt relief. Everyone was inside. But, at the same time, Jal was sad because the secret was out. Everybody knew about the lemonade. With his ear against the opening, he could hear Tucker yelling at Margaret.

"You're gonna get us arrested!"

Something was wrong. Tucker was mad, and he was hardly ever like that. Curious, Jal tugged open the heavy barn door and stood there in all his four-foot glory. Tucker stopped yelling and everyone turned and stared silently at little Jal.

After a beat, Margaret spoke in a sweet-sounding tone. "Jal, we need to get you some breakfast... Tucker, why don't you get him something to eat?"

"We're having a conversation." Tucker was annoyed.

"We can talk about this later," Margaret said. "Jal needs to get something in his stomach. I'm sure it's growling up a storm."

"Are you upset about the lemonade, Tucker?" Jal asked.

"Lemonade? What lemon…"

Margaret interrupted, "Mary, could you get Jal some breakfast?"

"Why can't I stay? It's not fair," Jal complained, as eighteen-year-old Mary led Jal to the house.

After Jal and Mary were gone, Tucker laid into Margaret. "Did you hear about the man from Morgantown? For Chrissakes, the Bureau pinched him."

"Oh, that's just neighborhood gossip. Plus, even if it's true, he wasn't the discreet type."

"You shouldn't be doing anything that requires discretion," Tucker yelled.

"I'm completely against discretion." Rose giggled.

"I'm starting law school soon. My mother can't be moonshining."

"See you later, Al Capone," Philip chuckled. "I'm getting some grub." He headed toward the house and everyone followed except Tucker and Margaret.

"Dad wouldn't have gone for this."

"Don't talk to me about your father. You know good and well we can't pay our bills. How are we supposed to get by?"

"We've always gotten by."

"This is real fine stuff. Not rotgut. I can get twelve dollars a gallon. I think the flatfoots will be customers."

"Are you nuts?"

"Most of them are probably alcoholics." Margaret poured sugar into a glass jar. "The Barney brothers have a first-rate network."

"I don't want to know about this."

"Oh, don't be a sack of sauerkraut."

"I'm staying on the up and up. And if the Bureau comes sniffing around, don't come crying. I won't be left holding the bag." Tucker shook his head and retired to the house for breakfast.

Margaret had no respect for the Volstead Act, the 1920 law that made the country "dry," and she was determined to profit from it. The Barney brothers who worked at the automotive shop on Ogden Avenue had helped her gather together the necessary tools, including the flake stand, thumper, copper still, and stir stick. They were only taking a twenty percent cut as her equipment suppliers and promoters. Plus, Margaret had all the ingredients: corn, prunes, whole rye, raisins, sugar, yeast, and apricots. The process involved putting everything into a fifty-gallon vinegar barrel, which was maintained at eighty degrees until fermentation. Then she drained the juice from the mash into a copper cooking still and heated it on a kerosene stove until it hit the evaporation point. In the end, Margaret would have 100-proof whiskey and gallons of clear alcohol.

There were thirty thousand speakeasies in the U.S. at the time, and lots of folks operated them out of their homes. Margaret knew there was high demand. Some rummies went on a toot for weeks and relied on booze from three or four stills just to keep them supplied. Margaret was not uptight about the coppers because she knew they would take a "granny fee" to keep quiet. The Barney brothers had told her so. They'd also said most would be paying customers. The lion's share got drunk on the clock.

But it was not just about extra income for Margaret. She had other reasons for starting her juice joint. Years prior, when she was a youngster in Italy, she had wanted to be an activist, to fight for a worthy cause. Some of her friends joined the nationalist movement, but not her. She had to survive, working twelve hours a day with a sore back, herding sheep and goats. Then she married Nick and her activist dreams were postponed due to their escalating debt and obedience to the

Genesis phrase, "Be fruitful and multiply." If children were a blessing, the couple was saddled with an overdose of blessings. One child came after another after another. But now it was 1928, and it was Margaret's time. It was time to join the anti-Prohibitionists. She would not be giving birth to any more young'uns and figured her makeshift "still house" could be the drop that makes the cup runneth over, knocking some sense into those federal lawmakers. She figured if the fuzz was to nab her, she would go kicking and screaming. Her caterwauling would reverberate from one West Virginia state line to the other like a raucous cow bell.

One might wonder why Margaret didn't focus her spare energy on something more important, like fighting the Klan. Clearly, the anti-temperance movement was a less urgent cause. Margaret had two reasons. First, fighting prejudice never occurred to her. It was on Margaret's radar, but only in an internalized way. It was buried deep in customs and language and thus was practically invisible. Margaret and many of the dark-skinned residents of Fairmont had been victimized for so long that they could not conceive of a different world. And, if the truth be told, Margaret was not even an advocate for one. This was her second reason.

Although she kept it quiet, Margaret agreed with the basic teachings of the KKK, despite disapproving of their intimidation tactics and periodic violence. She liked the orderliness of a hierarchical society, with Italians having status above coloreds and below whites. The system was easy to understand, and it was all she had ever known. She held unflattering views about women as well. She had been taught that they were lesser than men. For example, this was clear in the Bible, and she considered herself a good Catholic. She knew Timothy 2:11 by heart: "Let a woman learn quietly with all submissiveness. I do not permit a woman to teach or to exercise authority over a man; rather, she is to remain quiet." She had also memorized Colossians 3:18: "Wives, submit to your husbands, as is fitting in the Lord."

At times, Margaret's conflicting views made her feel like two separate people or like a train with two engine cars. She wanted to be active yet submissive. She wanted to fight for one cause but keep her trap shut about others. The bottom line was that Margaret was complicated.

"Ahhhhhhh!"

Margaret heard Mary scream and dashed out of the barn, running around the side of the farmhouse. In the front yard, she found all nine of her children staring at their bicycles. Only, they no longer looked like bicycles. They looked like chickens—Rhode Island Reds, to be exact. A black sticky substance had been spread all over the frames, handlebars, tires, and pedals, which had then been covered with a slew of reddish-brown feathers.

"Somebody tarred and feathered them," Mary said.

"Well, I told you children a hundred times… don't leave them out at night." Margaret folded her arms. "I'm not paying for new ones."

"Mischief-making kids coming around here like this." Philip shook his head.

"Or the Klan." Tucker shot an "I-told-you-so" in Jal's direction but mercifully did not rat him out.

Jal felt bad. He figured the bike-wrecking scoundrel was either Mr. Clark or the "finger-gun" goon. He aimed to atone for his sins.

"Don't worry, Ma." Jal plucked a feather from the sticky substance. "I'll make them all clean again."

Tucker began each morning in the same way: loading fruits,

vegetables, and flowers onto the running board of his Model T Ford while his siblings ate a hearty breakfast. In addition to "homegrowns," the family relied on packaged foods, such as Log Cabin Syrup, Grape-Nuts, Snowdrift Vegetable Shortening, Rumford Baking Powder, Nestlé's Milk Food, Dromedary Coconut, and Faust Instant Coffee. The Amoruso field hands, who came at six a.m. and left at noon, had limited duties because the family had limited funds. Their job was to till the land, pick the produce, and ready it for Tucker, so he could haul it into town for the grocer. Some days, there was tremendous output. On others, there was only enough to fill a couple of wooden crates.

The Amoruso backyard was home to a variety of fruits: apples, cherries, plums, melons, raspberries, figs, and peaches. There were also flowers: zinnia, pansies, geraniums, scarlet sage, and marigolds. As far as vegetables went, there were shelling beans, pumpkins, beets, radishes, squash, broccoli, carrots, cucumbers, celery, eggplant, spinach, garlic, potatoes, lettuce, and tomatoes. It was a regular cornucopia. Acorn squash was the biggest seller because it was a newly-introduced vegetable that required minimal fuss for the customer but melted onto their tongues with maximum flavor. Plus, it looked right pretty on the plate.

Margaret was no longer gawking at bicycles or in the back barn heading up what Tucker called her "criminal enterprise." She was baking bread in an outdoor oven, wearing a boater and arm stockings. A boater was a man's summer straw hat, and she kept hers in place with hairpins. The arm stockings were simply hose wrapped around her arms to prevent sunburn. Without protection, Margaret was a candidate for getting burned and blistered, and this would invariably lead to swelling, which doctors said could someday cause skin disease.

Margaret had a second reason for staying away from the

sun: she did not want her skin to darken. She did not mind looking Italian, but she did not want to look like a Negro. Regular exposure to the sun turned her the color of licorice. It was all about social status. Throughout the ages, light skin had been equated with class and aristocracy. It is true that things had recently changed. Since 1920, tanning had become a popular pastime. A magazine even featured French fashion designer Coco Channel bronzing herself on the Duke of Westminster's yacht during a cruise to Cannes. But Margaret paid this no mind. She was old-fashioned, and she rarely ceded to the latest trend, even when it involved a noted Sheba. She preferred to look Italian—not too dark and not too light—remaining solidly in the middle of society's yard stick.

"Mrs. Jackson's coming by for cucumbers today," Tucker hollered.

"Okay. Hold out a few extra."

Tucker plucked some produce from the crate and placed them on the back porch as James, Louis, and Rose stumbled out the door, laughing and being silly. Margaret was irritated because, with the exception of Tucker, her children always seemed to be fooling around rather than making themselves useful.

"Why don't you help your brother?"

"We can't," Rose replied. "We're going downtown. I'm introducing James and Louis to my new boyfriend. I'm gonna marry him."

"You're too young for a boyfriend, and you're not marrying anyone at fourteen."

Rose headed down the road with her brothers.

Margaret yelled after them, "Don't stay for long. If you're late for school, you're gonna get a whooping." She turned to Tucker. "You'd better hurry. We need to have everything at the store by eight."

After Tucker finished loading the goods, he donned his jacket and drove down the street and around the corner past a dilapidated house on a slight hill. This was the home of the twenty-six-year-old Ernie Yost, who was in his front yard. He was chiseling letters into his stone steps. Tucker stared straight ahead so as to keep his eyes on the road. He had no reason to look to the right at Ernie. Heck, he wouldn't have known him from any other stranger. But what Tucker did not reflect upon on that sunny morning was the unpredictability of fate and how it can turn a stranger into a close friend or even a mortal enemy. There was an amazing, unexpected, even shocking future waiting for Tucker and Ernie. The stars knew these two men would become intertwined. They would make history together. They would make the newspapers and be on the lips of generations to come. But on that particular day, they were separate. They were so separate that they had almost nothing in common.

Even though Ernie did not look up from his chiseling, he heard Tucker's car drive by and fade into the sound of the wind. Of course, he'd heard lots of cars that morning. He hadn't glanced up because he was immersed in his work. Some might say Ernie was making a mess of the stone steps, which had dazzling variations of color and a pleasingly rugged surface. His lettering made them look cheap and tacky. It was as if he was planting a "Saginaw Truck Equipment" sign in a rose garden or pouring urine into a crystal wine glass. But Ernie did not see it that way. He did not care about appearances. He cared about message, and he was pleased because the job was mostly complete. He stood back and stared at his work. He felt proud.

The chiseled words read: Hell's Half Acre.

Chapter 3

THE LOCKED BASEMENT DOOR

ERNIE WAS SOCIALLY invisible. He kept to himself, had few friends, and raised no eyebrows. Plus, he was an average-looking fellow of average height, who wore the most average type of 1928 duds. He had just one good suit: brown tweed with wide peak lapels and cuff bottoms. Although Ernie did not stand out in a crowd, he stood out to himself, and he liked being different. He had a beef with Christianity. Boy, was it a beef. He'd turn into a red-tailed scorpion when anyone mentioned the word. To him, the Christian faith was more than a bunch of hooey. It was an indoctrination hammer that turned his neighbors—the weasels of Fairmont—into a bunch of two-cent dummies. The preacher set the trance in motion, and the congregation swayed to the phony tune as if they were blotto.

After Tucker's car was out of sight, Ernie lit a cigarette. Lucky Strike was his favorite brand. The company's ad called them "toasted," and Ernie agreed. They were soothing like a winter fire. Ernie took a puff and stared at his masterpiece, the carving on the steps. His wife, Bessie, was fifty yards away, sweeping the front porch. She was paying no attention to Ernie or his chisel work—she knew better. She'd stopped asking years ago. She knew asking was risky. She was not the type to take a wooden nickel. Bessie was agreeable-looking, with soft brown curls and camel-colored eyes. She wore only cotton house dresses peppered with half-inch flowers.

Ernie's neighbor, Will Kleeman, came out of his house and saw the Yosts.

"Hey, it's the always-charming Bessie." Will waved and Bessie gave him a friendly "Hi-de-ho" back. Then, Will headed over to Ernie.

"What ya doing?" He read the carved words and laughed. "Hells Half Acre? You deeding the property to the devil?"

"Something like that." Ernie chuckled, flicking ciggy ashes to the ground.

"I always thought you were crazy." Will moseyed over to his car and drove off.

Ernie went into the house to see that Bessie had set down the broom and was tending to the couple's two infant daughters.

"You better get to work. You're gonna be late."

"Don't tell me what to do," Ernie barked.

Why was he in a bad mood? She had done nothing wrong. Despite her better judgment, she pressed on. "Ernie, I need some money so I can get my hair done."

She expected a flare-up, but there was none. Ernie did not explode. He calmly removed the special key from his trouser pocket. This was the key that unlocked the basement door. This was the key that Bessie was not allowed to touch. This was the key to his secret place, where he could do secret things, such as guzzling down his moonshine without being nagged by his wife.

As Ernie unlocked the basement door, Bessie figured it was safe to push a little harder. "What in heaven's name do you do in that basement? You don't need to keep the door locked. I would never go down there." The children began to cry.

"Tell your babies to shut up," Ernie said.

"They're your babies too."

Ernie descended downstairs, locking the door behind him.

"Wait... what about the money?"

Tucker arrived at the Great Atlantic & Pacific Tea Company, the main Fairmont grocery store. It was a "hole in the wall" with black, hand-written signage in the window: "Flour - $2.55 per sack," "White barley - $1.85," and "Catsup - 98 cents." Inside, there was a "Wonder Bread" sign, a potbelly stove, and a porcelain Toledo scale. Canned goods were lined up on shelves behind the counter. Tucker passed off a crate of produce to Jimmy Dee, an aproned clerk and the store's part-owner, who stood behind a pre-World War I, cast-metal cash register. Abe, another employee, sat on a wooden bench, looking drained.

"What are you doing sitting so early in the morning?" Tucker joked to Abe.

"Just resting my dogs." He laughed. "Guess I'm getting on in years."

"Aw shucks. I'd call you a spring chicken if it were spring."

Abe chuckled and roused himself. He headed for Tucker's

car to help with crate-toting. All of the produce made it into the store unscathed.

After Tucker finished his delivery and secured the payment envelope for his mom, he headed over to Fairmont State University, where he was wrapping up his bachelor's degree. Although he might have been accepted for a scholarship at Harvard Law School or at one of the other Ivy League schools, he had not applied. He needed to stay in the area. New England was too far. He could not desert his family. Margaret and his siblings depended on him. The crops would not get tended on their own. Plus, little Jal needed a firm hand, which only he could provide. So Tucker had filled out a last-minute application for West Virginia University College of Law, which was only a thirty-four minute car ride from his home. The school administrators had thankfully agreed to let him in, even though his paperwork was turned in a day after the admittance deadline.

Tucker was keen on becoming a lawyer. The idea was oxygen to him. But it would be more than liberation from poverty; it would be meaningful work. Tucker planned to be a generalist, taking on a broad range of cases with one common thread: they would all be vital in some way. That was the word: vital. The cases would be pivotal, necessary, or reveal some critical truth.

Tucker was the first Amoruso to go to college, and he would be the first to become a courtroom advocate or a "mouthpiece," as it was commonly called. Not many (or maybe any) Italians from the area had such "big cheese" aspirations. When he told folks from the community about his lawyering plans, he got baffled looks and grimaces. He imagined most believed that "good-for-nothing guidos" were only suited to be laborers, miners, bindle punks, or even gangsters like Lucky Luciano and the Genovese crime family of New York.

With books in tow, Tucker rushed into his Fairmont State

University Speech class, where two dozen students were waiting for the lesson to begin. He sat down in his usual spot next to his friend, George Rider, who whispered to him.

"Horsefeathers. I was hoping you'd be late so the doll would show me her legs. She never gives me the time of day."

George was referring to the teacher, Miss Dolly, who clearly had a crush on Tucker. She was twenty years his senior and so large in the brassiere that Tucker liked to say she was in the "sweater-stretching business." This was behind her back, of course, and only to George. Miss Dolly also wore short skirts, which Tucker called "loincloths." He'd say, "I like her purple loincloth," or "Poor Tarzan. He must be walking around in his birthday suit."

Miss Dolly sauntered over to Tucker and placed his graded exam on his desk. It was adorned with a big red A-plus. Then she spoke in her usual breathless way: "You did a swell job."

Tucker and George kept a straight face until she turned toward the chalkboard. Then they snickered like naughty boys. Tucker never felt so immature and free-spirited as he did in speech class with George. He could be roguish and juvenile. He could act like his brother, Jal.

Miss Dolly opened her book, but she was not quite ready to begin. She seemed to crave a little more attention from the Italian he-man on the front row. She mouthed to Tucker, "I like your jacket."

Tucker was embarrassed, but smiled politely. George gave him a playful kick in the shin.

The sign read, "Monongah Coal Mine." It was located in Marion County, only five miles from Fairmont, and it was the site of the worst mining disaster in U.S. history. This occurred on December 6, 1907, when Ernie was six years old. Many men, horses, mules, and boys died in underground explosions on that day.

In 1917, when Ernie was sixteen, he took a job as a slate picker at that very mine, but in 1921, he left the post to become an upholsterer. When "sofa stuffing" failed to rustle up a steady paycheck, he returned to mining. This time he worked at the shaft mine of the Consolidation Coal Company. He liked to say, "I'm appreciated here," which was an odd statement since most miners regarded breathing coal dust as a lousy way to survive. They also felt controlled by their bosses, who paid them partially in scrip rather than money, strong-armed them into buying goods at inflated prices from the company store, and required them to lease mining tools and other equipment. Plus, most workers lived in ramshackle company housing. This caused the vast majority to be "coal and coke," which meant they were virtually penniless. The mining site was like a small town with its own rules and language. There was a "coal-home," which was a cell where the sozzled were dumped until they could sober up, and there was the "coal scuttle," which was a punishment cell. The company store was stocked with clothing, groceries, furniture, and even coal extraction tools, and it was the social center of the community. People met there to play checkers or to shoot the breeze.

Ernie was peculiar in that he did not live hand-to-mouth, and he refused the company-owned housing. He had inherited a home from his parents—the one with the stone steps—and it was free of obligation. He was not cloth-headed. He had caginess and bargaining skills. He refused to accept scrip, taking only cash payments for his work. Plus, he owned excavating tools, which kept him free from leasing costs, and he never bought a darn thing from the company store. He got away with bucking the system for only one reason: because he was a capable man. In fact, he had heaps and heaps of talent. His shift bosses often said, "Ernie knows his onions," a compliment that made the other miners jealous. Ernie had the endurance and hardiness of a bull; plus, he could fix just about anything. When the crusher, ball mill, or some other contraption broke, Ernie got it running in a jiffy. He had that sort of mind.

Throughout the 1920s, the number of coal miners in the U.S. declined. Workers were cut right, left, and Sunday due to coal overproduction and inroads made by the oil industry. But Ernie never feared losing his job. He was indispensable, and he knew it.

While Tucker was in class with George and Miss Dolly, Ernie was having a smoke just outside the mine's manway where off-duty workers were milling about and chewing the fat. The shift boss, Sam Perkins, was checking out a detached anemometer, a tool that measures the amount of air entering and leaving the mine. A new hire ran up to him.

"Boss, we got a problem with the conveyer belt."

"We got a rule around here. Ask Yost." Sam did a visual sweep of the area and noticed Ernie fifty yards to his right with a Lucky Strike in his mouth. He called out, "Hey, Yost. I know you're on break, but get over here." Ernie approached.

"We need your help. It's the belt again."

"I've got ten more minutes."

"Do it now. Don't worry. I'm gonna retire one of these days, and you're gonna be in charge."

Ernie did not believe he would ever get propped up to boss man, but nonetheless, he always complied with orders. This was because it made him feel top-drawer and because it was his job. He threw his cigarette into the dirt and rubbed it out with the toe of his shoe. Then, he followed the new hire. One hour later, Ernie had fixed the conveyer belt as well as the wheel on the coal cart, which had also gone on the blink.

At the end of the day, he was paid in cash, as usual. Rather than head home to Bessie, he had to complete an unusual errand. Actually, it was a good deal more than unusual. It was important, and it had to be done in a covert way. He had to fetch a very special package. He could not breathe a word about it; folks would not understand. If they learned the truth, they would get all high-hat and preachy on him. He was especially careful as he drove to the ragtag neighborhood where the package was, periodically checking his rearview mirror to make sure he was not being tailed.

Ernie parked his car adjacent to a shed on a weed-filled slab of land. Then, he went to the front door and knocked. Otis Jones, a man who looked like a circus freak, peeped out through a crack in the door. When he saw Ernie, he opened the door six more inches and scanned the street to make sure no one was watching.

"Got it?" Ernie fanned out his payday cash.

Otis was not much of a talker. Plus, he was a snaggletooth, and his pearly whites bordered on yellowish-brown. He slid a mysterious brown bag into Ernie's hand and grabbed the dough. "I'll have more next month." He shut the door.

Ernie took a look inside the sack to see two pamphlets: *On the Writings of the Insane* by G. Mackenzie Bacon and *The Gospel of Satan*, which was, according to legend, resistant to fire. Ernie smiled. He had "ridden the goat." In other words, his purchase had made him a part of a secret and elite society. He threw forward his chest. He felt proud and knew things would be different from now on.

Ernie climbed back into his car and headed to his second destination. It was also a secret, but only from Bessie. He was visiting a young lady he had met in the multi-purpose room at the miners' music hall. Her name was Nellie, and she had been on the piano that night. She played real pretty. Her fingers were like tulip petals, and he had immediately become impressed. She was the cat's meow. He loved her silken bangs, full bottom lip, and the freshness in her wide brown eyes. He had not mentioned his marriage, and she had given out her street address. Nellie was only eighteen, whereas Bessie was twenty-seven. Nellie was single with no young'uns, whereas Bessie was always lugging around a screaming tot. Nellie was naïve, whereas Bessie was too smart for Ernie's liking.

Ernie did not have any firm plans to stray from Bessie. He was not set on making Nellie his honey pie. This was just a cordial and innocent visit. At least, that's what he told himself. He was bringing her a present as a friendly gesture. That was all.

Ernie turned onto Nellie's street, where there were rows of Sears Plan Book houses. It was a middle-class neighborhood, and Nellie lived with her mama and daddy. He found number "1842." It was a thin home with six front steps, a porch, a deep-pitched roof, and an upstairs balcony. Ernie grabbed the gift, which had been resting on the passenger seat, and headed for the front door. On his way, he took mail from the letter box. He knocked, hiding the gift and the correspondence behind his back.

Nellie answered with a coy smile. "Oh. Hi. I remember you."

"Ernie. Ernie's the name."

"Well, hello. Ernie."

He produced the letters from behind his back and handed them to her. "I brought up your mail."

"Well, that's awfully considerate."

"And I've got something else." Ernie revealed the present, which she promptly opened.

"It's a lid for your butter churn. I carved it myself. I'm pretty good at that sort of thing."

She examined it with admiration. "You sure are handy."

There was silence and awkwardness. Neither Ernie nor Nellie knew what to say next.

"Do you think I could visit you tomorrow?" Ernie was flustered. "Just to bring up your mail."

"Of course."

Nellie blushed and shut the door. Ernie felt snappy and confident as he strutted back to his car and headed home.

Class had ended, and Tucker was working his regular night job at the billiards hall or, as it was known around town, "The Recreation Parlor." The joint had rows of Brunswick "Vestal Steel" pool tables and v-shaped ceiling lights. On the walls were local area photos and sports team pennants. The sign behind the main counter read, "Welcome. Pool Hall," and there was a display case full of the popular brands of cigars and ciggys. Scattered around the establishment were trays of lime, which customers rubbed onto their leather-tip cues. Some of the country's best billiardists would pop in for a game when they were in town. These fellows were considered celebs; they were no less impressive than the great sports stars of the time, such as Babe Ruth and Jack Dempsey.

On any given night, "The Recreation Parlor" was full of smoke and plenty of good-time Charlies, servicemen, off-duty miners, and gamblers. This night was no different. There was a fiery game of poker going on in the corner. Although gambling was illegal, Larry Levers, the man who owned the joint, let folks bet as long as they stashed their loot when the heat showed up. On the subject of alcohol, he was less bendable. He insisted on abiding by the Volstead Act. No one understood why, because most pool halls doubled as "speaks." In other words, they served jag juice, foot juice, and other booze. Flatfoots were routinely bribed to look the other way. But Larry's place only served Coca-Cola, ginger ale, Bevo, coffee, Adam's ale, noodle juice, and other non-alcoholics.

Tucker was wiping down a table when a customer named Tim called to him. "Got something sparky in my flask. Want some?"

"Better pipe down," Tucker whispered. "Larry has better hearing than a poodle. If he finds out, he'll give you the bum's rush."

But it was too late. The poodle was already on his way over. "Tucker doesn't drink and I don't drink. In fact, nobody drinks in my joint. Give it over, Tim." Larry held out his hand.

"Oh, come on. I'm a regular."

"Give it over. You know I'll punch you in the face."

"You don't have to get scrappy." Tim reluctantly handed over the flask.

"Why are you dry, Tucker?" Tim asked.

"The kid's got ambition," Larry replied. "Plus, he takes his job here real seriously."

"You think it'll send you to Jericho?"

"Nope," Tucker said. "I've just never tried the stuff. Nobody in my family's a boozer. It's not in the blood."

"A Fairmontian with no hooch in the blood?" Tim laughed. "That's a hard one to swallow. What do you do for fun? You got a girl?"

"Nope, but I've got my eye on a pretty waitress down at the diner."

"Better get a move on. If she's a dish, she'll get snapped up."

Larry dumped out the contents of the flask and returned the empty container to Tim. The rest of the evening played out without a hitch. When closing time came, Larry and the others left Tucker alone to finish wiping down surfaces and sweeping the floor. The place had a weighty stillness when everybody was gone. Tucker liked it. He could be inward. He could mull over things without a whole bunch of racket. He thought about the pretty waitress, and he worried that Tim was right. Would she get snapped up? Should he get a move on? Tucker knew he was too wrapped up in his busy schedule: tending the produce, making the grades, and tidying the pool hall. He never left time for socializing. There was a cleft in his life, a hollowness. Things had to change. Tim's words lit a fire under Tucker that night. He decided that he would pay the waitress a visit, and it would happen on the following day. He would find out if she was as fetching on the inside as she was on the out. Tucker finished his chores and then did what he did most nights because he did not want to make the long drive home. He pulled out a pillow and blanket from the back-room storage bin, turned out the lights, crawled onto one of the pool tables, and went to sleep.

The next day began as usual. Tucker returned to the farmhouse, tended the crops, dropped the crates off at the store, and went to his morning classes. Just after noon, he moseyed downtown and sniffed around Liberty Restaurant. Was the chestnut-haired doll working that day? Would the place be too crowded for a proper introduction? Did she already have a steady fellow? Tucker moved from the middle of the sidewalk up to the restaurant's front window and peered inside. He immediately saw her, confirming once again that she was a Sheba. There were not too many customers, so he entered and took a seat in a booth.

Liberty Restaurant had tile floors, chandeliers, racks for men's hats, vase centerpieces, a "No Negroes" sign on the door,

and festive decorations hanging from the ceiling. This ornamentation, which was plastic or paper, was rotated based on
season and special occasion. At Christmas, there were dangling
sleighs and Santas. At Easter, there were bushy-tailed bunnies.
Spring meant garlands of flowers, and the fall brought orange
and red leaves.

The pretty waitress was Ginger Morris, the green-eyed,
eighteen-year-old daughter of a prominent West Virginia family.
She had just finished boarding school in New England. Her
father, Chester Morris, was a bigwig doctor at the Monongalia
General Hospital in Morgantown, West Virginia and an advocate for well-rounded meals and vitamin supplements. He followed the work of Dutch physician Christiaan Eijkman, who
had just published a thesis on how a lack of thiamine harms
the organ system. Chester also had investments, including fifty
acres of farmland and tenant-filled dwellings.

Ginger's mom, Faire Morris, was a mannered socialite, who
dressed to the nines and crowed on and on about the latest
magazine gossip. She expected her daughter to marry rich and
marry up, but first she would, of course, go to college. Although
the "hash house job" was an unlikely choice for a blue blood
like Ginger, it was only temporary. It was a summer diversion.
Faire and Chester billed Liberty Restaurant as a "delightful
vacation with the bourgeois." In truth, they wanted to keep
their daughter away from flapper trouble and teach her what
it felt like to get her hands dirty. Despite Ginger's otherwise
feisty nature, she went along with it because she thought waitressing was a ducky idea. Plus, it seemed better than spending
three months watching her mother play croquet and throw parties for the local stuck-ups.

Ginger noticed Tucker when he entered the restaurant but
paid him little mind because she was peeved about the lousy tip
left by the last customer. She pocketed the coins while mumbling

"cheapskate" under her breath. Then, she approached Tucker. She held out her pen and pad, ready to take his order.

"When life gives you lemons, turn it into lemon pie." Tucker smiled, having overheard her grumbling.

Ginger observed Tucker all matter-of-fact. "What can I get you, sir?"

"Lemon pie. It's my favorite."

This threw Ginger off-guard, making her laugh. Then she took a hard look at this fellow. He was downright handsome, although she worried that he might be a playboy. "Has anyone ever told you? You look like a movie star."

"I'm Italian," Tucker said. "I thought I should let you know up front."

"You don't look Italian."

"I know. I have light skin. My brothers and sisters are darker."

"You a coal miner?"

"No. I'm studying to be a lawyer."

Bingo. That was the right answer, and Ginger slid into the booth and talked a mile a minute. "My ancestor, Robert Morris, signed the Declaration of Independence, the Articles of Confederation, and the U.S. Constitution. He financed the American Revolution and, next to George Washington, he was the most powerful man in the eighteenth century."

"You're an aristocrat," Tucker said.

"No. Not really. But I am proud to be a Morris. My parents say my name's like bubbly—expensive and intoxicating."

"It's a fine name."

"Robert Morris was also a Pennsylvania senator. Are you gonna be a senator?"

Tucker laughed. "If you ask my mother, the answer's yes. But the first step is law school."

"My name's Ginger." Ginger held out her hand but then

jumped up before Tucker could shake. "Oh, I almost forgot. Lemon pie."

Ginger dashed into the kitchen. Tucker felt like he had been through a cyclone, but a good cyclone. Ginger had a barrel of energy. She was a bearcat—spirited and headstrong—but also dreamy.

Seconds later, the bearcat came roaring back into the room and placed a serving of lemon pie in front of Tucker. Then she was off again. This time, she flitted into the corner to engage in girl-talk with the other waitress, Matilda. It was clear that the two women were discussing Tucker. There were giggles and flirtatious glances in his direction. He was embarrassed but also flattered. He felt like he was in Speech class with Miss Dolly. When Tucker's plate was almost empty, Ginger slid back into the booth across from him.

"I have a really big problem. Maybe you can help."

"What is it?" Tucker put down his fork.

"I have this new dress. I bought it two weeks ago, and it's yellow with lots of daisies. You know, big ones. Bigger than real daisies. In fact, I named it Daisy."

"You named the dress Daisy?"

"Yeah. And around the daisies are striped ladybugs."

"Striped ladybugs?"

"Lots of them. More than you'd find in a typical garden. And the ladybugs are black and white. Kinda like little zebras."

"Zebra ladybugs?"

"Yeah. Anyway, the problem is this dress was really expensive, and I have no place to wear it."

"That's a difficult problem." Tucker played along, rubbing his chin.

"So I was kinda hoping you could take me out. On a date."

"Well, I wouldn't want to disappoint Daisy."

Chapter 4

A NEW NAME AND AN OLD MINE

ROSE TROTTED DOWNSTAIRS wearing a low-cut blouse and a short fringe skirt. Margaret was at the bottom of the stairs, ready to catch her like a fly ball. She regularly played umpire to her daughter's fashion choices, planting herself by the front door.

"You look like a hussy." Margaret folded her arms.

"I don't care."

"Well, you *should* care."

Philip entered the room with a cheese sandwich and plopped down on the couch while Jal raced through the room, almost decking his mom, on his way out the front door. The house was as hectic as Woolworth on price-cut Friday. Outside,

Jal scurried past Tucker, who was coming up the front walkway with a handwritten financial plan.

"Where do you think you're going?" Tucker shouted.

"To see my friends," Jal replied.

"Don't play near the construction site or the coal mine."

Jal was in his own world as he barreled down the sidewalk.

"Jal, do you hear me?"

"Alright," he screamed back.

Tucker entered the farmhouse to bickering. Philip was tossing out wisecracks boxing style.

"There's nothing wrong with my blouse."

"You're a dumbdora. No boy's gonna respect you if you dress like that."

"Uh-oh. She's on the ropes." Philip laughed.

"Why do you always pick a fight when my boyfriend's about to arrive?"

"It's a left hook." Philip took a bite of his sandwich.

"There's always a boyfriend arriving. It's a different one every week. Now go change your clothes."

"I will not."

"You've got a horse's behind for brains." Margaret grabbed Rose's arm and struggled to pull her to the stairs. The two tangled and there was some light swatting.

"Stop it. Let go of me."

"I will not have a strumpet living under my roof." Margaret gave a hard yank and Rose collapsed onto the floor like a defiant child.

Tucker broke up the skirmish. "I'll handle it, Mom."

"Damn, no one's been pinned," Philip said.

"Pipe down, Philip," Margaret said.

Tucker helped Rose up and pulled her aside for a heart-to-heart. "We just want to make sure you're happy.

"Oh, give me a break!" Margaret was miffed because Tucker was being a softy.

"If you ever want to talk, we're here to listen," Tucker added.

"Thank you. What do *you* think of my blouse?"

"It detracts from your beautiful face." Then, Tucker turned his attention to his mom. "I put together a financial plan. We have to think about getting ahead. And the first step is changing our name."

"What?" Margaret cried.

"Change our name?" Philip said. "Why would we want to do that?"

"I don't need a new name. I'll be getting married soon." Rose went upstairs.

"We're never going to be treated with respect as Italians, and forget about becoming aristocrats," Tucker explained.

"Aristocrats?" Margaret laughed. "Are you joshing?"

"No. I'm serious. We barely make it each month. I say we stop being the Amoruso family and go by Moroose."

"We're not gonna be successful, Tucker," Philip said. "And this whole lawyer scheme of yours is a waste of time."

Margaret was lost in thought. "Moroose... hmmm... Moroose..."

Everyone stared at her in silence. Margaret fudged and mudged for a full ten seconds. She was chewing on the idea. Then, she spoke: "Okay. If that's what you think is best, Mr. Tucker Moroose, then that's what we'll do."

"Come on, Mom. You're always siding with him," Philip said. "I'm not changing my name."

Rose skipped back downstairs. She had changed clothes and was now wearing a conservative blouse and a demure, ankle-length skirt. She glanced out the window, anticipating her boyfriend's arrival. Tucker and Margaret exchanged satisfied looks.

It was known around town as "Hangman Forest," and it was the most feared spot within Fairmont's city limit. Of course, not many folks had been there. It was all about rumor. Hangman Forest was deep in the woods, surrounded by thick brush and all sorts of critters, such as the big-eared bat, the eastern cougar, and the long-tailed shrew. There were even reports of scaly dragons, ten-foot snakes, and horned wizards. It didn't matter whether the hearsay was true. It gave the dark-skinned folks something to talk about over the dinner table. It brought them together against their common enemy: the Ku Klux Klan. Hangman Forest was the weekly gathering spot for the Klan. It had no other purpose. No one knew exactly what happened at secret meetings, but this did not prevent imaginations from going hog wild and coming up with stories about blood-drinking, torture, and human sacrifice. In truth, the Klan's activities were much tamer. The men in white robes and hoods mostly showed off their leaflets and made speeches about morals, Americanism, purity, and the importance of enforcing the Prohibition.

Jal had met up with his buddies, which included the nine-year-olds Ale, Alfio, and Amedeo and the leader of the group, the twelve-year-old Salvatore. The boys had trotted down streets, past businesses, and through grassy fields. They had been doing their usual "exploring" when they came upon the infamous Hangman Forest. They noticed burnt remains from a campfire.

"This is Hangman Forest. It's where they meet." Salvatore tried to sound spooky.

"No. They don't," Ale said.

"Yes. They do. My father told me," Salvatore said.

"Do they torture people?" Alfio asked.

"Only children."

"You're a liar," Alfio replied.

"It doesn't seem so scary." Jal wandered over to a piece of paper partially hidden under a cluster of leaves. He picked it up. It was a flyer that read, "The KKK Wants You." There was also a drawing of a hooded man. "What a goony simpleton." Jal laughed at the picture.

But suddenly, he heard a rustle. It was coming from behind a nearby tree. Jal froze. He swallowed hard. Could it be a Klansman? Would this fellow grab him? Would he hang him from a post? Jal's imagination was spinning. It was a locomotive without brakes. Jal tried not to breathe. Then, he turned toward his friends, but yikes... they were gone. *Oh, no,* he thought. *I'm alone in Hangman Forest.* He slowly backed away from the tree.

Then, he heard another rustle, but before he could let out a scream, a squirrel scurried out into the open. *It was only a critter,* Jal thought. He was relieved, but hightailed it out of the clearing just to be safe.

Jal caught wind of his friends, who were heading up a grassy hill near some tombstones. The property was a cemetery, which had not yet been fully developed. Graveyards and churches were the focus in Fairmont, and Jal did not like it. They seemed to be here, there, and everywhere, like freckles on a redhead's back. Jal thought it was lamebrain for the town to place so much attention on death. It was as if life's goal was to hurry up and get to the hereafter. Churches had an eye toward salvation, heaven, and hell. Jal was not sure whether there was a paradise or a pearly gate. But, if there was a gate, he figured it was made out of iron or metal. That made more sense to him. Pearls chipped too easily. Visiting dead relatives—such as distant cousins—was a weekly ritual for many folks in town. The Amoruso family was no different, except they went once a month. Jal resented this and complained. "This is malarkey." "This is boring." "I want to play ball instead."

Margaret always made Jal put on his one and only suit and go with the family to the cemetery. He had to hold her hand and move along silently from grave to grave. Margaret would shut her eyes and pray. Jal's siblings also prayed, except for Tucker. Tucker was a lot like Jal. They would eye each other as if to say the ritual was a pot of beans. Of course, Tucker got out of the ritual most of the time because he had chores. "Got too much work, Mom. Can't make it to the cemetery today." Jal did not think it was fair and would sometimes offer to help Tucker just to get out of the "dead people trip." But Margaret rarely agreed.

"I want to stay and help Tucker. I don't want to see dead people today."

"Oh, gibble-gabble. You must pay your respects to the spirits or you won't grow to be a fine young man."

Jal thought about this as he sprinted past a tombstone and up the grassy hill, where he caught up to Salvatore and the others.

"I was wondering when you were gonna get your spindles cranking," Salvatore said. "You were on edge back there."

"No, I wasn't," Jal lied.

Jal always acted strong, even with his best friends. He liked his school's dodgeball coach, who said, "Weakness is for losers." Jal knew any man worth his salt had big muscles and toughie strength. For those who didn't, pretending was important. Pretending to be a he-man warded off teasing and black eyes. Jal had one more reason for lying—because he had pride. In fact, he had enough to fill the Kingwood water tower, which he had seen once when his family was driving due east from Fairmont. His mom had told him pride was a sin, but on the other hand, she said, "Have pride in your appearance." Jal was confused. Was it good or was it bad? Was it a sin or not? At least if it was a sin and he went to hell, he knew his family would visit his grave. Heck, the whole town would visit his grave.

"I've got a nifty idea," Salvatore said.

"What?" Jal asked.

"You'll see." Salvatore took off running. Jal and the others followed.

The boys sprinted past the construction site that Tucker had mentioned. It was a rectangular two-story structure on a slight slope next to a pile of colored bricks. It was going to be the Dunbar School, and it was slated to open in the following year—1929. The boys also passed the Monongahela River, the Greenwood auto repair shop, the Esso gas station, the woman's club, and the First Presbyterian Church.

Twenty minutes later, Salvatore and the others reached their destination: The West Fairmont Coke and Coal Company. This was the mouth of the abandoned mine. Jal thought mines were dandy. Little boys were supposed to be all about snips, snails, and puppy-dogs' tails, but mines were even better. They were about dirt, soot, dust, coal cars, and shiny left-behind tools. Jal contemplated whether he should brush aside Tucker's warning to stay away. If he went inside and Tucker found out, he knew his brother would complain: "My words went in one ear and out the other." That's what he always said when Jal disobeyed.

There was a sign that read, "Brighton Yard." The opening, which was carved into the rock, was square and thirty feet wide. From a distance, it looked deep and dark inside, but when the boys got close, there was enough light to see iron tracks and two low carts filled with rocks and dirt. The mine extended for three miles and sloped downward in a slight manner. This is why it was called a "slope mine."

There were fans at the opening, but they were off and

possibly inoperable. There were also three helmets made of canvas with leather brims and lights on the front.

Salvatore grabbed one and flipped the light on. "Hey, it works."

Amedeo tried a second one, which also operated just fine. He put it on his head.

Salvatore moved into the mine. "Let's go."

All played follow the leader except Jal, who backed away from the opening.

"Jal, you coming? That one's for you." Salvatore motioned to the third hat.

"He's scared." Amedeo laughed.

"Hey, I've never been scared of anything. Let's check it out." Jal grabbed the hat, turned it on, stuck it on his head, and sashayed into the mine with the others.

The tunnel was braced with posts. The light emanating from the hats only gave about ten feet of visibility. The rest of the tunnel looked like hollow blackness.

The boys gleefully jumped back and forth over the iron tracks.

"Step on a line, break your mother's spine," Alfio said in a sing-song way.

Amedeo hopped over a crevice in the dirt. "Step on a hole, break your mother's sugar bowl."

"What's this?" Ale grabbed a black and white photo of a woman, which was resting in the v-section of a wooden brace.

"She's a spiffy dame," Amedeo said, referring to the gal's smart attire.

"No. She's a hooker," Alfio joked.

"Some poor cracker forgot it." Salvatore laughed.

The boys came upon a fork in the road. Salvatore veered left. "Come on. This way." Everyone followed.

"Do you know where you're going?" Jal asked.

"Sure."

The boys trekked along until Ale decided he wanted to lead the expedition. "It's my turn to be captain." He ran ahead, shoving Salvatore aside.

"It's getting darker," Alfio said.

"No, it isn't. You blockhead," Ale said.

It was time for Jal to show his mettle. "I bet I can go further than any of you." Jal ran past Ale and the other boys. He noticed a piece of equipment wrapped with a heavy chain and a soot-stained T-shirt balled up in the dirt.

"Jal. Slow down," Ale yelled. "I want to be leader."

"You can't beat me," Jal screamed.

Ale's words made Jal pick up his speed. He came upon three veins or branches. It was like a tree. Jal could either go left, right, or straight. He opted for the right vein and passed a pick and a shovel, both lying flat in the dirt. He could hear his friends' conversation. They sounded close but were actually lagging quite far behind.

Salvatore, Ale, Amedeo, and Alfio came upon the same fork in the road. They were not sure whether Jal had gone left, right, or center.

"Where are you, Jal?" Salvatore yelled.

There was a loud echo. "Over here."

The boys took the left tunnel because that is where they thought Jal was. However, they got no more than a hundred yards before becoming mystified.

"Where's that rascal?" Salvatore asked.

"I think we should head back. It's probably time for dinner," Ale said.

"Jal. Let's go back," Salvatore screamed.

There was no reply.

"Jal?" Salvatore tried again. "Jal?"

"He's fooling us," Alfio said. "I bet he doubled back."

"You think?" Amedeo replied.

"Sure," Alfio said.

"He's a sneak," Ale added. "He's always trying to fool us."

"You watch. He'll be waiting on the street, busting a rib," Alfio said.

"That creeper," Salvatore said. With that, the boys headed toward the opening of the mine. They had difficulty finding the right path, but were relieved when they stumbled into the open air.

"Look at my shirt. My ma's gonna kill me." Salvatore brushed soot off his clothes.

"Where's Jal?" Ale asked.

"Do you think he went home?" Amedeo replied.

"No. He wouldn't leave," Salvatore said. "He's still inside."

Suddenly, the boys noticed an old timer with a cane hobbling up the road toward them. "Don't say anything about Jal," Salvatore whispered to his friends.

The old timer had seen the boys emerge from the mine, and he doddered over to them. "There's carbon monoxide in there. You boys should be dead." The old man shook his head and mumbled under his breath, "Stupid boys." Then he continued on his way.

When the old timer was out of sight, Salvatore screamed into the mine, "Jal. Jal."

There was no answer. The other boys chimed in with their own calls. "Jal, Jal." "Jal." "Where are you?" "Come out, Jal."

It was getting dark and the boys became panicky.

"We can't tell a soul," Salvatore said.

"Why?" Alfio asked.

"Because they'll blame us," Salvatore said. "They'll put us in jail."

"Jail?" Ale was freaked out.

"What if he's dead?" Amedeo began to cry.

"They're gonna put us in jail?" Ale bit his fingernails.

"He's not dead. Now, don't tell anybody. Swear?" Salvatore put out his little finger.

The other boys reluctantly nodded.

"My mom's waiting. I gotta get home." Ale barreled it out of there and the other boys followed. They ran like the wind, leaving Jal's fate to the gods of the West Fairmont Coal Company.

Chapter 5

MINES OF DISASTER

JAL WAS STILL in the tunnel with only one source of light: his miner's hat. There were pools of water at his feet, which seemed to stem from a leak in an adjacent mine shaft wall. Jal figured there must be a creek nearby, or maybe the water was coming from a busted coal cleaning machine. Whatever the case, he had to jump over puddles in order to keep his shoes from getting soggy.

"Salvatore, where are you? Alfio? Ale? Amedeo? Where is everybody?" His voice echoed through the massive maze of tunnels. There was no reply.

His friends wouldn't leave him, would they? They could not have left him. It would be against the rules of the Musketeers Club, the organization they had formed. Their motto was "One for all and all for one." They were supposed to stick together.

"Salvatore?" he tried again. There was silence.

He became worried. His plan had soured. He could feel it. He was alone. He glanced at the closed-in walls of the tunnel and imagined it was a coffin, his coffin. He became scared and bolted in the direction of the exit. Seconds later, he tripped and fell—*plop*—into a pool of water.

"Ouch." His face was wet and his clothes were soaked. He could taste a sootiness in his mouth. He moaned and cried. "Ahhhh. Ahhhh. Ahhhh."

Although his ankle was throbbing, he pulled himself up and hobbled in the direction of the exit. When he arrived at the three-way fork in the road, he became confused. He could not remember which way to go.

Sobbing, he screamed, "How do I get out of here? Help. Help. Salvatore?"

He thought about Hansel and Gretel and how they'd got lost in the woods. *I'm a potato like them,* he thought. *I'm always messing things up. I can't do anything right.* Through his tears, he did eeny, meeny, miny, moe and chose a passageway. He did not know if it was the right one. He became incensed. "Why did I listen to you, black shadow? I hate you, black shadow."

Suddenly, the light on Jal's hat burned out. He was in complete darkness.

Jal's anger turned to hysteria and pleading. "I'm sorry, black shadow. I didn't mean to make you mad. Please, black shadow. Please get me out of here."

He felt for the wall of the mine but, in the process, tripped over something big, landing face-down in the dirt again. "Ouch." He sobbed, wondering what the obstruction was. It seemed sharp. He could feel a stinging on his leg as if he had been cut. He also noticed that it was getting harder to breathe, so he took short, shallow breaths as he got back onto his feet and once again searched for the tunnel wall.

Jal figured he was going to die. It was surely the end. He

thought about his family and how they would find the big box of candy he had stolen from the grocery store. He had gotten it for himself, but had also shared it with the Negro kids on Moyer Way because he felt sorry for them. They were not lucky like him. They had no mama and had to live in a house with a bunch of orphans.

Jal had stashed the candy on the top shelf of the hall closet behind the Christmas tree fixings. There was a train set up there; it always went under the tree. Plus, there were lights and ornaments. The lights were tungsten filament cone-shaped lamps. Jal liked December the twenty-fifth each year when his mom said, "Let's go to the Christmas tree." It was always a heavily branched cedar. Under it was all sorts of wrapped goodies, such as pencil sets, peppermint candy sticks, apples, and oranges. Rose had gotten a doll last Christmas. It had a china face and a sawdust body covered in a cotton dress. It had no shoes or socks.

Jal loved his secret stash of candy. Most nights, he would use the green stool to sneak a few pieces in the middle of the night while his mom and siblings slept. He had never gotten caught. The grocery store clerk, Jimmy Dee, knew Jal was a thief. He had even come to the farmhouse one afternoon to talk to his mother. Jal had denied knowing anything about the missing candy box, and luckily his mom had believed him.

Jal decided to set his thoughts aside and focus on getting out of the mine. His fingertips touched the wall as he moved along as quickly as possible, taking care not to fall. He was practically despondent. He figured he had chosen the wrong tunnel. He knew what would happen: he would be dead, his family would find the candy, Tucker would say, "Jal didn't listen to me," everyone would call him a dumdum, and the black shadow would win. Everyone would hate him. No one would visit his grave because he was a bad boy—a very bad boy.

It was time for prayer. Jal did not know what else to do. "Please, God. Get me out of here. I want to go to the pearly gates someday, but not yet. I'm only nine. Please don't let me go there now." Jal kept praying as he moved slowly along the wall of the West Fairmont Coke and Coal mine.

After slogging through a full day of work at the coal mine, Ernie picked up some candles from the dime store. He bought them for his "scythe room," or the private cubbyhole in the basement of his home. A scythe is a scary-looking, six-foot-long, knife-like device. It was once used in agriculture, and within thirteenth century mythology, it is depicted as the Grim Reaper's weapon of choice. The Grim Reaper (or death) is traditionally described as an eerie skeletal figure in a black hooded cloak with a scythe. Ernie had given the basement this strange name because he had a scythe hanging on the east wall. It was his only "decoration," so to speak. For years, he had planned to do a great deal more sprucing up, but he had never gotten around to it. Fixing had been stuck on the back burner. He had put his mind to accumulating money instead.

Ernie parked his jalopy in the driveway and tiptoed up to the house with his candles, hoping Bessie would not see him. He liked sneaking into the basement without fuss. Bessie always made a bunch of fuss. She was nosy. She'd ask what he wanted for dinner or how his day went. If he could get downstairs without notice, he could get a running start on privacy. Getting a running start was important. Privacy was important. He had one phrase that described his marriage: it was a cat and dog life. In other words, it was a bum deal. It was like ratty old socks, and conversing was to be avoided whenever possible.

Ernie slithered through the front door, taking a gander at the olive-green sofa, the piano bench with scrolled ends, and the inlaid wood end table with a Porto marble top and nickeled bronze hardware. He saw the gilt-framed oil painting, floor heater, small clock, letter opener, and three decorative platters, which had been wedding gifts from Bessie's parents. The front hall closet was open, and Ernie noticed his raincoat on its proper hook and the shelf that held his hats, such as his flat caps and felt trilbies. On the closet floor were shoes, lined up, with old newspaper stuffed inside to keep them fresh and stiff.

Ernie closed the front door all quiet like so as not to arouse Bessie. He could hear her in the kitchen fiddling with pots and pans. Then, he reached into his pocket, pulled out his special key, unlocked the basement door, and descended into his scythe room. The wooden basement stairway was irritating because, if Ernie was not careful, each step could result in a clippity-clop. It happened that way this time. Ernie made a faint clippity-clop, and Bessie thought she heard it. Ernie tried to be quieter as he slowly moved down the rest of the staircase.

"Ernie, is that you?" Bessie figured her husband was home from work. She popped out of the kitchen, noticing the basement door was shut. She placed her ear against the door, heard another muted clippity-clop, and realized Ernie was being weird again. Why was he always sneaking around? It was as if he had lard in his head. Sometimes Ernie could be normal and relatively considerate to her and the children. But, on other occasions, he was a monster. He could be stingy and unpredictable. He could be selfish. He could be cruel, shifty, and half-under. In fact, he could be more plastered than a hoary-eyed drunk.

Although nervous, Bessie put her hand on the basement doorknob. She took a deep breath and tried to turn it. It was locked. She was relieved. What would happen if he forgot?

What if she had access to his secret place? It might be tempting. She might want to see. She did not need the temptation. She did not want the temptation. She preferred to stay in the dark. She had never set eyes on his scythe room, and it was better that way.

Bessie decided to let Ernie think he was fooling her about not being home, at least for the time being. She went back into the kitchen with an idea to get back at him. She would "can dinner." Ernie liked home-cooked food, so she would give him something preserved. She opened the pantry to find Parkinson's Superfine Icing Sugar, Sainsbury New Potatoes, Heinz Baked Beans, Del Monte Sliced Pineapple, Harvest Fine Quality Salad Oil, a jar of Bovil, and Jal West Sardines. She decided to serve up a plate of canned beans and canned sardines to go with the corn she had already made. That would teach him. If he had a beef with it, she could say, "Sorry, Ernie. But, you didn't tell me what you wanted." She knew what would happen next because it had happened before. He would sit at the table, grumble under his breath about her failure to do home cooking, and lick his plate clean.

Ernie felt self-satisfied in the basement, figuring he had fooled Bessie. He relaxed in his tattered easy chair, staring at his scythe on the wall. The newly purchased candles were on a table in the corner next to the pamphlets he had gotten from Otis. He thought about how the room would look with new decorating and how he needed to get all the debris out of there: the rakes, boxes of unwanted clothes, paint cans, and whatnot. He even saw a couple of spiders that needed to be hotfooted out of the room. Ernie's planning turned into glassy eyes and then into sleep and outright snoring.

"Supper's ready." Ernie woke to Bessie's voice. It was half an hour later. Bessie had the table set and was not about to let the fixings get cold. She was still annoyed by Ernie's strangeness, but no longer cared about his ridiculous game of "who's fooling who."

"Ernie?" She pounded on the basement door.

"Okay, woman," he shouted back.

Bessie mumbled to herself, "I bet he's got another girl stashed down there."

"He's dead," Margaret said through her tears. "I can feel it. A mother has instinct."

"Calm down, ma'am." The police chief was at the farmhouse filling out a report.

It was midnight and had been over nine hours since little Jal had gone to play with his friends. The Amoruso family was filled with concern. At supper time, Tucker had gone knocking on doors. He even went to Salvatore's house, but the boy's mother said she had no idea where Jal might be.

"Salvatore says he saw him at Hangman Forest this afternoon but hasn't seen him since. We feel real bad for you."

Margaret paced the front room. "Lordy, the Klan nabbed him. What else could it be? He was at Hangman. What a numbskull place to be."

"We're looking into it," the police chief said. "I've got boys over there now."

Rose offered up some pound cake. "Want a piece?"

"That's right friendly of you." The police chief stuffed a slice into his mouth and made his way to the door. "Get some sleep. It won't do you any good to stay up fretting. We'll let you know when we hear something." He left.

The family could not sleep. They were as still as the furniture in the room. There were frowns, heads hung low, darting eyes, and worried looks. The clocked ticked, and they waited. It became one a.m. and then two a.m. At three a.m., when the family was feeling over-the-cliff hopeless, there was a weak knock at the door.

"Oh, no." Margaret held her breath, figuring the police had found Jal's lifeless body.

Tucker opened the door to find... Jal. He was bedraggled and filthy from head to toe. He appeared to have been through the wringer. In fact, it looked like the wringer was furious with him. Jal's pants and shirt were tattered and his knee was bleeding. His face was as sooty as a potbelly stove.

"What a mess," Philip said. "You're in so much trouble."

Margaret was in shock and more angry than relieved. "Where have you been? We had to call the cops. You look like a guttersnipe. Your pants are ripped. We don't have the money for a new pair. Don't just stand there. Explain yourself, Jal."

"Your leg's bleeding," Tucker said.

Margaret continued to chide Jal. "Tell me where you were. You're gonna be punished. Speak up right now. Then, I'm gonna whip you."

Tucker broke in, "Tell us what happened."

"I was just playing with my friends. I fell down and tore my britches. That's all. Nothing else." Jal could not hold back his tears and ran to his bedroom.

"I don't have money for this nonsense," Margaret said.

"I'll pay for it out of my wages," Tucker offered.

Margaret turned to Tucker, "Could you handle him tonight? I'm going to bed. And call the police so they don't waste any more time on my chowderheaded son."

Tucker entered the bedroom to find Jal face down on the bed, sobbing up a storm. "Let me see."

Jal pulled open the rip in his pants.

"It doesn't look serious. I'll get a Band-Aid." Tucker rummaged through the dresser drawer. "So, what *really* happened?"

"It was like I said."

"I don't think so. I've always been fair with you, but I will not tolerate lying."

Jal wiped his eyes.

"You need to tell me the truth." Tucker was stern.

Jal sat up on the bed. "Me and my friends... me and my friends, we went in the coal mine. I got in too far and my light went out."

Tucker placed a Band-Aid over Jal's wound. "Did you forget your promise?"

Jal shook his head.

"The worst coal mining disaster happened right here in Fairmont. Did you know that?"

Jal shook his head again.

"It was only twenty-one years ago. There was an explosion and hundreds of people died, including children. Most of them were Italian immigrants like us."

Tucker had seen a film about the disastrous day in 1907 when there was an explosion at the Monongah coal mine. Buildings shook, and sidewalks cracked. There were screams from those who were trapped. Smoke filled the tunnels, and shafts collapsed. Many believed the explosion was caused by an electrical spark that had ignited coal dust or methane gas.

"They lined caskets up and down Adams Street," Tucker continued. "And the bank was turned into a morgue. Mines are extremely dangerous. Do you understand?"

"Yeah."

"I worry about you. You're impetuous. You don't think about consequences. And the problem is compounded because of our heritage. People around these parts have a low tolerance for folks like us, so we have to be especially careful."

"But that isn't right."

"I know. And maybe someday things will change. But right now, we need to be measured in our actions, especially if we want to get ahead. We can't be riling up the Klan, wandering into coal mines, or failing in school. Did you do *any* homework this week?"

Jal nodded, but Tucker was not convinced.

"Jal, be straight with me."

"I don't like school."

"You got stuck in a coal mine today. Do you want to get stuck working in one for the rest of your life?"

"No."

"Then you need to get an education."

"Tommy, the clerk at the general store... he didn't go to school."

"He gets very low pay and works a lot of hours just to survive. Is that the kind of life you want?"

"Is that why you're studying to be a lawyer?"

"Yeah. I don't focus on my muscles or have a sassy mouth. I'm trying to use my brain to show people they're wrong about us. And, someday, I'm gonna get a pair of onyx cufflinks."

"Why?"

"They're a sign of success. Nobody can look down on a man wearing onyx cufflinks. Now, I suggest you get some shut-eye. The sun will be up soon. You can hit the books real hard after school today." Tucker glanced at the clock. "In about twelve hours."

"Are you gonna be home tonight?"

"Nope. I'm meeting up with a girl from the diner after she gets off work. Now get to sleep." Tucker left the room.

Chapter 6

THE BEARCAT AND THE FLAPPER

T HE WHITE, TWO-STORY colonial home with green shutters and manicured lawns was situated on fifty acres of land. It had been built in the late 1880s. The estate was occupied by blue bloods: Chester and Faire Morris. They were Ginger's parents and rarely let a week pass without a party or two. They called it "putting on the Ritz."

"Darling, we'll be putting on the Ritz this Friday and Sunday." Faire loved the word "darling." It was like salt to her. She used it generously and sprinkled it on everything. She bestowed it on friends and family as well as on the pharmacist, the milkman, and perfect strangers.

"You know I'm not a Ritz man," Chester often said. "What do you say we skip a week?"

Faire always laughed and brushed off his words

with, "Don't be silly," "You're such a card," or "Let me get you a fruit cocktail, darling." In other words, the idea of missing a party was utter bunk as far as Faire was concerned. Chester did not mind all that much. As long as he could read his paper in peace after work and get served a hearty meal by the butler, all was copacetic.

Sometimes Faire would rouse Chester for a different reason. She might ask for his opinion on a new curtain fabric or inquire as to whether he wanted the servant, Mr. Jingles, to press his suit. Chester tended to answer with "Jolly good," without lifting his eyes from his reading.

During the prior week, Faire had asked, "Do you tend toward blue or red napkins?"

"Jolly good," was his reply.

Faire put her hands on her hips. "Take off your cheaters and hear me out."

Chester removed his glasses. Faire held out the napkin samples, and he replied, "Red."

"You don't think blue might be better?"

"Blue. I meant blue," he said. Then, he put his cheaters back on and returned to the black and white print.

"Thank you, Mrs. Grundy," Faire said. This was her way of calling him a wet blanket.

This described their marriage in a nutshell, but it worked just fine for them. Faire was bossy and bound up in life's superficialities. Some of her girlfriends called her a face-stretcher because she tried too hard to look like a hotsy-totsy. Chester, on the other hand, was a much-respected physician with boo-coo beans in the bank; he was solitary, contemplative, and reserved.

Faire wanted to groom her daughter in her own image, but Ginger would have none of it. True, she fancied the finer things and loved getting dolled up, but she had no time for snobbery. She hated high hats—the tensed-up, highfalutin types that

Faire associated with. She preferred ordinary folks, which is why she was fond of her waitressing job.

Tucker seemed ordinary, but he was also a stand-out. He did not come from privilege but, on the other hand, had a strong eye toward success. This impressed Ginger. She wanted a beau with ambition. She wanted a beau who was not an upper-class bore, and she wanted a beau who was handsome with a silver tongue. Tucker was all that. Of course, Ginger knew her mother would throw a hissy fit if she knew her daughter was dating an Italian. Heck, her father might throw a hissy fit too. But Ginger did not care because she was the rebellious sort. She was independent and bold.

Ginger remembered the conversation two weeks prior when Faire talked up the Morgan boy, mentioning that he came from "good stock" and was set to inherit the family business.

"A little birdie told me Bobby Morgan has a crush on you."

"He's a toad," Ginger replied.

"But he's ready for a wife. And he's got a bankroll coming his way."

"He should go to Brandy's Pond. It's mating season, and that's where the female frogs are."

Faire crossed her arms in frustration.

"Anyway, I'm not sure I ever want to get married."

"Bite your lip, young lady."

Ginger was, of course, pulling her mother's leg, and giggled.

"You think you're a smarty pants. But if you don't start acting like the well-born that you are, you won't attract the right kind of boy. Or you'll end up a spinster." Faire left the room.

Ginger knew she'd rather be an old maid than marry a fellow she did not love. She was a mushy-hearted romantic. She put on her "Daisy" dress, brushed her long curls, dabbed rouge on her cheeks, and touched up her lipstick. She stared at herself in the mirror. Do I look like a babe? She was unsure, but hoped Tucker would ooh and aah and call her the bee's knees. Ginger ran downstairs to wait for his arrival. Unfortunately, her mother was standing at the front door, primed to be a nosy parker.

"So, who's this boy? Your father and I would like to know."

Chester was reading a medical book and let out a grunt.

"Oh. Just some fellow. It's a first date."

"Your father and I would like to meet him."

"I'm not introducing either of you to anyone until I'm in a serious relationship. Remember what happened with Jimmy last year? Dad, you don't ask a boy if baldness runs in the family. He never called me again."

Chester set aside his reading. "His hairline looked a little suspect. There were definitely some thin spots."

"Chester!" Faire said in a scolding way.

"Well, I don't want my grandchildren to look like marbles." He lit a cigar. "All right, it was an unfortunate choice of words. It won't happen again." He returned to his reading.

"I'm still not letting either of you meet him. Not yet."

Faire looked her daughter up and down. "You're a beauty, Ginger. Not one of those chunks of lead from your boarding school. You can have your pick of the crop."

"My friends are perfectly presentable, mother. They're..." Ginger was interrupted by the sound of the doorbell. "He's here." Excited, she scooted out the door before her mother could catch a glimpse of her date.

Faire ran to the window and got onto her tippy-toes. "I can't see a rotten thing, Chester. Do something." He took a puff of his cigar, ignoring her.

The front porch had wooden planks and lofty, white columns. Ginger was agog when she saw Tucker. He was the cat's pajamas, especially wearing his finest. Although it was too soon, she knew she was getting goofy over him.

"Nice to see you again, Ginger. And nice to meet you too, Daisy." He gave a slight bow to her dress. "Those *are* zebra ladybugs."

"I really wish we could've had dinner," Ginger said. "But, I only just got off work." The couple strolled to the car while Faire watched from the window.

"I think the soda shop is an ideal spot for a first date," Tucker said.

"Do you always dress so nicely?" Ginger asked.

"Only when I'm awake."

"You're so funny." She giggled.

Rose liked pulling the wool over her mother's eyes. "I'm going to Laura's house to study."

Margaret was in the kitchen wiping down the supper pots. "Don't stay out past ten. You hear?"

"Okay." Rose trotted out the front door with her mathematics book. When she got to the street, she glanced back at the farmhouse to make sure no one was watching. Then, she quickly shoved the book into the mailbox and sprinted behind a honeysuckle bush. From there, she tiptoed around the side of the farmhouse past the tomato plants, blueberries, and basil. She darted through the backyard and ducked into the old barn where her mom kept her bootleg stash. Once inside, she was taken aback by how dark it was. She could barely make out the objects in the room. After feeling around in the semi-blackness and almost knocking over the flake stand, she stumbled onto her mother's prized jugs of booze. Rose wasted no time, grabbing one and hightailing it out of the barn. In her haste, she failed to latch the door. In fact, she left it slightly ajar, an invitation to varmints in the area.

Back in the front yard with the moonshine in tow, she strutted down the road. She went several hundred yards and then turned left on to Yodie Street, where she saw it: a shiny 1928 Ford Phaeton. It was a four-door convertible and in her words, "absotively divine." Of course, the top was fastened shut so as to provide privacy. Privacy was needed. She smiled into the dark window of the vehicle and the door popped open.

"Ready for some boot knocking?" Thirt asked. "Boot knocking" was his word for lovemaking, and even though he asked, he knew she was a "sleep around" gal. He had met her in this very spot three times in the past month for petting sessions. Thirt's real name was Burt. His nickname was short for his age. He was a thirty-year-old tomcat with a lust for teenage girls.

"Where's your wife tonight?" Rose said flirtatiously as she stepped into the car.

"Visiting her sis." He closed the door, noticing the jug. "Where'd you get the alcohol?"

"My mom's a bootlegger."

"Really? She must be a cool cat."

"No, she's just full of prunes," Rose laughed. "Actually, she's looking for some extra kale. To pay the bills and all."

"Let's get drunk," Thirt said, opening the jug and taking a swig. "Then you can give me a freebie." Rose downed some booze as well.

Rose fashioned herself as a flapper. She was wild, boisterous, and deliciously disgraceful. No one in the family knew about Rose's secret life, although Tucker had his suspicions. A flapper was officially a woman who wore unbuckled galoshes, which, as legend had it, flapped in the wind. But it was about more than just galoshes for Rose. Her life flapped in the wind.

It was spontaneous and free. It was wild and unladylike. It was utterly immoral by society's standards.

Rose liked to flirt and refused to be bored. She smoked ciggys and loco weed. She was a full-on boozehound and enjoyed French kissing. She wore her hair in a bob with a choice pair of earrings, and wrapped her breasts to make them look smaller when she was not meeting up with a boy. She liked painting her lips scarlet red and putting black liner around her eyes. She had lost her cherry two years prior with one of her mother's field hands. He was also married. Rose liked two-timers because they were forbidden. She fancied dangerous men. When Rose was not meeting up with fellows in the back-seat, she was chewing the fat at speakeasies or meeting up with guys at Toby's, a makeshift jazz joint in town. Rose was quite an Oliver Twist. She could shimmy with the best of them and even do a dance called the Black Bottom. Rose remembered reading a newspaper article about the ten-year-old Mildred Unger. A year prior, this little girl had danced the Charleston on the wing of an airplane while it was two thousand feet in the air. This impressed Rose; she would have done it herself if given half a chance. *Live the high life or take a splat in a corn field,* Rose thought with a smile.

Rose knew there was more to being a flapper than wearing crazy clothes, being giddy, taking risks, and having swanky good times. There was the serious side. Rose thought of herself as a liberated gal, the type who could parallel a man. She supported the suffrage movement and admired the National Woman's Party. She sometimes flipped through the radical publication *Equal Rights* at parties when she came across it on a coffee table. Rose was pleased that womankind had been given the right to vote in 1920 and wanted to see females do more than clean the house and take care of the young'uns. She did not want any young'uns herself. She had a distaste for their late-night wailing and messy faces. Her friend Laura Smith felt the same way. They had decided to be "decadent baby vamps" forever. They had vowed to get married but have no children. Laura lived nearby and was Rose's alibi when she was meeting up with a fellow. If her mom was ever to come calling, it was Laura's obligation to say, "She just left. She's on her way home." Then Laura was supposed to track down Rose and light a fire under her to get back.

"Let's go berserk, honey." Thirt had had his fill of liquor and started taking off Rose's clothes, beginning with her felt, bell-shaped hat. Then he rolled down her rayon stockings.

"The bank's closed," she replied and pushed him back.

"What?"

"Butt me first."

"Now? Before sex?"

"Yeah. Give me a cigarette. I'm a modern-day bird."

Thirt sighed, pulled out a ciggy, and lit it for Rose. She reclined, resting her feet in Thirt's lap and blowing airy smoke rings toward the roof of the vehicle.

"At least show me your bubs."

With that, Rose lifted her top, fully exposing her breasts. His eyes got real big.

Rose liked Thirt all right, but from her perspective, there was a drawback to necking with him. She did not get any cabbage for her piggy bank. She fancied being pampered. She wanted a sugar daddy. But where could she find such a fellow? The courtesan way of life piqued her interest.

While Rose was doing unladylike things with Thirt in the back seat of the Ford, Margaret was marching through the backyard, curious as to why the barn door was ajar. She had been wiping down the kitchen counter when she glanced out the window and saw the door was not fastened. She had shut it herself that very afternoon. This was peculiar. Who might be messing around out there? Was somebody getting into her hooch?

When Margaret stepped inside the barn, she turned on a light. All looked normal. There was nothing out of place and not a darn thing was broken as far as she could tell. Then, she counted the moonshine bottles, and the number came up short. Just to be sure, she counted a second time and a third. "Damn, there's one missing," she said to herself. She stormed back into the farmhouse.

"I won't stand for thievery." She confronted Philip while tearing through his bedroom in search of the missing jug.

"What are you talking about?"

"You've been fiddling around in my bootleg."

"No. I haven't. Why do you blame me for every blasted thing?"

"No one in this family's a rummy. You're the only one who might be sneaking a sip. I know you coal-mining types."

"Well, it wasn't me."

Margaret could find no proof that Philip was the crook, so she left. "I'd better not find out you're fibbing."

When Ginger and Tucker entered Dixie Soda Shop, all eyes focused on them. They looked like cinema stars, all fetching and glamorous. They could have been Hollywood upper crusts, dropping in to wet their whistles before hitting the popular night spots in Paris or before skiing in the Catskills. To the common-stock patrons in the place, Tucker was a sheik with light skin and dark hair, while Ginger was a babe in her splashy daisy dress.

The place was cheery. There was a marble counter, a black and white tile floor, half-a-dozen tables, bakery items on trays with glass covers, an ornate brass soda dispenser, and display cases crammed with a vast assortment of merchandise. The couple sat on red stools at the counter and the soda clerk greeted them, speaking first to Ginger.

"You look like that actress... what's her name... from *Pollyanna* and *Daddy-Long-Legs.*"

"Mary Pickford?" Tucker replied.

"You betcha. Mary Pickford." Then, he turned to Tucker. "And you must be Douglas Fairbanks."

"Nope. I'm just the lady's chauffeur."

"Oh, Tucker," Ginger laughed. "You're such a card."

The soda clerk smiled. "What can I get you two lovebirds?"

"Vanilla shake and four straws, please," she said.

Tucker and the clerk looked puzzled.

"I'll have chocolate with one straw," Tucker replied. "Thank you."

The clerk wandered off to fill the order.

"Why do you need four straws?" Tucker asked.

"Four's my lucky number."

"But you don't do everything in fours."

"Are you a philosopher?"

"No." Tucker laughed. "You didn't bring me four pieces of lemon pie."

"Four pieces of lemon pie would've made you fat. I'm a practical person... a butterfly goes through four stages of metamorphosis. And I'm looking to spread my wings and realize my full potential."

Ginger was nothing like any of the girls Tucker had dated. She was a little whimsical and a whole lot fascinating.

"What do you hope to do?" he asked.

"Travel to every continent and become the world's best ballroom dancer."

"I can't dance," he said.

"I can teach you in four steps. You can go through meta-morphosis too."

"You're a beautiful girl. I think you're already a butterfly."

The clerk placed the couple's drinks on the counter and leaned in real close to Tucker. "Seems you've got a feisty one on your hands."

"Yep." Tucker laughed. "She's a bearcat all right."

Ginger glowed, basking in the praise. Being a bearcat was just about the nicest thing a fellow could say about a gal in West Virginia in 1928. Following the sodas, the couple enjoyed a stroll down Adams Street and some hand-holding. At the end of the evening, Tucker gave Ginger a respectful peck on the cheek on the front porch of the Morris estate. The bearcat and the Italian were off to a real fine start.

The relationship gained steam quickly. In fact, it could have been likened to the popular flick, *Wings*, which won "Best Picture" at the first Academy Awards in 1928. Both the movie and the relationship had immediate lift-off. Ginger and Tucker managed to keep their romance private. No one knew much about the mysterious "squeeze" who occupied their time each weekend.

"She's a beauty. That's all you need to know," Tucker told his mom.

"He's not bald, and there's no baldness in his family. I won't be dragged into a talk-fest," Ginger said to her parents.

The couple only dated on Friday or Saturday nights each week due to Tucker's obligations, which mounted quickly once he began law school. Not only did he have to juggle his farming work with his clean-up duties at the pool hall, but he had scads of homework. To top it off, it was a grim time going into 1929. The stock market crashed and the Great Depression spread over society like sticky smog. While there was less lettuce to go around, Tucker had rising financial burdens. His schooling alone cost a whopping four hundred dollars per year. Plus, he spent fifty dollars on books and one hundred dollars on gas, oil, and tires for his Model T Ford, which was his only means of getting to class. Thank goodness Tucker was able to avoid the dormitory fee by living at home. Of course, moving out would have left his mother in the lurch. She relied on him, and he knew it.

Margaret's hooch business brought in meager sums. Sure, it helped the family limp through tough times, but it added up to a lot less than expected. The Barney brothers had promised Margaret that she would get rich off her homemade brew, but this was an out-and-out lie.

"They told me a tall tale," Margaret confided in Tucker. "I work my fingers to the bone fermenting, mashing, buying fixings. I end up with bupkis. They end up with all the money."

"Plus, you risk getting thrown in the slammer," he said. "You should give it up."

"For crying out loud, without those extra pennies, we'd end up ragamuffins!"

"I'm almost done with school. Then I'll get a fine lawyering job."

"I hope so. God knows we need more clams in the cupboard." Margaret had a worried look. "Do you really think they're gonna hire you?"

"Sure they will. Of course they will. Don't you worry," Tucker replied in a rosy way, but deep down he had doubts. He figured the numbers were bleak, that the odds were no better than gambling on a racetrack horse. At law school, he'd seen the figures on Negroes. There were a handful of colored lawyers in West Virginia at the time and not all that many in the country. Most were employed in northerly states of New York, Ohio, and Michigan. West Virginia was "borderline southern," especially when it came to mindset. Colored female lawyers had it even worse. There were twenty-four in the entire United States.

Were any Italians working in the Marion County courts? Tucker had no idea. Maybe he would be the first. But he *would* be the first, if necessary. He would definitely get a job as a mouthpiece. No one could tell him otherwise.

There was one detail that would work to his advantage: his name. He was pleased that his family had made the change from "Amoruso" to "Moroose" and that the transition had stuck. Even Jimmy Dee at the grocery store called him "Tucker Moroose." So did the patrons from the pool hall. Tucker knew lots of them figured he was white. He'd heard them having bull sessions behind his back. His new name was his ace in the hole. It would help him get ahead.

Ginger had no financial obligations during her courtship with Tucker, but she stayed busy. Rather than attend college in New England, she remained near Tucker by enrolling at the University of West Virginia, where she studied for a liberal arts degree. She had asked her parents to let her attend this school by saying, "I need to be near my new beau. You're going to be mighty impressed by him." They went along, assuming this fellow was top-of-the-line, a well-to-doer from old money who would someday tie the knot with their daughter.

Like most folks in the early 1930s, Faire and Chester believed the proper role for "the fairer sex" was that of wife and mother. It was widely accepted that college hurt women by distracting them from their main goal: marriage. Plus, it was thought that universities corrupted gals into thinking they were equal to men. Ginger did not think she was equal; she knew she was equal, but refrained from discussing the subject with her parents for fear of flare-ups.

Ginger lived in a dormitory where rules were strict; students could be expelled for breaking them. The curfew was ten p.m., and boys were never permitted in the girls' rooms. At dances—which Tucker often attended with Ginger—both feet had to be flat on the floor at all times. When the music stopped one night, a Johnny-on-the-spot protested the silly rule: "What if I've got gum on the bottom of my shoe? Do they really think we want to boff under the punch table?"

In the dormitory, meals were provided, and laundry was done by university staff. Smoking cigs was so popular that butts had to be swept away from the Woodburn Hall entrance six times a day. Elizabeth Moore Hall was a lounge and gymnasium for women, while the men's gymnasium was in the Field House. Ginger settled into university life, even joining a sorority. Tucker had been a member of Tau Beta Iota when he attended Fairmont State University, but did not have time for this sort of socializing at law school.

After three years of painting the town red, countless picnics and dinners, twenty trips to the cinema, twelve college dances, a couple of canoe expeditions, and a wobbly ice skating adventure, Tucker and Ginger were thinking about tying the knot. But they were only thinking, and they were thinking about it separately. Neither had broached the subject out loud. Ginger was in love with Tucker. He felt the same about her, but wanted to finish up his schooling and snag his law license before wading into family life.

One afternoon, Ginger and Tucker were strolling down Adams Street when they came upon Adams Fashion Shop. There was a Victorian-style wedding dress in the storefront.

"That's right pretty. Isn't it?" Ginger hinted, pointing at the dress. But Tucker paid her no mind because he had wandered over to the jewelry shop next door. He was staring at a pair of onyx cufflinks in the window.

She joined him. "I didn't figure you for a cufflinks man."

"Onyx comes from the mineral chalcedony," he said.

"Why are you such a know-it-all?" She giggled.

"My mother thinks they're gonna find onyx on the new planet," Tucker said.

"What new planet?"

"The one they just discovered: Pluto. It was named after the ruler of the underworld."

"Pluto's a ridiculous name. They should call it Plateau."

"Why?"

"Because it sounds better. Plateau's a French word. Everything sounds better in French."

Tucker chuckled as the couple continued down the sidewalk.

"By the way, I had a talk with my parents," Ginger said.

"About what?"

"Now, I haven't told them anything… but they want to meet you for dinner."

"They do?"

"Tonight at six."

"That seems awfully soon."

"Tucker, we've been dating for three years."

"But I have 'meeting your parents' written on my calendar for 1942."

"That's in ten years! Oh, come on. They'll be at the country club. They want us to drop by so they can introduce you to their friends."

"Their friends?" Tucker felt his nerves prickle but agreed to go along with the plan.

That evening, Tucker picked up Ginger and they drove to the country club, a three-story white mansion surrounded by rolls of green grass, flowery bushes, and a Titanic-sized front porch. The couple was dressed to the nines. Ginger's shoulders were wrapped in a black feather boa. They left the car in the parking lot, a hearty distance from the main dining room, and walked toward the entrance.

"I was here last year," Ginger said. "There's a nice view of the golf course, and I love the artwork in the main hall."

"I'm not sure I'm prepared to meet your parents." Tucker squeezed her hand. "What if they don't like me?"

"They're gonna love you. Everybody loves you."

The couple turned down a pathway that led up to the regal building. But as they got close, they came face to face with a sign in bold black print. It read, "No Dogs. No Negroes. No Italians."

Ginger jumped in front of Tucker, hoping to block his view.

"You know... I've changed my mind. Maybe you should meet my parents another time when you feel more prepared."

Ginger pulled Tucker back toward the car. She was pretty sure he had not seen the hateful sign.

She was wrong.

Chapter 7

BESSIE AIN'T NO PUTTY HEAD

"**S**HH. THE GIRLS are sleeping," Bessie whispered.

Ernie, who had just gotten home from work, said nothing because he was in a "keep to himself" frame of mind, plus he was shaking a leg. He wanted to hurry to his basement scythe room in time for the *"Vic and Sade"* radio show. It always gave him a laugh. He also liked *"The Carnation Contented Hour,"* *"Amos 'n' Andy,"* and the *"A & P Gypsies."* Ernie spent more time with his radio than his wife.

"Like my hair?" Bessie asked in a hushed voice. "I visited the hairdresser today."

"You're always wasting cabbage, woman."

"Don't you want your honeybun to be a Cadillac?"

"You could be a battle-axe or a bug-eyed Betty. I wouldn't give a damn." Ernie dug into his pocket for his special key and moved to the basement door. He suddenly became confused. The knob did not look right. The keyhole was always sideways, not vertical. Could it be unfastened?

He slowly turned the knob. It opened. The door was unlocked! Ernie felt his heart racing. His anger shot upward like the gauge on the strength-testing game at the carnival. He became rattled, suspicious, and outraged all at the same time.

"Have you been in my basement?" he roared.

"No." She was taken aback.

"Then why is the door unlocked?" His voice grew louder. "I always lock it. If you've been down there…"

Bessie interrupted, "I haven't. Shh. Pipe down. You're gonna wake the girls. You probably forgot to lock it this morning."

Ernie stared at her, seething. "I don't believe you." Then he pushed her against the wall. "Tell me the truth, woman." His eyes were all squinty and scary-looking.

"What are you doing?" she cried out.

Ernie grabbed her wrists and held them much too tight.

"Stop. You're hurting me." Bessie was on the brink of tears.

Ernie slammed her arms against the wall above her head and gave her the evil eye. "If I find out you've been down there, I'll fucking kill you." With that, Ernie let go of Bessie and clamored down the steps.

Once downstairs, he ran to a toolbox hidden behind a mound of building materials. He dug through it, emptying a hammer, nails, screwdrivers, pliers, and a tape measure onto a work table. At the bottom of the toolbox, he found his stash: a large roll of twenty dollar bills. It was more moolah than most folks could ever hope to see. Ernie counted it. When all was accounted for, he sighed. He was relieved. Then, he scanned the room. It looked normal. Bessie had not been down there. He was pretty sure.

Ernie headed back upstairs to make sure Bessie was not mad. He found her packing. A suitcase was open on the bed.

"I don't think this marriage is working out. I've called my parents. They'll be here in two hours."

"Jeepers creepers, sweetie pie. You want to call it quits?"

Bessie nodded, trembling. "I think it's best. My father knows somebody who can handle the divorce."

"But I didn't mean it. You know how I am."

Bessie ignored him, carrying stockings from the dresser and placing them in the suitcase. Ernie did not know what to say. He was not even sure how he felt. He was a little peeved that Bessie had the gall to leave. On the other hand, part of him wanted her to breeze off to a new life. She was a flat tire, boring and drab. She was no spring chicken anymore. Plus, he thought about his favorite skirt, Nellie. He still carried a torch for her.

After he'd given Nellie the butter churn lid several years prior, he had visited her twice to bring up her mail and chat. He had never gotten any sex. He had not even stolen a kiss. She got wise. She found out he was hitched. He ran into her at the company store, and she said, "I know you're married, Ernie. Please don't come around anymore." It turned out some of Ernie's mining buddies had spilled the beans about his wife. He'd never forgive those good-for-nothings.

Divorcing might be a good thing, Ernie thought. He watched Bessie tuck her favorite pair of high heels into the suitcase. He had visions of becoming a ladies' man, lingering on Main Street and picking up flappers. But mainly, he wanted to be free to date Nellie. She was ducky, and she *was* a spring chicken. Maybe they could even make whoopee.

Suddenly he remembered his bankroll and got worried. Was Bessie aiming to leave him high and dry? Was that her plan? Was she going to steal his stash like ex-wives do? His temper flared. It was a match snuggling up to a jug of kerosene.

"I'm not giving you any money. You don't think I'm giving you any money, do you? I don't have any money." Ernie stepped toward Bessie in a menacing way.

But Bessie was no dunderhead. She was focused on escape. "I'm not asking for any money. You don't have to give me anything. I just want to go." She remembered her four-year-old daughters. "*We* just want to go."

Ernie backed off. He was fine with letting her haul off the young'uns. Holy hot cakes, he wouldn't have known what to do with them anyway. He'd never even changed a diaper or warmed a bottle of milk. *Children should be with their mother,* he thought.

Ernie returned to his scythe room to relax in his easy chair and catch the tail-end of the *"Vic and Sade"* show. He also lapped up some of his brown plaid. He got drunk. In fact, he got so drunk that he slurred his words and walked with a weave, sort of the way a paper airplane glides into a tailspin. Eventually, he sauntered back upstairs to check on Bessie.

She was standing in the middle of the living room next to two suitcases and staring out the window in anticipation of her parents' car. The couple's little girls played with their "Abigail" dolls at her feet.

Ernie leaned against the doorway, swigging his moonshine and glaring at Bessie. "You're lit up like a Christmas tree, Ernie."

"Says you." He took another gulp of his booze.

"There's some coffee in the kitchen." She hoped he would sober himself up, but she knew all too well that Ernie was not reasonable when he was half-cocked.

"Oh gibble-gabble, woman."

Ernie continued to stare at her with a resentful expression.

He looked a little like a leopard ready to pounce. Bessie kept glancing back and fidgeting. She was uncomfortable. She was worried. She shot him a partial smile in an effort to calm him, but it did not work.

"My parents will be here soon." She glanced back at his sinister expression. "It shouldn't be too long." There was more uncomfortable silence. "I think we'll wait outside."

"I'll give it to you, Bessie. You ain't no putty head."

Bessie tussled with her suitcase, trying to get it out the door. Ernie did not offer to help. He just leaned against the doorway with his bottle of rotgut and a smug look on his face. He enjoyed watching her struggle. It was right good entertainment as far as he was concerned.

Five minutes later, Bessie stood in the front yard with her suitcases and daughters. It was coming up to dusk. She noticed the headlights of a vehicle heading toward the house. Was it her parents? She hoped so. She thought so. But she was wrong. The vehicle did not stop. It was just a stranger in a Model T Ford.

Tucker was in that Ford. He was heading home from the pool hall. As he passed, he glanced over at the woman standing in the front yard with two children and two suitcases. He had no idea who these folks were. They looked like average Fairmont residents waiting for a taxi to take them to the train station. Maybe they were going on vacation to Boston or Miami, or maybe they were heading to Playland on Long Island, a popular spot for kids.

After Tucker's car was out of sight, Bessie's parents, Joseph and Virginia Clayton, arrived and parked in the driveway. Relieved to see them, Bessie burst into tears. She had been holding back her emotions, afraid to let Ernie get the better of her.

"Are you all right, honey?" Virginia ran over and hugged her daughter.

"Yes, Mama." Bessie wiped her eyes.

Joseph was carrying a flashlight and grabbed a suitcase.

Virginia bent down and spoke to the children. "You're gonna spend the night in the blue bedroom."

"Really, Grandma?" one exclaimed.

"What the hell is this?" Joseph screamed. He was shining his flashlight on the chiseled stone steps. "Hell's Half Acre? What's this supposed to mean?"

"I don't know. Let's just go." Bessie did not want to know about the steps. She did not want to think about Ernie. She just wanted to get out of there before something bad happened.

"He's creepy," Virginia said. "I don't know why you married him in the first place."

Everybody climbed into the car. As they drove away, Bessie saw Ernie peering out at them from behind the living room curtain. He looked bizarre. His eyes were wide. They did not blink. They were the eyes of a cold and cunning man. They were the eyes of a distrustful and erratic husband who she no longer knew.

Tucker was not thinking about the woman and two children he had passed. He was thinking about how the farmhouse was a right big mess. He had walked through the front door to a slipshod disaster: pillows, playing cards, jacks, flower clippings, and newspapers all over the floor. It reminded him of recent radio reports about the thirty-six tornados that had damaged hundreds of homes, displaced families, and even killed three dozen folks all the way from Illinois to Mississippi. Had a tornado hit his living room?

"Mom, you forgot to tidy," Tucker shouted. There was no answer. "Mom? She'll be here in ten minutes."

Frustrated, he spruced up a bit and pulled out what his

mother called the "Hoover upright," a vacuum cleaner that had cost a hard-to-come-by sixty dollars. He pushed it across the rug and over patches of dried mud that did not come out. The mud had been tracked in by Jal after clowning around in the garden with Salvatore. *These spots need a forceful rubbing with Sunlight soap,* Tucker thought to himself. That is, if the wool weaving could take it. In truth, the rug was getting thin and needed replacing. It had been bought in 1924 out of the fancy Bigelow-Hartford catalog but had never seemed to be as high-quality as the catalog itself.

After vacuuming, Tucker dusted the tables and took a slew of dirty dishes into the kitchen, piling them up in the sink. He thought about Ginger while he tidied. It had been several months since the couple's encounter with the "No Italians" sign at the country club. Neither Tucker nor Ginger had mentioned the awkward incident and neither had met the other's family. Their courtship had continued in a smooth and merry way. But this was the big night. After almost four years of courting, Ginger—the bearcat to end all bearcats—would finally meet Tucker's family. He crossed his fingers that the evening would go swimmingly.

Tucker fixed his hair in a hanging mirror in the hallway as Margaret, Philip, Rose, Jal, Mary, and James burst through the kitchen door. They had been in the back barn labeling the bootleg for the next day's pickup. The Barney Brothers were coming at six a.m. to get the latest batch of hooch.

"Good timing, everybody," Tucker joked. "Thanks for helping me clean."

"Sorry," Margaret said. "We were tagging the tarantula juice."

"Mom likes being a whisper sister." Rose giggled. "Or we could call her a 'lady legger.' My mom, the lady legger."

"When's your broad coming?" Margaret asked Tucker.

"She's not a broad," Tucker replied. "She's lovely. She's an upper crust."

"An upper crust? You never told me that." Margaret poured herself a glass of juice. "I don't like upper crusts."

"You'll like Ginger. She's got spunk."

"What kind of name is Ginger?" Margaret sat at the table with her juice.

"It's a fine name. It comes from Genevieve."

"That's French," Margaret said. "I don't like anything French."

"Why are you being like this? You know it's important to me."

"Hey, Tucker. Where's your hot mama from?" Philip plopped down on the couch.

"She's not a hot mama."

"I hope she's not from Genova," Margaret chimed in. "Those folks are hard-boiled."

"She's not Italian."

"What?" Margaret said. "This is baloney. Have you gone crazy? You know you're supposed to woo Italians."

"Is she a Negro?" Philip asked.

"No. She's English and German by birth."

"I already don't like her," Margaret folded her arms. "I bet she isn't Catholic."

"She's Baptist. It's close."

"No, it's not," Margaret shot back. "Baptists have no respect for the saints. I can't tolerate a person who has no respect for the saints."

"You're being prejudiced. And this is exactly why I didn't introduce you sooner."

"She's gonna force you to convert if you keep seeing her. Just you watch."

"Mom, you know I'm not religious."

There was a knock, and Tucker excitedly opened the door to find Ginger, wearing a brightly colored party dress and white gloves. She looked like a peacock among the simple-looking Moroose family. Tucker put his arm around his bearcat and led her into the living room.

"Everybody, this is Ginger."

The Morooses stared at her in silence for a full five seconds, and then Philip broke out in laughter. The cloddishness of the situation did not deter the always-sociable Ginger.

"It's such a pleasure to meet you. Tucker has told me so much. I just adore that you have a magnificent plot of land and oodles of vegetables. If the General Store ever goes out of business, I think you could survive for at least fifty years."

Margaret looked Ginger up and down. "You going someplace fancy?"

"Nope. Just coming here to meet you. I wanted to look my best. A girl should always look her best."

Tucker pulled Ginger close and took a deep breath. "Ginger and I have an announcement."

There were another five seconds of deafening silence.

Tucker sighed. "We're getting married."

"Married? What?" Margaret was beside herself. "You never said anything, You can't just spring this on us."

"Wow." Jal was wide-eyed.

Rose looked dejected. "You're getting married?"

Tucker had proposed to Ginger on the banks of the Monongahela River three weeks after the country club incident because he'd feared losing her. What if she ditched him over his Italian blood? What if her well-to-do parents put their foot down? What if she found a more suitable gent, such as a dashing doctor from good stock? Tucker was not a "chance-taker" so he had invited Ginger for a picnic and proposed to her before the pumpkin pie. He was all too pleased when she became overjoyed, wrapped her arms around his neck, and said "Yes." He presented her with an inexpensive ring, but promised to replace it with a bigger stone when his mouthpiece job got going. The couple had agreed not to let the cat out of the bag until the right moment. And this was that moment.

"Attaboy!" Philip said with a smile, feeling it was an achievement to land a flashy babe in a poofy party dress.

Margaret stood with a concerned look on her face. "You're too young, Tucker. You need to get your law practice started and you have responsibilities. You can't just up and leave us."

"I'm not moving out of town, Mom. I'm just getting married. We've already set the date."

"What?" Margaret said.

"You've set the date?" Rose looked miserable.

"It's gonna be so beautiful, with lots of pinks and purples," Ginger gushed. "I've ironed out all the details, and I've been teaching Tucker how to dance." She turned to him. "Let's show them."

The couple waltzed, while Ginger whispered into Tucker's ear, "One, two, three, four. One, two, three, four. One, two, three, four..."

The Moroose family watched in disbelief. A bundle of thoughts dashed through Margaret's head. Who would tend to the chores? Could she handle the bills on her own? Who would keep little Jal in line? How could her favorite son abandon her? She inched over to Philip and whispered in his ear.

"He's gonna end up Baptist. Just you watch."

Chapter 8

TWO WEDDINGS AND A SNITCH

"**W**HAT DO I need to know?" Tucker asked as he and Ginger headed up the walkway toward the Morris home.

"Well, my father's a tad reserved, but my mother's chatty."

"What does she like to talk about?"

"Fashion, movie stars… she bumps her gums about the Ritz, the Stork Club, and the Rockefellers."

"Hmm. I don't know much about the Rockefellers, except one of them's a bigamist."

Ginger was horrified. "Don't be bringing that up. She'll get the wrong idea."

"So you don't think I should mention my three wives?"

"Oh, Tucker. You're such a rascal."

As the couple stepped up to the front porch, Faire threw open the door, ready to roll out the welcome wagon.

"You must be the handsome Tucker," Faire gushed. "I'm tickled to finally meet you."

"It's a pleasure, Mrs. Morris." Tucker shook her hand and entered the home with Ginger.

"My boy, it's about time," Chester was in the front hall ready to greet them. "Seems Ginger's been keeping you a secret." The two men shook hands.

"No I haven't, Daddy. I just didn't want to be premature."

"Premature?" Chester replied. "Lucky we're not dead. We've been waiting for... what is it, Faire? Four years? Long enough to get cancer, go through treatment, and full-on die."

"Don't be morbid, darling," Faire said.

"I'm just saying our bodies could be rotting in Woodlawn Cemetery."

"Why don't we sit?" Faire said. "Our butler, Albert, has an out-of-this-world dinner planned," Faire called out, "Hors d'oeuvres, Albert... Albert?"

Everyone took a seat in the living room.

"Have you been to the Waldorf Astoria, Tucker?" Faire asked.

"No ma'am, I haven't."

"Well, there was a splendid party there last month in the Jade Room. Herbert Hoover attended and..."

"Mother," Ginger interrupted. "I don't think we should talk about that. Don't you want to know about Tucker?"

"I have a question," Chester spoke.

Everybody stared at him. "So, tell me about your father. He has brown eyes, I assume. And a full head of hair?" Chester saw that Ginger and Faire were annoyed. "I'm only asking so as to get a mental picture of the man."

"Actually, my father died a while back."

"Deary me, how did that happen?" Faire asked.

"It was a heart attack, ma'am."

"I'm so sorry. Probably too much stress at work. Chester knows about that. He's a doctor. So what industry did your father control?"

"Well... he didn't control anything. He was a miner."

"A miner?" Faire laughed. "You're quite the ham. Everyone knows only coloreds and Luigis work in the mines."

"Mother," Ginger spoke. "Tucker's Italian."

"Oh, don't tease." Faire laughed, but then realized Ginger was serious. "Actually, that's just dandy. We love the Italians. Don't we, Chester?"

Chester nodded.

"Tucker's very smart," Ginger bragged. "He's finishing up law school. Someday he's gonna be a senator."

"Great ambition is the passion of great character," Chester replied. "That's from Napoleon. A squat man, but shrewd nonetheless."

"Mother and Daddy, I'm gonna burst if I don't tell you the rest. Tucker and I are dizzy in love." Ginger snuggled up close to Tucker on the couch.

"That's nice, darling." Faire had no interest. "Where's that tardy Albert? He's always tardy, and he's always forgetting the hors d'oeuvres."

"Mother..." Ginger started.

"Albert?" Faire screamed.

"Mother, we're getting married."

"What? That's impossible." Faire was certain Tucker was a grifter, cozying up to her daughter for the suds. "You barely know each other."

"They've been dating for four years, Faire," Chester said. "We could be rotting in the cemetery."

"Stop butting in, dear." Faire smiled at Tucker. "It's too early. My daughter has plenty of options. I'm sure you understand."

"I'm over the moon, Mother."

"Is this a shotgun wedding?" Faire was worried that her daughter was pregnant.

"Of course not," Ginger replied.

"Well, we like you very much, Tucker. We've always liked the Italians, haven't we, Chester? But my daughter's not ready to get married."

"I *am* ready to get married. Stop treating me like a child."

Albert appeared with a towel draped over his forearm. "Dinner is served, madam."

"Oh, fiddle-faddle," Faire said. "Let's retire to the dining room. We can discuss this later."

Tucker and Ginger followed Albert, while Faire pulled Chester aside. "Take her out of the will."

"What?"

"I'm not letting a foreigner get his hands on our bank account."

"Oh, come on, Faire."

"He's a gold digger," she said.

"I don't think a boy can be a gold digger."

"That Luigi would be digging in the mines like the rest of his lot if he didn't have his shovel in our bank account."

Faire plastered a smile on her face and sashayed into the dining room.

It was the third week of November, 1933. It was a day Margaret would never forget. It was the day she was arrested.

Clotheslines crisscrossed the farmhouse backyard like garlands on a Christmas tree. There were dangling socks, shirts, pants, skirts, sheets, pillowcases, and towels. It looked as cluttered as a West End, Cincinnati slum. At least, that was Margaret's reckoning based on a television program she had seen about poverty in the Ohio city with its measly sixteen-foot wide lots and apartments holding up to twelve families at one time.

"Gee whiz," she muttered, taking a gander at the wet clothing. "It ain't exactly as neat as a pin." But Margaret knew being practical required looking rubbishy now and then. Full-time beauty was only for full-time highborns with their servants and such.

Margaret moved on to tackling two small rugs. She laid them over the wooden porch railing and banged on them with a broom. It got the dust out better than the "Hoover upright." Plus, it reduced tension; the "slapping around" was a release. Margaret had been tense since learning Tucker was fixing to marry the highfalutin Ginger Morris. She knew she would never accept this silly upper crust who came from the phony world of matching purses and pool parties. This high-class chippy was not good enough for her precious Tucker. He needed a salt-of-the-earth type, not a ballroom-dancing crackpot twirling a pink feather boa. There were more important matters than shimmying across the floor or bending into a Tango dip.

Plus, Margaret was beside herself over the wedding being held at the First Baptist Church instead of St. Peters. Who would have thought her right and proper Catholic son would be getting hitched in a pit of sin? Her poor husband was probably turning over in his grave, or trying to claw himself out in order to stop this lapse from decency. A non-Catholic wedding was a slap in the face, a brickbat to her, her ancestors, and her Italian homeland.

Tony G., a cop from the local station and a regular hooch

customer, came running around the side of the farmhouse. He was huffing and puffing, out of breath.

"I smell bacon," Margaret laughed.

Tony G. ignored her "pig" joke. He was frantic. "Margaret, the squad cars are on their way. You've got to get a wiggle on."

"What are you yapping about, T.G.? You looking to get soused before lunch?"

"No. You don't understand. They're coming. You've got to get out of town."

"Who's coming?"

"Rudy and the others from the station. You're gonna get pinched. They know about your stash. Benito snitched. They're gonna take you to the big house." Tony G. hightailed it back in the direction from which he had come.

Margaret was in disbelief.

Tony G. stopped and turned. "Hey, don't tell them I was here. You'd better hustle." He disappeared around the corner.

A dozen thoughts flew through Margaret's head, such as, "Could I hide the bootleg in time?" "Who's gonna handle the farm if I get thrown in the can?" and "Will my young'uns turn into waifs?" Margaret was paralyzed by her clashing emotions. Fear, worry, self-preservation, duty, confusion, and desperation buzzed around her head like a pack of bent bees. She would have leaned on Tucker for advice, but he was in class. In fact, she was the only one home.

Margaret's first thought was to conceal the rotgut gadgets, but realized they were too bulky. Plus, she lacked muscle to lift the boiler and was fuzzy about how to detach the thumper and flake stand. Her second idea was to dash into the back barn and hide, but figured this was a goopy plan because she would be butt up against her stash and look even guiltier. "Oh my goodness, where did all this hooch come from?" "No officer, I've never seen this still before." "A friend has been renting this barn, so you can imagine my surprise." Every blasted excuse sounded fishy. As a third option, Margaret thought about scooting from room to room in the farmhouse, locking windows and turning the place into a fort. But this was not Little Bighorn. It was not Custer's Last Stand. The fuzz would just knock down the door. It was their job to knock down doors. They were professional door knocker-downers. In the end, Margaret felt like a rattletrap: old and broken down. She was tired and lacked the spunk to fight on. She accepted defeat right then and there. She plopped down on the living room couch and placed her head in her hands. She was like a turtle crawling into a shell. Minutes later, there was a pounding at the door. She was hesitant, but answered it. To her surprise, it was little Jal, rubbing his nose.

"What are you doing here?"

"The teacher sent me home. I've got the sniffles."

"Let me see." Margaret put her hand on Jal's forehead. "You're steaming. Get yourself upstairs."

Jal felt ill from top to bottom, so he put on his pajamas and dragged himself into bed. Margaret handed him a cup of orange juice.

"You need the vitamin C," she said as she left the room.

Downstairs, she settled back on the couch. New thoughts came into her mind. Was Tony G. wrong? Maybe the coppers were not coming. Could he have been fibbing? She remembered the time he'd phoned her with "This is May." When she said, "May who," he replied, "May-onnaise." It was a silly prank, especially for a grown man and police officer, but it had given her a belly laugh nonetheless. Was this another joke? Was Tony G. pulling her leg?

Suddenly, there was a knock. Margaret held her breath as she answered the door. This time, it was bad news. A brood of policemen glared at her, "Benito the snitch" and the loyal Tony G. among them. Some coppers fanned out over the property in search of her illegal stash. They found it within minutes. Then, Rudy put cuffs on Margaret's wrists and escorted her to a waiting patrol car.

"I see you've got your bean shooter, Benito." Margaret noticed the scumbag weasel was packing heat. "You planning to gun me down?"

"No, Margaret," Benito cackled. "Not today. I'm just gonna turn you over to the feds. You'll be in stir for years."

Jal had heard the commotion from his bed. He ran downstairs and into the front yard, where he tugged on his mother's skirt just before she got into the car. "What's going on? Why's the fuzz here?" Jal knew they had come about the back barn still but did not want to say it out loud.

"It's okay, Jal." Margaret pretended to be calm, even though she was sweating up a storm. "Just wait in your room until Tucker gets home. He'll handle everything. You hear?"

"Where are they taking you?" Jal became teary-eyed.

"We're sending your mama up the river." Benito flashed a smug look.

"They're taking me to the station," Margaret replied. "Now, go back to your room, son."

"I want to come with you," Jal begged.

"I'll handle him," Tony G. said, putting his arm around Jal. "Don't you worry about a thing, Margaret. I'll wait with him until the others get home."

Rudy pushed Margaret into the cop car while Tony G. consoled Jal.

No one on the scene noticed the 1928 Renault parked across the street. No one realized there were two members of the Ku Klux Klan in that car. And no one had any idea that it was Mr. Clark and his long-time buddy, Henry. As former detectives, they had been given the scoop about the arrest. They knew Margaret would be nicked at noon for her "rummy hut." It was not so much about seeing the notorious "guido bootleg queen" in hot water with the law. It was more about her lying, thieving, and mischief-making son, Jal. He had caused headaches for coppers, detectives, and townsfolk for years. He was beyond the pale. Mr. Clark had a particular hatred for Jal ever since the kid egged his house. It was two years prior. Jal had done it for revenge. Mr. Clark had hoped to haul Jal into the station and throw him in the slammer, but lacked proof to make the charges stick. Jal denied being the culprit, the smart alecky liar that he was. "I didn't do nothing, Mr. Clark, but you deserve it for being in the Klan. You're just a shriveled-up yokel." It took Mr. Clark hours of scrubbing to get that sunbaked egg off his red brick. He was glad he had tarred and feathered those bicycles back in 1928.

Mr. Clark gloated as he watched Jal sobbing over his mother's arrest. Jal's misery was a delicious sight, a satisfying treat. It was like candy.

"One less whisper-sister wreaking havoc on the good folks of Fairmont," Henry said.

"Scofflaws," Mr. Clark said. "That whole cotton-picking family's a bunch of scofflaws. Especially that slippery eel of a kid."

"We should invite him to Hangman..." Henry laughed. "For a goon's grab."

"Nah, better to stay on the level."

"We could at least paste him one." Henry punched the air with his fist.

"I don't figure being on the wrong side of the law." Mr. Clark started up the engine. The two men headed to the station to watch the heavies book Margaret.

Five hours later, Tucker arrived home to chaos and a nest of worry warts. His siblings had given in to panic, tears, room-pacing, and nail-biting, except for Rose who loved the "*Bonnie and Clyde"* or *"Dragnet Girl"* drama of the ordeal. From her perspective, crime was dark and murky, risky and thrilling, absorbing and romantic.

There was relief when Tucker walked through the door because he was the "Bruno" or "man of the house," as Margaret liked to say. His presence was calming. He was the steady captain of the ship. He was the anchor that kept his family from veering off course.

"They took her away," Jal screamed. "They took mama away for the bootleg."

"What?" Tucker removed his coat.

"She's in the slammer," Philip said. "And they want ten Cs for bail."

"We don't have that kind of money," Tucker replied.

"Let's crush her out," Rose laughed, eager for some down-home titillation. "My boyfriend's got a getaway car."

"I wonder if Jimmy Dee could lend us some," Tucker contemplated. "He knows I'm square. I can pay him back after I get the mouthpiece business going."

"Where would he get that kind of cash?" Philip asked.

"He's half-owner in the grocery." Tucker put his coat back on.

"He is?" Philip was surprised.

"That mug dresses too rinky-dink for a well-heel," Rose said, referring to Jimmy Dee's weather-beaten, "stray-dog" look. "No dame would date that guy."

"Trust me. He's no pauper."

Rose's face lit up as she chewed on the idea of turning the grocery clerk into a sugar daddy.

Tucker headed over to Jimmy Dee's house and it was not long before he had signed a contract with the well-to-do grocery clerk for half the needed greenbacks. There was a steep payback schedule and lofty interest just in case Margaret got it in her mind to duck out of the state. Plus, Jimmy Dee helped Tucker snag a bond for the other five hundred dollars from The Lexington Company. Following the business dealings, Margaret was released from the can. As Tucker and Margaret walked out of the station, they passed Benito, who was doing paperwork at the front desk.

"Hey, Margaret. Don't be drifting off to Canada." Benito chuckled. "I wouldn't want to have to hunt you down like a bush rat."

"You're the only rat I know," Margaret snapped at him.

"I'll be turning the file over to the feds in three weeks," Benito said. "I'm second string. But them feds… they'll put the screws on you."

"Your mother knows what you did, Benito. She's looking down at you and thinking what a rotten squealer she raised." Margaret marched out of the station with Tucker.

Benito had been a cellar-smeller. In other words, he'd been bumming hooch off Margaret for months before the bust. She could not figure why he'd tattled. It was not in his interest. But whatever the case, she hoped she'd never see that vile, snake-in-the-grass snitch again.

Less than two weeks later on December 5, 1933, there was big news. Congress passed the Blaine Act, which lifted the prohibition. In other words, Margaret's hooch lab in the back barn was no longer illegal—that is, if it had not been taken apart and hauled off by the coppers. The bad news was that the new law seemed to come too late to help the Moroose family. Margaret already had a court date on the Marion County calendar and her case was set to be referred to the feds in only a few days.

Although Tucker had not yet finished law school, he decided it was time to put some of his learning to work. He donned a black suit and garnet tie so as to look all official-like. Then he marched down to the Fairmont police department to have a one-on-one with Rudy—the station supervisor and bull who had gone on record for arresting Margaret.

"Are you aware of the Blaine Act?" Tucker asked him.

"Yep, but that's got nothing to do with your ma. She broke the law and she's got to pay for her crimes."

Tucker paced as if he was in a courtroom. "First, my mother has nine children and no husband. Who do you think is gonna feed, clothe, and take care of the young'uns?"

"You could do it, Tucker. You'll be a mouthpiece real soon... bringing home a decent wage." Rudy kicked back in his chair and rested his feet on his desk. He was not going to be nudged.

"You're right. I'm about to get my law license. I'll have it in a few months. But what you don't realize is I plan to lawyer the hell out of this case. Plus, I will push it forward on the calendar again and again. So when the jury eventually sits to hear it, the prohibition will have been over for a very long time. They will have no appetite for putting away a single mother with nine children who did something that has been perfectly legal for some time."

"I think they'll have an appetite. Folks don't like lawbreakers. We've got a new prison for dames over in Alderson, so you can visit..."

Tucker interrupted. "Maybe you're unaware, but your men were my mom's customers. Not one. Not two. Not even three. Almost the entire station were boozehounds. I doubt you want it known... even though I'm sure the Fairmont Times would be interested."

Rudy fidgeted. He looked on-edge. "That's nonsense."

"I've got witnesses who will swear under oath. And one of your men feels guilty. He's all ready to confess. So, you've got a choice. Lose the case and, of course, don't refer it to the feds. Or the Fairmont Police Department's going down."

Rudy dropped the case.

Tucker felt good about the triumph in Rudy's office. He had walked in with sweaty palms and a nervous twitch and come out feeling like he was no longer a flatwheeler with pie-in-the-sky dreams. Smooth talking was critical in the world of legal wrangling, and it was possible that maybe—just maybe—he would not be a complete washout in the field. But it was not just his self-confidence that got a lift; so did his reputation. Those around town "in the know," such as former hooch customers, were flabbergasted that an Italian, who was not even a bona fide lawyer, could pin the Fairmont Police Department to the mat.

The Moroose family was also impressed. Margaret routinely bear-hugged Tucker, saying "My son, the hero." Plus, she called him a swashbuckler, a lion, a big gun, and "My very own Jesus Christ." Of course, "Jesus Christ" was a sacrilegious slip, which required scooting over to confessional and asking the Lord for forgiveness.

Although Tucker liked the praise, his attention was not on the past. It was on the future because his wedding was in view. In fact, it was that very day. He was excited but also taken aback by the sky-high cost of it all. He called it "Daylight robbery," adding, "Our bread and butter's getting snatched away for five minutes with a preacher man and a drop of organ music." The flowers were an exorbitant seventy-five dollars, Ginger's dress was sixty-two dollars, the lime green attendant dresses were ninety-one dollars, and the engagement ring was eighty-three dollars. Gifts to attendants were twelve dollars, and decorations were sixteen dollars. The "special help coordinator" was an extra twenty dollars. There were other fees for music, drinks, Tucker's tux, the church reception room, photos, cake, and the bridal bouquet. A high cost was not uncommon.

Couples routinely spent twenty-five percent of their yearly income getting hitched. Tucker and Ginger were lucky; Faire and Chester were bearing the brunt of the fees.

Ginger wore a long-sleeve, high-collar wedding dress, hemmed to lightly kiss the ground. Woven into her perfectly bobby-pinned hair was a lacy veil. Tucker wore a tuxedo with a satin tie and flower pin. A handkerchief peeped out of his pocket.

"Your hanky's hiding," Margaret said in a last-ditch effort to get Tucker to come to his senses. "It's against you getting married."

"Oh, Mom," Tucker laughed and gave her a peck on the cheek.

Similarly, Ginger had a testy conversation with Faire, who had been pouting round the clock.

"Come on, put on a rosy face, Mother. Be bright-eyed and bushy-tailed. This is my big day."

"I'm not gonna trot around like a gay fox."

So that was how it went. Both mothers were dead-set against their young'uns tying the knot. They stood on opposite sides of the church, listening to the traditional Mendelssohn "Wedding March" and shooting each other with the evil eye. Margaret equated the Morrises with something poisonous like arsenic or hemlock, while Faire walked around with her nose in the air. She was a purebred poodle, unwilling to mix with bloodhounds.

A graceful reception followed the ceremony. It featured food and drink, cake and dancing. Guests oohed and aahed as Tucker and Ginger waltzed to a medley of romantic tunes, including Irving Berlin's "Blue Skies" and George Gershwin's "Someone to Watch Over Me."

However, all was not the oyster's earrings. In the midst of

the harmony and winsomeness, there was a blustering blow-up at the cake table.

"This one's mine," Jal screamed, grabbing a plate of cake. He was dressed shabbily in lightly stained pants, a partially unbuttoned vest, and a wrinkled shirt with rolled-up sleeves.

"You lunkhead. You already had cake," Salvatore yelled back.

"Tucker's my brother. I can have all the cake I want, and I want the chocolate bell!"

"I'm the guest." Salvatore snatched the piece of cake from Jal's saucer and dropped it onto his own plate.

Guests were flabbergasted. The boys looked like mugs in a bar brawl.

"Hey, put that back, you simp," Jal hollered.

"No."

Then, Jal walloped Salvatore in the mouth. It was practically a knockout blow. Salvatore went reeling backward. Then, Jal jumped onto his friend, punching him like crazy. The boy's plates toppled to the ground and cracked. Cake flew across the room.

"Goodness gracious," Ginger said. "What's all the fuss?"

Tucker was incensed. He marched over and broke up the tussle, grabbing his little brother by the shirt collar. "Jeepers creepers, Jal. This is my wedding. Can't you behave for one day? And you have a swanky suit at home. Why do you look like a guttersnipe?" Exasperated, Tucker released Jal and returned to Ginger.

Jal felt bad. His black shadow had gotten the better of him. He did not mean to steal Tucker's thunder. This was his marriage day, and he had botched things yet again. Jal fled the church while Salvatore got back on his feet. A guest took it upon himself to pick up the broken glass and cake from the floor.

Outside, Jal drifted down the sidewalk, asking himself why he always caused trouble. He wiped a tear from his face. He was fourteen years old now. He was almost a grown-up. He should not be acting all hotheaded. He wanted Tucker to be proud of him, but he had wrecked everything. Would he always be a flop? Would he ever get his fiery temper under control? Would his life ever be more than one scrap after another?

Jal kicked a pebble. It rolled into the sewer.

It was not long before there was another fancy hullabaloo. It was Ernie and Nellie's wedding. They were finally getting hitched after a drawn-out but sunny courtship. The simple event with twenty guests took place in Ernie's backyard with an improvised altar. Nellie wore an ankle-length, pale yellow frock and carried a bouquet of daisies and sweet pea. There were no attendants and a justice of the peace headed up the vows. Ernie refused to let Christianity worm its hideous little commandments into their special day, and Nellie did not put up a fuss about the lack of "God" in their vows.

Nellie wanted an unusual keepsake, so Ernie suggested she take a photo in a tree. He pulled out a ladder from the garage and she climbed up a sugar maple. Ernie snapped pictures with his Kodak. In some shots, Nellie's ankles were crossed. In others, her legs were crossed at the knee and her arms were open to the sky. In still others, she waved her grosgrain hat in the air.

After what Ernie called "frolicking in the sugar maple," Timothy—a miner with an operatic voice—sung "At Dawning" in the yard. The guests (as well as all neighbors within earshot) listened attentively.

Ernie liked being a rascal so he got onto one knee in front of his new bride and sung along with Timothy. "When the dawn flames in the sky, I love you. When the birdlings wake and cry, I love you..."

Nellie blushed. Ernie's voice was raspy and off-key, but she loved that he gave her so much attention. He made her feel like a wolfess: powerful yet feminine.

Of course, she knew about his previous marriage and that he had gotten a divorce. But she was deaf to the details, including the fact that Bessie had claimed "severe mental cruelty." Divorces at the time were frowned upon and tended to be granted solely for abandonment, mental illness, cruelty, or adultery. Some states were more lenient than others. For example, divorces were easier to get in Indiana, Nevada, and Utah. The court also ruled that Bessie should raise the couple's young'uns. The judge stated, "The children are of tender age and female. Therefore, the mother is preferred as their custodian. She has been shown to have parental affection for the children."

Ernie's daughters, who were now of kindergarten age, visited him three times a year. Nellie liked that he took pains with them on those occasions. He would push them on the swing, make them gingerbread and Jell-O, and even play their favorite game, "doll house." On Halloween—Ernie's most beloved holiday—he would buy his daughters costumes and take them trick or treating. Nellie found it striking that he showed such sensitivity and playfulness. This was the side of Ernie she knew: the good side. She had no knowledge of his mood swings because he had kept them under control. She knew nothing about the scythe room with the locked door and the roll of scratch in the toolbox. He had kept them out of sight. Nellie had no reason to question Ernie. She had no reason to fear him. She was in the dark about the coldness in his soul.

After Timothy finished singing "At Dawning," the guests congregated in the living room for an after-ceremony buffet.

There was fried chicken, pineapple salad, mashed potatoes, overcooked string beans, Parker House rolls, spumoni ice cream, and champagne.

Sam—the supervisor from the mine—was so sozzled that he weaved around on his gams like a factory cart going down an incline. He almost toppled over a footstool as he toddled over to Ernie and Nellie. "My boy." Sam slapped Ernie's back. "I'll be your best man at this wedding and the next."

"We already got hitched," Ernie said. "Remember? But you were a befitting first man. You were."

Sam scratched his head. His face was a question mark.

"I won't be taking any more wives," Ernie said. "Nellie's a keeper and a lovely bit of fluff. Aren't you, dollface?"

"Oh, Ernie." Nellie swooned, and Ernie kissed her on the cheek.

"Guess I'm all balled up." Sam staggered away.

A guest scampered over. "It was a lulu of a wedding! And that bride of yours… she's lovely."

Nellie adored being fawned over.

"Yep. She's a rare dish." Ernie was then motioned over to the gift table by Otis. "Be right back, honeybun," he whispered to Nellie and headed over to Otis.

"Wanted to give you this up close." Otis handed Ernie a present. "It ain't nobody's business. Don't want to louse it up for you by leaving it in the open."

"Much appreciated." Ernie took the package. "What do I owe you?"

"Zip. It's your nuptials."

"Help yourself to some vittles."

"Sure enough." Otis headed over to the food table.

Ernie checked to make sure nobody was watching and stashed the package inside his jacket. Then he skirted over to the basement door and unlocked it with his special key.

Once downstairs, he opened the present to find the book, *"Archfiends and the Dismembering of Children."* He savored the title, but then noticed something else tucked inside the box. It was an actual dead human hand. *Great sassafras,* he thought. *This is aces, a first-rate gift.* It was blackish red, slightly shriveled, child-sized, and frozen in the shape of the "horned god." In other words, the pinky and the index finger were pointing out, while the other fingers were tucked under the thumb. Ernie held it up to the light, examining it from every angle as if it was an heirloom. He knew the "horned god" symbolized the journey to the underworld. Had Otis been chopping up young'uns or did he have a pal at a funeral home? Ernie was unsure how his friend had come up with such an offering, but he was over-the-sun impressed.

He walked over to what he called his "rite shelf." He placed the book and the dead hand on top of the other books and pamphlets he had gotten from Otis over the years. He had not examined them with any seriousness, but he knew it was time. It was time to buckle down. He had not fixed up his scythe room like he'd always planned. He would start redesigning on Sunday. Now that he was settled with a new wife, there could be no more shirking and backsliding, no more song and dance. The world was waiting. Blackness was waiting. The demons were waiting. He would not be a muttonhead and let them down.

Chapter 9

THE KEWPIE DOLL

THE NEXT SEVEN years moved like a sailfish in salt water. They shot by like crazy, even though nothing key happened. Ernie settled into married life and took to sprucing up his scythe room behind Nellie's back. Tucker finished school, snagged his mouthpiece license, and became the lowliest tenderfoot on the "McNeer and Highland" law firm's food chain. He made a decent but not eye-popping wage of $300 per month, but got stuck writing briefs, doing legal research, and making routine appearances in court. Essentially, anything that did not appeal to the senior advocates became Tucker's burden. This gnawed at him. He had not gone into law to handle trifling matters. He had not gone into law to be somebody else's pygmy goat. He had not gone into law to become a sad sack.

Tucker yammered on about his frustration until 1941 when he up and quit. He was thirty-three.

From then on out, he went solo. Lots of clients hired him as their courtroom advocate. He was saddled with a mighty case load, yet lacked a supply of junior attorneys and assistants to pick up the slack. Plus, he had no office. His apartment became his "law firm." Ginger was not pleased as boxes of legal files piled up in the bedroom, then in the living room, and eventually in the kitchen. Ginger called Tucker "a professional pack rat."

"Honey, I'm making dinner between the Miller car accident and the Bailey eviction," Ginger hollered from the kitchen.

"And don't think I don't appreciate it," Tucker replied.

The next day, Ginger complained, "Don't come crying if the Peterson annulment smells like tomato paste."

"Tomato paste's fine," Tucker joked. "I think Mr. Peterson's allergic to pineapple."

On the following day, Ginger bellowed, "Maybe we should get on the horn to the Olympics to see if they have a 'professional pack rat' contest."

Tucker yelled back, "I already called. I'll be competing in Helsinki next week."

And so it went, month after month, until the young'uns started popping out. First there was Sharon. A year later, there were the twins: Sheila and Shirley. And, finally, they adopted a dog: Fido. Tucker found himself in a skimpy, two-bedroom apartment surrounded by a wife, three babies, a mutt, and at least a hundred file boxes.

"You think it's getting a little cramped in here?" he asked Ginger one night in late 1947, when the children were of nursery school age.

"Do you want to know the truth?"

Tucker nodded.

"I feel like a finger in a thimble."

"A middle finger?" he asked.

"Yes, dear."

So, the next morning, Tucker and Ginger got toggled to the bricks and met with Mr. Hughes at the bank to see if they could afford a home. They were hopeful. Tucker's earnings had increased considerably since he had ventured out on his own. He'd been bringing home the bacon to the tune of a sizable $850 each month. He could almost touch affluence.

Mr. Hughes—a pencil-pushing, showboat type—tapped on his calculator for ten minutes with a furrowed brow and a grimace.

Ginger became uneasy. "I know you don't like handouts, Tucker, but if worse comes to worst, we *could* ask my parents…"

"Sweetheart," he interrupted. "Able-bodied men don't need the Red Cross."

Suddenly, Mr. Hughes grinned real big. "This is gonna blow your wig, folks."

Tucker and Ginger held their breath, wide-eyed.

"You can swing it. We can lend you some cash for a real swell house near the glitterati.

"Near the glitterati?" Ginger was jubilant.

Tucker was mystified. "But the silver screen stars live in Hollywood. I don't think we have any in West Virginia."

Mr. Hughes leaned in close to Ginger and pointed at Tucker. "He's a thinker, isn't he? That's why he makes the big clams."

"That's right. He's an intellectual."

Mr. Hughes turned to Tucker. "All I'm saying is this. You're not exactly behind the eight ball. If Mickey Rooney or Montgomery Clift were to move to Marion County, they'd be smack-dab on your street. Maybe even right next door."

"Right next door?" Ginger was elated. "Did you hear that, Tucker?"

The couple bought a roomy place in a swanky area where crime was only seen on television or talked about on the radio.

Their new home on Sunset Drive was white, two-story, and comprised of wood with a charming front porch. It also had a right nice view. In the sprawling front yard, there were manicured, cone-shaped bushes, a rock walkway, and a crescent-shaped bench.

On move-in day, Tucker drove the family to the new place. Ginger was in the passenger seat and the children were in the back with Fido. A Mayflower Transit truck was parked on the street, and movers were lugging the couple's furnishings and boxes, including the mess of legal files, through the front door.

Pete Palin, a dapper fellow who lived next door, was plucking letters from his mailbox when the Moroose's Plymouth pulled into the driveway. He waved. "Howdy, new neighbors."

Ginger returned the kindness. "Hi there. Nice to meet you."

Tucker parked, opened the trunk, and began unloading small appliances, bags of shoes, and other personal items. "I'm glad the movers are here. Maybe they'll finish before lunch."

"Come on girls. Out of the car. Let's go, Fido." Ginger hustled everybody out, but eight-year-old Sharon was distracted by her kewpie doll.

"Mommy, my doll's broken."

Ginger removed belongings from the trunk.

"Mommy?" Sharon tried again, and then turned to Tucker. "Daddy, can you fix my kewpie?"

Tucker set a pair of boudoir lamps on the driveway. "Not right now, honey."

"This is a beautiful neighborhood," Ginger said. "I can't believe we're gonna be living in such paradise."

"Mommy, my doll!"

"Look." Tucker pointed at a building at the bottom of the hill. "The round house... where Jal works. It's right over there."

"That's so very convenient," Ginger replied.

Sharon came to life with excitement. "Uncle Jal works there?

Does Uncle Jal work there, Daddy?" She tugged on Tucker's jacket. "Does he?"

"Yes, he does."

"He can fix my doll." She was off.

"Wait," Tucker yelled. "You can't go down there."

"Sharon," Ginger screamed. "Sharon, come back here. Right now."

Sharon's forty-one-inch body disappeared into the distance.

"She's got some moxie, that one," Tucker said.

"Oh fiddlesticks," Ginger said. "I'm always chasing after that girl."

The B&O Roundhouse was a mechanic's shop for trains. It was a semicircular building with a turntable for steam engine locomotives, a slew of windows, and sixteen top hat-like ventilation shafts on the roof. It was butt-up against the railroad tracks on one side and the Monongahela River on the other, where a suspension bridge stretched over the water to connect up with downtown Fairmont. There had been an incident years prior when a worker left the cylinder cocks closed on a locomotive that had a leaky throttle valve. When it came down the track, it did not change direction. It veered straight across the turntable and through the wall of the roundhouse. Thankfully, nobody was killed. A couple of workers ended up with some cuts and scrapes.

Jal, who was now twenty-nine, had been working there, measuring and fine-tuning brass bushings, since graduating from high school with a sticky D average. He was proud of himself for not turning into a gold brick or a "loafer type" like some of his former bunkies. He wished he'd had a hankering for college, but the notion of sitting through four more years of classes made him want to flush his hash. He also regretted that he had never picked himself up and found a career, but there were few jobs for the unschooled. Plus, he was low on spare time, working forty to fifty hours per week for a pitiful seventy dollars per month. It was barely enough to cover the rent for his shoddy one-room apartment on run-down Pennsylvania Avenue.

Jal's life was on the skids, or at least it was one notch away from it. He could not shake his black shadow. It popped up a lot, usually at the wrong time. Once, Jal got nasty-mouthed with Butch, the roundhouse foreman, who had asked him to stay past working hours. "Shove your clutch. I'm going home." Then, he punched Butch in the jaw. Jal got lucky. Butch was not hurt and did not fire him. He was short on laborers at the time.

Then there was Herbie, Jal's best friend of ten years who worked in the cubbyhole one over and to the left. Jal routinely hammered him as "a bucket of bilge" and "a bit freakish," while Herbie lobbed back his own insults, describing Jal as a "lazy dewdropper," "ugly like a blobfish," and "Mr. Phonus Balonus." But when Herbie confessed out loud that he found dames "scary," three of the roundhouse boys teased him as a "percy pants" and a "poof." This angered Jal, so he popped the prigs in their snouts, saying that nobody but him had a right to call Herbie names. Butch did not take kindly to the violence, calling Jal a "ruffian" and docking his pay.

Jal was like Herbie in that he had no wife or young'uns, but this was not to say he did not date. The roundhouse boys were always on skirt patrol at the local bar, getting pickled, being obnoxious, and fancying themselves as tomcats. But Jal did not drink and stayed mostly to himself. It was a rare Friday night when he could be found at the local diner with his arm around a gal. Jal's relationships were always short-lived. He could not be serious because he did not have the bucks to be serious. He did not want to snag a dish to call his own without a better job, a better apartment, and a better paycheck.

"A penny a day keeps the dolls away," Jal told Herbie one afternoon. "But with ten dollars a day, it'd be a different story. I'd be hitched to a slick chick and living in the suburbs like my brother."

Jal was in his windowless cubbyhole smoothing brass fittings with his electric sander when Butch appeared.

"Jal? Hey, Jal... turn that thing off."

Jal shut off the machine and removed his goggles.

"You've got a visitor. In the front room."

"A visitor?" Jal was confused. He'd never had one of those, except for the time Tucker surprised him on his birthday with a chocolate cupcake.

Jal mopped up the fittings with his hand, pushing them to the middle of the work table so they would not fall to the floor. Then, he headed to the front room where he found little Sharon.

"Sharon, what are you doing here? Where are your parents?"

"At our new house. My kewpie's broken, Uncle Jal. Will you fix it for me?"

Jal took the doll and studied it. The left arm was dangling. "I suppose I can, but then we have to get you home. I bet your mom and dad are worried." Jal grabbed a container of glue, dabbed a little on the doll's arm, and popped it back into the socket.

"What do you do here?" Sharon asked.

"I work with brass fittings. I fix broken trains."

"Trains get broken just like dolls?"

"Yes, they do."

"Do you like fixing trains?"

"It's a job, I guess."

"My daddy's a lawyer. Why aren't you a lawyer?"

Jal handed Sharon the fixed kewpie. "I'm not smart like your daddy."

"Yes you are. You fixed my doll."

Ginger dashed through the door, out of breath. "Sharon, you can't just run off like that. I'm sorry if she's bothering you, Jal."

"She's no bother."

Sharon showed off her kewpie. "Look, Mommy. He fixed my doll."

Ginger put her arm around her daughter. "Come along, Sharon. We have to get home."

"Bye, Uncle Jal." Sharon waved.

"Bye-bye Sharon."

"We'll see you at the party next Saturday," Ginger said to Jal. "I'm making a delicious sponge cake."

"Sounds swell." Jal returned to his cubbyhole, donned his goggles, and went back to work.

It was Saturday at the Yost house, and it was the day following Sharon's visit to the roundhouse. Ernie was 45, Nellie was 40, and the couple had settled into a regular routine. This is not to say there weren't bumps and skirmishes here and there, but Ernie had stayed on top of his fury. He was like a sweater; he would start to unravel from time to time, but then catch himself. He would take out his scissors, snip off loose threads, and all would be copacetic for a month or two. The problem was that as the years went by, the sweater began to fall apart. The wool became frayed at the sleeves, at the neckline, and near the waist. Ernie could not trim the fabric fast enough. A complete collapse seemed imminent. It was clearly on the horizon. Even Nellie knew it on some level, although she did not want to admit it. She told herself that her marriage was all peaches and cream. It was rosy and sweet like cotton candy. And, by golly, she could control Ernie if need be. Things could never get out of hand because she was a perfect wife and he was her "sugarpuss."

"What are you making?" Nellie was cheery as she swept the front walkway.

"A whistle." Ernie was sitting in a wooden kitchen chair in the yard, whittling away with a carving knife. The shavings fell into an unkempt flowerbed of buttercups, dayflowers, and crippled crane-fly orchids. Ernie's black cocker spaniel, Tutu, sat at his feet.

"My goodness, I married a genius."

"I like to tinker around, Nellie-cakes." Ernie shot her a wink. He called her "Nellie-cakes" when he was in a chirpy mood.

"Maybe you could fix the porch light this afternoon."

Ernie ignored the remark. He had no interest in abandoning his hobby for a chore.

"Did you hear me, Ernie?"

He wanted to shout, "Mind your potatoes, woman," but thought better of it. It was another one of those loose threads on the sweater. He quickly snipped it and grunted, "Uh huh."

"Well, maybe next weekend." Nellie decided it was better to put the topic to rest.

"Yep," Ernie mumbled.

Nellie continued sweeping until she got to the stone steps, where she saw the eerie carved lettering. "Oh my goodness… it says, 'Hell's Half Acre.'"

Ernie did not speak. He was hatching up a good excuse.

"Ernie?"

"It was there when my parents bought the house." He tried to sound casual.

"Really? What do you think it means?"

"Beats me. Come on over here, Nellie-cakes, and try out the whistle. Let's see if it works."

She ignored him. "It's loathsome. Maybe you could scratch it out."

"I'm not gonna scratch it out, woman," Ernie barked, but then caught himself. He calmed down and smiled. "Pay it no mind. Now, roll up your flaps. You should get inside. Looks like it's gonna rain pitchforks."

Nellie got on her knees and ran her fingers over the carved words. "Whoever did this is a few peas short of a casserole."

"Nellie, don't make me tell you again!"

Nellie was alarmed by Ernie's bossiness and cross tone.

"Nellie! I told you to get your tookus inside."

She was not normally one to let herself get bullied, but she composed herself, dusted off her dress, and retreated into the home.

Chapter 10

THE MOUTHPIECE AND THE PHARMACY BUFF

TUCKER REMEMBERED THE first time he'd set foot inside the Fairmont courthouse. He was fourteen and thought it looked like a chapel for politicians. It felt solemn, like a place where the soul could get thrown for a loop. A preacher could call a fellow "full of sin" from a soapbox, but so could a judge, except the judge could mete out a shellacking in the process. Pictures of former presidents —George Washington, Thomas Jefferson, and Abraham Lincoln—hung in the front altar section of the courtroom. A slatted, wooden barrier separated the judge's modest desk and jury area from the public observation seats. There were hooks on the wall for men's hats, and an American flag balancing on a stand. All in all, the place was not fancy because, as Tucker figured it, West Virginia was not a fancy state. It was down-home and not fussy. He imagined big city courtrooms in New York and Chicago full of carved wood, gold trim, and other frou-frou ornamentation.

The Fairmont court looked much the same in 1948, except a picture of the West Virginia seal had been mounted on the wall. It was two days after moving to Sunset Drive, and Tucker was arguing a pressing case about spousal abuse to a judge and a room full of onlookers. His client, Mrs. Carlton, sat next to him, while Mr. Carlton fidgeted at the defense counsel table with an attorney named Redkin.

Jal, who was dressed in his usual scruffy clothes, sneaked into the courtroom and sat in the back row to watch. It was his day off. He was proud of his brother for making so much of himself and wished he could do the same. Tucker had a refined life, conversing with upper crusts. Jal had a grubby life, working with his hands. Tucker had a dishy wife and swell children. Jal had a potted plant and an empty refrigerator. Tucker had potential for hitting the big time. Jal had potential for ending up in a soup line.

Unfortunately, Jal could not see his brother as a catalyst or motivating influence because he lacked self-confidence. He regularly told the gang at the roundhouse, "I'm damned useless." The boys clamored back with "Stop looking for pity," "Go jump in a lake," or something equally dismissive. One time, Herbie had tried to be nice, saying, "You're plenty useful." However, Jal had struck back, "Much appreciated, but you know you're an oil can like me." That put the lid on it for Herbie. It was the last time he tried to help.

"Your Honor." Tucker stood and spoke with a loud and self-assured voice. "This is an egregious case of cruelty. Mr. Carlton not only abused Mrs. Carlton emotionally but, on one occasion, he attempted to strangle her."

"I object," the opposing attorney, Redkin, yelled. "There's no evidence."

"Objection overruled," the judge replied. "Please continue, Mr. Moroose."

"The apartment manager was witness to this disturbing incident. In addition, a police report was filed."

Redkin whispered to his client, "Why didn't you tell me about this?"

"The apartment manager was unavoidably detained today," Tucker continued. "But he will be in court tomorrow at nine a.m., Your Honor. I respectfully request a recess until then."

Redkin jumped up with his fist in the air. "I object. My client and the opposing attorney failed to inform me about this witness or the police report."

"He's listed, Your Honor," Tucker said with aplomb.

Redkin grabbed the witness list and found, to his dismay, that Tucker was right. "Well, I need time to prepare, Your Honor."

The judged stared at Redkin. "That's just too bad, isn't it Counsel?" Then he shifted his gaze to Tucker. "Your request is granted, Mr. Moroose. We will resume this case tomorrow morning at nine."

The judge banged his gavel and Redkin tossed his legal file onto the table with disgruntlement, albeit tempered so as not to be found "in contempt."

"See you in the morning," Tucker said to Mrs. Carlton as folks filed from the courtroom.

"You handle neighbor disputes?" A man startled Tucker from behind.

"Sure do."

"Can I ring you next week?"

"I'm changing offices, but the courthouse knows where to find me." Tucker handed the man a business card.

As Tucker slid paperwork into his briefcase, he was approached by Jal.

"You spying on me?" Tucker joked.

"Just wanted to see my spiffy brother in action. You always said to drop by anytime."

"I'll show you my new office... then buy you some lunch."

"You're not gonna be taking cases out of the house anymore?"

"Nope. It doesn't look professional. I finally saved enough dough." Tucker pulled a paper from his briefcase and flashed it. "I signed a lease this morning."

"Gee whiz, it looks really official," Jal said.

"That's because it is official." Tucker led Jal out the door.

As the brothers strolled down Adams Street, Tucker thought about his new office. Soon, he could pull the plug on fibbing. He could stop pretending that his law firm was under remodel or that he was caught between locations. Ever since stepping out on his own, he had met with clients at the courthouse, at the coffee shop, at the park, or at their residences. He had been hiding the truth: that he worked from home. He was a busy and pricey mouthpiece and did not want folks to find out that he had files stacked up in his breakfast nook, in his master bedroom, and in the tub of his pink guest bathroom.

The brothers passed a slew of shops until they stumbled upon Crane's Pharmacy.

"Do you mind if I pick up my medicine?" Jal asked.

"What's wrong?"

"Backaches, but the doctor gives me this stuff."

As Tucker and Jal entered the pharmacy, a bell rang, alerting the druggist, Mr. Crane, to a new customer. Tucker noticed a long counter, a clock on the wall, rows of labeled bottles on shelves, and two benches where patrons could sit to converse or wait their turn. This was more than a place to pick up medicine; it was a gathering spot for the community. Patients often swapped gripes about their ailments or listened to a lecture by Mr. Crane. He dished out medical tips without hesitation, even though he wasn't a doctor. In those days, this was considered as harmless as rubbing Jergen's lotion on a patch of dry skin.

In the 1940s, there were eighty thousand pharmacies in the U.S. and three hundred million prescriptions were doled out each year. 70 percent came from pre-manufactured dosages. The remainder was compounded by druggists, who took raw ingredients and mixed them to come up with creams, capsules, and tablets. Mr. Crane had a strict duty to take care of the strength, purity, and quality of the substances he made. It took a lot to become a registered pharmacist. A fellow had to graduate from an accredited college and then pass a state board examination.

"I'll be with you in a jiffy," Mr. Crane said as he poured tablets into a bottle.

Jal was riveted. He was like a tightrope walker focused on not falling. "Dang nabbit! It's fascinating to watch. A pill is kind of like a bullet, except it's used for good. It goes into a great, big body and bang... the person's cured. The pill is so tiny." Jal was keen-eyed as Mr. Crane sat on a stool and created a label on a typewriter.

Tucker was jarred by the sight of his brother taking an actual interest in something instead of being his usual flub-the-dub self. "Have you ever thought about becoming a pharmacist?"

Jal laughed. "Come on, Tucker. I'm a meatball. I practically failed high school."

"It's not too late. I could set aside some money for you... kind of like a college fund."

"I'd rather be mauled by a mule."

Mr. Crane came to the counter. "May I help you?'

"I'm here to get that reddish-brown stuff," Jal said.

Tucker looked at the shelves. There seemed to be at least

five hundred bottles of reddish-brown stuff, and each had a different label.

"And you are?" Mr. Crane asked.

"Jal Moroose."

Mr. Crane flipped through a stack of papers until he found Jal's name. "That would be laudanum. It has opium alkaloids. It's tincture number twenty-three. You take ten to thirty drops depending on the severity of the pain."

Jal was impressed by the way the pharmacist whipped out mystifying tidbits. He was a wiz at terminology, chemical names, and dosages. Mr. Crane grabbed a bottle from the shelf and affixed a label to it. Then, he returned to the counter.

"Put your address and John Henry here." He turned a thick ledger toward Jal.

"I think it's 'John Hancock.' Not 'John Henry.'" Tucker interjected, but Mr. Crane and Jal paid him no mind.

"Eight dollars and twenty cents," Mr. Crane said.

Jal rummaged around in his pocket and pulled out a handful of bills. "I've got five aces. No, six."

Tucker placed nine dollars on the counter. "Don't worry. I've got this one."

The brothers' next stop was the Deveny building, which was, in effect, a sanctuary for law offices. Both legal giants and legal dwarfs did business out of the four-story edifice, which was managed by the owner himself: Mr. Deveny. Tucker led Jal into a vacant suite of three rooms.

"This is it," Tucker said.

"Wow, it's big."

"My secretary will be in there and my assistant over there." Tucker pointed at two adjacent rooms.

"Smooth, but you don't have a secretary or assistant."

"I'll be hiring them, knucklehead."

"Where's your furniture?"

"They're dropping it off next week."

Mr. Deveny poked his head into the room.

"Hey, I'm showing my brother around."

"I need to speak with you, Mr. Moroose." Mr. Deveny had a long face.

"What is it?"

"In private."

Baffled, Tucker stepped into the hallway, but Jal, being the mischievous piker that he was, put his ear near the doorjamb to eavesdrop.

"I'm sorry. I didn't realize," Mr. Deveny said.

"I'm dumb to the fact," Tucker replied.

"I like you," Mr. Deveny continued.

"I don't understand."

"I just didn't know. I had no idea you were an inky-dinky."

"I'm not. I'm Italian."

"That's what I mean. You're so light-skinned. I'm sorry. I can't lease to an Italian. I'd lose my other tenants. I'm sure you understand. You need to drift on."

Before Tucker could respond, Jal burst onto the scene. "You can't do this to us." He slammed his fist into Mr. Deveny's stomach.

The building owner doubled over, dipping his head within a foot of the ground.

"Put up your dukes, crab patch." Jal reared back, ready to pound him a second time.

Tucker grabbed Jal and tried to square things. "I'm sorry. He didn't mean it."

Mr. Deveny was furious. He stood up and fastened his eyes on Tucker. "This is exactly why folks don't lease to Italians. And tell your brother to clean himself up. He looks like a hooligan."

"We have a signed lease," Tucker said.

"And your brother just assaulted me." Mr. Deveny, who had mostly recovered from the punch, sashayed out of sight.

"Honestly! You can't attack folks, Jal. He could file charges against you."

"I don't care. That lowlife was going on and on about you being Italian."

"A gentleman uses his brain, not his fists."

Jal did not seem to be paying attention, so Tucker put his hands firmly on Jal's shoulders. "Look at me. A gentleman uses his brain, not his fists. You hear?"

Jal nodded. "I fouled things up."

"It's not your problem. Let's grab some lunch."

The brothers ate at Jim's Steak and Spaghetti, where Jal went back and forth between apologizing and giving Mr. Deveny a verbal thrashing.

"Sorry, I mucked it all up. I'm such a dimwit. But that fellow, Deveny, is low-down. He's Hitler's work, he is."

"It's in the past, Jal. Just forget it."

"You must hate me. I'm a right big screw up."

"No. I love you. You're my brother.

"I'm not up to scratch."

"Yes, you are. But what's it gonna take for you to get your temper under control?"

"I don't know. Maybe an extra scoop of ice cream."

"I wish that's all it took."

After lunch, Jal made tracks back to his hole-in-the-wall apartment, where he found a "three-day notice to pay rent" affixed to the door. He got one of these almost every month because his paycheck came a few days after the rent due date. Jal knew he'd once again be suckered into late fees. The apartment was dark, dingy, and depressing. Jal likened it to living in a tree trunk. The windows were pint-sized and above eye level. The place was a good ten notches below the roundhouse, which had more of a cheery feel. Plus, at work, he could shoot the breeze with his buddy, Herbie. He felt lonesome at home.

Jal balled up the landlord's notice and chucked it into the trash. This did not satisfy his antsiness. He thought about how he did not have jack, how he was always tapped out of beans. Plus, he hated that he was getting up there. He was almost thirty. Jal stepped into the bathroom and took note of the sink, toilet, Pears soap, scrubbing brush, pumice, and wooden bathing rack. Then, he took a gander in the mirror and noticed his aging lines. He also saw that he needed a shave and muttered to himself, "Holy mackerel! I'm turning into a whiskbroom."

Jal thought music might calm his nerves, even though he had a bit of a tin ear. He went back into the main room and put Perry Como's "Prisoner of Love," on the record player. The lyrics "She's in my dreams, awake or sleeping" reminded him of a sweet patootie, Mary Lou, who he had met at the movie house one afternoon. He had been straight-up with her from the start, confessing, "I can't be all lovey-dovey till I get more rooted." He was not in the "breaking hearts" business like some of his buddies at the roundhouse. He fashioned himself as honest when it came to gals. Jal had once taken Mary Lou out for a soda. She was kind of cute, and she would be company. She would divert him from his troubles. She would make him less jittery. He decided to phone her to see if she might like to sit on the Tygart Valley River bank and chat.

Tucker left lunch with Jal and went directly to the McCrory building, which was across the street from the courthouse. He had visited it a week prior when scouting out leases. It was his second choice after the Deveny building.

The manager of the property, Mr. Olden, was just like his

name: ancient. Tucker figured he had more lines than a bay scallop sea shell. Plus, he moved slower than a three-toed sloth, a woodcock dragging a boulder, a bubble in a box, or even Ernie Lombardi running to first base with his shoe laces tied together. Tucker liked coming up with funny images. He knew he could entertain Ginger with them later at home.

Tucker signed a lease for a small suite of rooms in the back of the building. Then, he followed Mr. Olden to an oversized closet to get a copy of the contract. This proved to be challenging.

"Hooey, I can't ever get this thing to work." Mr. Olden struggled with the Eastman Kodak Photostat machine. "My secretary, Mildred, says it's just plain lazy."

"I like this location because it's across from the courthouse," Tucker said.

Mr. Olden hollered, "Mildred, this thing's all janked up again."

"The carpet is a tip-top color and the wood paneling is classy."

"I'm sure you'll be happy here. There are lots of legal types in the building." Mr. Olden pressed scads of buttons but nothing happened.

"I really need a copy." Tucker was worried that he might once again get chiseled out of the lease.

"Damn, it just won't work." Mr. Olden kicked the side of the machine. "It looks like a handshake will have to do. But I'm a man of my word. The office is yours."

The two men shook, but Tucker was concerned.

When Tucker got home in the early evening, his daughters were playing chase. They bolted past the grand piano in the living room and the framed posters of Fred Astaire and Ginger Rogers on the wall.

"Settle down, children," Ginger yelled. "It's time to get

ready for bed." She noticed Tucker had arrived. "We already ate, dear. Did you want me to fix you a sandwich?"

"I'm not hungry."

"Well, tell me. I'm so excited."

"Tell you what?"

"Did you sign the lease with Mr. Deveny?"

"Oh, yeah. Sure." Tucker did not have the heart to tell her that he'd been rejected, and he was afraid to mention the McCrory building in case the deal fell through.

Tucker and Ginger spent the evening reading and listening to a special radio presentation of Alberto Ginastera's "Duo for the Flute and Oboe," but Tucker could not shake his nerves. He was on pins and needles about the lease. In fact, he was so "on pins and needles" that he could not sleep when the time came. He lay in bed with his eyes wide open. After an hour, he put on his bathrobe and tiptoed into the living room. He sat in a wing chair and stared into the darkness.

Chapter 11

EAT, DRINK, AND BE JEALOUS

MRS. JOY NEUBAUM had the Midas touch when it came to back tacking, basting, rantering, satin stitching, whip stitching, and darning. It did not matter whether a dress needed to be hemmed or a suit needed to be tailored. She was so good that folks called her "The Turtle's Neck," which was similar to calling her the cat's meow. Her Singer "hand crank and treadle" sewing machine got more use than her stove, and she had won the "Harrison County Dressmaker Tournament" five years in a row. Her trophies—all six inches tall with two-inch bases—were lined up on her living room mantle. She was proud of them and figured someday she would show them off—if and when a visitor came calling.

Mrs. Neubaum also had a knack for other kinds

of textile work: from knitting and needlepoint to quilting and crocheting. Although she was sixty-five, her blinkers were in fine shape. She did not need eyeglasses and could even make out the thin loop of the needle-threader. It went beyond her sight: Mrs. Neubaum was a picture of health. Her doctor liked to say her arms, legs, and meat hooks could "spar with any thirty-five-year-old," and her heart "stayed on beat better than a Conga drummer."

Mrs. Neubaum had once married a soldier who had gotten himself killed in the First World War, leaving her strapped and widowed at the tender age of thirty-four. He was one of the 53,402 killed in action; Mrs. Neubaum had memorized the number. After her husband died, she needed some gravy, so she landed a job at the cotton mill, where she worked for two decades. She eventually got fed up with factory conditions— the summer's heat, the winter's cold, bad lighting, reduced pay, and pressure by the boss for bigger turnout. So, she quit. A week later, she became the "alterations lady" for the Adams Street bridal shop.

This was still her place of employ, but she worked from her house most days. There were always two or three wedding gowns hanging in her coat closet, along with a mess of madcap bridesmaid dresses. She called them "madcap" due to their bright and goofy colors: canary yellow, lilac, azure, lime green, and fire engine red. To her mind, these dresses were designed to outshine the bride, and this was full on poppycock. Mrs. Neubaum had her opinions about weddings, starting with the fact that the bride should be the headliner and her attendants should dovetail into the background as the rhythm section.

Mrs. Neubaum's best friend was Freckles, a gold and white Himalayan cat who rarely left her side and who enjoyed tussling with the odd ball of yarn. He was such a deft wrestler that Mrs. Neubaum likened him to the flamboyant and legendary

Gorgeous George who had beat Enrique Torres to win the World Heavyweight Championship.

"I should've named you George," she often said while stroking Freckle's ears. "You're a blonde hunk of heartbreak just like him."

Besides sewing and caring for Freckles, Mrs. Neubaum had one more pastime, but it was more of a peccadillo: she was a chatterbox and a snoop. As Dale Carnegie might have said, being the neighborhood busybody is not a way to win friends and influence people. She had moved into the house on Chesapeake Hampton Road only a month prior and spent the lion's share of her spare time peeping at neighbors, deciphering clues about their goings-on, and trying to pry out secrets. For example, she knew Mr. Paulson from the end of the road was teetering on the brink of divorce and had a saucy honey pie on the side. She knew Mrs. Cooper, who lived in the corner house, had a secret part-time job so as to get extra spending money; her husband had a tendency to be all close-fisted. She also knew the Baker young'uns had broken the church window with a rock. She had tattled to their parents, and they had gotten a whopper of a whooping. Plus, they had to reimburse the minister out of their weekly allowance.

But one neighbor was strange. He was an odd egg, a hayseed, and a loner-type—not an average Joe. He had icy eyes and kept a basement light on in the wee hours of the night. What was he doing down there? There was something fishy about this fellow and his cagey ways.

This fellow was Ernie, and he lived smack-dab across the street.

Mrs. Neubaum had first tried to engage him in conversation when he was fetching his mail. "What's your story, morning glory?" she said, all chipper-like.

Ernie pierced her with a spiky stare and grumbled, "Yeah,

lady." He was expressionless and withdrawn and headed back to his house.

"Don't take a powder, mister," she yelled. "Tell me about yourself. You look right interesting." Her ploy to draw him out of his shell failed. *Drat,* she thought to herself. *That wet smack gave me the slip.*

So a few days later, she moved on to plan two. When Ernie and Nellie were not home, she tiptoed across the street to do some poking around. But when she got up close to the house, she was thunderstruck. The two basement windows were covered with thick black paint. There were only a few thin spots where light could escape, as well as an unpainted strip on the right side of the westernmost one. Mrs. Neubaum put her nose up real close to the glass, but she could not see a darn thing. The gaps were too tiny. The strip was too thin. Why would somebody paint over their windows? What might this grafter be hiding? Suddenly, Tutu—who was inside the home—began to bark, so Mrs. Neubaum hotfooted it out of there. She was not about to let her buttinsky nature get her in a heap of trouble with the law.

Mrs. Neubaum was trimming her rose bush when she next saw Ernie. It was the day after the "Deveny spat" and Tucker's lunch with Jal. Ernie was dressed all spiffy and was coming out of the house with Nellie. They were heading to Palace Restaurant for dinner. Mrs. Neubaum jumped behind the Sycamore in her front yard and peeped around the tree trunk all cryptic-like.

Ernie noticed her right off and became paranoid.

"Come along." Nellie hurried her husband to the car.

Ernie settled in the driver seat. "Who's that old woman?"

"What old woman?"

"Tree lady. Over there."

Nellie turned to see Mrs. Neubaum. "Oh, she moved in last

month. She's the neighborhood gossip. She knows everybody's business." Nellie laughed. "I don't pay her no mind."

A busybody? Venom shot through Ernie's veins. What was this old crow up to? Why was she peeping at him? Did she know about his scythe room? He was jittery about leaving home. Would she find a way to sneak inside? The sweater that was his temper was unraveling. Ernie's mood was suddenly lousy, and he was right sure it would spoil the evening. Ernie backed his car slowly out of the driveway with his eyes fixed on Mrs. Neubaum in the rearview mirror.

Tucker and Ginger were already sitting in a booth at Palace Restaurant and dressed to the nines. They were inspecting menus while a waitress stood over them with a pad and pencil.

"I'll have the Caesar salad," Ginger said. "Julius Caesar was a general and a statesman, but the salad was invented by Caesar Cardini. I heard that on the radio. Anyway, no croutons and only a little dressing. Actually, put the dressing on the side next to the rolls. And no butter please."

"Vegetable soup. Thanks." Tucker said. The waitress collected the menus and left.

"It sure is nice having time away from the kids," Ginger said.

"You're a stunner tonight." Tucker smiled.

"Oh, Tucker." Ginger blushed. "You're a bit of a dreamboat yourself."

"You thought I'd forget." Tucker had a look suggesting tomfoolery on his face.

"What are you talking about?'"

Tucker reached in his pocket, brought out a small present, and set it on the table.

"Oh... you remembered our anniversary!" Ginger tore open the package to find a jade necklace. "It's stunning. How did you know? You've been reading my mind. I'm very keen on jade. Last Wednesday I was thinking how a jade necklace would match my Christian Dior. Oh, Tucker. I just love it."

Ginger gave Tucker a tiny but passionate smooch. Then, she got a sly look on her face and pulled a present from her purse. She set it on the table.

"I think you're gonna like it. Actually, I know you're gonna like it. Hurry up and open it. I just can't stand the suspense."

Tucker pulled apart the wrapping paper and lifted the lid off of the box inside to find just what he always wanted. "Onyx cufflinks? Sweetheart, they're gorgeous. This is the perfect gift."

While Tucker and Ginger were acting all lovey-dovey, Nellie and Ernie were walking down the sidewalk. They were only steps away from the eatery, and Ernie was still in a foul mood.

"Restaurants are a waste of money. I wish I'd known you were a crummy cook before we got married. You deceived me. Don't think I don't know about your trickery, woman."

"Oh, Ernie. Don't be a grouch."

Ernie held the restaurant door open for his wife despite his crabby disposition. A waitress seated the couple at a table next to Tucker and Ginger.

"What do you want?" Ernie looked at his menu. "Something cheap, I hope."

"Ernie, let's have a nice evening. Don't be a spoilsport."

"I just don't like frittering away my suds."

"Call me Nellie-cakes and put on a jolly face."

Ernie stonewalled.

"Come on now." She gave him a tickle under his chin.

He squirmed and chuckled. "Nellie-cakes, I just don't like frittering away my suds."

"It's only one night. It's important to get gussied up from time to time." Nellie glanced around the room and whispered to Ernie, "He's a lawyer." She pointed at Tucker. "I can tell by his suit."

Ernie became cranky all over again. "That's foolish, Nellie. You can't tell a man's line of work by his suit."

Nellie caught Tucker's attention. "Excuse me, sir. Are you, by any chance, a lawyer?"

"Why yes, I am." Tucker smiled. "How did you know?"

"I could tell by your suit."

Ernie was jealous. "Don't get into his business. He doesn't want to talk to a complete stranger."

"Oh, I don't mind. I'm Tucker and this is my wife, Ginger."

"Nice to meet you," Ginger chimed in. "This is a lovely restaurant, isn't it?"

"It's a fine place, ma'am," Nellie replied, and then she asked Tucker, "You work around here, sir?"

"Why, yes. I'm moving to a new office, but the courthouse always knows how to find me. This is my card if the two of you ever need anything." Tucker handed Nellie a business card, but Ernie snatched it out of her hand and stuffed it into his pocket.

"It's time to order, Nellie-cakes. Stop bothering these fine folks."

Both couples went back to their separate conversations. Forty-five minutes later, Tucker and Ginger got up to leave.

Ginger spoke to Nellie. "Have a nice evening."

"Bye Ginger and Tucker," Nellie said.

"I don't understand you," Ernie spoke after Tucker and Ginger had left. "Why'd you keep talking to him?"

"I was just being friendly. What's eating you? You've changed lately. You're always complaining and bossing me around. I'm starting to wonder why we're together."

"Maybe you're hoping to meet him when I'm not around."

"What are you talking about? Are you off your nut? This is

about you and me and the problems in our marriage. Irene says I should leave you."

"This is none of Irene's business."

"She's my sister. She cares about me."

"What have you been telling her?"

"Just that we fight. She's got a right to know."

"Are you saying you want a divorce?"

Nellie was taken aback by Ernie's pivot from a tiff to an outright cutting of ties.

"Yes, I think I do." Nellie did not mean it.

"Well, tell it to the chaplain, dollface. You can't have one." Ernie folded his arms in front of his chest.

"I can have one if I want one," Nellie said all sassy-like.

"In a pig's eye."

"You can't tell me what to do. You're just a dreadful bully."

Ernie and Nellie drove home. There was an uncomfortable silence in the car, except for Ernie periodically calling the dinner "a trip for biscuits." His sour mood shifted at home when he realized Nellie might be serious about the divorce. He turned on the sweetness, folding down the bed linens and making her a hot cup of chocolate.

"Honey pie, come get your dessert."

She obliged, but did not speak.

"I only get upset because I love you, Nellie-cakes. You know that, right?" Ernie fed Tutu a Milk-Bone under the table.

Nellie nodded but, deep inside, she was starting to have doubts. Ernie's outbursts were happening more frequently. One moment, the marriage was smooth like eggs and coffee, but the next, her husband would hurl insults or act all fruity. She did not know what to think. She figured she would run it by Irene. Irene was a good listener. She was an Ann Landers of sorts.

Chapter 12

THE DEVIL COMES TO ALL WHO WAIT

"WHAT SAY, GLAMOURPUSS?" were the words of endearment Ernie uttered to Nellie first thing on Saturday morning. The couple was still in bed. Nellie was not ready to greet the day, so she turned her body away from her husband, burrowed her head into her pillow, and went back to sleep.

Ernie was peppy that morning. He got up, raring to dig his paws into the roll top desk he was carving for the living room. It would be a perfect fit for the northerly wall, where there was a sizable gap between the china cabinet and a mahogany Hepplewhite chair.

Once out of bed, Ernie went to the closet to fetch his shirt and pants, but a large Sherry's box caught his eye. It was nestled on the floor behind Nellie's purses and shoes. Sherry's was a chichi New York clothing store, and the writing on the container said, "Designed to fit you to a T." Ernie opened the box, dug through the tissue paper, and found a gray and lime Leslie Fay dress, which was low-cut and fell wickedly above the knee. The tag was still attached, and it read $12.98. There was also a silver fox collared coat with a price of $34.98. *Holy Joe,* Ernie thought. *That little bitch of a wife has been sneaking around behind my back.* He was incensed. She was spending like a grabby fat cat.

But a second thought sent him round the bend. Why did she need a hotsy-totsy dress and fur-trimmed coat anyway? He became suspicious. Did she buy it for that Casanova from the restaurant? He figured these were the sort of clothes a fancy lawyer would like. Then he wondered if Nellie was having tons of affairs. Maybe there were scads of fellows, just like there had been in the past. Was she getting all gussied up for them? The door that was his mental state suddenly became unhinged.

"What the hell is this, you rusty hen?" He threw the clothes at Nellie. "This ain't hay."

She woke, first looking confused and then becoming apologetic. "I was gonna tell you. I was. I was waiting till you were in a good mood. They came out of my grocery money."

"What are you talking about, woman?"

"I saved for over a year. I got them from New York. You know I always wanted something nice from New York."

"You betrayed me. And who'd you get them for? That high-falutin' mouthpiece?"

"What are you talking about? I got them to wear for you."

"I don't believe you, woman."

"It's the truth."

"I won't never trust you again." Seething, Ernie stomped out of the house, slamming the door behind him.

Ernie drove to the local fabric store, where he picked out

five bolts of linen—blue, black, red, white, and peach—and five packages of pillow stuffing as well as some notions. He lugged them over to the checkout counter.

The clerk looked him up and down. "You rattled about something, mister?"

"Nope. Just had trouble finding the right color."

"How much you want?" He took out some scissors and lay down the white linen next to a tape measure.

"Three yards."

"On all five?"

"Yep."

"I wouldn't have figured you for a seamstress." The clerk chuckled.

"They're for my wife."

"You want me to cut your apron strings, too?"

Ernie did not crack a smile.

"I'm just a-funnin' you," the clerk said. "Don't get all bent out of shape."

After buying supplies, Ernie headed home, where he scooted through the front door all furtive-like. He hoped to sneak into the scythe room without his wife noticing, but on his way, he heard someone talking. It was coming from the bedroom. It was Nellie on the phone with Irene. He inched up close where he could hear but not be seen.

"Yeah, I know there are plenty more fish in the sea, and some dishy ones at that, but I want to give it one more try. Ernie may be rough around the edges and a bit of a dogface..." She laughed. "But he needs me. Trust me, I can handle him. He'll do whatever I say."

Dogface, my eye! Ernie was having none of it. Maybe Nellie was not talking about splitting up, but he had no use for a wife calling him a mutt and playing him for a stooge. He was ready to ditch the whole shebang: Nellie's face, her lies, her bad cooking, her sagging breasts, the increasingly chunky drumsticks that she called legs, and her round-the-clock nagging. He was ready to end their salty marriage once and for all. Ernie was an emotional man, and once he filled up with rage, he was like a volcano. His upset was not going to be stuffed back down. Honest-to-God, it was going to boil over.

Ernie was positioned cattycorner to the bathroom and noticed Nellie's bright red lipstick resting on the side of the sink. "Well, looky there," he said to himself and snatched it. He jammed it into his pocket. Then, he quietly unlocked the basement door, descended into his scythe room, and placed his sacks of fabric and notions on a shelf.

Ernie had been fixing up the basement for years, and it had become downright impressive-looking. First, there was his "sorcery mat." This was a thin piece of rubber that stretched over a sizable portion of the concrete floor. On it was a reversed pentagram. In other words, two points of the shape projected upward; this signified "evil." Ernie had drawn it himself, copying the image from a book written by Eliphas Levi, a nineteenth-century French author, magician, and practitioner of the occult.

Levi had also written *Dogme et Rituel de la Haute Magi* in 1856. Inside this book was a picture of the Baphomet: a horned and winged human monster. Ernie had made a replica of this image, turning it into a life-sized poster and taping it to the wall.

Levi's *Dogme* book—which was open on a card table—read, "Mysteries of other worlds, hidden forces, strange revelations, mysterious illnesses, exceptional faculties, spirits, apparitions, magical paradoxes, hermetic arcana, we shall say all, and we shall explain all. Who has given us this power? There exists an occult."

Ernie had other books on the card table. There was the 1933 edition of *The God of the Witches* by Margaret Murray, which had fine-spun prose and a delicious picture of a horned devil on the cover. There was an array of other works, such as *The Testament of Solomon, La Chef de la Magie Noir, Science Occulte et Magie Pratique, Might Is Right, Concerning Freemasonry,* and *The Handbook of Magic and Witchcraft.*

The final book on the table was *History of the Devil,* written in 1900 by Paul Carus. It discussed the sacrifice of children and stated, "Fifteen of the most prosperous young boys, between ten and fifteen years of age, were painted white. Having brought them forth, the people spent the forenoon in dancing and singing about them with rattles. In the afternoon, they tied those children to the root of a tree." The passage then went on to talk about beating their naked bodies while their mothers cried and prepared their funerals. In the end, blood was sucked from the young'uns and they were killed and eaten.

At least, this is what Ernie thought it said. He was the first to admit he might be a smidgen off. Maybe the children were tortured and not eaten. Maybe they were eaten and not tortured. He was a little wobbly about the details because the words in these polished books were like wheels within wheels. They were complicated, and Ernie lacked a gilded education.

Ernie's scythe room was filled with more than just books and drawings. There were knives, gargoyles, broken crosses, a gun, and dozens of black candles. When not lit, the candles were a little like dust; they covered every surface. When lit, they resembled a blanket of glittery dots or downtown Fairmont at night as seen from the steeple of the Mount Zion Methodist church. Of the tiny disfigured dolls, one was a hunchback with a single eye, while another had a horn and a body shaped like a snake. Hanging in the corner of the scythe room was the eeriest thing of all: a noose. It was made of coarse rope, had been fine-tuned to fit a human neck, and swayed like a corpse when the floor fan was turned to "high." Ernie had never used the noose, but figured there could come a time. In his mind, "people kill-ing" was central to the craft of "devil ritual."

The scythe room would not have been complete without a non-voodoo section, which Ernie nicknamed "the patching place." This is where Ernie kept his saws and screwdrivers, as well as his planks of wood and scraps of metal. It was where he did his carving, repairing, and inventing. It is where he put what he called his "devil-given talents" to work. His special toolbox was also kept in this area. It still hid a huge wad of bills, which had been getting thicker over time. Ernie was flush and how! But, of course, Nellie knew nothing about his secret stash. She also knew nothing about the inside of the scythe room, except that it contained tools for whittling and for mend-ing broken contraptions. Plus, she had been told about the easy chair and radio adjacent to "the patching place," which Ernie used when he wanted to take a load off and shilly-shally the time away.

"A man can't be fixing and communing with the devil all the time," he would mumble to himself. Then he would plop down in his chair and flip on one of his favorite shows, such as *The Shadow, Blondie,* or *Captain Midnight.*

Ernie was a hermit when it came to spells, rituals, and "deviling around." He doubted he knew anyone who relished this sort of thing other than Otis, whom he rarely saw, partly because he lived on the other side of town and partly because he liked keeping to himself. Of course, he had an acquaintance-ship with the big cheese himself: Dr. Herb Sloane, a hypnotist, numerologist, and tea leaf reader who acted as the priest of the satanic church, Our Lady of Endor Coven. He had only a handful of disciples, but these folks were no-nonsense when it came to dabbling in sorcery and participating in rituals. Ernie had met Herb in the flesh once, and had talked to him twice on the blower.

The evening they'd met was six months prior. Herb had driven for three-and-a-half hours from his home in Cleveland with four tag-a-long members of his group to meet up with Ernie and Otis. The seven men converged at the Esso filling station and then headed over to Hangman Forest—a place they knew only by rumor as the KKK's gathering spot of yore. The Klan was not so active anymore, but a few local folks, such as Mr. Clark, still donned their hoods for weekly meetings in their homes.

Herb was six feet tall, forty-three years old, and rugged-looking, with large hands, a thin goatee, and a chrome dome for a head. Baldness was the tradition in the occult world, even though Ernie had never taken a liking to it. Herb was loquacious, with a full and contagious laugh. Even though he was a bigwig, he was no high muck-a-muck, and Ernie idolized him almost immediately. He longed to speak like him, to preach like him, and to become privy to the dark world's secrets that were tucked under his lapel.

"We're following the path of Cain and the serpent," Herb said all somber-like as the seven men fought their way through the thick brush toward the Hangman clearing. Each carried a Ranger brand flashlight because it was dusk.

Ernie didn't have a clue what the priest meant, but kept his trap shut for fear of sounding like a boob.

Otis was less chickenhearted. "I ain't no wisehead, Dr. Sloane. What in cod's name are you talking about?"

Herb chuckled. "Cod! I like that, Otis. Well, Cain was the first satanic priest, and the serpent represents the vessel of knowledge."

"Our coven got its start from the Bible's story of Cain and Abel," Arnie explained. He and his buddy, Eugene, were walking side by side and taking swigs of soda pop.

"Abel was a bad egg, out there bumping off beasts," Eugene said. "Cain was innocent. He made an offering of fruit."

Ernie was cloudy-headed on scripture but was eager to get some learning.

"The Lord praised Abel's gift," Herb said. "And shunned Cain's peaceful bounty."

"Well, that don't sound right," Otis piped up.

"Like I always say, God's a vile no-goodnik," Ernie finally spoke. "And Christians are a bunch of crackpots. I'd like to boil me up a few."

"You're a card, Ernie," Eugene said.

"The newshawks think Herb's the crackpot." Arnie glanced at the priest. "They're always writing bunk about you."

"True. They call me the flimflam man." Herb chuckled. "But I don't sell flimflam. I sell truth. Ever read the Bible, Ernie?"

"Blasted. Can't say I have."

"Well, you aren't missing a damned thing," Arnie said.

"You can't speak about your enemy's faults until you master their lies," Herb said. "Remember that."

"You bet I will." Ernie devoured the advice with a smile.

"I hope it gets dark soon." Herb glanced toward the heavens. "The invocation's better at night."

"Too bad there won't be a full moon," Arnie added.

The seven men galumphed through a final thicket and then came upon the infamous Hangman clearing.

"Shhh!" Herb stopped abruptly. He became still. "The devil's in our presence."

"Holy mackerel!" Arnie said in a hushed tone as he and the others stopped in their tracks.

"Poor stiff," Eugene whispered.

"What?" Otis was wide-eyed. "What's going on?"

Eugene pointed at a dead snake. It was smack-dab in the middle of the clearing. Then, Herb and the other coven members hightailed it over to the lifeless reptile, chanting "Dies irae, dies illa. Nema. Nema, Nema." They got onto their knees, repeating the chant over and over. Ernie and Otis were at sea about what was happening, but joined in with the ritual.

Five minutes later, the chanting stopped, and Herb pulled a hankie from his pocket. He wrapped the snake up carefully so as not to crinkle it in an unnatural way.

"This is a sign," Herb said to Ernie and Otis. "I saw a horned god when I was a mere child of three, and tonight I see a scaly god."

"What are you gonna do with it?" Ernie asked.

"Cook it into a thick brew," Herb said.

"Then we pour it around the outside of our church," Arnie added. "It draws the spirits to us."

Next on the agenda was a full-on satanic ceremony, complete with supplication, communion, and benediction. Herb spoke with the confidence of a politician and the grace of a poet. Ernie had never seen anything quite like it. Herb's coven members did their part by swaying, repeating chants, and waving their flashlights. The flashlights created inspirational trails of light in the darkness. Ernie and Otis even recited special passages so as to become bona fide members of the group.

The evening ended with a trip to a local coffee shop, which specialized in ham and eggs. Its slogan was "The Bite That's Right. Mornin', Noon, and Night." The seven men ordered some chow while jabbering amongst themselves. Ernie got an earful from Herb, who was sitting next to him.

"This is my April Belle." Herb trotted out a photo from his wallet.

Ernie looked at it real close. It did not look like a woman. It wasn't a woman. It was a life-size doll! A grown man with a doll? Egad! This was a curious notion as far as Ernie was concerned. April had brown straw-like hair, a peach complexion, and brown eyes. She wore a white blouse and a plaid skirt. Her mouth was a small circle, which gave her face an unsettling expression.

"A friend in Cleveland made her for me."

"What do you do with her?" Ernie asked.

"We communicate, and she helps me with séances. After April came into my life… all was divine."

Ernie thought having a grown-sized dolly was plenty peculiar, but who was he to question the master of the occult? Who was he to quibble with the devil's right-hand man? Ernie wanted to soak up some big ideas rather than come off as a heel, so he held his tongue real tight.

Ernie's thoughts of the merry time he'd had with Herb and the others faded, and his mind came back to 1948. He looked around to find himself still in the scythe room. He plucked Nellie's lipstick from his pocket and set it on the shelf next to the fabric purchases.

Grawgurgpurg. Ernie's tummy gave him a jolt. Grawgurgpurg. Then, it rumbled again. These were hunger pangs, and Ernie remembered there were Hydrox cookies in the kitchen. He liked scraping off the center cream with his teeth and then eating the outside chocolate part. Was Nellie still on the phone? Could he nab the cookies without getting caught? Ernie was not sure. He tiptoed up the basement steps and peeped out through a crack in the door. He could hear his wife in the bedroom, still running her trap, so he made a bee-line for the kitchen and grabbed the box of Hydrox. Then, he scuttled back to the basement door, where he could make out the tail-end of Nellie's conversation.

"You'll have to visit sometime with your daughter. Well,

I'd better get off the ol' Ameche. Ernie will be home soon, and I need to do my face. He complains when I don't wear makeup."

Her sideswipe rankled him. *What a filthy liar,* he thought. *I've never forced her to do her face. She always looked just fine to me.* With that, Ernie descended back down into the privacy of the scythe room.

Nellie was none the wiser about her husband's sneaking around. She hung up the phone and headed for the bathroom, where she noticed her lipstick was missing. She got on her knees and inspected the floor behind the toilet and tub. She rummaged through her purse and then searched the medicine cabinet. She was in a full-blown muddle. She put her hands on her hips. "For heaven's sake, where could that confounded thing be?"

Chapter 13

STRIKE WHILE THE IRON IS HOT

TUCKER AND GINGER'S new, swanky four-bedroom home on Sunset Avenue was 2648 square feet with hardwood floors and had been built in 1939. The living room was decorated with Kroehler Davenport chairs, Jacques Bodart designer lamps, a West Branch cedar hope chest, a Simmons Hide-A-Bed, a Baldwin baby grand piano, and an assortment of tables from Brunovan Antiques. It had clearly been designed for up-and-coming blue bloods.

This was the evening of the house-warming party, and Sharon, Sheila, and Shirley were nowhere to be seen.

"Where are those rascals?" Tucker was kidding around. "Oh well. I guess they're not gonna get any candy."

With that, the girls came running out of their makeshift fort in "The Andes." "The Andes"—as the family called it—was a brown monstrosity that looked like a mountain range, comprised entirely of Tucker's jillion or so legal files. It swallowed up a full quarter of the living room. The children had burrowed secret tunnels through the maze of boxes.

"What kind of candy?" Sharon was eager-eyed.

"Junior mints." Tucker hid the box behind his back. "But they're all gone now."

"No, they're not." Sharon giggled as she tried to snatch the candy. The other two girls joined in until the four of them fell to the floor in fits of laughter.

"Tucker, could you please help me with the food," Ginger hollered.

"She's such a fuddy-duddy," Tucker quipped.

"Yeah," Sharon yelled. "You're a fuddy-duddy, Mommy."

Tucker went into the kitchen. The room was green and yellow with white St. Charles steel cabinetry and a white Buck stove. The walls were covered in Bradbury & Bradbury wallpaper that depicted blenders, spoons, crockpots, graters, knives, and rolling pins.

"Could you put toothpicks in the cheese squares?" Ginger removed a casserole from the oven.

"Sure thing. I'm good with tiny spikes of wood," Tucker joked.

"Then maybe you could put the cocktail napkins on the table."

"Actually, my real talent is small bits of paper. I bet that's why you married me."

Ginger glanced at the clock. "Di mi! They'll be here in fifteen minutes and the potatoes aren't even peeled."

"Don't get the jumps. It's just our families. There's no one to impress."

"Your mother already hates me. I don't want her thinking I'm a complete jelly bean in the kitchen."

The doorbell rang and Tucker answered it to find the Moroose family: Margaret, Philip, Jal, Rose, and the other brothers and sisters, plus a couple of their spouses. Two of Tucker's siblings were hitched, and one had a "main squeeze." But Philip and Jal were still single, and Rose had a mysterious boyfriend who no one in the family had ever met.

"Hi Mom." Tucker gave Margaret a hug.

"Good for you. You've got some meat on your bones." She pinched Tucker's arm skin. "You must be doing better than us."

Tucker knew this was a not-so-subtle plea for cash. Margaret was always short. But Tucker was ready that night. He had prepared envelopes full of hard-earned dollars to dish out to his mom and each of his siblings.

"This is a humdinger of a house." Philip headed over to the record player.

"Except for that pile of cardboard in the corner." Mary pointed at "The Andes."

"Ginger's quite a woman if she hasn't complained about all these boxes," Mary's husband, William, added.

"She's a trouper. She hasn't put the kibosh on them yet," Tucker replied.

Ginger popped her head into the room. "Tucker just leased an office. These will be out of here in no time. Right, dear?"

Tucker nodded, although he was still in worry over whether he actually had a deal.

Philip put on the song, "Boogie Woogie Bugle Boy" by the Andrews Sisters and Rose lit up like a fireworks display.

"Let's make this party a gas. Let's dance, Philip." Rose offered her hand to her brother.

He shook his head. "You know I'm a cement mixer."

Rose hoofed it over to Robert and again put out her hand. "You want to dig the jive?"

"What?" Robert replied. "With my own sister?"

"Oh, balderdash. You're all full of tripe." Rose pranced into the middle of the floor and got in the groove all by herself. She shimmied around the room in a frenzy, creating a right big spectacle.

"Hey, sis. You're cookin' with helium," Philip shouted. "You're a real pepper shaker."

"Hey, don't fall on your keister, Rose." Jal laughed. "You wouldn't want to break Tucker's new floor."

"She's just like Gene Kelly," Margaret mumbled to Tucker. "Too bad she hasn't made something of herself."

"She's doing all right, isn't she?" Tucker was concerned.

Margaret shrugged with an expression that said, "She's a bit of a free spirit, but I'm just an old fogey in a hair net."

"Mom, tell me. Is she getting along okay?" Tucker pressed.

"How would I know now that she lives in Detroit? But I can tell you one thing. She's gone back to dressing like a hussy."

Tucker grabbed the pre-stuffed envelopes. "This is for you." He handed Margaret the one marked "Mom."

She was tickled when she found the slew of v-spots. Tucker handed over the rest of the envelopes. "And these are for the others."

"You're so good to us." Margaret flipped through them, noticing that one was addressed to Rose and another had Jal's name on it. Then she gave Tucker one of her famous bear hugs.

"There's food and quenchers on the table," Ginger yelled, competing with the loud music.

Everyone—except Sharon, Sheila, and Shirley—moved to the dining area, where the dinner was laid out all pretty. The children stayed in the living room, playing a game of knucklebones on the floor. Suddenly, there was a knock at the front door.

"Somebody's here," Sharon hollered, but then realized there were no grown-ups in the room.

"I better get it," she said to her sisters as if she was a grown-up herself. She wore no shoes and dashed into the entry hall, sliding into place in her socks.

She stared at the door handle. It was jiggling as if the person on the outside was trying to turn the knob. She felt a burst of nerves and remembered that her mother had told her not to talk to strangers. Was this a stranger or a party guest? Should she open the door or fetch her parents? Sharon got up close with her ear against the door. She could not hear anything. The knob continued to jiggle. Maybe it was an emergency. Maybe this person was in a hurry. Maybe it was a party guest trying to get away from a stranger. Maybe he needed to get inside real quick.

Sharon threw open the door and found herself staring at Faire and Chester.

"Hello, Sharon."

"Hi Grandma."

"We're here for the party, but Mr. Morris needs to use the little boy's room. Could you show him where it is?"

"This way Grandpa." Sharon, full of energy, galloped back into the living room, moving her arms through the air as if she was swimming. Faire fastened the front door.

After Chester ducked into the bathroom, Sharon slid in her socks over to the piano where the dog was sitting. She picked him up. "Come play with me, Fido." She carried him over to the knucklebones game and resumed playing with her sisters.

Meanwhile, Ginger was conversing with Rose, who was nibbling on a deviled egg. "I'm taking piano lessons. And I'm getting pretty good. It compliments my ballroom dancing."

"I once dated someone who played," Rose replied. "But the fellow I see now, he's into money. You know, business. Not artistic. Did you know he's married?"

"You're dating a married man?" Ginger was appalled, but became distracted when she noticed Faire and Chester had joined the party. "Oh, for goodness sakes. My parents are here. Excuse me, Rose." Ginger scooted over to greet them.

"Mother, I'm so glad you could make it." Ginger hugged Faire.

"Hello darling. The place is truly lovely."

"Hi Daddy." Ginger embraced Chester. "I made a delicious sponge cake. I know how you like sponge cake."

"Jolly good." Chester chuckled, and Ginger escorted him to the food table.

Margaret edged herself over to Faire. "I didn't think you'd be here. I know you and Mr. Morris are busy folks."

"We wouldn't dream of missing it. Ginger has absolutely transformed this place. And the baby grand in the corner is a delightful touch."

"It's all because of Tucker," Margaret responded. "He's been doing very well, buying up vacant lots and becoming a big shot. Did you know he won the state orator competition?"

"Yes. Ginger told me."

"He's eventually gonna run for the Senate."

"Really?"

"And the man from the newspaper wants to do a story on him."

Tucker heard his mom bragging and wanted to toss a rug over any potential flames.

"Come on Mom. Stop it." Tucker put his arm around Margaret. "It's nice to see you, Mrs. Morris."

"This is an excellent street," Faire replied. "The director of my garden club lives on the next block."

Margaret rolled her eyes.

Tucker held out his wrists. "Did you see the cufflinks Ginger gave me?"

"Very tasteful." Faire examined them.

"Tucker gave Ginger an expensive jade necklace," Margaret crowed. "It's a one-of-a-kind."

"Come on Mom," Tucker pulled his mom away. "Let's get some chow. Ginger is a dandy cook."

"I bet you two rubes to a chocolate sinker that she can't make sweet potato pie like me," Margaret said as the two of them headed for the food table.

Ten minutes later, the doorbell rang. Sharon was still playing games on the floor with her sisters and hollered, "Somebody's here." She once again had wild thoughts about whether the visitor was a dangerous stranger or a party guest.

But this time, Tucker had heard the bell. "I got it Sharon." He answered the front door to find a broad-shouldered salesman selling irons.

"Hello sir. Could I interest you in the finest product?" The salesman was a crackerjack at peddling his product. "This is not just any steam iron."

Tucker noticed lettering carved into the appliance. It read "KKK."

"What does this mean?" He pointed at the letters.

"KKK?" The salesman was chirpy and convivial. "It stands for the Klan. Our company has no affiliation, but we find irons sell better with the insignia. The Klan has five million followers."

"We're not interested." Tucker started to close the door, but the salesman blocked it with his foot.

"Don't let the insignia bother you. The iron will get the crease out of your shirt. And that's what matters, isn't it?"

Margaret and Jal became curious about the commotion in

the front hallway and moved in behind Tucker. The salesman noticed their dark skin.

"Oh… are you folks… Italian?"

"Yes, we are," Tucker replied.

"Oh. Sorry. Have a fine evening." The salesman stuffed the iron into his leather bag and scurried away. Tucker shut the front door.

The salesman approached the next house on his list. This was where the Palins lived.

The salesman rang the bell and spoke to Pete. "Hello, sir,"

"Hi. What can I do you for?"

"Uh… did you know you're living next door to Italians?"

"What?"

The housewarming party was wrapping up. Faire and Chester had already left and the Morooses were heading home. Rose was on the dance floor, boogying and twirling to Glen Miller's "Chattanooga Choo Choo."

"Are you coming, Rose?" Margaret yelled.

"Just call me Ginger Rogers." Rose swayed to the music, ignoring her mom. "Look at this." She spun around three times with her arms open wide as if they were ribbons on a maypole.

Margaret put her hands on her hips. "Miriam Rose Moroose. Are you coming?"

"No, mom. My fellow's picking me up here. We're driving back to Detroit tonight."

"That's six hours in the middle of the night." Margaret sighed.

Rose paid her no mind.

Margaret turned to Tucker. "Is it alright if she stays here until that scumbag boyfriend fetches her?"

"How do you know he's a scumbag?"

"A mother knows."

"Sure. I'll be up for a while."

Everyone left. Ginger cleaned up the dishes and put the children to bed, while Rose and Tucker had a heart-to-heart on the couch.

"I know you're grown, but mom's worried about you," Tucker said.

"Oh, she's full of prunes. I'm doing fine."

"Who is this fellow you're dating?"

"I can't talk about him."

"Why not?"

"Just can't."

"Are you sure? I'm a real good listener."

Rose was itching to let someone in on the big secret. "Okay, but you have to promise never to tell. It would be bad if you told."

Tucker nodded.

"Double swear with a cherry on top?"

"Okay. I swear."

"Triple swear on daddy's grave?"

"Yes, Rose."

Rose leaned in real close. "He's a big shot in the mob. They call me a moll. Doesn't that sound neat?"

"You're dating a gangster?"

"Officially, I'm his mistress."

"How long has this been going on?"

"Six months. He's a bigwig in Detroit, and my life's all the mustard. I have a fancy place to live and gobs of fancy stuff. Bill and I drive around in a limousine with a spiffy driver and all."

"But the danger, Rose."

"He's no cad. He'd never let anything happen."

"Being a chippy or a strumpet is not…"

Rose interrupted. "I'm not a strumpet. I'm a moll. There's a difference."

Suddenly, there was honking. It startled Tucker, but Rose jumped up all peppy-like. "That's him. I gotta go. Nice seeing you. The party was romping good fun." Rose was out the door.

Tucker inched over to the window and pushed aside the curtain. He saw Rose climbing into a black Fleetwood Cadillac limousine. The car looked important. It looked menacing. It looked like something he did not want to mess with. A tall, strapping fellow in blue jeans with straight brown hair stood next to the vehicle.

All of the sudden, the man turned and locked eyes with Tucker. It gave Tucker a chill. Was this Bill? Was this a Detroit mobster? Was he aware Rose had spilled the beans? The man winked at Tucker in a confident but intimidating way and then climbed into the backseat of the car.

Tucker mumbled under his breath, "You better believe your cuffed bottoms. I won't tell a damn soul."

The limousine sped away. Tucker closed the drapes, reflecting on how Rose was impulsive and drawn to living in quicksand. But he knew there was nothing to be done. Even as a youngster, she had shrugged off words to the wise. He used to say, "Put on your ears, Rose. Don't be a deafie like your Madame Alexander doll." He could never knock good sense into that pretty little head of hers. And now it was too late. She was a mafia tart.

Tucker locked up the house real tight that night. He double-bolted the front door and made sure the windows were firmly sealed. Then, he hit the sheets. But before getting any shut-eye, he lay in bed wondering if the Detroit mob might one day pay him a little visit.

"Missed you, doll," Bill said to Rose in the backseat of the limousine. He straightened out his peg leg. He had been run over by a milk truck as a ten-year-old. "What did my little cuddler do tonight?"

"Peachy things."

"What kind of peachy things?"

"Shimmying and twirling. You know I like to boogie."

"For three hours?"

"There was some eating, too."

"Who was that guy?"

"What guy?" She hated being edisoned with questions, but Bill was a jealous cat.

"That Casanova at the window."

"Oh. It must've been my brother, Tucker. He's no Casanova."

"Tucker. Hmm… you didn't mention me, right?"

"Of course not. I'm no tattle muffin."

"That's my toots." Bill planted her one on the mouth.

The drive toward Detroit involved a whole lot of smooching and petting in the backseat of the car. The driver, Dom, kept his eyes on the road because he knew better than to test the patience of "Billy Jack" Giacalone, who Rose called "Bill" or "Billy." Bill was well-liked by most folks both inside and outside of "The Partnership" and La Cosa Nostra family. However, there was one group who was not a fan: the bulls at the Federal Bureau of Investigation. In fact, the Bureau had a three-inch file on Bill and another four inches on his gangster brother, Tony or "Tony Jack," as he was most commonly known.

Bill was married to "Stella Rose" and Tony Jack was married to "Jennie Rose." In other words, there were a whole lot of

Roses in their lives. Rose Moroose hoped for a fairy-tale ending to her love affair, but knew tying the knot was unlikely. It was not the Italian way. The mob did not look kindly on divorce. Stability of family was foremost, and intermarriage (between cousins, sisters, brothers, etc.) was promoted and practiced. It was seen as a means to keep loyalty. Since most gangsters were tied by blood, weasels and double-crossers were uncommon. It was virtually impossible for informants to infiltrate the Detroit mafia.

Bill's limousine was as lavish as a king's chamber. Next to Rose was a velvet throw pillow and under her feet was a miniature oriental rug. In front of her was a gold-plated drink holder. It was circular with a center hole for bubbly and slots for glasses.

"No champagne?" Rose giggled when she saw the empty champagne hole. "You're slipping, Billy."

"Hey, Dom. Let's pull over for some Taittinger when you get a chance."

"Sure thing, boss."

"And turn on some music for my Jane here."

"Sure thing."

Dom switched on the radio to Dinah Shore's "Buttons and Bows."

An hour and a half later, the car veered through Pittsburgh. It was still the middle of the night, so businesses were dark and streets were mostly empty. Bill glanced out the window and got an eyeful of a bum who was catching forty winks on a park bench.

"Hey, Dom. Pull over next to that miserable gutterpup."

"Sure thing, boss."

Dom stopped the vehicle. Bill rolled down the window, put his fingers to his mouth and made a piercing whistle noise. "Hey, clodpole. Get over here."

The bum roused himself, confused, and then schlepped over to the car.

"Get yourself some grub and a room." The gangster handed him ten clams. "It's too cold out here for the likes of you."

"Hat tip to you, sir." The man smiled, eagerly pocketing the money. Then, the limousine pulled away from the curb.

Rose snuggled up close to Bill, who wrapped his arms around her as if she was a jewelry store sparkler. Her mind wandered. She reflected on the time they first met. It was six months prior.

Chapter 14

THE ASYLUM FOR THE CRIMINALLY INSANE

IT WAS SIX months before the housewarming party, and Rose and her flapper friend, Laura, were slopped up on scotch, vodka, daiquiris, and just about every conceivable form of alcohol. They had attended a bash at the Minard's Inn in Clarksburg, which was thirty miles southwest of Fairmont. They had danced and shot the breeze at this frolic pad, but had also spent slathers of time fending off rednecks, two-timers, and skirt chasers. At the end of the evening, Laura was so lathered she could barely track down her car.

"Hot damn! Where's that lame-brain Chevy of mine?" Laura weaved through the parking lot.

"Over here." Rose walked in front of her. "No, wait. Your car's green, right?"

"I think so." Laura rubbed her eyes.

Five minutes later, Rose screamed, "Here it is. It's blue."

"That's right. It's blue."

The women climbed into the vehicle and took off. Rose was in the driver's seat. They got no more than ten miles before smoke started billowing out from under the hood.

"Oh, no. It's steaming," Rose said.

"What?" Laura's eyes had been closed but she perked up.

"The engine's steaming. What do I do?"

"Pull up behind those cars." Laura pointed at a black Buick and a pale yellow Frazier, which were parked at an abandoned filling station. "We need to find ourselves a fine gentleman with motoring skills."

Rose parked and she and Laura got out. There was nobody inside the vehicles or in the boarded-up structure, but they heard voices coming from a woodsy patch.

"Maybe they're having a picnic," Laura said.

"It's the middle of the night, Laura. No one has picnics in the middle of the night. You're as boiled as an owl. Let's get out of here."

"Come on." Laura motioned for Rose to follow as she staggered toward the trees.

"I think we should mind our own business. The car will go a few more miles. Maybe all the way to Fairmont."

Laura disappeared into the blackness of the woods. Despite her better judgment, Rose followed. The women quickly stumbled upon three goons. They were standing over a dead man, who was sprawled out on a patchwork quilt. The whole scene was utterly bizarre as far as Rose was concerned. It was like being thrown into a James Cagney film. Rose was also scared because she could tell these were hatchet men who had bumped off this poor old patsy. Laura, on the other hand, was too soused even to realize the poor schmuck was pushing up daisies.

"I told you, Rose. It *is* a picnic." Laura pointed at the quilt, which looked a little like red and white gingham. Then she spoke to the goons. "Our car broke down. Hey, why's that guy taking a nap?"

The men were silent for a full five seconds, unsure how to handle the situation. They seemed to be wondering if anyone could actually be this foggy-headed, stupid, or loaded on booze. Then, they whispered to each other.

Rose hoped to squirm out of the situation by turning on the charm. "You seem like fine fellows. We didn't mean to interfere. Looks like you and your sleepyhead friend here are having a real fine picnic, so we'll just be on our way."

"Not so fast, dame." Vince, a gorilla in a pinstripe suit, placed his hand firmly on Rose's shoulder. It was clearly meant as a threat. "You can't be running off. We're your pallies. We can help. Right, boys?"

Joe, another one of the goons, nodded.

Ten minutes later, Rose and Laura were scrunched in the backseat of the Buick between Joe and the third thug named Thomas. Vince was at the wheel, and the "sleeping" corpse was in the trunk. Rose was on the brink of tears and secretly cursing her bad luck, but nobody could tell. She pretended all was peachy-keen.

"We'll get you home, ladies." Vince smiled.

"Can he breathe alright back there?" Laura was still muddle-headed about the dead man.

"He'll be fine," Joe replied. "There's plenty of oxygen." The three men chuckled.

As the Buick wound down the street, Rose figured she was going to die. She knew the car was going *away* from Fairmont, not toward it. Nobody was taking her home. Why hadn't they killed her in the woods? Why was she being snatched? Maybe they were going to hold her for ransom or sell her into white sex slavery. Maybe they planned to cut her into tiny pieces and feed her to crocodiles. Anything was possible, and she felt like she was going to puke. She did not think there could be a rosy ending to this night that had gone so dreadfully wrong.

Thirty-five minutes later, the Buick rolled through Weston, West Virginia and pulled up to what looked like a mansion. But a double-headed load of fear came crashing down on Rose when she realized it was not a mansion. It was the Trans-Alleghany Lunatic Asylum. Rose knew all about this hospital of horrors because she had heard the ghost stories as a child and seen pictures of the structure in the newspaper. The building was made of hand-cut stone masonry, and it looked like a ghoulish, old haunted house. It was supposed to house 250 patients, but there were an astounding eighteen hundred being kept there at the time—many against their will. These folks had been tagged "mentally impaired" or "unfit for society," sometimes by nefarious-minded relatives who aimed to steal their bankroll. Rose had heard folks were admitted for most any ridiculous reason, such as for reading novels, venereal disease, marriage problems, promiscuousness, masturbation, laziness, consuming whiskey, or having an interest in politics. Some of the inmates lived in cages. She knew people went in but seldom came out. She figured two flapper-types (Laura and herself) who had made love to countless flyboys, glad lads, and big-time operators were prime candidates for "madness," at least as far as society was concerned.

"Where are we going, fellows?" Rose feigned a sunny face.

"We're gonna introduce you to Bill. He's a big-time wise-head," Thomas replied.

"A top dog," Joe added.

"That's sounds truly splendid, but I need to get back to Fairmont. My mama's gonna be worried."

"Ish Kabibble!" Vince said. "We'll get you there soon enough, dream-puss."

Rose thought about escape. But how? If she made a run for it when the car stopped, these fellows would nab her. She was in high heels and they were tough and burly. Yelling would do no good—certainly not at a looney bin where screams were as common as straightjackets. And if she pled her case to asylum staff, would they believe her?

Rose imagined a nurse saying, "Another lie by a fruitcake whore. Put the nutjob in the cage!"

Rose figured the thugs were planning to stash her in the asylum. That would keep her quiet, all right. It would prevent her from snitching about the murder or fingering anybody. Laura's car would be found on the side of the road by the coppers in a day or two and the police chief would make a public statement: "Two young women just up and vanished." Because Rose had lived unconventionally, the Morooses would assume she had bolted out of town and was living the high life in California or New York.

Vince parked the Buick, and everybody got out except Laura, who was fast asleep.

Thomas tried to rouse her, but she was not having it.

"The bitch is catching some Z's," he reported to Vince. "You want me to carry her?"

"Nah. Stay here with her." Then, Vince gave Rose a shove in the direction of the building. "Let's go, dilly."

Rose felt like she was stepping off a cliff as she walked along a thin stone path. Vince and Joe were close behind and seemed ready to rough her up if need be.

"This way." Vince pointed to the left. Rose obeyed.

The three of them passed a cemetery with loads of weeds and unmarked graves. Rose figured this hell hole of a graveyard was her future—her final resting place. But she knew she would not rest; she would be tossing and turning until the devil snatched her out of there.

"Honey, over there." Vince pointed at a structure marked, "Medical Building."

She and the hoodlums went up a ramp and through a set of double doors, which slammed all eerie-like. She could hear the distant screams and moans of patients. Then, the threesome turned down a dingy hallway, where Rose noticed green tiled walls, a metal gurney, and half-a-dozen metal doors with food slots. From there, they descended down steps into what seemed to be a basement with a moldy smell and what looked like blotches of green vomit on the walls. She saw a door marked, "Autopsy Room."

"This way." Vince held a door for Rose, and she went into a freezing cold chamber with brick walls and a concrete floor. It was the morgue, although there was a smaller "bunk bed type of freezer" for storing corpses. There were bars over a ventilator-sized window and padlocks on the bars. She turned to find Vince and Joe were still in the hallway.

"Wait here." Vince slammed the door.

Rose was alone in the room and spiraled into a full-on panic. She began crying. "Come back. Don't leave me. Please." She pounded on the door.

What was going on? Why were they doing this? Would she die in this death-infested room? She noticed a trash can in the corner. When she got close and looked inside, she saw a pile of rotting dolls with missing eyes and noses. Suddenly, she heard a sound. The door opened and in walked a man.

Rose was immediately shocked, but not by anything bad. She was shocked by the looks and sexy demeanor of this six-foot-tall fellow. He was over-the-top dreamy with caring brown eyes. Rose was positively agog, and realized she'd never been so attracted to someone at first sight. Although he had a peg leg on his right side, this gorgeous man carried himself in a confident and commanding way. She wiped the tears away from her eyes, careful not to smear her mascara.

"I'm Bill."

Rose felt all feminine, and her fear faded into the brick and concrete. She figured her attraction was palpable to any ghosts or demons in the room.

"I'm Rose." She was serene in her tone.

"This room is cold. Do you know why that is?"

"No."

"Because they can't bug a cold room. I'm partial to freezers 'cause the cops can't listen in."

"That makes a lot of sense."

"What did you see when you were in the woods with my pals?"

Rose did not know how to respond. She wanted to give the "right answer," mainly because she wanted Bill to like her.

"I didn't see very much."

She watched Bill's expression turn into a frown and figured she had better be honest. "But I did see that your henchmen killed some sucker and stuck him in the trunk. He probably had it coming. I figure you will be burying him in that ratty, old graveyard out back. Nobody would ever find him there. I'd bet my lace garters on it."

Bill seemed amused as he digested each and every word.

"Frankly, I don't care what you and your pals do," she added, sensing she was no longer in danger. "It's not my business... so, are you married?"

Bill was stunned by the question. He had never met a gal so brave and calm in the face of squalor and death. Her intensity and moxie were downright intoxicating. Plus, this sweetie pie was a solid sender with a real pretty face.

"Uh... yeah. I'm married." He felt off-balance for the first time in years, and he liked it.

"That's too bad."

Suddenly, the door opened, and Vince popped his head inside. "That flap in the car's awake. What should I do with her?"

Bill stared at Rose as if seeking advice.

"She didn't see anything. She was loaded to the muzzle." Rose giggled. "She thought the sad sack was asleep. It was a riot."

Bill and Vince were deadpan as they watched Rose roar with laughter. They could not believe her candor.

"Drop her at the nearest bus stop with a couple of bucks," Bill said.

Vince did not like the answer. "But Billy, we can't…"

"Just do it."

"Fine, boss." Vince shook his head and left.

"As for you…" Bill took Rose's hand. "I'm leaving for Detroit in an hour. You want to come?"

"Oh. Uh…" Rose was taken aback. "Why Detroit?"

"That's where I live. You want to come?"

"I do, but I don't know. It's such short notice. I mean, we met five minutes ago, and I need to tell my mother and…"

"You can call her from Detroit."

"What would happen if I couldn't go?" Rose stared at Bill.

He looked at her all serious-like. There was silence, and then he spoke. "Vince would drop you off at the bus stop with your friend."

Rose smiled. "That's what I figured."

There was another bout of silence.

"I don't mean to rush you, kitten. But I'm on a tight schedule."

"One more question… what would I do in Detroit?"

"Whatever you want, baby doll. I could set you up in a suite at the Book Cadillac."

"The Book Cadillac?"

"Yeah. It's a spiffy hotel near Michigan Avenue."

Rose put her arms around Bill's neck and whispered. "Okay, Mr. Killer Man. I want to go." Then, she gave him a whopper of a smooch on the kisser.

On the following afternoon, Rose found herself settled into a cushy suite at the Book Cadillac, a Neo-Renaissance-style hotel on Washington Boulevard. It had over 1,100 guest rooms. She immediately phoned her mother to say she was not coming home.

"I've got a snazzy place to stay here in Detroit. I'm living the life, mom. It's the real McCoy."

"That's all and good, Rose. Just remember... there's a bed here with your name on it if you're ever strapped."

Margaret was not all that surprised to get the call. She had always figured her "looker of a daughter" would someday up and move to the big city. She had never been a small-town gal. Margaret did not ask Rose how she was coming up with enough dough to get along, but figured some well-heeled lollygagger of a fellow was footing the bill.

Detroit was a hopping place in 1948, especially compared to the sleepy town of Fairmont. There were approximately 1.6 million residents. It was the center of industry, with oodles of factory jobs, wooden tenements, assembly lines, rooming houses, opium dens, brothels, illegal gambling parlors, and saloons. It was the sort of city where anything could be had for a price: legal or illegal.

Gangsters from all over the country had come to Detroit during the Prohibition, including Al "Scarface" Capone, who had reportedly taken in a staggering $105 million in just twelve months. Back then, the Detroit River had been a conduit for bootleg whiskey from Canada. Then, the mob got into the heroin trade and became a supplier for the New York underworld, despite the fact that many figured it was the other way around. The Detroit mafia had deep ties with Sicilian crime families in Italy, who in turn had links to opium growers in Turkey and other parts of the Middle East. Michigan mobsters also had a cozy relationship with the labor unions and the trucking industry, thus were "in the prime" when it came to distribution.

The Eastern Market district of Detroit was a hotbed for the mob. Bill, whose family came from Italy, headquartered his operations there, often directly out of his father's (legitimate) fruit company, which was called Farm Fresh Produce and was on Riopelle Avenue. When Bill called meetings—including on scorching hot days—his crew knew to bring along their winter coats. This is because the gatherings were held in the company's walk-in freezer, which was kept at a brisk thirty-five degrees Fahrenheit.

"Billy, you should join a twelve-step recovery program," a member of his gang ribbed him. "You got an unhealthy obsession with freezers."

But Bill knew his obsession was keeping him out of the slammer. He was careful and meticulous if he was anything. He did not blab at the wrong place or time. He was not one to get caught with his pockets full of stolen cash or his finger on the trigger.

Rose lived at the Book Cadillac week after week, never asking her gangster boyfriend about his capers or "special business," which she sensed mostly had to do with gambling, extortion, and racketeering. However, she made it clear in subtle ways that she was willing to be the Bonnie to his Clyde. Bill got the hint, but never took her up on it. He was against dames getting involved. They could get in over their heads. He did, however, spend gobs of time with her, sometimes in the hotel's grand dining room, feasting on his favorite dish: cherry bruschetta. This was a gourmet, sandwich-style dish filled with mozzarella, bell peppers, green onions, and sweet cherries.

It was one fine Saturday morning only two months after moving into the Book Cadillac. Rose was taking a bubble bath and sipping on Dom Perignon. Bill, who had his own key, entered the suite and came into the bathroom in his golfing duds.

"Hey," Rose smiled. "What's my sexy fellow doing here? I'm looking forward to dinner. I bought a nobby new dog leash to go with that tight red skirt you like."

"Why do you need a dog leash?"

"It's a belt, silly." Rose laughed. "I didn't think our date was until six."

"I got some news today." Bill looked torn up, and it made Rose on edge.

"About what?"

Bill sat on the side of the tub with a glum face. "Your friend... your friend... Laura."

"My friend from Fairmont?"

"Yeah. Did you ever try to get her on the horn?"

"Uh... no. Why?"

"Well... Vince never took her to the bus. That lowdown rat's on probation with me."

"What do you mean?"

"Your friend didn't go to the bus."

Rose started to speak, but Bill covered her mouth with his hand and looked around the room as if to advise her to take care when choosing her words. Then, he removed his hand.

"I just thought you might want to know. He's a fucking eel. A greaseball. A twit. That Vince is... I'll see you after my game, sweetie."

Bill gave her a honey cooler of a kiss on the lips and left.

Rose swallowed hard, realizing she could be dead like poor

Laura. She could be rotting in that ratty graveyard at the hospital of horrors. Beetles and earthworms could be munching on her internal organs, or whatever was left of them.

She loved Bill, but appreciated him with extra gusto at that very moment. Becoming a gangster's moll had full-on saved her life.

It was the morning after the house-warming party, and the Moroose children were playing in the front yard. Fido was on the porch with his attention on a bone that barely fit into his mouth.

"Everybody loves Slinky. Winky, dinky, winky, dinky, doo." Seven-year-old Sheila was trying to invent a catchy tune while making the spring-filled contraption "step" along the concrete walkway.

Sharon and Shirley were on the grass, playing catch with a red, white, and blue rubber ball. It was covered in patriotic stars and stripes and had been purchased by Margaret during World War II—it had been part of a campaign to raise greenbacks for America's troops. She had given the toy to the Moroose girls for Christmas.

Shirley hurled the ball with all of her childish might. It landed out of bounds in the bushes between the yard and the road.

"Oopsy daisy." Shirley laughed.

"Throw straight. Not at the street." Sharon retrieved the ball. "I don't want to have to bench you."

Shirley screamed, "Noooo. I don't want to be benched." Then, she giggled.

The fifteen-year-old neighbor boy, Roy Palin, watched the girls from his parents' driveway. Roy was Pete's son, and was a low-life and a big mouth. He could badger the britches off a baby.

"Mongrels are really noisy," Roy taunted the girls. "My papa says you have to move."

"What?" Sharon headed in his direction.

"Only whites are allowed. My papa's talking to the judge and getting you kicked out of your house."

"Liar! You're just being a meanie."

"Hey, don't get all sore, guido girl. I just don't want you to be in a dither when they haul you away."

"Nobody's hauling me away."

"There are deed restrictions, dummy. You're in violation."

While Sharon was being mocked, her parents were in the kitchen. Tucker was eating breakfast while Ginger was whipping up a batch of Maxwell House.

"That party sure did beat all," Ginger said. "Want your coffee blonde and sweet?"

"Yep." Tucker was glancing over the newspaper.

"I'm real glad Rose could make it down from Detroit," Ginger continued. "She's such a stunner. Cute as a bug's ear."

"Yep."

"But I'm concerned about the fellow she's dating."

Tucker put down the paper, alarmed. "What do you know about him?"

"Well... Rose said he was married."

"Did she say anything else?"

"No. I think that's quite enough."

"Yeah." Tucker was relieved and returned to his reading.

"What do *you* know about him? Are you holding something back?"

"I don't know a darn thing, sweetheart. I just think we should mind our own business. Rose is a grown woman."

"We should say something to your mom. She could set her straight about dating a two-timer."

"We need to leave her be. You hear?" Tucker could tell Ginger was not paying attention. "I'm serious, Ginger."

Suddenly, Sharon burst into the room in tears. "Daddy, Daddy. I don't want to move."

Tucker lifted his daughter into his lap. "What are you talking about? We just got here."

"What are deed restrictions?"

Ten minutes later, Tucker found himself knocking on the Palin front door. Pete answered.

"Your son said some unkind words to my daughter."

Pete smirked.

"It was beyond the pale. She's only eight. You need to teach your boy some manners."

"You're in violation, Mr. Moroose. Check your deed. As a lawyer, you should know about such things. I could probably get you disbarred. If you don't move, the property owners on this street will make you." Pete closed the door.

Tucker was appalled by Pete's rudeness, but also curious about his claim, so he spent the next few days researching deed restriction law. He found a troubling clause in his title paperwork that forbade an owner to sell or rent a house to anyone not of the white or Caucasian race. In addition, it said, "Negroes, Jews, Italians, Ethiopians, Orientals, American Indians, and Mongolians are not permitted on the property with the exception of chauffeurs, gardeners, and domestic servants."

"This is absolute rubbish," Ginger said when Tucker revealed his findings. "You should tell that droop, Mr. Palin, and those backward neighbors of his to go jump in a lake. We're not leaving."

"The problem is… Mr. Palin's not all janked up. He is on the level about the law. There's a special ruling in West Virginia."

"A special ruling?"

"It allows Italians to own property, but it bars occupancy."

"We can't live in our own house?"

"It seems that way."

"I can't believe the law would be so asinine."

"Plus, civil case law's rather bleak. Mr. Palin could sue us for bringing down his property value."

"What? I've never heard of anything so ridiculous."

"But there's one glimmer of hope."

Ginger leaned in close.

"The Supreme Court's looking at a case right now: Shelley vs. Kramer. It might mean we could stay. It was argued in January, and they're gonna rule on it real soon… probably in the next couple of months. Maybe we'll be in the clear."

"Oh my goodness. I hope so. Otherwise, I don't know what we'll do."

"We'll have to move."

"But, where? I can't go back to that scrunched-up apartment, Tucker. I'd get the screaming meemies."

"We could build a house on some of the land we bought. Maybe on Cleveland Avenue. On the hill. Problem is we'd have to live in that shack on the property… at least for a while."

"I don't want to live in a shack. I'm not a shack kind of woman."

"I know you're not, honey bun. I know you're not."

A week later, Tucker had full-on changed his mind about waiting for the Supreme Court decision. He needed to get his family moved. It all started when he was fetching letters from his mailbox and found a hand-written note tacked to a newspaper clipping. It read, "From your friendly neighborhood Kommittee." Tucker knew what this meant. It was a threat from the Klan. The KKK was known for inserting random Ks into correspondence.

The accompanying article, dated December 16, 1945, was meant to scare the bejesus out of him. It read, "Black Family Killed in Southern California House Fire after Refusing to Move from White Neighborhood." According to the story, Mr. and Mrs. Short and their two children (seven and nine) had perished. The intentionally-set blaze was attributed to "quite a bit of Ku Klux Klan activity in the area."

Tucker folded up the clipping and stuffed it in his pocket. He figured there was no use worrying Ginger. He hoped the warning was more of a paper tiger than a real one. But the next morning, the situation got ratcheted up considerably. When Tucker opened up the front door to head to work, he found a gasoline can on the porch next to a box of matches. He knew the Morooses could not stay. Tucker could not duke it out for his rights while the Klan was threatening to set his family on fire.

Chapter 15

SCARING OFF THAT OLD CRATE OF SEAWEED

ERNIE WAS STILL dull-eyed about Nellie. His feelings were on the skids, and he no longer noticed her charms. To his mind, the marriage was treading water near the shallow end of the pool. Soon, his feet would scrape bottom and he'd suffer stubbed toes and other wounds. Ernie wanted to push the marriage into greater depths, avoiding a split. He knew what was required. He needed to harness his temper—fighting the laws of science if need be—and remain Nellie's all-weather friend. Tantrums and bickering would only lead to more tantrums and bickering. Ernie planned to be cordial when his wife was cordial... and stoic when she was acting surly or carping at him. It was a fine sunny morning. Ernie was getting dressed, and Nellie was once again searching for the missing tube of Revlon. Buying a replacement was out of the question to her mind because it would require asking Ernie for money, which would no doubt set him off and lead to a conniption fit and sulking in the scythe room. She knew her way around his moods better than her kitchen.

"Ernie, are you sure you haven't seen my lipstick? It's not a cotillion girl. It couldn't have waltzed off on its own."

"Cotillion girl." Ernie laughed, trying to be jovial. "That's a knee-slapper, Nellie-cakes." He buttoned up his shirt.

"Well, have you?" She figured he had tossed it in the trash just to be cruel. It was the sort of thing he might have done in a fit of rage.

"Nope. Can't say I have."

Frustrated, Nellie left the bathroom, dumped her plastic cosmetics bag on the bed, and sifted through the mishmash. "I told Irene to come for a visit."

"I don't want her here."

"You agreed not to push me around anymore."

"I'm not pushing you around. I just don't want her in my house."

"It's our house, remember? We hold title in joint."

Ernie almost burst an artery, but caught his tongue in the nick of time. He wished he hadn't stuck Nellie on the deed. At the time, he was ill with pneumonia and thought he might die. He had not wanted his wife to be squeezed by the courts or, worse, to be sucked dry by Bessie.

"Don't be a dog biscuit, Nellie. Be the level-headed bit of fluff I married."

"Look, if we get a divorce…"

"We're not getting a divorce, woman," he interrupted. "Why do you keep bringing that up when I'm trying so hard to make things right?"

"I know you're all practical with your hands and with

putting things together. But you're not being practical about our marriage. It's Humpty Dumpty. I'm not sure it can be put back together again."

"It's not Humpty Dumpty. It's a slightly used Dodge with a dent on the fender. It'll be good in no time if you just give me a chance to hammer things out."

Nellie had a one-track mind. "Well, if we *do* get a divorce, you're gonna have to pay me seventy-five dollars a month. Irene thinks that's fair."

Ernie had absorbed a bellyful and spiraled out of control. "Did you marry me thinking you were gonna steal my house and all my cabbage? Did you? Was that your devious plan? Was it, bitch?"

Nellie knew she had pushed too hard.

"I don't have any money. See?" Ernie emptied his pockets onto the dresser. There were a few loose coins, a comb, the basement key, his driver's license, chewing gum, and Tucker's business card from Palace Restaurant. The business card fell onto the floor beside the dresser, face up, but neither Ernie nor Nellie noticed.

"You've drained me dry, woman. And if you keep pushing, you're gonna pay for it. I suggest you just shut the hell up, be a good wife, and everything will be fine." Ernie snatched the basement key from the dresser, leaving everything else behind, and stomped out of the room.

He headed for the kitchen, where he aimed to pour himself some grapefruit juice and whip up some pancakes. But, on the way, he caught wind of an unsettling sight outside the living room window. It was that old hag he called "Mrs. Meddle-Face." Yes, it was that pesky mossback of a neighbor, and she was standing smack-dab on his land. She was inspecting the stone steps. How dare she snoop around! Who did she think she was? He could have her arrested for trespassing!

Ernie hid behind the curtain and eyeballed her every move. Mrs. Neubaum brushed leaves away from the stone carving, and read the words, "Hell's Half Acre." She was shocked, but became full-on terror-stricken when she caught a glimpse of Ernie ensconced in the folds of curtain fabric. She swallowed her screams and scooted back across the street, periodically turning to make sure she was not being tailed. Then, she ducked into her house and locked the door.

Thirty minutes later, Nellie walked into the kitchen, carrying her jacket and handbag. She found Ernie scarfing down pancakes.

"I made some extra goo and moo."

"No thanks," Nellie said. "I've got some errands. I'll be back in a couple of hours."

"Okey-dokey." He poured too much maple syrup onto his plate as Nellie left the house.

A little later, Ernie rinsed off the dirty breakfast dishes and set them on the wooden drying rack. Then, he passed back through the living room, where he could see Mrs. Neubaum across the street loading a wedding dress into her car. He watched her drive off. He knew she lived alone and liked the idea of tinkering with revenge.

"Tit for tat... for that old bat," he mumbled. Snooping was a two-way street, and Ernie was itching to scare the girdle off that old crate of seaweed. He would teach her to mind her own beeswax, or else.

Ernie grabbed his lock-picking tools, which he kept in a shallow drawer in the basement. He had made them himself by trial and error. Some of the boys at the coal mine called him "the worm gypsy" because he could worm his way past any barrier. Plus, the boss was always ordering him to go here, there, and yonder like a nomad to open doors. When the storage room lock jammed, Ernie was summoned. When the bath house door handle went on the blink, it was Ernie's job to fix it. When Andy Joe lost the keys to the lamp house, the post office, and the recreation room, Ernie had to get those dang doors open. As the mining company's top mechanic, Ernie had a regular cornucopia of special tools, including those for lock-picking.

Ernie marched across the street all confident-like. He was not worried about getting caught because the only house with a clear view of his nefariousness belonged to Will Kleeman, who was out of town for two days.

First, Ernie went around tugging on all of the windows and doors, but came up dry. Mrs. Meddle-Face had fastened them with precision and even added extra security in some spots. Ernie figured she was a goody-goody with a stick down her throat or as paranoid as one of those charlatan fortune-tellers. But when he noticed the back door had a regular pin tumbler lock and no extra bolt, he smiled and pulled out his tools. It was a whiz to crack open, and Ernie made his way inside in ten minutes flat.

He skulked around the house, peering at odds and ends. He found family photographs, gold jewelry, and a stash of women's briefs and brassieres. The undergarments made him queasy. Then, he stumbled upon a diary, which he opened. It read, "The world is a gosh awful mess. The war has ended, but seventy million folks are dead. So is Hitler. So is Roosevelt..."

"Boring drivel," Ernie mumbled, dropping the diary back onto the table. "I don't need no history lesson."

Then, he saw the gold and white cat standing next to a food dish. He wore no collar. "Hey, Goldilocks, is this your porridge?" He noticed a small plaque over the water bowl, which read, "Freckles."

"Oh, your name's Freckles. The old fossil named you after a skin disorder. If anything happens to the busybody, you can come live with me." He gave the cat a wink.

Ernie passed Mrs. Neubaum's bedroom and then wandered into her dressmaking studio. There he found a work table, mannequins, a wedding dress in a plastic bag, rolls of fabric, a sewing machine, a pile of Simplicity patterns, trims, buttons, a pin cushion, and a turquoise and black package of Puritan Brass Rustproof Dressmakers' Pins. There were also several books on a shelf: *Home Handicrafts Needlework and Repair, Drafting and Dressmaking* by Claire Neylon, and *Vogue's Book of Smart Dressmaking.*

On a desk was a newspaper clipping. It was an advertisement for the Woman's Institute in Scranton, Pennsylvania. The title read, "Learn Dressmaking: $15 to $40 a week." Next to it was a box of OMO dress shields, promoted as "absolutely odorless." Ernie had no idea what their purpose might be and, frankly, he did not want to know. He opened a desk drawer to find spools of colored thread and "pearl head corsage" straight pins. The pearl bulbs on the ends of the pins were red, yellow, blue, or pink. This gave him the lick of an idea.

He went to Mrs. Neubaum's bedroom. He spelled out "RIP" in blood-red pearl straight pins on her freshly ironed white pillowcase. The message looked eerie and foreboding. It would give her a fright. Ernie felt a tinge of pride and figured Herb and the satanic coven members from Ohio would give him a "good going" slap on the back if they knew.

Then, he searched for Freckles, whom he found hiding under the dining room table. The feline tried to flee, but Ernie nabbed him and wrapped red thread around his neck. He made twenty passes; the finished product resembled a collar. He kept it loose, so as not to choke him. After all, it was not Freckles's fault he had a nasty-faced meddler for a master. Then, Ernie departed, locking the back door behind him. He whistled as he crossed the street. He hoped Mrs. Neubaum would see the handwriting on the pillow case and the threat to Freckles's life and stay the hell away from his house. He did not aim to be ruthless, but knew he could—and would—if need be.

The Morooses called it a shack, but it was really a two-bedroom cabin nestled in an iffy part of town between a steep incline and the bustling Cleveland Avenue. The dwarfed, one thousand-square foot structure was comprised of stone and wood and had no yard, although it was part of a generous forty-acre parcel. There was a section at the top of a hill that was the size of a dance hall, but it was out of reach without pitons, a climbing rope, and other mountaineering tools. In other words, it was of no immediate use to the family.

"You've got forty acres but no stinking mule," Jal joked on move-in day. "Oh, wait. You do have a mule. It's me."

"If only we had the semblance of a house." Ginger sighed while fighting through a blanket of cobwebs.

Tucker was at the courthouse arguing a case, so Jal was helping the movers get Ginger settled. In addition to hauling and heavy lifting, Jal was in gear to do some nailing and fixing. He had been a decent student in his high school shop class and remembered some of the basics. He planned to patch up the floorboards; they were weathered and creaky.

"The place sure is rough around the edges." Ginger noticed bent nails poking out from the window frames.

"Looks a little rough in the middle too." Jal pointed at a sag in the center of the ceiling. "I'll start with the bedrooms." He headed toward the back of the house.

Three Atherton Company moving men struggled to get Ginger's baby grand through the door. They had taken off the legs and pedals. They were panting and grunting up a storm.

They angled it here and tugged it there. It was as if they were wrangling a bear into submission.

"You can put it in the corner," Ginger said.

"Lady, this thing's gonna take up most of the room."

"That's fine. Did you know baby grands weigh five hundred pounds?"

The movers looked peeved.

"Some baby grands weigh as much as eight hundred pounds."

They looked even more peeved.

"I read that in a magazine," Ginger added. "Those magazines are so informative."

The crew placed the piano in the proper spot and reattached the legs and pedals.

June, a black woman and professional candy-maker who lived across the street, knocked on the open door. "Hello?"

Ginger perked up when she saw there was a visitor who seemed to be bearing a gift. "Can I help you?"

"Are you the new owner?"

"Why, yes I am."

"I'm the neighbor from over yonder." June pointed at her house. "I made a casserole to welcome you to the neighborhood." June handed Ginger a tomato cobbler in a rectangular dish covered with aluminum foil.

"Why, thank you. That's awfully sweet. You are such a friendly person."

June noticed the movers. "Goodness, they're hard-workers."

"Yes, they are." Ginger smiled. "They're plenty rugged."

"I've got a canopy bed that needs to go in the garage," June said. "You think you fellows could move it? It can't be too much heavier than a piano."

"Of course they can," Ginger volunteered. The men looked all bent out of shape.

Hours passed. The movers hauled belongings. June went home. Ginger cleaned. Jal did some fixing. Tucker made arguments at the courthouse. Ernie dilly-dallied in his scythe room and Nellie wrapped up her errands. In fact, all the residents of Fairmont puttered through their regular routines that day, but not one of them was aware of something stunning: Tucker's shack on Cleveland Avenue was within spitting distance of Ernie's place. It was around the corner, but in the opposite direction from the Moroose farmhouse. It seemed Tucker had gone full circle. He had moved back to Ernie's neighborhood. The two men were in each other's grasp—not only physically, but also on a spiritual or philosophical plane. Circles are a right big part of life. They are natural. The earth turns. The sun rises. Clocks tick along in a cycle. The beginning is the end. Oedipus could not escape his mother. Perhaps Ernie and Tucker were pawns of fate in the same way. They were being shoved along predestined paths. They had destiny—a destiny to be interknit in a curious and powerful way. That day was fast approaching, but no one realized it... except, perhaps, for the gods and devils of the universe.

Mrs. Neubaum returned home from the bridal shop with a batch of dresses that needed hemming and tapering on the sides. All seemed normal as she went to her dressmaking studio and hung the gowns on hooks. But then she noticed the drawer to her desk was slightly adrift. It was cracked open. It was where she kept her thread and straight pins. "That gripes my cookies," she said to herself, thinking she was getting old and forgetful. She was normally the meticulous type—clean, kippy, and efficient. Mrs. Neubaum shut the drawer and headed to the kitchen for an apple. But on her way, she caught wind of her bed and the word "RIP" spelled out on her pure white pillow case.

Fear overtook her. Her heart shuddered. She began to sweat. Somebody had been in the house. Maybe he was still there. She was all nerves as she began poking around in closets and cupboards. Was he crouched behind the radio table? Was he hiding in the shower? She searched, but came up empty. Then, she remembered her beloved cat.

"Freckles, where are you?" She dashed around in a frenzy. "Lamb pie, where are you? Freckles? Freckles?"

The feline strutted out from behind a chair all calm-like, and Mrs. Neubaum whisked him into an embrace, relieved—that is, until she noticed the red string wrapped around his neck. Was this a threat on her baby's life? She grabbed a pair of scissors and quickly snipped off the makeshift collar as if it was tainted by evil.

Then, she returned to her bedroom and stared at the wording on her pillow. What was "RIP" supposed to mean? Was it short for "Rest in Peace"? Was the intruder going to kill her? Was he going to kill Freckles? Or did "RIP" have to do with cutting and slicing? Was this wet smack going to rip up her skin, rip open her heart, or send ripples through her spine? Maybe the straight pins themselves had meaning. Maybe the intruder was going to stick them into her eyes.

One thing was for sure: Mrs. Neubaum was not in a muddle over who had done it. The intruding had not been done by just anybody. Ernie had been in her house. She was right certain. She knew his name because she had been conversing with Nellie out by the mailbox a few days prior, and Nellie had mentioned it in passing. At the time, Mrs. Neubaum had thought that the word "Ernie" was a lot like the word "eerie." Did Nellie, who seemed like a perfectly respectable woman, know her mustard platter of a husband was breaking into other people's homes?

Did she know he was a loon who left cryptic messages on pillows and wrapped string around cats' necks? Did she know he hid behind curtains, peeping out like a deranged owl? Did she know about the creepy carving on the steps and the black paint over the basement windows? Mrs. Neubaum had a feeling she knew a lot more about Ernie than his own wife did.

Mrs. Neubaum also felt like a weasel in a hole. She was a sitting duck. Ernie knew where she lived and was skilled enough to get inside. She thought about getting on the blower to the cops, but then stopped herself. Maybe this was a bad idea. She had a speeding ticket that she had not cleared. She had failed to appear in municipal court for the proceeding because she'd had an emergency alteration that day. Plus, she had ignored the follow-up notices in the mail from the traffic bureau. Would the fuzz figure her for a scofflaw and throw her in the pokey?

Also, Mrs. Neubaum was worried that snitching could send Ernie around the bend. It could lead to recriminations—possibly deadly ones. If peering at the stone steps had upset him so, what might he do if she alerted the police? Ernie had not stolen anything as far as she could tell, so what could she prove? She could hear the officer being all doubtful. "How do you know it was him, ma'am?" The copper would surely ask why she did not suspect an escaped patient from the Weston lunatic asylum, a vagrant hunting for a warm meal, or a teenager playing a prank.

Mrs. Neubaum sat on the couch and did some thinking. She made a swift appraisal of the situation. She figured Ernie would have killed Freckles if he meant business, or he would have waited for her to get home and popped out of the closet with a shiv or a gun. Frightening her was his goal. He was sending a message to leave him be.

She decided not to make waves. This would, of course, be challenging because she was fond of waves. She had a hankering for the foam, the swells, the spray, and the ripples. She fancied the way they crashed into her life, giving her a thrill and making her feel less ordinary. They got her adrenaline going. Plus, making waves was part of her nosey parker nature. She had a compulsion to know what was going on around her, to be on top of neighborhood news. The grapevine was her lifeline. But going forward, she would have to make an exception with Ernie. She would stay in the dark about his doings, no matter how foul or seedy they might seem. She would keep her peepers shut real tight and stuff temptations down into her gut when they were itching to flare.

Mrs. Neubaum was determined. She would not let "RIP" be her fate.

Chapter 16

RUN, NELLIE, RUN

ERNIE WAS ACTING all devious and bent. He was in his scythe room, stroking a pink pillbox hat. He found the velvety softness pleasing and the shape fetching. It looked like a strawberry cupcake from a swanky afternoon tea. It was more of a fashion piece than a head covering. Ernie had secretly nabbed it from Nellie's side of the closet while she was in the shower. It had been on the shelf above her matching pink party dress. To his mind, his wife could no longer lay claim to it. It full-on belonged to him.

It was strikingly dark in the basement that day. A faint beam of light jetted out from the corner where there was an Isamu Noguchi lamp fitted with a low wattage bulb. The room looked like a maze of shadows or, for somebody with Ernie's colorful imagination, a den of misshapen monsters.

Ernie was ready to get down to business, so he set aside the pink hat and edged up close to his "guest."

"You're not listening. Sit still." Ernie suddenly became incensed because she kept tilting to the left. "Sit up straight, you scrag, or I'll smack your hussy face."

He shoved his "guest" upright but, seconds later, she fell to the left again.

"You think I'm fooling? I'll snap that ugly neck. I'll cast monsters on you." Ernie glanced around the room at the behemoth shadows on the walls.

Then, he put his hands on his "guest's" shoulders and positioned her up straight.

"Don't move a hair, woman." She stayed put. "Now, I want you to hold your horses on the divorce. You hear?"

She did not answer because she could not answer.

Ernie was out-of-whack with himself. He had stepped into a queer world. It was the world of his occult readings. It was a world he had craved for years. It was a world that sprang from the hideousness of his most base intentions and from the slatternly corners of his mind.

Ernie's "guest" could not talk because she was not a woman. She was not even a person, although she was a dead ringer for his wife. She was a creepy, life-sized doll. Ernie had named her Ella May (or Ella, for short), and she was the product of hours of stuffing and stitching using excelsior and other materials from the fabric store purchase. Making an effigy was a breeze of a task for Ernie due to his previous work as a sofa upholsterer. Ella's face was flesh-colored with black pen marks drawn to look like eyes, a snoot, a kisser, and eyebrows. She wore Nellie's lipstick and hairstyle. Her mane was actually a brown wig of ringlet curls that Ernie had pulled from his mighty stash of Halloween costumes. His daughters had been devoted trick-or-treaters back when they were of school age, and Ernie had showered them with a slew of spooky guises. Ella wore a skirt and a modest button-down blouse, covering her cleavage. His Ella was no trollop and, by golly, she would not dress like one.

"Lunch is ready," Nellie hollered through the basement door, jolting Ernie back into the real world. "Ernie? Ernie?"

"Patience, woman," he screamed.

"The food's getting cold."

"Damn it. Pushy broad," he muttered to himself. Then, he yelled, "Keep your bloomers on. I'm coming."

Ernie roused himself. Why all the fuss? Why was Nellie being so pushy? It was not normal for her to be impatient. On the other hand, he would be pleased to get some nourishment in his tummy. It had been growling like a rankled honey badger.

But when Ernie got upstairs, he peeped into the breakfast nook and his mood turned sour all over again. It was clear why Nellie was in a hurry. That pesky Irene and her ten-year-old daughter, Shirley Anne, were sitting at the table all polite-like with napkins folded in their laps. They looked like ghastly Puritans.

"What in Sam Hill is this? I told you. I don't want that rock of ages in this house," Ernie whispered to his wife.

"Just try to get along." Nellie gave Ernie a friendly shove into the room. He took a seat at the table, looking miffed.

"Hello, Ernie." Irene smiled.

"Hello, Irene." He steered clear of eye contact, instead focusing his attention on Tutu, who was under the table.

Nellie removed a tray of rolls from the oven.

"Shirley Anne's sprouting up like a vine." Irene put her arm around her daughter.

"I'm hungry," Ernie grumbled.

"Irene, do you want some Adam's ale?" Nellie placed the rolls on the table.

"No thanks, sis."

Nellie took a chair and set her napkin in her lap. "It's your turn, Ernie. Etiquette is the linchpin of civilization."

Ernie shot daggers but complied, tucking his napkin into his shirt like a bib.

Irene turned to Shirley Anne. "Would you like to show us what you learned?"

The child smiled, shut her eyes, and folded her hands in front of her as if she was at Sunday school. "Dear God, thank you for this meal…"

"What's she doing?" Ernie interrupted. He was piping hot with fury.

"Saying grace," Irene said.

"Dear God…." Shirley Anne began again.

"Shut up. Shut up." Ernie went ballistic. He stood, threw his napkin onto the floor, and began howling. "Arrrrg. Ugggh. Grrrh. Arrrrg. Ugggh." If there was one thing that irked him, it was being fed Christian gobbledygook.

Nellie and Irene looked at each other in horror and bewilderment. Ernie sounded like a deranged demon. Then he high-tailed it out of the room. They heard the basement door slam and Ernie's stompers going down the steps, followed by more shrieks of anguish. "Arrrg. Ugggh. Arrrg. Ugggh."

"For heaven's sake! That was quite a display." Nellie was embarrassed and felt like crawling under the rug.

"It was plumb strange, but that void coupon of yours has always had splinters in his head." Irene was always happy to condemn her sister's heel of a husband.

"Hush your mouth, Irene. You shouldn't say such things. He's never done this before. I just don't know what's come over him lately. He has such wild mood swings."

"Arrrg. Grrrh. Ugggh." Ernie's voice echoed through the house.

The two women picked at their food. Irene decided to keep her trap shut for fear of pushing Nellie into a tailspin. Shirley Anne gobbled down her lunch, oblivious to the tension.

"Arrrg. Grrrh. Ugggh."

"I'll put on some music." Nellie went to the radio and turned on "Stormy Weather" by Ethel Waters. Then she reclaimed her seat. "He's gotten angrier this past year."

"He should see a doctor," Irene said.

"He doesn't like doctors."

The women took a few bites in awkward silence.

"He's been stealing from me too."

"What?" Irene was horrified. "You never told me about this."

"My pink hat's missing. And I'm pretty sure he stole my lipstick."

"Jeepers creepers. What would he want with *them*?"

Nellie shrugged.

"You think he's a homo?" Irene was mortified.

"Ernie's a swish." Shirley Anne giggled.

"I don't think that could be right. He's not freakish." Nellie shook her head. "Maybe he's just in a springtime slump."

"Arrrg. Grrrh. Ugggh." Ernie's moans drowned out the sound of the radio.

"A springtime slump?" Irene could no longer hold her tongue. "You need to file for divorce. I've told you at least a hundred times."

"I know, but he doesn't want a divorce. He gets all upset when I mention it."

"All upset? Oh, take my long johns down the river," she said sarcastically. "And what's he doing now? Acting peachy?"

"I can't get a divorce if he won't give me one."

"Yes you can. Be a tough canoe. Lay down the law."

Nellie thought for a second. "Maybe you're right."

"Arrrg. Grrrh. Ugggh."

"Maybe we should be going." Irene put down her fork. "So you can tend to him."

"That would probably be best."

After Irene and Shirley Anne were gone, Nellie shut off the radio. She was unsure how to proceed. Part of her felt brash and able-bodied, but another part felt like a white flag waving in the wind. She placed her ear up against the basement door. She listened hard but could not hear a thing. There was a lull in Ernie's moans and shrieks.

Then, Nellie placed her hand on the knob. She was rattled when it turned. He had forgotten to lock it. Ernie had left his sacred place unsecure. His precious scythe room was an open highway to strangers and prying eyes.

Nellie was tentative. She hemmed and hawed. She was beside herself with confusion. Should she tiptoe downstairs or not? Should she try to soothe Ernie or leave him be? Should she bring up divorce or wait until he was chipper? She went back and forth, under and over, here and there about what was best. She did this for a full ten minutes.

Finally, her curiosity won out and she convinced herself that she *needed* to go in the basement. It was her duty to be at her husband's side, to help him through the hodgepodge of emotions. Never mind that he had made it clear that his secret place was forbidden. Never mind that he was foaming at the mouth like a can of spoiled whipped cream.

Nellie removed her shoes and tiptoed down the staircase, hoping the creaky steps would be her pal rather than a stoolie. She heard one more chorus of "Arrrg, grrrh, ugggh," during her short but strained journey into the dark and damp basement.

When she got to the bottom of the steps, she froze, petrified. It was a nightmare, a bloodcurdling jolt, a "knock-me-for-a-loop" shock of a lifetime. Nellie was eyeball-to-eyeball with a carnival of horrors. To her mind, the room was like one of those traveling freak shows, featuring sword-swallowers, man-monkeys, bearded ladies, and deformed dwarves. Nellie felt sick to her stomach. She noticed lit black candles, devil-worship books, a horned gargoyle, knives, broken crosses, her missing lipstick, disfigured dolls, the child-sized hand, and the drawings of pentagrams on both the floor and walls. But that was not the worst of it. She was most horrified by the noose hanging in the corner and the creepy life-sized doll. It was her spitting image and wore the stolen pink hat.

"Hey, cut yourself a piece of cake, precious," Ernie said softly to Ella while brushing bits of fluff from her blouse. He was wearing a red devil mask with white fangs. "You're my honey pie." Ernie had his back to Nellie and was unaware that she had intruded on his private space.

Oh nausea! My husband is having a conversation with a doll, Nellie thought to herself. *It's bonkers. His sanity has run amok. There's no paint on his canvass.* Nellie had already seen too much. She knew she dare not make a peep or, for that matter, breathe. She was trembling in her socks. She wished she could sneak back upstairs to the comfort of her humble kitchen and forget about the frightfulness of it all. But it was too late, and she knew it was only a matter of seconds before Ernie would turn. He would catch her with her peepers as big as a spook fish and her mouth as open as a bottle of Old Crow.

All sorts of ideas were upside down in Nellie's head. For one, she scolded herself for living in a fog, for not catching the strangeness sooner. How could she have been such a dodo? Who was this sinister man she called her husband? What kind of sub-zero was he, skipping down the primrose path to hell? How could she have not known he was a monster, a deranged turnip, a perverted eel? She had dutifully swallowed his lies for years like a young'un taking sugar pills. She hated herself.

She was not just naïve; it was worse. She was blind. She was a weak sister with a lamppost for brains.

Then, the dreaded moment came. Ernie turned, saw Nellie, and removed his mask. His face got all red and bloated. He was a raging geyser of fire and it looked like he would mushroom into a giant serpent. He plowed toward his wife, screeching like a siren. "How dare you come into my room?"

Nellie tried to scramble up the basement steps, but was yanked backward and thrown onto the concrete floor. Ernie dragged her toward the noose.

"You bitch. You ugly bitch. Who do you think you are?"

"Please, Ernie. Stop," Nellie bawled. "Please, Ernie. Please, don't hurt me."

"You cheesy whore. You goo-ball of a wife."

"Ernie, let me go. I won't tell, I promise."

Ernie pulled her hair and bit her upper arm as he struggled to pry her neck into the noose. She kicked and squirmed with the fierceness of a woman facing death. Ernie reached for a knife, but Nellie kicked over the table where it rested. The knife fell to the floor. This outraged Ernie, who set out to fetch it. He briefly let go of Nellie in the process, and she took the opportunity to bolt toward the stairway. He lumbered after her, caught her, and hurled her across his haunted playground. She hit a wall. She felt dizziness and a throbbing in her head. When she opened her eyes, her face was right smack-dab up against the ghoulish doll.

She shrieked and heaved the effigy with all her strength. It flew through the air and landed all cockeyed like a heap of junk.

"No." Ernie was distressed to see his beloved Ella hurt. He ran to tend to her while Nellie made a beeline for the stairs. She bolted upstairs, but Ernie caught wind of her escape and followed.

The struggle was not over. Nellie was bloody and bruised as she stumbled into the bedroom and tried to shut the door behind her. But Ernie outmuscled her and belted her again. Her body hit the dresser with a thud, and she sunk to the ground next to Tucker's business card.

"Where's my fucking gun?" Ernie mumbled as he scampered back down the scythe room steps.

Nellie grabbed the business card and made tracks through the living room, only to tumble over an ottoman. She heard Ernie scaling the steps. Nellie got to her feet just as Ernie appeared. He pointed his gun, but she darted out of the house in the nick of time.

Ernie shouted into the front yard, "Don't be telling no lies, woman. No one would believe a bitch like you."

Ernie eyed her through the window as she scampered past Will Kleeman's house and down the road. "Look at those stubby stilts dusting out of here." He cackled. "That eyesore of a wife has a right big screw loose... coming into my scythe room like that."

Nellie ran as if her feet were on fire. She was aiming for the phone booth outside Hartley's department store on Adams Street. She veered down Chesapeake Avenue and made a hard left onto Cleveland Avenue, where she dashed past Tucker and Ginger's shack (although she had no idea who resided there). Nellie's legs felt weak and rickety and the bottoms of her socked feet stung due to the small bits of rock on the road. But she dared not stop. Survival was on her mind.

Back at the house, Ernie was blaming his cheeky tart of a wife for the whole beastly kit and caboodle, for the whole nasty blowup. *She brought the whole damn thing on herself,* he thought. *She shouldn't have been sniffing around like a hound dog.* He knew cause and effect had taken hold. Once the glass was tipped over, the water could not be stuffed back in. Once the domino got tapped, it had to hit the next domino. Once the branch that was his privacy got broken, it had to fall. It had fallen on Nellie, and rightly so.

There was no going back, and in part, Ernie was pleased about this peculiar turn of events. Now, he was a genuine disciple of the dark. He could fly into the night without chains. He could be a new man—a full-fledged devil in the basement. There would be no hiding behind husbandly lies and locked doors. Ernie knew his wife would tattle to Johnny Law and anyone else who would listen, but he was not fretting over it. *Nobody will believe that cluck,* he thought. *She's just a lowly woman, and nobody gives a damn what women say.*

Chapter 17

LONGING FOR A LEG UP

IT WAS GOING to be a whopper of a day, and Tucker was chomping at the bit, gung-ho about settling into his new law office. He put on his spiffiest suit and showed up at two p.m. on the dot, in line with the arrangement made with Mr. Olden, the building's manager.

The Adams Street offices were positioned above McCrory's dime store but, nevertheless, they had a reverent and commanding feel, just like the courthouse across the road. Tucker was keen to be within shouting distance of the judge. He would never be late for trial. Not that this was a concern, of course; he was simply not a tardy fellow. Punctuality was innate. It was stitched into his brain matter. He had been the man of the house since he was knee-high to an asparagus plant. Of course, responsibility could be aggravating and akin to dragging around a sack of sugar, but he was used to it. Plus, he had a knack for taking charge, tending to details, and not letting others down. There were no ifs, ands, or buts. To Tucker's mind, letting others down was no peccadillo; it was a big-league defect.

"I'm here to get settled and pick up a copy of my lease." Tucker smiled at the secretary, Mildred, who sat at a desk, shuffling invoices.

"Mr. Olden's upstairs, sir. Second floor."

"Thank you very much, ma'am." Tucker tipped his hat and headed to the elevator.

Tucker caught sight of Mr. Olden in the second-floor hallway chatting with J. Worley Powell, who was known around town as "a doozy of a fellow." He was robust, forty-four years old, and more generous with sloppy handshakes than most folks were with smiles. When meeting a newcomer or an old friend, he would offer one paw and then come around with the other for good measure, turning a routine shake into a fancy, double-decker greeting. Essentially, Worley was a big lug with brains and probably better-liked than any man, woman, or child in Marion County. He had been a mouthpiece for many years, having gotten his law degree in 1927.

"There's a stain on the carpet in my outer room," Worley said. "Could you inform the cleaning crew?"

"Sure thing, Mr. Powell. It'll be handled in a jiffy," Mr. Olden replied.

"Sorry to interrupt," Tucker said. "I'm here to fetch the keys. And maybe you could ferret out a copy of my lease. I'm all set to move in."

"I don't know what you're talking about, mister." Mr. Olden plucked a handkerchief from his pocket and blew his nose.

Tucker was jarred by his words and on the verge of fury. He could not believe this was happening again. He wanted to wallop that cauliflower of a manager for pretending to be dumb, for acting all ignorant about the lease. For a moment,

Tucker wished he was Jal. It was clear that Mr. Olden was not just old-looking. He was old-thinking and had been apprised of Tucker's Italian blood.

Besides being peeved, Tucker was heavy-hearted. Success was that bubble that floated away each time he tried to grab it. He had spent his life being disciplined and responsible, attending classes, taking jobs, and working his way up from having mere pennies in the bank. He had been climbing that mountain for so long, but was always getting whacked back down to the base. It was not the natural elements—the wind, rain, sleet, and snow—that were weighing on him. It was those that were manmade: the backwardness, the prejudice, and the old-fogey attitudes. They kept biting him in the leg and throwing him off balance. Tucker wondered if Jal had been right to back away from the mountain in the first place. Maybe it was wiser to stay at the bottom, shoveling rocks and signing onto modest "guido jobs." Why expend brainpower if white-haired relics like Mr. Olden were going to trip a fellow up and bury him under the rubble?

Plus, how would he break the news to Ginger? This rejection would be the third—a triple whammy of misfortune. He imagined saying, "Ginger dear, remember how we lost our movie-star home? Well, Mr. Deveny also sent me packing, as well as some prune-faced dullard on Adams Avenue. Aren't you glad you married a guido?" He figured Ginger would cry up a storm and criticize the Klan-like mentality of some Fairmontians. But she might also regret marrying an Italian. That would, of course, hurt Tucker's heart. He watched Mr. Olden blow his nose for a second time and wondered how much a fellow could swallow before he just up and burst. He figured one day he might stop climbing that stupid mountain and instead just blow up the whole damn thing!

Despite the barrage of unsettling thoughts, Tucker hoped he

was wrong about this man. *Maybe that old box of bird seed has faulty recall*, he said to himself. *Maybe he just needs a little shove to jiggle his memory*. So, Tucker prodded him.

"Remember, the copy machine was broken. You called it 'lazy,' and we shook. You gave me your word."

"Nope. Don't recognize you."

"Well then, I'd like to lease an office." Tucker tried one last time, remembering how persistence was the pony that Paul Revere had ridden into the history books.

"Nope. No openings. You need to peddle your papers elsewhere." Mr. Olden turned to Worley. "I'll have the cleaning crew get right on it, Mr. Powell." Mr. Olden moseyed over to the elevator without giving Tucker a second glance. Tucker dropped his head, defeated.

Worley had a smile that could warm a greenhouse and he was itching to grow a new friendship. Plus, he did not like seeing a man feeling low. He held out his big, warm meat hook in search of a handshake. "I'm J. Worley Powell." He always sounded like he had a megaphone.

Tucker had no spunk left so his grip was limp.

"I know who you are," Worley said in a coy way. "You're Tucker Moroose. I've seen you in the courthouse. You're a very impressive trial lawyer. You say you need an office?"

"Uh…"

"I've got just the place for you… in my office. Come with me."

Tucker was reluctant, but accompanied Worley down the hall and through a door with gold nameplates, identifying the "esquires" in the suite. They ankled into an outer room where Worley's secretary, Wanda Corley, was preoccupied. She was making copies at a Photostat machine behind her desk. She was a shorty in her early sixties and had a tight bun that made her face seem stretched.

The outer room had six walnut Bergere chairs with nail head trim, three matching mahogany tables embellished with brass decorative bands, two Genet and Michon lamps, an American flag, a large fern, an array of framed seascapes on the walls, and a fist-sized stain on the carpet.

"I have a suite of six rooms and there's a vacancy because Ronald Simpson—do you know him?"

Tucker shook his head.

"Well, he just moved to Charleston."

Tucker backed away. "I don't want to waste your time, Mr. Powell. I think I should let you know up front…" Tucker hesitated.

"Well, what is it? Spit it out."

"I came through Ellis Island when I was three. I'm Italian." Tucker anticipated a song and dance about why the place was not available after all.

"So? What's your point?"

"Well… some people don't want to lease to…"

Worley interrupted, "Hey, they won't bother you anymore." He put his arm around Tucker and winked. "You're with me."

Worley led Tucker into an office with oak baseboards, weighty brass fixtures, a mahogany desk, two armchairs, an empty walnut bookcase, and a framed picture of an old shoe. There were two windows that were a trifling sixteen inches off the floor and sixteen inches down from the ceiling. They allowed for a right fine view of the courthouse. There was also a six-foot by three-foot swatch of speckled, obscure glass between the office and the reception area. This permitted Wanda to keep tabs on her boss if she was so inclined, although she could only identify shadows and general shapes rather than the nitty-gritty or particulars.

"This would be your office. Your law license could hang right there instead of that ridiculous shoe." Worley shook his head. "An old shoe? Makes no sense to hang something like that in a law office. Don't know what Ronald was thinking. Anyway, what do you say?"

"May I inquire as to the fee?"

"Whatever arrangement you had with Olden will be fine."

Tucker was impressed with this kindly man who had given him a leg-up, a much-needed boost. Worley was unlike most folks in West Virginia, or anywhere else for that matter. He was a rare bird, a four-leaf clover in the forest, a Rolls Royce in a dime store parking lot. He had turned a bum rap into a cotton candy of a day, and Tucker was eager to get home and feed the good news to Ginger. Tucker flashed a wide smile and held out his hand. He was hankering for a whale of a shake.

"Okay. Thank you, Mr. Powell. You have a deal. I really appreciate it."

"Call me Worley."

The two men returned to the outer area to find Wanda typing a letter.

"This is Mrs. Corley," Worley said. "She'll be your secretary. Helps all the lawyers in my suite. She's a crackerjack employee... and Mrs. Corley, this is Tucker Moroose. He's our new associate. He'll be occupying the front office. Please call the courthouse and give them his new address."

"Yes sir." Wanda made the call.

Worley led Tucker over to a team-autographed baseball ensconced in a display case. It was a fresh addition to the outer room and part of Worley's effort to spruce the place up a bit.

"This is my pride and joy." Worley picked up the collectible. "Just had the case made. I'm a Pittsburgh Pirates fan. That Dixie Howell's got golden hands. Golden... oh, Christopher Columbus. That reminds me..." Worley escorted Tucker back to the suite's main entrance as Wanda hung up from the courthouse call.

"I almost forgot." Worley pointed at the gold-plated plac-ards on the door, listing the lawyers in the suite. "This is where your name goes. Plus, I'll get it added to the directory downstairs."

He shouted at Wanda. "Could you ask maintenance to take care of this?" She nodded as she answered the ringing phone.

"Yes, he's here," Wanda said into the receiver. "Could I get your name?" Then she shouted, "You already have a call, Mr. Moroose. It's a woman... a Mrs. Nellie Yost."

Nellie had more nicks than a football helmet and more scratches than an old frying pan. Her face was bruised, her socks were filthy, and her hair was unkempt. Her day dress was ripped and bespattered with blood. All in all, she looked like she had been through a garbage disposal. After bolting out of her house, she had run directly to the pay station (or phone booth) outside Hartley's department store and begged a nickel off a stranger. She'd dialed Tucker straightaway, who instructed her to file a report with the constables at the Fairmont police station.

"Wife-beating's a crime, Mrs. Yost," Tucker told her on the phone. "And the penalty for attempting to kill a spouse is as much as eighteen years in the clink. I'd advise you to hustle on down to the station."

The Fairmont police department was situated in a three-story red brick building on Monroe Street. As Nellie dragged herself through the door, she saw two cops at the complaint counter and two more behind desks. There were scattered wooden chairs, cub-byholes for forms, commendations on the walls, and bars over the window. The bars seemed curious to Nellie since lawbreak-ers were not likely to be roaming the joint; they would surely be wearing bracelets.

The police uniforms were navy with white buttons and a tin on the left side of the torso, inscribed with the words, "Fairmont Police." The officers were divided into two shifts: day and night, both twelve hours. Gumshoes—who wore street clothes—made up 15 percent of the department's staff. Their job was investigating the nuts and bolts of a case.

"I'm so hungry my spare tire's deflated," Sergeant Red Walsh said.

"You did that one last week," Officer Angus Digman replied. "It's Bing Crosby in *Road to Singapore*."

"Okay, smart aleck. Give this one a spin." Red chuckled. "Love is like champagne. Marriage is the headache and divorce is the aspirin tablet."

"Beats me." Angus shrugged.

"*Look Who's Laughing*. Charlie McCarthy."

The men were playing a game in which they linked pithy phrases from motion pictures with the name of the flick and the actor who delivered the line.

The officers suddenly noticed Nellie. Although she was a wreck, they made no mind of it, figuring she was a down-and-out. They had seen their share of street urchins and derelict types, and these folks were not exactly gussied up when they waltzed through the door.

"Morning, ma'am. I'm officer Digman," Angus said to Nellie, who exploded in a hullabaloo of tears.

"My husband. He hit me. He tried to kill me. He's got a creepy doll. I'm such a stupe. How could I have not known?" Her voice squealed like wind against a steel fence. "I hope you're gonna arrest him. You need to arrest him. I don't know what I'll do if you don't arrest..."

Angus interrupted. "Take it easy, ma'am. What's your name?"

"Nellie Marie Yost."

"And your address?"

"Address? Oh, my lord. I don't know. I can't go home. I guess I'll be staying with my sister." She buried her face in her hands, sobbing.

Angus passed her a handkerchief. "Never mind the address for now. What's the story? From the top. Take your time."

After Angus got the particulars, he hoofed it into the back room and chased down Frank Ganges, one of the station's gumshoes. He was poring over a newspaper.

"Family trouble. Got a frail woman out there whose husband has been mistreating her. Bruises on her throat, shoulders, and arms. Some cuts. No eyewitnesses. This is the address." He handed him a piece of paper. "I'm gonna ship her on over to Fairmont General."

"Almost finished with my mud." Frank pointed at his cup of coffee. "Then I'll swing on by."

"Husband's a white male, American, approximately 175 pounds, forty-five years old, brown hair, regular features. Name's Ernie Lee Yost. Oh... and he's got a gun."

An hour later, Frank parked his patrol car in front of Ernie's house and knocked on the door. Ernie answered with Tutu at his feet.

"Good day. Are you Ernie Lee Yost?"

"Yep. How can I be of use?" He was in good spirits.

"I'm Detective Frank Ganges with the Fairmont Police. I have a complaint." Frank studied the paper in his hand. "Assault. Battery. Attempted murder of Mrs. Nellie Marie Yost. I need to have a look around."

"Sure, detective." Ernie opened the door as wide as a shotgun. "Look all you want. That broad's a nut. We're in the midst of a divorce, and she likes to whistle Dixie. She told me she was gonna make up stuff so she could swipe all my money. I didn't think she'd go so far as contacting you nice folks. Crazy chucklehead. Don't know why I married her."

"You packing a heater, sir?

"Got one in my sock drawer."

"Mind if I take a look?" Frank had his hand on the gun in his overcoat pocket and was ready to drop the hammer if need be.

Ernie led Frank to the bedroom, extracted the piece from the drawer, showed it was not loaded, and set it on the dresser next to Nellie's lipstick and pink hat. He positioned it just so, with the barrel pointing at her belongings—a symbolic act of spite and done for kicks.

"Want to show me the rest of the house?" Frank motioned Ernie into the hallway, gesturing that he would follow. Leading was a thorny proposition. Leading was for suckers and greenhorns. Leading was against department policy. It could put a copper on a collision course with death. He might fall prey to a knife in the back, a bullet in the brain, or a rope around the throat.

Frank sniffed around the house, peeping into rooms and cupboards while keeping a tight eye on Ernie. Despite this fellow's genial disposition and welcome wagon style, Frank did not full-on trust him. Was Ernie being framed by Nellie? Or was he a hothead who had tried to grease his wife? Frank was full of questions, but he believed in caution. To his mind, Ernie was cagey until he wasn't. He was full of malarkey until he wasn't. He was a chiseler until he wasn't. Frank was no halfwit. He was as devious as Ernie and not about to be sweet-talked or bamboozled.

"There's a basement?"

"Yep." Ernie pointed. "But nothing down there except a mess of cobwebs and some tools."

Frank opened the basement door, which was unlocked.

"After you, Mr. Yost." He motioned for Ernie to go first. The two men descended into the scythe room.

The place was like Pygmalion. It had been transformed. It was no longer the equivalent of a bedraggled, Cockney flower girl. It was now a normal-looking basement with a respectable amount of dust, tools, scruffy bags of household odds and ends, and prominently displayed materials—such as wood and metal—for fixing and inventing. Ernie's "patching place" was still intact, but had been spread out to take up most of the room. The only fluky items were the easy chair and radio.

"I listen to *Family Theater* down here. And *You Bet Your Life*. That show's a riot. But, that greedy, dog-faced wife of mine doesn't like it. She wants me working my fingers to the bone night and day so she can buy fancy dresses from New York."

Frank pushed aside a rake and poked his nose behind a wheelbarrow and a pile of wood. "The place looks right typical. Don't see anything out of the ordinary."

Ernie was playing hide and seek with his devil worship props. The books and pamphlets were squirreled away under the living room couch. The black candles and the noose were tucked under dirty clothes in the bathroom hamper. The posters of pentagrams, symbols, and charts were lying flat under the large throw rug in the kitchen. The deformed figurines and human hand were in paper sacks in the freezer behind the Birdseye vegetables and frozen orange juice. The effigy was in the storage loft near the ceiling of the scythe room.

"Do you have some sort of curly-haired doll?"

Ernie rubbed his chin as if he was thinking. "Oh, yeah... Nellie and I used to set that damn thing up in front of the window. You know, to make it look like someone was home. To keep away porch-climbers and picklocks."

"Do you know where it might be?"

"Nope."

Frank moseyed over to an open box of screwdrivers, hammers, and other tools.

Suddenly, Ernie became on edge. He could see the storage loft out of the corner of his eye and a piece of Ella's skirt was hanging down! He knew an emergency "diverting of attention" was in order, and grabbed a football from a metal bucket.

"You play?" Ernie juggled the ball from hand to hand.

"No. Never been the 'sportsy' type."

"Well, I was a right good punter back in high school." Ernie led Frank back to the steps. "It's getting drafty. What do you say we head on up?"

The men went upstairs.

Frank was confused about the whole deal. Things just were not adding up. His report said one thing, but Ernie was a slick stick about explaining it all away. He plowed into one final question. "You got some kind of a pug-ugly devil mask?"

Ernie chuckled. "Detective, I've got a whole slew of masks." He waltzed over to a trunk in the spare bedroom and opened it. He explained how his daughters from his first marriage were red-hot trick-or-treaters. Ernie yanked out props, hats, masks, and costumes, one after another. There was a fairy princess, a Mickey Mouse, a clown, a skeleton, a bunny, a witch, and a werewolf, among others.

"A devil, you say? I don't seem to have anything like that." Ernie dug deeper in the trunk. "Well, hot peppers. This is probably what you're looking for, detective." He pulled out a bull mask. It did not look like a devil.

The detective knew he did not have the goods on Ernie, even though he was quite sure this fellow was a skylarker. There was something about his eyes that gave Frank the willies. They were so dark brown as to be black. They were like cauldrons of spiky bayonets. But a "bad feeling" was not good enough for a respectable sleuth. Having the heebie-jeebies had nothing to do with evidence. Gumshoeing was like geometry; it was not mushy. It was not about sensibilities or butterflies in the tummy. It was a darn tootin' science.

Frank headed for the front door. "I don't mind saying… this case confounds me, Mr. Yost. I mean, why would your wife just up and invent all this?"

Ernie laughed. "I already told you. Nellie's trying to make me look bad for court because I have a lot of money."

"*You* have a lot of money?" Frank looked skeptical.

Ernie plucked a wad of twenty dollar bills from his pocket and waved them through the air like a showboat. "Seventeen hundred bucks. Just in my pocket alone."

Frank was shocked. It was a whopping stash of clams like nothing he had ever seen. "I guess you *do* have a lot of money." Frank was unsure whether Ernie was a straight arrow, but he figured his wife was probably to blame. She had no doubt been gumming up the marriage and looking to score. Maybe she'd fashioned him as a sugar daddy. After all, this fellow was on the level about being loaded. "Sorry for the inconvenience, Mr. Yost."

"No problem, detective. I appreciate the Fairmont police department. You folks do a fine job."

"Have a nice day." Frank headed out the door and down the front walkway. He did not notice the chiseled steps.

"Hey, root for me. In the divorce, that is. Us menfolk have to stick together."

Frank waved and climbed into his patrol car, where he wrote the word "closed" on the file. Then he drove away. He was no longer chewing on the bit about whether Ernie was a wife-abuser. He was no longer bothered about the curly-haired doll or the elusive devil mask, and he was no longer wondering if he had been hoodwinked. Instead, Frank was thinking about the cabbage—seventeen hundred clams of crisp pulchritude—enough to buy a real pretty car. Enough for a sizable down payment on a house or enough to jet around the world like Cary Grant. Being a well-heeled upper crust was Frank's rainbow—a rainbow that he hoped someday to touch.

Frank wore an eerie smile as he turned on the radio and mumbled to himself, "A fellow like that Yost character... walking around with all that loot. He's not safe around these parts. He's just not safe."

Chapter 18

FATE AND THE PHONE CALL

ANGMAN FOREST WAS particularly creepy that day. It was noon, and the trees looked like bony ghosts. The sky was dark and sullen. It seemed to be giving Fairmont the evil eye. It was raring to drop canisters of water onto the mountains and valleys.

Ernie was engaged in a bizarre private ceremony in the clearing with his beloved Ella. In his mind, he was marrying her. He was ditching his nagger of a wife and connecting his trigger-happy soul with the life-size doll.

"The god of one people is the devil of another," he read from *The Black Book*. "Lucifer says a loaf of bread shall be taken from the house of Kochak and divided between bride and bridegroom, each to eat one-half."

Ernie tore into a chunk of French bread with his teeth and then offered some to Ella, who was across from him and leaning against a log. In his mind, she took a bite. Then, he set down the loaf and continued with the reading.

"Marriage in March is forbidden, for it is the last month of the year." Ernie smiled and spoke in his own words to the doll. "It's April, pumpkin. The start of a new year. A right fine beginning for us, Ella-cakes." Then, he returned to the text.

"A bride must visit the shrine of every idol she may happen to pass. The bridegroom must hit the bride with a small stone in token of the fact that she must be under his authority."

Ernie then picked up a thumb-sized rock and used it to rap on Ella's head three times. What he did not know was that two women had stumbled upon the Hangman Forest clearing and were watching this freakish ceremony unfold from behind a hazelnut bush. They had wide eyes and rattled expressions. They had no idea Ella was made of hay, fabric, and make-believe hair. They saw her from the back and assumed she was real.

Ernie continued reading. "It is the law that the bridegroom must pass a razor over his bride's face."

Ernie put down the text, donned his devil mask, and grabbed a John Deere pocket knife. He slashed at Ella's face. This petrified the Peeping Toms, who believed a madman was dicing up a living, breathing person.

"Holy mackerel! He's killing her," one whispered to the other.

"Let's make tracks." The other moved, causing a rustle in the bushes.

Ernie heard the sound and was peeved. He shouted, "Who's there?" as he caught a glimpse of the two women darting away. He bolted after them, still in his mask. He planned to lay into them with his knife. But, after scuttling past a dozen trees, he realized the broads had given him the slip.

"You nosey skirts," he shouted into the woods. He figured he had better head back to the clearing, pack up Ella, and hightail it home. He knew these meddlesome scrags would be wagging their clappers and telling young and old about his special ceremony. He could not fathom why folks were always poking their schnozzes into his privacy. What was the matter with all these loopy-headed dips who would not leave him the hell alone?

Back at the house, Ernie put Ella in a chair at the breakfast room table, where he tended to the knife wound on her face. His gun was on the table as well as some books on astrology and ritual. He stuffed hay back into the doll's gap and sewed up the hole with needle and thread. He remembered how he had stolen the hay from the Madison family's barn on Fleming Avenue two days following the purchase of the fabric store supplies. It had been around midnight, and the horses neighed like crazy. It was as if they thought Jack the Ripper was tearing them asunder. Of course, maybe they were just cross about losing their breakfast. Luckily, the Madisons did not wake. Ernie stuffed fistfuls of hay into his duffel bag. Then, he sneaked back to his car and sped home. The whole kit and caboodle was duck soup. The Madison family was none the wiser and the horses were no doubt offered extra chow the next morning to make up for their "peculiar filly feast" in the dead of night.

"Don't go into decline, Ella-cakes. We'll finish our ceremony real soon."

While whipping up a lunch of eggs and tomatoes, Ernie thought back to his wedding day with Nellie and how she had niggled him from the start about the locked basement door. He remembered toting her over the threshold after the backyard ceremony and setting her down in the hallway. Like a rogue homing pigeon, she zeroed in on exactly the wrong thing.

"What's this?" She yanked on the scythe room door.

He brushed away her hand. "It's not safe for you down there, honey pie."

"Why? What is it?"

"It's the basement. You have to promise me you won't go down there."

"But why?"

"There are all sorts of sharp tools and things not befitting a wife. Now, promise me."

"Oh, phooey… I'm not making a promise like that." She was sassy and playful. "You can't keep secrets from me."

"Nellie," Ernie said in a stern voice. "Nellie, I'm not playing hopscotch."

"Okay, I promise." Then, she giggled, pulling her crossed fingers out from behind her back like a child. She waved them in his face. "Oops-a-daisy. I might be fibbing."

Ernie's emotions were in high-gear, but he took pains to act calm. "I'll just keep the door locked so you're not tempted."

Later that day, Ernie caught Nellie peeping through the crack of the scythe room door. He pulled her away, shook his finger in her face, and said, "No, Nellie." He realized that Tutu was better behaved than she was. That's the moment Ernie should have known it would be a "hits and fits" marriage. That's when he should have realized his wife could not keep her peepers to herself. That's when he should have figured the whole blasted relationship would explode all over the floor like a shook-up bottle of soda pop.

Ernie finished whipping up his eggs and spooning them onto a plate next to the tomatoes. Then, he took a seat across from Ella and ate, holding the fork in his usual primitive way. He was hunched over and shoveling the grub into his fly trap like a cave-dweller.

"You look pretty today, toots. But you don't want to catch a cold." He fastened the top button on the doll's blouse.

Scruuuutchhh.

What was that? It was an odd scratching noise. Ernie froze as he scanned the room all cagey-like. He was motionless for a full fifteen seconds with his ears cranked up like an organ grinder's box. He heard nothing else, so he went back to his lunch. Seconds later, he heard the suspicious sound again.

Scruuuutchhh.

Ernie was sweating and all janked up with paranoia. He whispered, "You hear something, Ella?" He figured there must be a snooper in his midst, so he rose, brushed back the curtain, and peered into the garden. All looked normal, so he returned to his seat.

Scruuuutchhh.

There was a third bizarre scratch. Ernie tiptoed to the back door and threw it open with a forceful snap, thinking he would catch the scoundrel red-handed. But there was no scoundrel. It was just Tutu, itching to come inside. She was a house dog, not a yard dog, and Ernie had forgotten she had gone out to do her duty.

"Don't go knocking the wind out of me, Tutu." Ernie chuckled as the dog wandered in and plopped down under the table. Suddenly, the phone rang. Ernie answered it.

"Hello?"

"Mr. Yost?"

"Yep."

"This is Attorney Tucker Moroose. We met at the Palace Restaurant. I gave you my card a time ago. You may recall."

Ernie's adrenaline was pumping and his mood was gloomy. It was that highfalutin' mouthpiece! What the hell did he want?

"Well... I wish I was calling with pleasant news, Mr.

Yost. But... I'm representing your wife, Nellie. She's filing for divorce."

Ernie was so blistering mad that reality was getting all foggy. It was starting to fade into the floorboards.

"I'll be meeting with her on Wednesday morning at nine. I need to ask you some questions about your finances so I can get the papers in order."

By this time, Ernie had plummeted into his own crazed world. He stared at Ella and mistook her for Nellie. He set down the receiver.

"What are you looking at, bitch?" He ignited. "Don't stare at me with those ugly black eyes."

Tucker's voice could be heard coming from the receiver. "Hello... hello?"

Ernie shoved his plate at Ella. "You need to eat, bitch." Then he slammed her face into the food again and again and again. "Eat, bitch. Eat!"

"Hello? Mr. Yost?"

Ernie seemed to be in a trance as he picked up his gun and pointed it at the doll. "This is all your fault. See you in hell. Bang." He pretended to shoot Ella and then he cackled.

"Mr. Yost? Are you still on the line? I think we may have a bad connection."

Ernie hung up the phone. When Tucker rang back a few minutes later, Ernie was no longer there. He was on his way to the hardware store to fetch bomb-making supplies. He bought colored wires, wicks, two timers, kerosene oil, balance scales, two alarm clocks, and two batteries. He already had paper, wood, gasoline, and other necessary combustibles. He was aiming to construct two bombs that would scare the bejesus out of Nellie and her lovey-dovey mouthpiece, as well as the rest of Appalachia.

Ernie was no dunderhead when it came to this sort of thing. He knew about the physics of blasts due to his work at the coal company. Plus, he had a technical mind matched by no other. He understood how energy, explosive materials, compressed gas, and exothermic reactions could come together to produce a walloping bang. He was also well-versed on how to keep the materials stable; he knew how to coop them up so they would not erupt before he could give the green light.

He lugged his hardware store purchases to the basement where he aimed to construct the bombs. He also gathered together the rest of the materials he needed, including the noose, which he used for rope, and the gasoline, which was in his Chris-Craft Cabin Cruiser in the garage. He loved this power boat and its pristine wooden finish. He had bought it the year prior for twenty-five hundred dollars and had skippered it onto the Tygart Valley River with Nellie at his side.

After grabbing the Protectoseal gas can from the cockpit of the boat, Ernie admired the yellow lettering on the vessel's stern. It read, "Hell's A Poppin'"—a macabre phrase that had always thrown his wife into a tizzy, embarrassing her in front of strangers. Ernie had given it this name based on his favorite musical, *Hellzapoppin'*, a 1941 Universal Pictures flick that had received a Best Song nomination for "Pig Foot Pete." The movie opens with an array of finely-dressed folks going down a staircase that collapses into a funhouse ride and slides them into hell. This idea was plumb appealing to Ernie. He liked thinking that high muckety-mucks who saw themselves as the bee's knees could be slapped on the fanny by the devil and roasted up alive. Ernie was also pleased by the notion of his boat floating toward Hades, much like his house with the chiseled steps. To his mind, he had deeded them both to Satan, and this was better than letting that greedy crate, Nellie, get her claws on them.

Ernie settled on the basement floor and began piecing together his bombs with a fine touch here and firm grip there.

There were twists, pushes, pulls, and even a smidgeon of frustration. They would be masterpieces. Ernie was the Picasso of technology, a craftsman of the nether world, an "artiste extraordinaire," as the French might say. He could imagine television and radio announcer Ken Roberts introducing his bombs to an eager-eared audience. "Mr. Yost's explosive works of art are shaking the world." *That's a right big knee-slapper,* Ernie thought.

Despite the occasional tummy-chuckle when an idea sprouted, Ernie remained in a fit of rage for most of the day. He vowed never to be tethered to Nellie. That spook of a wife was not going to get the better of him. No siree. He had told her "no divorce," and dadgummit, he meant it. Obviously, Nellie figured she could do all sorts of nasty stuff with that fancy lawyer—even go necking into the sunset with him—but Ernie knew he'd rather see her dead. He was also convinced that the two lovebirds were in cahoots, planning to flimflam him out of his house, his boat, and his secret stash of cabbage. As far as Ernie was concerned, there would be no waffling or fumbling about. He would put the brakes on that ruse real damn fast.

Tucker was beat. He had been bickering up a storm at the courthouse for most of the day. Arguing cases often felt more like engaging in a rhubarb with his siblings than participating in an above-the-fray display of lawyerly skill. Tucker crossed the street and headed up to his second-floor office, where he planned to scrape together his belongings and shove on home. Instead, he found three serious-looking Italian fellows in swanky business suits seated in the reception area. They looked like sodbusters or arm-twisters. Tucker got a chill. Were these goons from Detroit? Were they Rose's gangster pals?

Had she spilled the beans? Maybe she'd been *forced* to give the game away. Maybe these fellows wanted to make sure his beak stayed shut or give him a whack upside the skull.

Wanda greeted Tucker at the door, talking low. "These men won't leave. I told them to make an appointment."

"What do they want?" Tucker whispered.

"They won't say. But my husband's waiting, Mr. Moroose. It's after five."

"You can go on home." Then, Tucker spoke to the men. "May I help you gentlemen?"

"We need to drag our hocks into your office, Mr. Moroose. It's a confidential matter."

Wanda grabbed her purse and sweater and headed out the door.

"It's closing time. Folks don't usually show up all unannounced, and…"

"Mr. Moroose, we drove four hundred miles."

Tucker figured that was about the distance to Detroit. But he also knew it would do no good to cause a flap. Gorillas have a way of getting to a fellow—any fellow—and causing duress. So Tucker opened the door to his private office and the men sashayed in.

"I'm Tito Rossi and these are my brothers, Luka and Marcello." The men pulled up chairs while Tucker settled behind his desk.

"It's nice to make your acquaintance. Now, what can I do for you gentlemen?"

"We've been watching you," Tito said.

"Why would you be doing that?" Tucker figured these wet noodles—whether they were from Detroit or not—had some sort of axe to grind.

"We'd like to mitt you, Mr. Moroose," Marcello spoke up.

"Mitt me?" Tucker's face was mapped with worry.

"We want to congratulate you," Tito clarified. "You're a solid mouthpiece and a Johnny-on-the-spot debater. My old geezer brother here…"

"Hey…" Luka objected to the insult.

"My hunk-of-heartbreak brother here caught the state orator competition."

"I said to myself," Luka interrupted, "'hot diggity dog, we've got ourselves a winner.'"

"And we've watched you in the courthouse, finessing the judge," Marcello said.

"We drove here from New York to talk to you about politics, Mr. Moroose," Tito said.

"Politics?" Tucker was confused.

"Are you a Democrat or a Republican?" Tito continued.

"Well, I've never really thought about it," Tucker replied. "The Democrats are the party of the Klan. So, I suppose I'm a Republican."

"Swell." Marcello's eyes were the size of hubcaps.

"That's music to our ears, Mr. Moroose," Tito said, "because we're from the drafting committee of the Republican Party. We want to…"

"Groom you. Lick you into shape," Luka interrupted.

"What?" Tucker was confused.

"We think you'd make a fine candidate for Congress," Tito said. "Down the road, that is. Then, we'd move you on up to the Senate."

"Bless my aunt Bessie. You might end up in the White House," Marcello added.

"This is bananas, fellows." Tucker figured the whole thing was a gag. "Are you playing the banjo behind my back? Did my mama put you up to this?"

"Ever heard of that grandstander, John Pastore?" Tito asked.

"Nope. Can't say I have," Tucker said.

"Well, he's the governor of Rhode Island. The only Italian in major office."

"That's the crop," Luka said. "We want our kind to get some influence. What do you say, Mr. Moroose? Ever thought about throwing your hat in the ring?"

"Well... not really... well, maybe a little... but not seriously."

Tito handed Tucker a booklet. "Here's some information about the party platform. Run your eyes over it and let us know what you think. I'll ring you next week."

"Honestly, I'm really flattered, but I don't know that I'm the right..."

"We think you'll be a fine candidate," Tito interrupted. "You've got the style and smarts to pull it off." The men offered their goodbyes and left.

Tucker drove home, thinking about how politicians have truckloads of influence. They can put a dent in mindset, repeal slipshod laws, and even chip away at the gangrene of prejudice. A statesman's life was about making a difference, a notion that Tucker found appealing.

The Cleveland Avenue residence looked more like a doll house than a shack now that it had been hammered into shape by Jal. It had a fresh coat of paint on the walls, moldings, and window sills. Tucker entered and set down his briefcase. He was greeted by his daughters, who were itching to get out the door. Ginger was at the piano, flipping through a songbook.

"Where are my little angels going?" Tucker asked.

"We're getting candy canes from Miss June!" Sharon said.

"Yummy in the lumpy tummy." Tucker grabbed his daughter and tickled her.

Sharon giggled. "My tummy's not lumpy."

Out the window, Tucker could see June stepping onto the porch to fetch the girls.

"One each," Ginger said. "You hear? You don't want to spoil your supper."

"Okay Mommy." Sharon and her sisters left.

"How's my bearcat?"

"Just ducky." Her eyes were fixed on a songbook. "Did you have a productive day?"

"Yeah, but the judge on the Jones case is both off the cob and a sourpuss. I don't know how a fellow can be both. That takes some real doing."

"Did you cancel the conference?" she asked.

"Yeah."

"Sorry about that," Ginger said. "But you know how important my lessons are. My teacher says if I miss even one, I'll regress."

"I wouldn't want you to regress."

Tucker had planned to drive to a three-day legal conference in Wheeling, West Virginia, which started the next morning. But Ginger needed the family car for her Wednesday morning piano lesson, so she had asked Tucker to stay in town.

"I'm behind on my workload anyway... hey, I picked up a divorce case. Do you remember that couple from the restaurant?"

Ginger was tinkering on the piano and adrift in thought. "Do you want to hear what I learned? My teacher's very impressed."

Tucker sat on the couch while Ginger played a sequence of chords followed by a short ditty.

"Hot damn. That's good. There wasn't even a smidgeon of regressing."

Ginger blushed with pride. "The C flat and the B sharp are a little shaky, but I always get the F."

"I wouldn't call it an F. It's an A-plus."

"Oh, Tucker. You're so corny."

Tucker was unsure whether he should mention politics and the New Yorkers. Maybe it was a bad idea to get Ginger all zipped up over what might amount to a pipe dream. On the other hand, she had a right to know. His future was her future. His obstacles were her vicissitudes. His failure could become her blanket of tears.

So, he gently held her hands and gave her the dope about the Republican Party offer, admitting that he was on a "seesaw of confusion" over what to do. "Should we embark upon politics or stay the course in law? Should our future be roulette wheel or a two-sided coin? Should we risk sinking in an ocean called Washington or stay in the tiny pond of Fairmont?"

Ginger was no timid buttercup and believed in swinging for the stars. "Tucker, are you nuts? There's not a dad-blamed thing to think about. Of course you're gonna say 'yes.' You can help folks and show off that top-notch brain of yours. Plus, I hear Washington is absolutely dreamy. Now, I don't want to hear another word about it. Dinner's in an hour." She turned her focus back to the piano.

"Okay. I'll give it some thought." Tucker shrugged and moseyed into the kitchen. "Anything sweet in the house?"

"You can have the carrots in the icebox."

"Carrots?" Tucker grimaced and opened the fridge. He snarled at a platter of raw vegetables. Then, he tiptoed over to the cupboard, where he quietly and artfully opened a package of Town Toast fruit delight cookies, advertised on the wrapper as "deliciously different."

Tucker peeped into the living room to make sure Ginger's attention was on the baby grand before settling down at the table, scarfing down cookies, and mulling over the pluses and minuses of becoming a baby-kissing statesman.

Chapter 19

THE DEVIL GETS HIS DUE

OOM WAS IN the air. It was on the edge of its seat, ready to flatten Tucker like a tractor. Doom lived in slow motion. Every trifling movement seemed significant. Every sigh conveyed symbolism. Every second was an hour.

Tucker did not know about the future and neither did Ginger, although she'd had what she called a "bad feeling" weeks prior when the family was on vacation. Ginger and Tucker were in a Florida hotel room when she let the rabbit out of the hat.

"I know this sounds like abracadabra, but I'm worried about going home."

"Why, sweetheart?"

"I have a feeling something horrible's gonna happen."

Tucker laughed. "Well, something horrible's gonna happen if we *don't* go home."

"It is?"

"Yeah. We'll be in the poorhouse before you can say, 'Please don't sell my baby grand.'"

"Tucker, I take my premonitions seriously."

"And I take the poorhouse seriously."

That was it. There was no more prattling on about prophecy or hocus-pocus.

Now, it was the morning after the meeting with the New Yorkers, and Tucker had decided to dive into the gutter called "politics." He was dressing for work at his normal pace but, to the universe (that knew about the lurking peril) he was moving slower than a mud turtle. He put on his shirt, tie, and onyx cufflinks. He looked in the mirror and caught sight of a pesky gray hair just above his forehead and a wrinkle next to his eye. He was only forty, so why the heck did his body think he was a weather-beaten warhorse?

Tucker ventured into the kitchen with his briefcase to find his daughters at the breakfast table, drawing pictures and eating cereal. There was a box of Cheerios on the counter with a picture of the Lone Ranger on the front. The masked lawman had two guns drawn and stood adjacent to a red and white special offer about Frontier Town.

Ginger was baking a pie. "I see some Town Toast cookies are missing."

"It's a downright scandal." Tucker acted all serious. "There's a cookie thief in town. I heard about him on the radio." Ginger rolled her eyes.

"No, Daddy. You ate the cookies." Sharon laughed.

"Me? I might be a carrot thief, but I'm no cookie thief."

Sheila and Shirley were drawing scenery shots with their crayons, but Sharon's picture showed her family next to a big tree. Below each image was the corresponding name: "Daddy," "Mommy," "Sharon," "Sheila," "Shirley," and "Fido."

"Worley will be here soon. He's giving me a lift."

"What about breakfast?" Ginger said.

"I'll get a bite later."

"Mommy's making your favorite for dessert tonight," Sharon said. "Lemon pie!"

"Lemon pie? I wasn't gonna come home tonight," Tucker joked, "but now… you can bet your britches I will."

"I drew you a picture." Sharon held it up. "See? It's all of us. And there's a lemon tree so you'll always have lemon pie."

"It's beautiful, Sharon. I'll hang it in the office when I get to work."

"Bye, honey." Tucker gave Ginger a kiss.

"Maybe I could come by and watch you in court this afternoon. I'll be downtown running some errands."

"I don't know. You might distract me."

"How could I do that?"

"By being too pretty."

"Oh, Tucker." Ginger blushed while waving him off, as if to say, "Stop it."

Sharon spoke in a no-nonsense tone to her sisters. "Daddy thinks Mommy's too pretty." Then, she wrote the words "Too Pretty" above Ginger's name on the family picture and handed it to her father. Tucker gave each of his daughters a kiss and left with his briefcase and the drawing.

These moments at breakfast seemed trivial at the time, but would later prove pivotal. They would be memorized by heart and replayed again and again like a favorite song. They would leave an imprint on Tucker's family until their final breaths, until they were folded into the earth, never to be heard from again.

Ernie was a tornado. He was in a blustery lather, whipping around his house and rounding up his ritual tools—the pentagrams, gargoyles, books, candles, and such—and dumping them in a pile in the basement next to his two bombs. As far as Ernie was concerned, the explosives would deliver a spine-chilling roar from his place on Chesapeake Hampton Road to the fire-and-brimstone corners of the lower world.

His plan was a humdinger. He had set the timers to go off a full seven hours after popping in on Nellie at that varmint of a lawyer's office. If she would agree to come home and make the marriage all peachy keen, he would diffuse the bombs. But, if she refused, well, then he could not be held responsible for the hideousness, for the unleashing of death that would hit Marion County like a bloodthirsty beast. Ernie did not mind that his house, his boat, and his worldly possessions would be incinerated. He knew he'd rather be dragged behind his neighbor's pickup than let Nellie and her two-timing Casanova get their hoggish hands on his stuff.

After the bomb timers were set to a tee and the basement looked hunky dory—at least, from the standpoint of a fiend bent on destruction—Ernie went upstairs to check on his beloved Ella. The doll was beloved when she was Ella, but "Hitler's work" when she was Nellie, a perception that hinged on Ernie's mood and the fluctuations of his spasmodic mind.

"You haven't touched your grub, lamb pie," Ernie said to the doll, who sat at the breakfast room table in front of a bowl of North Dakota rice and a glass of Sunsweet prune juice. There was also a platter of Ritz crackers and fruit within arm's reach.

"You don't need to girdle that girth. You ain't no tub of fat. So eat up, Ella-cakes. It's our big day."

Ernie had decided it was the "big day" partly due to

two pamphlets on the living room sideboard that purported to foretell future events. They implied it was a swell day for action, and Ernie figured "killing" and "wreaking havoc" certainly qualified as "action." The first pamphlet had the following notation for that day, April seventh: "Favorable. You have twenty-four hours of variable planetary aspects." The second one was titled, *What the Stars Forecast*. It read, "It should now be possible to reach settlements and clear up matters that have been troublesome... there are indications of possible loss, trouble through papers, figures and mistakes, as well as talk and intrigue..." Ernie figured this soothsaying swarm of pages was referring to the divorce and his lousy situation with Nellie.

Ernie extracted the slew of twenty dollar bills from his pocket and fanned them out on the coffee table. He loved gazing at the seventeen hundred suds, pretending he was a golden-coated king. He fancied thinking of it as chump change. He liked imagining himself as a big shot, wading through a bank vault.

It was sweeping up time. This was the final chore before getting dressed for what could be the dastardly deed to end all dastardly deeds. Ernie lugged the broom out to the chiseled steps and swept away the leaves. This was not a day for hiding. It was not the time for "Hell's Half Acre" to be veiled like a timid bride. Instead, it was a day for elbowroom, for a fresh sweep on life, and possibly for an unleashing of thunder.

While Ernie was tending to the steps, Mrs. Neubaum was peering at him from her window. She had kept her nosy parker tendencies under control, at least as far as Ernie was concerned. After he had tampered with her place, she had taken care to shush her mouth and throw away the key. But she was no longer free from temptation. That dang key was back in her hand. On the previous night, after making "s'mores"—a dessert of fire-roasted marshmallows and chocolate sandwiched between two graham crackers—she'd almost broken down and sneaked across the street. She'd gotten as far as her front walkway, but had thought better of it. If Mrs. Neubaum had her druthers, she would leave Ernie be. There was no question about it. But she did not have her druthers. The devils inside her were restless. They were stirring the pot. They were fidgety. They were tossing and turning. They wanted to come out and snoop. They wanted to get the lowdown on eerie Ernie, the fellow who always seemed to be up to no good.

When Ernie finished sweeping and went back into his house to don his suit and tie, Mrs. Neubaum inched onto her front lawn and then hightailed it across the street. It was an impulse, a compulsion, a stunt she figured she'd probably regret. She ducked into Ernie's bushes and counted to ten. Then, she held her breath and sprouted up next to his front window. She looked inside. As her peepers scanned the living room, she caught wind of the slew of bills on the coffee table.

"Well, eat my hat. That tin can robbed a bank!" she mumbled to herself.

It was true that the scene looked fishy. But it was equally true that Mrs. Neubaum had no proof of pilfering. She paid this no mind because she did not hang her hat in the regular world where folks were innocent until proven guilty. She lived in the "busybody world" where proof was a luxury. Guessing, reading between the lines, and taking pokes in the dark were a part of the game. A hunch was good enough, and Mrs. Neubaum had a right deep hunch about this hinky fellow and his salad of Andrew Jackson bills on the coffee table.

Suddenly, Mrs. Neubaum saw Ernie's image come into the living room. Terror-stricken, she ducked below the window-sill and hunkered back down in the bushes. *Holy hot socks*, she thought to herself. *Why am I such a dingbat?* She was in a stew and scared from her hair (which was now standing on end) to her tippy-tippy toes. She prayed to God and the angels in heaven that Ernie had not spotted her.

He had not. All seemed regular, even copacetic, from his perspective. Ernie, who was now wearing his suit, moved over to the coffee table and stuffed the seventeen hundred dollars into his trousers.

Mrs. Neubaum stayed crouched in the bushes for a full five minutes. She was zeroed in on only one thing: scampering back across the street as fast as her geriatric gams would take her. But, in readying herself for the frantic dash, she had a mishap. Her foot, which was resting on a large rock, wobbled, throwing her against Ernie's house. This created a thud. Ernie cocked up his ears. He listened. He listened some more. He peered out the window at his front lawn. He saw nothing out of the ordinary. There were no more thuds, so he ditched his suspicions and went about the business of retrieving his gun from the fireplace mantle, loading it, and stuffing it into his jacket pocket with a pouch full of shells.

Finally, Mrs. Neubaum cut loose and ran from the bushes to her front door. But she lost her four-inch-long, silver-coated pin in the process. This was a clasp for her plaid shawl. The shiny piece of jewelry fell onto the grass near Ernie's front footpath. The biggest problem was that it was in a visible spot, only five feet from Ernie's Chrysler Desoto, which was parked in the driveway.

"Shucks," Mrs. Neubaum muttered after locking herself inside her house and realizing the pin was gone. She knew retrieving it was more than a ticklish prospect. It was a hot potato of a bad idea and plumb out of the question.

Ernie was now in the kitchen. He glanced at his pocket watch. It was 8:40 a.m. He was raring to pop in on Nellie's nine o'clock appointment at Tucker's legal office. He had no stomach for being tardy, so he quickly gave Ella a final peck on the forehead.

"See you later, alligator. Maybe in this life. Maybe in the inferno of the next."

Then, he grabbed a blue pen and drew pentagrams on the palms of his hands. This was for luck. This was to help him shoot straight if need be. This was done as an invitation for Satan to serve as his handmaiden.

Ernie's final thought was of Tutu, who spent most of her time on the couch and in a special corner of the kitchen. She did not deserve to die, so Ernie toted her outside and set her on the porch. He locked up the house. Tutu wasted no time pawing at the door. She seemed to think that the trees would swallow her up or the sky would plummet to the ground. She did not realize the porch held promise for a new life, while the inside might become a cauldron of smoke, flames, restless ghosts, and caustic memories.

"Now, don't be scratching, dog. This is for your own good." Ernie gave her a goodbye pat on the head. She crouched against the back door.

Of course, Ernie figured the farewells to Ella and Tutu were unnecessary. He was ten-cocks-to-a-barnyard sure he would be sweet-talking Nellie into coming home. Then, he would be able to diffuse the bombs well ahead of their blast time.

As Ernie walked to his car, he saw a curious glare in the yard. It was a shimmer like a lighthouse lamp, but it was coming from the grass not far from his walkway and front window. He edged on over to inspect and found the shawl pin. That was when he knew the meddlesome old biddy had been up to her tricks again. She had been nosing around his windows! His emotions were on the skids. He shot daggers at Mrs. Neubaum's house, but knew he would have to tend to this wretched crank later. He was not going to let this buttinsky gnarl up his day or squeeze him off-track. He had set his sights on righting things with Nellie and, like Cupid's arrow, he needed to stay on course.

Ernie's mood improved during the short drive to downtown Fairmont, where he parked his car on Quincy Street, only two and a half blocks from Tucker's office. He then strutted down the sidewalk, whistling and lobbing "Howdy" at strangers on the street.

"Nice morning to you," he said to a hayseed waiting for a bus.

"Hi-de-ho, sir." The man smiled.

"Fine day, isn't it?" he said to an informally slacked and bloused lady.

"We're having some right fine weather for April," she shot back with a grin.

At last, Ernie stumbled upon his destination. It was a three-story beige building with a flat roof. McCrory's dime store was situated on the ground floor. No one, including the tree and lamppost out in front, could have suspected Ernie's twisted plans and his faith in the powers of darkness. There were gold placards on the brick of the building, identifying the suites inside. One read, "Attorney Tucker Moroose." Ernie checked his appearance in a darkened window. It was crucial to look killer-diller. He wanted his Nellie-cakes to swoon and jump into her husband's arms like a good little wife. He had decided to forgive any indiscretions with the highfalutin' mouthpiece, as long as she agreed to come home and behave.

Wanda had arrived at the law office suite at 8:45 a.m., and the bandaged and bruised Nellie had arrived at seven minutes before nine. Wanda was confused because there were no clients noted for the day.

"Are you sure you have an appointment?" Wanda scoured the date book.

"I think Mr. Moroose was supposed to be at a legal conference, but it got cancelled," Nellie replied.

"Well, then... I guess you should take a seat."

Nellie was reading a magazine when Ernie strolled through the door. It was nine a.m. on the dot. Wanda was typing a letter.

"Excuse me." Ernie caught Wanda's attention, but then noticed Nellie. "Oh, never mind. There's my wife."

As before, the universe was privy to the weightiness of the day. So, from its point of view, every keystroke, every hunt-and-peck on Wanda's typewriter, reverberated as if in slow motion, as if to convey a warning of doom.

Nellie squirmed at the sight of Ernie, who slid next to her with puppy-dog eyes.

"What are you doing here?" she asked.

"Let's forget about all of this. Come on home, honey bunch."

"No, Ernie."

Ernie scrunched up close to his wife, but she scooted away. Wanda tried to eavesdrop on the couple's conversation while pretending to be working.

"I won't push you around. Just come on home. I need you, Nellie."

"No." She pointed at the bandages on her body. "Look what you did to me. You're a vile and hateful man."

"I'm sorry, Nellie-cakes. I get passionate sometimes. It's because I carry a torch for you. You're my dreamy, little black-out girl."

"You're off your rocker, Ernie. You tried to kill me and you made that... that awful doll."

"I only made that doll to keep away burglars. You know... to set in the window."

"You were talking to it."

"No, I wasn't. I was reciting a poem. Remember the poem I recited when we first met?"

"There's something wrong with you, Ernie. You're half-cocked. You're nuttier than a squirrel's breakfast."

"I still remember a few lines." Ernie began the poem. "What's the best thing in the world? June-rose, by May-dew impearled. Sweet south-wind, that means no rain. Truth, not cruel to a friend. Pleasure, not in haste to end."

Nellie was not impressed. "Plus, you have all that creepy stuff in the basement. Black candles, monster drawings, a rope for hanging."

"I just like to decorate in the medieval style. I was experimenting... trying to make it look like a dungeon or a feudal manor."

"A feudal manor? Oh, horse feathers! You're full of propeller wash!"

"There's lots you don't know about me, sugarpuss. Let's go home. The basement's back to normal. I did that just for you."

"You're not gonna get me to change my mind." Nellie went back to flipping through the magazine. She was thinking about how Ernie was a stinking liar and how she would never again be suckered into his jiggery-pokery and his phony trail of excuses.

"Well, don't come home if you don't want." Ernie folded his arms. "But I won't agree to a divorce."

"Tucker says you have to."

Ernie was suddenly ruffled. "Who is this mouthpiece anyway? What do you know about him?"

"He's been practicing law for fifteen years. He comes from Italy, and he's only once lost a case."

"He's a fucking guido?"

"Don't talk like that."

"You're messing with a fucking guido? Next thing, you'll be sloshing around with niggers."

"Ernie, stop being a dim porch light and go home or I'll call the cops. I already told them what you did to me. They'll be arresting you real soon."

"I can't pay you any money."

"You're gonna have to. Tucker says it's the law. Plus, I'm entitled to half the house."

"What are you talking about, woman?" With this, Ernie became a blustery biscuit of venom. The mention of finances had set him off. His black eyes glared at Nellie and his blood pressure gurgled through the roof. He was frothing at the mouth and nursing a silent but powerful snarl. Clearly, his plan for a reunion had hit the skids. And, to his mind, this left him with only two options. Both involved pandemonium and a load of bloodshed. He could kill his bitch of a wife and shake a leg over to Ohio with the seventeen hundred clams, or he could kill his bitch of a wife and everybody else in sight, including possibly himself. He yearned to see Nellie's cold, dead body all raggedy on the cold, hard floor.

Just then, Tucker arrived for work with his briefcase and the drawing. He marched through the outer room and into his private office. Nellie followed. Ernie followed Nellie and shut the door. Wanda knew the couple had been bickering and kept her eyes fixed on the opaque glass window, where she could see the outline of her boss and his clients.

Tucker sat at his desk in front of the divorce paperwork. "What are you doing here, Mr. Yost?"

"I know the two of you are plotting to steal my house and all my money," Ernie growled out the words. "And I know you're having an affair."

"That's a damn lie." Tucker's voice was cranked up so high that Wanda could hear. "I will call the police and have you thrown out of my office."

The time for pitching pennies had passed. Ernie was ready to transform into a crowning horror, to become a full-on demon.

He wore a cocky sneer as he extracted the death revolver from his pocket and pointed it at Nellie.

"What are you doing?" she cried.

"Are you crazy?" Tucker stood, ready to intercede. "Put that thing away."

Wanda could see the image of the gun through the opaque glass and, seconds later, she heard the roar of gunshots—a sound that tore past the outer room and reverberated through the building. Then, she heard the thud of a body falling to the ground. Wanda screamed and ran out of the suite. She bolted down the hall and into the law office of Ogden and Ogden, where she flagged down the receptionist, Okey Hawkins.

"They're firing shots."

Ernie had punctured Nellie's throat. Blood stained her beige blouse and she fell to the floor. Tucker then tussled with Ernie, who got off another shot. This bullet blasted through the middle finger on Tucker's right hand and went on to shatter the glass of his law license hanging on the wall. It was inside the frame that had once held the picture of the old shoe.

Then, Ernie shot Tucker four more times: in the right shoulder, in the chest, in the left side of the neck, and in the right side of the head. Tucker fell to the ground in a trough of his own blood. Ernie was downright pleased. He did not give a donkey's behind about this high-and-mighty guido who had probably been necking with his wife and plotting to rob the pants off of him.

Tucker was in bad shape, barely alive, and figured he was set to die. His body was burning, throbbing, stinging, and aching. The pain was nothing like he had ever felt. It was as if a band of psychopaths had slashed him into pieces. Despite the discomfort, he was able to open his eyes without Ernie noticing. He first glanced at the onyx cufflinks on his wrists and then focused on the black-eyed barbarian he knew as Mr. Yost.

Tucker imagined floating away from the earth, and he mulled over "absence." Death meant he wouldn't grow old with his beloved Ginger or watch his daughters graduate from college. Death meant his mother would be left with a hole in her heart and that Washington really *had* been a pipe dream. Death meant Jal was likely to remain an emotional bramble bush who might never get his life under control. Death would put an end to so much. It would impact so many souls, rupture so many rainbows, and smash so many dreams. Death would be more than an unexpected visitor; it would be an explosion of boundless pain.

Ernie reloaded his revolver with three more cartridges and waltzed over to his dead wife. He was acting all smug, self-righteous, and even relaxed. He put the barrel of his gun against the pale skin of Nellie's forehead, just as he had done with Ella in the kitchen. "See you in hell. Bang." Ernie cackled, and then he blasted her between the eyes.

Ernie was pleased with the ritual, but displeased to find a large black mark on his right hand. It was the residue of gunpowder. "Oh cripes!" he muttered as he rubbed his palms together. He was like Lady Macbeth, trying to wash blood off her hands and yelling, "Out, damned spot! Out, I say!" Ernie was annoyed to find that his "cleaning" smeared off the pentagram drawings but did not disturb the pesky black mark.

Ernie turned his attention to Nellie's dead body. "You were never doodly-squat," he said. "I don't want to ruffle your feathers, honey. But now, you're just an ugly sack of bones. Plus, you should know. You've been giving me a Nellie-ache for years. Nellie-ache! That's a knee-slapper." Ernie let out a tummy chuckle.

Ernie was suddenly pensive. He thought about the years of fighting his nature, of living as a bird with clipped wings, of feeling like a gagged voice, of being a campfire without flames.

For the first time, Ernie felt at ease. He was calm and serene. He was himself. He was a screw in a slot. He was the devil that he always knew he could be.

Ernie glided over to Tucker's desk and took a look at the divorce paperwork. Then, he grabbed Sharon's drawing. He sat in a wooden straight chair and studied the artwork for a period of time before releasing it in the air. The paper floated to the ground back and forth, back and forth, like a pendulum. It came to rest on the floorboards next to Tucker.

Ernie took in the fullness of the room. He was pleased with his handiwork. It was another stunning masterpiece, much like the bombs that were set to blow in six and a half hours. Ernie knew the police would be bursting in soon and figured he had better get a crack-a-lackin'.

"I'd walk a mile for a Camel." He smiled and plucked a smoke from his pocket. He lit it.

He took four puffs. Then, he placed the revolver against his right temple and fired. The bullet went through his brain and hit the far wall of the room. His gun dropped to the floor with a thud. Ernie fell forward into a slumped position with the ciggy still dangling from his mouth. It was a bizarre sight, the kind of thing one might see in a horror flick about demons or voodoo. He was leaning in at a crazy angle. It was a fitting pose for the "devil in the basement." Ernie's blood trickled onto the floor in a stream. It was nourishment for maggots.

Tucker shut his eyes, but he was not dead. And neither was Ernie.

Chapter 20

BODIES, BOMBS AND DRANO

DETECTIVE FRANK GANGES was in the field when he was radioed by headquarters about a melee at the McCrory building. He skedaddled over to the location in his scout car, parking a block-and-a-half away due to roadwork on Adams Street. Then, he sprinted down the sidewalk, into the structure, up the staircase, and to the end of the second-floor hallway. At first, he felt like Jesse Owens at the Berlin Olympics. But, by the end of his journey, he realized he was more of a deflated balloon. He was out of breath.

He came upon the carnage in Tucker's office and froze. He had never seen anything quite like it. It may have been a Wednesday but, to his mind, it could have passed for Bloody Sunday, a day of rampant killing during the Second Boer War. He had studied the saber out of this battle and others like it as a history buff back in college.

Detective Don West and Police Chief John Austin arrived a minute later.

"Oh my God." Don was shaken by the brackishness of the situation.

"They look to be in pretty bad shape."' Chief Austin scooted over to Nellie's body, as if police protocol had a "lady's first" provision. He took her pulse. "The missus is deceased."

Don plucked the still-burning ciggy from Ernie's lips and checked his heartbeat. "He's alive."

Chief Austin monitored Tucker's pulse. "He's alive, too."

"This one's yours, Frank. I'm up to my eyeballs in assignments." Don was itching to wiggle out of the investigation and wanted the *other* house dick to do the work.

"I don't see any coffee sergeants around here," Frank said, hinting that he was nobody's fool or errand boy.

Chief Austin took Don's side. "That's a whale of an idea, West. You take this one, Ganges."

Frank mumbled, "Right, chief." He was down in the mouth and even a bit peeved, but he was an ace at masking his frustration.

Although Frank's motto was, "I'll get to the bottom of a case if I have to dig to China," this time he was not so sure. He felt wobbly about unraveling the sequence of events. There were so many gunshot wounds and so many barrels of blood. Plus, the bodies were all twisted up like garbage bag ties. He was used to clear-cut cases with one or two shots fired and only one victim. This was not a boilerplate assignment.

Chief Austin took charge, doling out tasks. "West, call for ambulances. I'll track down the secretary. I believe she's a witness. And Ganges, check their IDs."

Frank nodded as the other two men left the room.

"So, what's the story, folks?" Frank said out loud, hoping the two breathing stiffs would jump to their feet and start yammering on and on about the particulars. There was obviously no response, so he searched Tucker's pockets and Nellie's purse, taking care not to disturb evidence. He found their names and addresses.

Then, he moved over to Ernie, who was still slumped forward. Apart from the grisly crater-like hole in his temple, he looked like a fellow taking a nap or a churchgoer bored with a minister's sermon. Frank got up close, tilted Ernie's head upward, and took note of this fellow's facial features.

"You look familiar. Why do you look familiar?" Frank furrowed his brow, all wistful-like. "Wait. I remember. You're Mr. Rockefeller."

Frank's adrenaline was pumping. Suddenly, he was glad Don had backed off the case. *Santa might be coming down my chimney,* he thought. *Maybe I'm getting a golden pom-pom. My wallet could be coming up roses.* He was drooling over the prospect.

Frank did a quick looksee to make sure he was alone and that neither the chief nor Don had tiptoed back into the room. When he saw the coast was clear, he turned into Mr. Greedy Fingers, feeling around in Ernie's right pocket. To his dismay, he found only an empty wallet and a driver's license. "Dammit," he said to himself as he peeked at the door again to make sure there were no prying eyes. All looked good, so he dunked his hand into Ernie's left pocket and bingo... he found it: the fat wad of clams.

Hot lead on a sled! he thought. *Seventeen hundred buckaroos—enough sawbucks to give me a real boost up in the world.* Frank was over-the-rainbow thrilled and jammed the cash into his trousers. This was the biggest moment of his life. It was more rousing than when he made detective or got a commendation from the West Virginia legislature for fine police work. Frank had been bringing home the bacon to the tune of three thousand dollars a year, so these greenbacks amounted to almost seven months of salary!

This was not the first time Frank had grabbed a little extra on the side. He was always willing to bend the rules to make a buck or two. After all, he deserved it. He was putting his life on the line for pin money. The community should be grateful. They should be willing to close one eye and put a mitt over the other. Plus, God did not want him to be poor.

Despite his petty pinches here and there, Frank had never been blessed with a stash like this. He had never taken more than a few bucks when snooping around a house or emptying the pockets of a pigeon or jigger man. He had never come up with anything like seventeen hundred whoppers!

"Feast or famine?" Chief Austin startled Frank from behind.

"What?" Frank stuttered, afraid he had been caught with his feelers in the diamond drawer.

"Feast or famine? Did you get the names or not?"

"Oh. Sure, chief. This here is Attorney Moroose." He pointed at Tucker. "This is Nellie Marie Yost." He pointed at Nellie. "And this fellow is Ernie Lee Yost, but I don't think he's gonna make it."

"Why do you say that?"

"Oh, well..." Frank tripped over his words. "He's... he's holding on by a thread."

"Are you a doctor?"

"No, sir."

Of course, Frank *needed* Ernie to die. If he were to survive and start wailing about the missing cash, Frank could be in a whopper of trouble. To be on the safe side, Frank was quickly contriving a cover story.

"I know this Yost fellow," Frank added. "He's a lying sack of potatoes."

"What are you talking about?"

"I was sent to his house. Family trouble. You know, twenty percent of the calls that come into the station are family trouble. Ninety percent are resolved on the spot. But the statistics..."

"I know the statistics, Ganges. You think I've got a hole in my head, too?"

"No sir. Anyway, his wife filed a complaint for abuse. When I went there, I could tell this fellow was a lying sack of potatoes, but I didn't have the goods on him. No evidence to arrest, sir."

Chief Austin nodded as ambulance workers rushed into the room and loaded Tucker and Ernie onto gurneys. It was 9:38 a.m.

"Over there, Dusty." Chief Austin pointed out Nellie to the coroner, Dusty Kidd, who had just arrived. Then he glanced over the paperwork, including a court order, on Tucker's desk. "Looks like a divorce. Mr. Moroose was representing the wife."

Frank listened eagerly while the chief read from the court order. "It is likewise adjudged, ordered, and decreed that the defendant be hereby enjoined from striking, threatening, or annoying the plaintiff until the further notice of the court."

"That low-down scalawag was beating that poor dame." Frank acted more torn up than he really was.

"Looks like the court date was slotted for June, and Yost wasn't allowed to sell his property. Plus, he was gonna have to pay his wife temporary alimony of seventy-five dollars a month," Chief Austin said, still reading over the paper.

"He was probably short on money and just snapped." Frank was still stitching together a cover story in case Ernie was to regain consciousness. He knew painting this fellow as a dishonest down-and-out could come in handy down the line.

Chief Austin and Frank remained in Tucker's office to continue the investigation, drawing on the assistance of lesser-ranked officers. Nellie's body was covered with a white cloth.

A crowd gathered on the sidewalk outside the McCrory build-ing. They watched Wanda as she was escorted to a squad car by a policeman who planned to drive her home. She was a foun-tain of tears and mumbled, "Please God, don't let Tucker die."

All the while, two McIsaac company ambulances zipped around corners and barreled through the morning traffic with sirens blaring as they made their way to State Hospital, hoping to save Tucker and Ernie's lives. At 9:49 a.m., both vehicles pulled up to the facility's entrance, where doctors and nurses were poised to spring into action. Each hospital employee wait-ing in the street had been assigned to one of the two vehicles.

The rear door of one ambulance flew open and a bleeding man on a gurney was whisked into the facility. A contingent of eager-beaver staff members, including nurse Joy Penton and Dr. Phillip Johnson, tended to this man's wounds as he was wheeled into surgery. They did not know the identity of the patient, but it was not their job to know. It was their job to heal.

The other ambulance had also stopped at the entrance, but it was closed up like a clam shell and as silent as a snowflake. Only an idling or a low hum of the engine could be heard. Dr. Jake Waters, along with a bevy of concerned attendants and nurses, were chomping at the bit. They were confused. Some cocked their heads. Others tapped their feet in a show of impa-tience. It seemed like the driver was on a coffee break.

Infuriated, Dr. Waters banged on the back door of the ambulance. "Hello? Hello? Hello?" There was no answer, so he thumped even harder. "Hey, what's going on in there? Hurry it up."

Finally, the door tipped open and an attendant stepped out wearing a sullen look. "Tucker Moroose is dead."

While Tucker was struggling for his life between nine and 9:48 a.m. (when he officially died), Ginger was being a twinkling high-brow. She was in fine fettle at her piano teacher's house, learning how to play the popular song, "Wrap Your Troubles in Dreams," which had been recorded by Bing Crosby in the 1930s. At 10:15, she arrived back home, none the wiser to the carnage at the law offices. She parked in the driveway and hollered at June, who was across the street snipping daffodils for a table centerpiece.

"Hey, pretty lady. Want to take a break and come on over for some noodle juice or Mountain Dew?"

"That sounds like a fine idea." June put down her clippers and removed her garden gloves.

The two women enjoyed iced tea in tall glasses and some stimulating small talk. Then, Ginger rehearsed her latest piano tunes on the baby grand while June flipped through fashion magazines: *Vogue, Companion,* and *Bazaar.* There was a freshly baked lemon pie on a table.

Suddenly, there was a knock. June answered the door to find a police officer.

"I'm looking for Mrs. Tucker Moroose."

"Ginger, there's somebody here to see you."

Ginger left the piano and approached the door, all perky-faced. "Well, hello. Can I help you?"

The officer was out of sorts and seemed unsure of his words. "I'm sorry to inform you, ma'am. Your husband..." He stopped, swallowed hard, and tried to collect himself.

"Yes?" Ginger was the essence of friendliness. "Do you know my husband?"

"Your husband was shot this morning. He's dead, ma'am. I'm sorry."

"What?" Ginger was in a state of confusion. "You must be mistaken. That can't be right. You must be wrong. Maybe you are talking about somebody else's husband. There are lots of husbands on this street. We just moved here. You probably got the wrong house."

"His name was Tucker Moroose. He died in the ambulance on the way to the hospital. I'm sorry, ma'am."

"What? This can't be right." Ginger burst into tears. "No… no… no. This can't be right." She sunk to the floor. June ran to console her. Ginger's pain was searing. It was almost unendurable. She did not think she could go on.

While Ginger was in a ball of anguish on the floor of the Cleveland home, Sharon was at school. The teacher, Miss Anderson, was quizzing the class on the multiplication table. Sharon was a crackerjack student. She had memorized her eights and nines. She knew nine times seven was sixty-three, nine times eight was seventy-two, and nine times nine was eighty-one.

Suddenly, Miss Anderson was motioned to the door by the principal. "Turn to page thirty-two and do the problems at the top of the page. I'll be back shortly."

The class became as quiet as a library. Most students did not follow the instructions, but instead eyeballed the two women in the doorway. They seemed to be whispering about Sharon.

Sharon was thrilled. She figured Miss Anderson was talking about giving her a gold star. She deserved one for getting a high score on her test. She already had a red one and a blue one for turning in her homework on time. She knew her daddy would be proud. He loved it when she brought home stars.

He would say, "Star light. Star bright. You're the first star I see tonight."

Sharon would reply in a sing-song voice, "I wish I may. I wish I might. Have the wish I wish tonight."

"So, what does my little star want?" Tucker would flash an exaggerated grin.

"Toll House!"

Then, he would pluck three chocolate chip cookies from the bread box when Ginger was not looking. He would pretend to be a quarterback after a scrimmage, handing them off behind his back. He had to be sneaky because Ginger was a sweet tooth grump. Tucker was a sweet tooth fairy.

Miss Anderson finished up the conversation with the principal and approached Sharon. She scrooched down at the child-sized desk. "You need to get home, Sharon. Your mother's waiting."

"But school's not over."

"Collect your things. Your grandma's picking you up."

"But why?"

"Do as I say, Sharon."

She gathered together her books.

Sheila and Shirley were already in the car with Faire.

"Why are we going home? School's not over." Sharon settled into the back seat.

"Your mama needs to talk to you."

"Why can't she talk to me after school?"

"Because it can't wait. Now, no more questions. I'll get you home in a jiffy."

While the three girls were heading home, Philip was bursting through the front door of the farmhouse, out of breath. He found Margaret home alone, knitting a sweater.

"I can't believe it. I still can't believe it."

"Can't believe what?" Margaret shook her head. "What are you muttering about, Philip?"

"The man at the gas station... he told me Tucker was shot by a client."

"What?" Margaret stood, horrified. She visualized her son

in the hospital, but also figured he would be patched up and as good as new.

"He was handling a divorce. He was shot five times."

"Five times?"

"He's at the morgue."

"What?"

"The man that killed him is at State Hospital."

"No! I don't believe it, Philip. Some looney tune tells you this sort of thing. What kind of cruel man…" Margaret cut herself off, picked up the phone, and dialed Tucker's office. "That man at the gas station is downright cruel," she said to Philip. "He should be hung by his tongue."

Chief Austin answered the law office phone. "Hello."

"I'm calling for Tucker Moroose."

"Uhhh… who's this?"

"This is his mother. Where's my son?"

"I'm sorry ma'am. There was an incident. He's deceased."

She let out a scream to end all screams and dropped the phone. She ran to the kitchen, hysterical, and started poking around inside the cabinet under the sink. She was in tears and making all sorts of ruckus, knocking over bottles of cleaning products. Oxydol, Vel, Johnson's Glo-Coat floor polish, and a box of Ivory Snow fell onto the floor.

"Mom, what are you doing?" Philip stood over her.

She did not answer. She just kept searching and making a right big mess.

"Mom, answer me. What are you doing?"

Margaret finally found it: Drano. The product was no slouch at unclogging pipes. It churned away dirt, grease, lint, soap-fat, hair, and vegetable matter. Margaret clutched the container and sprinted to the bathroom.

"What are you doing, Mom?" Philip was at sea, but tagged along.

Margaret had plans to swallow the whole hog—every last drop. She just wanted to die. She could not live without Tucker. He had always been her favorite, the red-breasted robin of her existence, her buttress, her only hope for a future. Plus, the other children (even though they were all grown by this time) depended on him. Robert was prepped to go to college and then apply to law school—because of Tucker. Betty was out of debt—because of Tucker. James got a hefty promotion at the coal mine—because of Tucker. Mary had started hair-styling classes—because of Tucker. Louis had a few clams to start a furniture business—because of Tucker. The farmhouse bills were never late—because of Tucker. Rose and Jal had not gone completely askew, and this was, by and large, because of Tucker. Tucker had always been the brakes to Jal's runaway sled.

Margaret was beside herself with grief. She had been knocked from her horse. Without Tucker, the oasis was a mirage. Without Tucker, life was a dark ditch. Without Tucker, there would be no inspiration, no loving pats on the back, and no special shoves away from poverty and slothfulness.

Margaret did not realize that swallowing drain cleaner was a particularly unpleasant way to die. The first reflex was gagging followed by a vomiting up of blood. This was not normal, run-of-the-mill blood; it would include huge black chunks of the stomach. Then, the person's eyes would leak blood like a weeping statue or a zombie from a horror flick. The small intestine would shrivel and there would be facial disfiguration. The person would end up blind, unable to smell, and have to undergo surgery—that is, if she survived at all. Margaret knew about none of this as she tore the cap off the Drano and tried to pour the solution into her mouth.

"No," Philip screamed, whacking the container out of her hand. It tumbled across the room and splattered all over the floor, walls, toilet, and sink. Less than a thimble-full made it onto her tongue.

"Spit it out. Now!" he screamed. "Spit it out."

She was crying and held her lips shut, like a toddler refusing to eat okra.

"Spit it out." He slammed Margaret's head down to the toilet. "Spit it out! Now."

With that, Margaret opened her mouth, and the drain cleaner mixed with saliva dribbled down her chin and onto her blouse.

Philip grabbed a wash rag and handed it to her. "Dry out your mouth! Now! Hurry up! Then, I'll get you to the hospital."

She was on her knees crying.

"Do it now!" Philip pulled her back by the hair, pried open her mouth, and dried it out himself. Then, he let go of her. "Get your sweater. I'll drive you."

She stood, still sobbing. "No. You don't understand, Philip. My precious son is gone. There's nothing else for me."

"What the hell are you talking about?" Philip backed away, incensed. "You have eight other children. Think about us." He shook his head and stomped out of the room.

A few seconds later, Margaret inched into the living room and found Philip peering out the window. She was still sobbing, but took baby steps over to him and gave him a hug.

"I'm sorry, son. I'm sorry. I know I haven't treated you right all these years. I know you have a different mother, but you're my son too. You're my son too."

Chapter 21

CUT OFF MY LEGS AND CALL ME SHORTY

T HE DEMONS WERE gnawing on the ropes, ready to let loose with a mad and ear-piercing growl. It was the afternoon "witching hour." It was four p.m. on the dot, and the start of the second phase of Ernie's dastardly plan. Would Fairmont fall victim to the uproar to end all uproars? Most folks who knew about the double murder in Tucker's office that morning agreed with Mayor Silbert F. Robinson when he said, "This is the most shocking incident in the history of our state." But nobody could have suspected more violence could come crashing down on this God-fearing and well-behaved town.

The hands of the clock ticked along at a steady pace and it became 4:01 p.m. Did the bombs explode? Or had there been a glitch? Was the house on Chesapeake Hampton Road a blistering stockpile of flames? If so, would the inferno stretch out its arms, roasting the whole of the neighborhood and perhaps the east end of the county? Only one living soul possibly knew the answer to these questions: little Tutu, who had been crouched against the back door. That is, if she had not been devoured by the barbaric blaze or scared into the woods by the deafening and limb-severing blast.

Some might say setting one's property ablaze in this way amounted to a Viking's funeral—the pagan ritual that allowed folks to perish along with their belongings. In Norse mythology, this was necessary so that the deceased would have possessions in the afterlife. After all, Ernie might need his scythe, his boat, his doll, and his trove of fixing tools. While dilly-dallying with the devil and flirting with the spirits of the netherworld, he might want to whittle harmonicas, make butter churn lids, or slice up little girls. He might want to take a ride in *"Hell's A Poppin"* or share a meal with his beloved Ella.

Ernie's oldest daughter, Vivian, knew about the shooting because Chief Austin had phoned her at one p.m. She lived in Morgantown, but made tracks over to the hospital to find her father unconscious. He was hooked up to tubes and a ventilator. Ernie had always been good to her and her younger sister, Edwina, although he only visited them three times each year: in the spring for a picnic, at Halloween for a trick-or-treat adventure, and on "tree day" (which most folks called "Christmas") in order to lavish upon them buckets of goodies. Ernie had always made good use of the short and infrequent visits, which had begun when they were toddlers. He'd been attentive, loving, and playful with his young'uns.

Of course, Vivian had suspicions about her dad, mostly due to his obsessive secrecy about the scythe room. When Vivian was eight, she tried to pry open the locked basement door with a table knife, but Ernie caught her. He told her, "There are hungry dragons down there. They eat up children." From that day forward, Vivian and her sister walked on the far side of the hallway—often clinging to the wall—in order to avoid the basement door.

After visiting Ernie at the hospital, Vivian appeared at the Fairmont police department in a fit of worry. "I need somebody to go with me to my father's house. There's a dog, and she'll die of neglect."

When the boys in blue saw Vivian at the front counter, they fell all over themselves to talk to her. They were bug-eyed and aching with lust. Vivian was a solid sender, a dream puss, a peach of a beauty. She was tall, slim, and in her twenties, with a regal nose, sparkly blinkers, and full lips. She took after her mother rather than her devil-in-the-basement dad. She was a dog-lover and often cared for as many as six strays at a time while seeking homes for them.

Vivian had been at the Fairmont police station for less than ten minutes when Chief Austin emerged from the back room. Although it was not routine to search a hooligan's house—even after he'd shot up a law office and snuffed out two folks—taking a peek could not hurt. Why not give the place a once-over? Why not pry around for clues, such as scribblings on notepads or not-yet-mailed letters? They might point to a motive. So Chief Austin hollered out, "West. Ganges. Accompany this young lady to the Yost property. See what you can find."

"Yes, sir." Detective Frank smiled. He had a reputation for being lap-happy with the ladies.

"I'm on it." Gumshoe Don was gung-ho as well and grabbed his hat. The other officers looked plenty jealous.

"It's the old Harvey Adams farm," the chief added.

By 4:15 p.m., Don, Frank, and Vivian were riding in the police car on what they thought was a leisurely mission to Chesapeake Hampton Road to fetch Tutu and snoop around the property. The detectives were in the front seat while Vivian was in the back. But the trip became less leisurely and more panicky when they arrived to find scads of thick smoke. The house was smoldering like a meatloaf in an oven. The structure was buried in a caked cloud of the devil's handiwork, a whirl-pool of resentment and ruin.

"O Lord and butter! It's on fire!" Vivian shrieked. "The house is on fire!"

"Call for a truck," Don yelled at Frank as he leapt from the vehicle and bolted toward the front door. "I'll get the dog, ma'am, and make sure there's nobody else inside." Don's quick-footedness was partly due to a hankering to impress Vivian and partly because he was an action-aligned fellow. He was that way by nature. He could be counted on in a pinch.

Frank radioed the central station while Vivian paced the street in a stew.

"Why do you think your father shot those folks this morning?" Frank asked.

"You might not know it by looking at her, but Nellie had a gooball reputation from way back. She was a bit of a billboard, if you know what I mean. My dad was never quite trusting her. So it wasn't completely his fault."

Frank wanted to say, "Throw away your tears, lady. I've got no sympathy for your thug of a dad." But instead he held his tongue with both hands. He was not keen on straddling the sticky barricade between a jealous stepdaughter and her dead stepmom.

Meantime, Don was scooting from window to window and from window to door. He was pushing, pulling, prodding, and yanking. He was searching for any sort of opening, and was just shy of breaking into the joint. The place was closed up tighter than a jam jar. When he moved to the back, there she was: the beloved Tutu. She was a sight for sore eyes and was butt-up against the back door. She seemed oblivious to the smoke swirling around above her head. Don picked her up and scampered back around to the front, screaming, "I've got her. I've got the dog, ma'am."

Vivian took Tutu into her arms and slobbered her up with kisses. "Sweet little baby Tutu! You gave us a right big scare!"

Frank was, of course, still anchored to the squad car. He was willing to let Don take all the risk, but felt surges of guilt. "I'll be waiting here when the truck shows," he announced so as not to look like a slacker.

There was not a second to squander, so Don bolted back toward the house, stopping short when he saw the curious lettering on the steps. *What in God's name is this?* he asked himself. *Hell's Half Acre? This would raise the hair on a bald man's head!* Don knew he had to leave "deciphering the carving" until later. Duty was yawping at him, so he dashed to the house.

There was no way inside without a whole lot of breaking or a fair amount of jimmying. So, Don grabbed a brick in the garden and heaved it at a front window. Then, he brushed away the broken glass with his police baton and wriggled through the opening like a centipede. He landed in the living room. The place was a fog of pea soup. It was so thick and chalky that he had to feel for the walls and let them guide him from room to room.

"Is anybody here?" He choked out the words as he inched along. "Hello? Anybody here?" The place smelled like burned wood.

He made his way to the kitchen, which was less smoky. He could see the room just fine, but almost crawled out of his skin when he noticed the creepy doll sitting at the table in front of a bowl of cereal and a beverage. She had a napkin in her lap and a sardonic stare on her painted face. She looked like a mad woman! He wanted to climb up the wall with his fingernails!

Don yanked down a curtain and wet it in the sink, but kept glancing back at Ella, fearful that she could spring to life and strangle him. Then, he placed the damp cloth over his mouth and nose and headed for the back of the house.

"Anybody here?" Don checked the bedrooms and bathroom, but found no one. Then, he came upon the basement door. It was unlocked.

"Hello? Anybody there?" he yelled down the scythe room staircase, realizing this was the starting point for the fire. Then, he descended the creaky steps. The walls were seared. There was gasoline on the floor, which had mostly evaporated. There were burned household items (including costumes and a devil mask) piled up between two bombs. *Two bombs! Oh shit,* Don thought. *What if there are more explosions? What if I get caught up in a big one?* He figured he had better open the throttle and get the hell out of there. He turned to run but a lone pamphlet caught his eye. It was partially singed; the corner was in flames.

Don picked it up and read the title: *The Devil's Helper.* He was baffled. Why would any self-respecting fellow have literature like this? Suddenly, the small fire mushroomed, engulfing the whole of the pamphlet. It scorched Don's hand, causing him to drop the publication onto the concrete floor. Then, *poof...* it turned into ashes before his eyes. It was the queerest thing he'd ever seen. He was creeped out and figured he had better dangle it out of the house as fast as his sticks could take him. He was relieved when he made it to the street.

"There are two firebombs in the basement. We need a munitions expert," Don said to the volunteer firemen, Albert Angelelli and W. J. Morgan, who had arrived in the city emergency truck. They got on the blower to the pumper and to a fireman named Sine, who was an expert at disconnecting wires. Minutes later, two engines arrived from the Grant Town volunteer fire department. There was a whole lot of commotion.

The street and nearby yards were filled with onlookers, including Mrs. Neubaum. First, there were a dozen spectators. Then there were two dozen, and eventually there were over a hundred Fairmont residents watching. But they kept their distance so as not to be in harm's way in case there were more blasts.

Nine-year-old Johnny Stafford was keeping tabs on the mystifying situation. He had brown curly hair, brown eyes, and had stepped off the school bus near the Mount Carmel Catholic cemetery as he routinely did on school days. He had walked home by way of Chesapeake Hampton Road and happened upon the fire. He lived with his parents in the house behind Ernie's property. They had moved in a year prior.

Johnny's father had always been stern with him about their "odd bird" neighbor. "Never get near that Mr. Yost, you hear? He doesn't like kids. He's a pot of stewed rhubarb. He's cutting out paper dolls." Johnny had heeded his father's advice, and only crossed through Ernie's property once in a while to get water from the well.

After the basement bombs were disconnected, Johnny and the other onlookers watched as a booster line was carried from the pumper truck to Ernie's house. As water sloshed over the flames and quelled the smoke, it became clear the structure would be saved. The actual damage would be minimal, except in the basement where all had been destroyed.

Don pulled Ernie's speedboat out of the garage in an effort to get it out of the way, and *"Hell's A Poppin'"* rolled into view. It stuck out like a sore thumb and led to a flurry of whispers in the crowd. Johnny heard the words "infidel" and "Beelzebub."

Mrs. Neubaum, who was standing beside the rose bush in her front yard, was not surprised by the nutty name of the boat. She was not surprised by the blasts, the smoke, or the fire. She had known from the start that eerie Ernie was up to no good, that he was a slimeball, a mad hatter, and that he was skipping down the primrose path to angry land. She watched. She was inquisitive but smug. She was eagle-eyed but vain. She was delighted but also blue. She was tickled that the coppers had their tentacles in her bogeyman of a neighbor but sorry that she would not be able to meddle in his business again. Surely, Ernie would be hauled off to jail and never heard from again.

There was a newcomer to the scene. This woman had come from the house at the road's end and knew Mrs. Neubaum was a full spice rack when it came to gossip. "Do you know what's going on?"

Mrs. Neubaum drew her close in her usual cliffhanger way. "You want to know a secret?"

"Sure do." The woman was peppy and saucer-eyed.

"You promise not to tell?"

The woman nodded eagerly.

"The good-for-nothing wurp who lives there... his name's Ernie... I'm pretty sure he robbed a bank."

"He robbed a bank? Well, cut off my legs and call me Shorty!"

Chapter 22

THE WILTED ROSE

THE GARTER WAS scarlet red, the color of wine. It was resting on the dresser next to lace bras, silk teddies, satin slips, stockings, and other fetching lingerie. Rose was alone in her room at the Book Cadillac and wearing a teal corset with a ruffled, see-through petticoat. She was pretending she was a peacock—posturing, twirling, strutting, and being all cheesecake in the mirror. She was giving herself a fashion show. Although she had never modeled for a calendar, lithograph, or magazine, she knew the basics of posing—how, for example, to show the ideal amount of cleavage and leg. Too much was dog soup. Too little was stuffy and a complete bore. Like Goldilocks, everything had to be "just right" for her Billy bear.

My hunky fellow's about to arrive, she thought to herself. She wanted to bowl him over with beauty, whisk him into a fantasy, and make him forget about the drudgery of the day. She felt this was her devoir, her charge, her reason for being alive at this time in her life. Some women prepared dinner for their families. Others toiled away at glove factories. Her job was to be all sugar and spice and everything nice.

When Rose was content with her seductive garb, she focused on cosmetics and hair. She needed to convey charm, gaiety, and feminine mystique. She needed to look like a Vargas girl—a glossy, seductive beauty with unparalleled allure. She began by making victory rolls on top of her head by twisting two sections of her hair and securing them with bobby pins. Then, she sprayed both the rolls and the ends of her long, luscious curls with Helene Curtis Spray Net. She topped off the pièce de résistance with a dishy teal flower.

As she applied rouge to her cheeks, she thought about Laura. She felt like green vomit when she thought of her friend's corpse rotting at the lunatic asylum. How could this have happened? How could Jesus, Buddha, or whoever ruled the cosmos let a slick chick like her end up in a weed-infested cemetery alongside crazy-heads and psychopaths? Rose was not one to wallow in cheerlessness, so she willed herself into happier times.

She remembered the final "doll-up date" with Laura—the one that had taken place on the night she'd died. An hour before the shindig at Minard's Inn, the two women had been raring to lavish love on their brows, lashes, and lips.

"I'm Houdini. I'm on time for our date." Rose entered Laura's house, where she lived with her parents.

"Hey, Houdini," Laura joked. "You're not really my type, but if you bought me a corsage, I'll forgive you."

With that, the women made a beeline for the bathroom, elbowing each other for first dibs at the mirror. They giggled and put on their party faces, using pancake foundation, lip liner, an eyelash curler, a brow pencil, a powder brush, and eye shadow.

They gave their peepers a winged look like foxy-eyed cats. This was a popular style that month. They finished their doll-up session with Russian red lipstick, lash cream, and black mascara.

"We're real dazzlers," Laura said, showing off her sexy pout.

"We'd be the gnat's eyebrows if gnats *had* eyebrows." Rose laughed.

The girls skipped out the door and slid into Laura's blue Chevy for that final wingding of a night. If only they had known what would happen. If only they had stayed home.

Days later, after Rose had gone to Detroit with Bill, she got a curious call from the Fairmont police department. It was curious because she could not understand what the fuzz wanted with her.

"Miss Moroose, this is Chief Austin of the Fairmont police."

"Yes?" Rose twirled the phone cord nervously.

"We're trying to track down Miss Laura Smith. We believe you may have been the last person to see her."

"She's missing?" Rose was bewildered.

"Yes, ma'am."

Where was Laura? Did Bill's goons *not* drop her at the bus? And if they did as they were told, why was she gone? Had she made tracks out of town for a thrill in line with her khaki-wacky nature? Maybe she was living the high life with a movie star or professional athlete. But if so, why hadn't she called her parents?

"How'd you get my number?" Rose asked.

"From your mother. I understand you were at Minard's Inn with Miss Smith. Do you have any idea why she would vanish along with her car?"

"Her car's gone?"

"Yes, ma'am."

Where was the blue Chevy? Why wasn't it parked on the

side of the road or sitting at a mechanic's garage? Had a Mafioso taken it? God forbid it was cozying up to a catfish at the bottom of a lake or racing around Canada with a new paint job and a fake license plate. Rose was full of questions and fears, but thought it wise to keep her pie hole shut.

She was a touch paranoid, figuring the call could be a set-up. *Is this one of Bill's mugs trying to trap me?* she wondered. *Maybe this guy is pretending to be a police chief. Maybe it's all a trick to find out if I'm tight-lipped or a snitch. Maybe Laura is at home with her parents. Maybe she is not missing at all.* Rose figured she had better play it safe. She did not want to end up in the trunk of a car or under a lump of concrete. She knew only chowderheads put themselves on the wrong side of the Detroit mob. Plus, if this was a real copper, she did not want to get her hunk of heartbreak in trouble. She was in love with Bill.

"I was at Minard's with her, officer," Rose finally said. "But I left the party with a fellow."

"Did you see her talking to any grifters? Anybody suspicious?"

Rose was jittery. She was unsure what to say and stumbled on her words. "There were... uh... lots of snazzy guys... uh... all sorts of fellows at Minard's that night. But I didn't see anybody particular."

"Her parents can't understand why she would up and leave without taking her clothes."

"Well... uh... she always had a hankering to move to California. And... uh. She was spontaneous."

"Hmm. Maybe you could come by the station for a statement. Are you going to be in Fairmont any time soon?"

"No, officer. I... uh... I live here in Detroit."

"I see. Well, thank you for your time, Miss Moroose."

Rose hung up. She was in a knot of confusion. Her emotions were all twisted like the earlobe of a misbehaving child.

She called Laura's house, but was told she had never come home from the party. It was not until months later when Bill revealed that she had *not* been dropped off at the bus that the whole ghastly story made sense.

There was a knock. Rose quickly snapped out of her melancholy and her memories of Laura. She set all sadness aside, powdered her face, and opened the door. She was ready for a ring-a-ding-ding good time.

"What's buzzin', big boy?" Rose smiled and planted a passionate smooch on Bill's lips.

"Wow." He looked her up and down. "You're toggled to the bricks, darling. You look dynamite... like a pin-up girl."

"Nothing's too good for my sugarpuss." Rose did a graceful turn and then grabbed Bill's hand. She led him into the room for some kissing, fondling, and sex. After an hour of love-making and cuddling, Rose whispered in his ear.

"I thought we might try the Holly restaurant tonight. It's supposed to be haunted."

"Gee, Rose. I can't stay."

"What?" She pulled away from him. "I haven't seen you for three days."

"I have to attend one of those dinner parties." Bill flashed a look of dread.

"You could take your sweet patootie. I don't think my dance card's full."

"No, dreamboat. I can't."

"Why not?"

"I have to go with my wife."

"Your wife?" Rose acted a tad hurt, but, in truth, she was totally and completely crushed. He had never before mentioned the other Rose in his life, or any of the other mistresses (of which there were many).

"Wipe away that long face. Let's enjoy the time we have,

dollface. We can do the ghost thing on Friday." Bill got out of bed. "I'm gonna grab a shower."

It was time for Rose to do some smoking, drinking, and television watching. This was her ritual after sex. She lit a ciggy and poured herself some gin. Then she switched on the box to NBC because she liked the show *Kraft Television Theatre*, which came on at 7:30. It was only 7:20, so the news was playing. A broadcaster was babbling on about red-letter events around the nation.

That was when she heard it. That was the moment she learned the devastating truth.

The man on TV said, "Prominent West Virginia attorney Tucker Moroose was shot and killed in his law office at nine a.m. this morning by a client's husband. Mr. Moroose will be memorialized at a special meeting of the Marion County Bar Association on Friday." Then, the broadcaster moved on to other stories.

Rose was in shock. She could barely breathe. She dropped her gin and cigarette on the table. Her favorite brother was dead! He was only forty. How could this be? Why had nobody in the family called? She knew her mother must have cried buckets, squeezing out every ounce of liquid from her body.

It was then that Bill came out of the bathroom, freshly showered and dressed. "Gotta get going, honey."

Rose suddenly became hysterical and bowled him over with a hug, sobbing.

"Hey, hey, hey. What's the matter, Rose?" he said, thinking she was getting a little too clingy with the relationship.

"I just heard on TV. My brother… my brother, Tucker. He was killed today."

"Gee. That's horrible. I'm so sorry, sugar." He stroked her hair. "But I really gotta go. We'll talk about it on Friday."

"Please don't leave me, Billy. Not right now." She wiped her eyes with the palm of her hand, smearing her mascara.

"Rose, you know my family comes first. I'll see you Friday. You can tell me the details then." He gave her a peck on the lips and left.

Rose had never felt so alone. Once again, the world seemed to expect her to wipe away her anguish, dry her eyes, and put on a sunny face. First, there was Laura. Then, there was Bill's wife and the stupid dinner party. And now it was Tucker. Rose felt like a soldier being forced to set aside her pain every time there was a bombshell, a wounded friend, an explosion of bad news.

She wondered if her whole life had been a mistake. Maybe she was a dingbat for sharing another dame's man, for being satisfied with leftovers. Maybe Tucker was right to tell her to go on the straight and narrow, to give up being a chippy and a moll. Maybe she should have settled down with a man of virtue in the first place, rather than sneaking around with a hoodlum who did God-knows-what with God-knows-who. For gosh sake, the FBI was even on his tail!

Rose downed a glass of gin to soften the blow. Then she walked over to the mirror and studied her mascara-smudged face. She looked like a clown, a tart, or a battered wife. She even noticed wrinkles on her forehead and under her eyes. She was a beaker of self-pity as she extracted bobby pins from her hair and set them on the dresser.

Rose's youth was fading. She was a wilting flower. Her bloom was in the rear-view mirror.

Margaret and Philip were beside themselves with worry. They had been on the blower all over town, trying to track down Jal in order to give him the news about Tucker. They had called his apartment, some of his pals, the roundhouse supervisor, and local dives and gin mills, but nobody knew of his where-abouts. They feared he already knew about the shooting and had done something rash. He was no milquetoast; it was in his nature to do something rash, something he would later regret. Tucker had always been Jal's role model, confidant, and "chin-up man." When Jal was down, Tucker did the heavy lifting, doling out doses of inspiration. Jal had a heap of thanks for this and often remarked, "Tucker's the only damn reason I'm not in jail or hanging from a rope in the barn."

In truth, Jal had no knowledge of Tucker's death that day. He had an altogether different reason to hang his head low, to be in the dumps. He was as certain as the sun would rise tomorrow that he was fixing to lose his job at the roundhouse. In an effort to ease his pain, he had been playing poker with low-lifes at a hole-in-the-wall in Preston County, which was an hour due east of Fairmont. The game was being held there because Marion County folks had rules against letting Negroes, Italians, and bohunks in on the betting. This applied to both under-the-table games and those organized a little more formally through the Masonic Order or the Elks Club. The "no Italians" rule was not official. It was not written down in the annals of the court-house or nestled in a signed document at the limestone State Capital in Charleston. It was a casual rule of prejudice against darkies getting in on the gambling action.

Jal had been holed up with five good-for-nothing gamblers since 9:45 a.m. that day, three minutes before Tucker's time of death. They had gone through hands of stud horse poker as well as "draw" variations on the game. Jal did not drink, so he had his wits about him, but the others were intoxicated. Their snoots were plumb full. Jal could not understand why they were winning. How could a man who was sozzled to the gills sit up straight, hit on all six, and walk away with a bankroll? This was baloney as far as Jal was concerned. It pissed him off and made him feel like a lunkhead. He figured he was a slug-burger while his gambling buddies were rib roast steaks.

Jal had lost almost all the money in his bank account, most of the change in his pocket, and had gone into serious debt by the time he left the game to head for his six-p.m. shift at work. He knew where his rump would be on the following day: in Tucker's office. He would be begging his brother for scratch, confessing that he was under water and could not pay his April rent, which was already a week past due.

After Jal got into his jalopy and started sputtering toward the roadhouse, he wondered how many more days he had left. Was it seven? Was it ten? Was it a full three weeks? He didn't figure it could be much longer. He knew he'd soon be out of work, kaput on cash, and sleeping on his mama's couch. He thought back to the talk he'd had with Herbie on the previous afternoon.

Herbie had slid into Jal's workstation all furtive-like to give him the scoop. "Hey, Jal. It's not gonna be announced till next week, but I want to let you in on the secret."

"What secret?"

Herbie peeped out of the cubbyhole to make sure there were no eavesdroppers around. "It's bad news."

"What's bad news?" Jal took off his goggles and put down his electric sander.

"They're talking about layoffs and pay cuts. Down to forty cents an hour."

"What?" Jal's insides went into a cold sweat.

"They're phasing out the steam engine. They're going over to diesel."

"That's a bunch of bunk."

"Most of us are gonna be let go, including you and me. I heard it from the boss man himself."

"Butch told you?" Jal's heart sank.

"Yep. You can't say nothing. But, there's good news."

"What?"

"They're hiring at the mine. There's a slew of openings."

That was *not* good news as far as Jal was concerned. He knew he'd rather be rolled in batter, chopped into bite-sized pieces, and put on a skewer over a blazing fire than work in a dirty, rotten coal mine. As a youngster, he had decided he would kill himself before getting all grimy and lung-sick inside one of those death holes.

The hour-long drive from the gambling game in Preston County to the roundhouse in Fairmont drew to an end, and Jal's thoughts returned to present day. He parked his car and jetted inside to his work stall. Less than five minutes later, Butch poked his head into the cubbyhole.

"Your mom's been trying to reach you. She called at least five times."

"I'll get back to her at the break."

Jal did not figure it could be anything important. His ma was always phoning, keeping tabs on him. Even though he was a grown man, she wore motherly worry like an apron. More so than her other children, she felt like Jal needed to be checked on, fiddled with, and fretted about. His impetuousness and self-destructive urges needed to be reined in like a wild horse.

Break time came at eleven p.m. There were fifty men on the night shift, but only a dozen were taking a breather or a recess. They always went to the "ketchup room." It had gotten this name because it had a red rug, it was where the men had a bite to eat (often a burger smothered in Heinz), and it was where they would "catch up" on juicy stories, mostly about hanky-panky with broads.

Jal opened his sack dinner and pulled out a peanut butter sandwich. He noticed the other men in the ketchup room were gossiping about him. He was unsure what the big mystery was, but decided to pay it no mind.

Finally, a worker named Saul piped up. "Jal, what are you doing here?"

"Eating my vittles like the rest of you bums."

There was another huddle of whispers.

"Why aren't you at home with your family?" Saul asked.

"Why would I be home with my family?" Jal wondered if he had already been fired and everybody knew it except him.

"Did you hear about your brother? Tucker?"

"What are you talking about?"

"It's all over the news. I'm sorry, Jal. He was shot this morning. He's dead."

"What?" Jal jumped to his feet. "Tucker's dead?"

Other men chimed in with, "It's true, Jal," "I'm sorry," "Yep, heard it on the radio," and "My condolences."

Jal was devastated. His heart was pumping up a storm. His eyes were watery and he felt dizzy. He seemed to be in a nightmare.

"The killer's still alive at State Hospital," Saul shouted as Jal bolted out the door.

Jal jumped into his car and sped away. He was ready to wreak havoc on the town—or for that matter, on all of West Virginia. He did not care what was legal or moral. His temper was out of control. It was not about to be tamped down. It was a racecar without breaks. Nobody was going to calm him, cut him off, or bring him to a stop. Jal knew only one thing: he would get his fill of revenge if it was the last goddamn thing he ever did!

Chapter 23

THE DEVIL BIRD
OF REVENGE

JAL THUNDERED THROUGH the streets. He was seething, snarling, and screeching, much like an Irish banshee or a Sri Lankan devil bird. He had worked himself into a lather. He had no regrets, no qualms, no plan to bridle his passions. His fiery soul was shackled to his fiery body. They were riding the rapids together. Jal was set on killing that scum-sucking lowlife who had murdered Tucker, and no feeble-minded fool or yellow-bellied jellyfish could tell him otherwise. His car ripped past the fire station on Odell Street, turned right, and then hurtled down Hampton Road until he got to Dewey Street. Jal slammed on the brakes in front of the farmhouse and blasted through the door like a madman.

Margaret was unaware of the hubbub in the

front room because she was tucked away in bed, snoring up a storm. Philip was on the couch, sipping soup and perusing hospital paperwork.

"Jal, did you hear what happened?" Philip perked up when he saw his long-lost brother. "We've been trying to track you down all day."

Jal shot into a bedroom and plowed through dresser drawers.

"Jal?" Philip came into the room." Did you hear? Tucker was killed. The fellow's name is Yost. He's in critical condition at State Hospital."

The dresser was a bust, so Jal moved over to a wooden foot locker and dug through it. In his haste, he threw can-can garb, sailor-style clothes, and an eye patch onto the floor.

"Where's the fire?" Philip joked. "You late for a date with a pirate?"

The foot locker came up short, so Jal darted to the closet and felt around on the top shelf.

"What are you doing?" Philip was at sea. "What are you looking for?"

The closet shelf was also a washout, so Jal hightailed it upstairs. Philip tagged along, feeling like the invisible man.

"What's going on?" Philip was balled up with confusion. "Talk to me. I'm beating my chops here. Did you know mom tried to kill herself? The doctor says her taste buds are shot. We're taking turns babysitting, helping her through this rough patch."

Jal paid him no mind, throwing open drawers. He tossed out clothes, right and left, making a humdinger of a mess.

"You're acting all goopy, like you have a screw loose." Philip pulled a sweater from the floor, folded it neatly, and placed it on the bed.

Suddenly, there was the flicker of triumph in Jal's eyes. He had found it. It was a beauty. It was his henchman. It was a sight for sore eyes in all its black and silver glory. It was a .32 Short Colt revolver and a box of bullets.

"What you got there?" Philip was confused, but then he got a load of the piece and panicked. "No, Jal. You can't."

Jal stuffed the revolver and bullets into his pocket and darted back downstairs. He flew out the front door with Philip still on his tail.

"You're gonna end up in the slammer or dead." Philip blocked his brother from the car. "Damn it, Jal. You're half-cocked. Stop being a knucklehead. I don't need another brother in a Chicago overcoat." As far as Philip was concerned, it felt like déjà vu. He'd had to knock sense into his mom that morning, and now his little brother needed a whack upside the head.

Jal maneuvered, getting to the car door handle, but Philip shoved him backward. Jal became peeved, drew back his fist, and belted his older brother in the mouth. It was a whopper of a smack, a real snow plow, and it sent Philip flying. He ended up all twisted up in a patch of pink rhododendrons. Philip was slow to get back on his feet, which gave Jal time to jump in the driver's seat of his jalopy, turn on the ignition, and barrel down the road. He barely escaped playing footsies with an elm tree as he made a wide swerve around the bend.

Although Jal was long gone, Philip screamed into the moonlight, "Come back here. You're gonna ruin your life."

Jal weaved through the dark streets, almost crashing into a trail of parked cars. Everything looked blurry because he was crying so hard. He was sweet on the notion of an eye for an eye, a bullet for a bullet, a cadaver for a goddamn cadaver. Jal was drenched in sweat—the sweet sweat of revenge.

Meanwhile, the hospital had been in a state of mild bedlam since that morning when Ernie was admitted. Nurse Joy Penton had the grumbles because she did not think the staff should be caring for a scoundrel. She'd had a run in with Dr. Johnson.

"I say… let him die." Nurse Joy folded her arms all sassy-like.

Dr. Johnson shot daggers. "You do your job and I'll do mine."

Sure, Ernie was bandaged, hooked up to a bunch of tubes, and looked like he wasn't going to make it. But Dr. Johnson had a duty to heal, not to play God. He planned to do his best to save Ernie's life, despite snooty stares from Nurse Joy and other holier-than-thou members of the staff.

The waiting room looked mostly regular that night, with a few folks biding their time and flipping through magazines while their loved ones were in the back being fussed over by doctors. There were twelve chairs, two tables, and a bookcase. The white tile floor was so clean that a white glove test would not find a single particle of grit. A long counter was manned by two admittance secretaries.

It was almost midnight when Jal stormed into the place, waving his gun in the air. He was ready to crush Ernie, pulverize his rancid face, and pummel him with bullets. Although he had never set eyes on this oil can, he imagined him as a sack of chicken droppings with the brains of a stick and the moral compass of a… well, a portable compass.

"Where's the crazy man?" Jal shouted. "Where's the crazy man?" Folks who had been minding their own business saw a stranger brandishing a pistol and screamed. Most bolted out the door.

Jal scooted over the long counter to get to the patient area, frightening the pants off the admittance secretaries, who made a beeline down the hallway. Nurse Penton was the only one not alarmed by Jal's anger or his weapon. She reckoned he was a hero. She had been praying for a white knight, a vigilante, a

Zorro of sorts who would be willing to take from the vile and give to the pure.

"Where is he? Where's the man who killed my brother?" Jal was sobbing.

Nurse Penton pointed down the corridor to room number four. Jal dashed in that direction, but was blocked by a male orderly.

"Come on, fellow. You don't want to do this."

Jal, being a bit of a John Wayne when it came to sparring, shoved the orderly to the side like it was nothing and gave him a Hindenburg-sized pop in the kisser. This sent the man against the wall, where he dropped to the floor, bruised.

With that, Jal had a clear path. He lumbered down the hallway and scooted into room number four to find Ernie unconscious and looking pretty rough around the edges, possibly on his last limb. Dr. Johnson—who was bedside writing notes on a clipboard—was terrified when he saw Ernie's revolver. He backed against the wall. Nurse Penton peered in to watch the showdown.

"Put down the gun, son," Dr. Johnson pleaded from the corner. "Come on, put it down."

"Is this him?" Jal was a Niagara Falls of grief. "Is this the man who killed my brother?"

"I knew Tucker," the doctor mumbled. "He wouldn't want you to do this."

Jal was having none of it and barked, "Is this the man who killed my brother?"

Dr. Johnson nodded reluctantly.

"Nobody kills my brother." Jal shoved the gun up against Ernie's bandaged forehead with his finger on the trigger, ready to blast the good-for-nothing to kingdom come. "Nobody kills my brother," Jal repeated, tears streaming down his cheeks.

Dr. Johnson noticed that Ernie's chest was no longer moving and threw his arms into the air. "Wait! Wait! Wait! Don't shoot!"

Jal kept his revolver fixed on Ernie's forehead, but did not fire. He waited patiently while Dr. Johnson examined the pulse.

"He's dead!" Dr. Johnson exclaimed. "Ernie Lee Yost is dead!"

Ernie died only seconds after midnight on April 8, 1948. This would have pleased him. He would have puffed up his torso like the noble cobra. The serpent had upset the apple cart at a most perfect time. Midnight was the hour when warlocks rolled up their sleeves and dabbled in hocus pocus. Midnight was the hour of the netherworld, of cryptic ceremonies, and of grisly nefariousness. Midnight was an ideal time for a devil in the basement to take his last breath and be bathed in flames for the rest of eternity.

Ernie's corpse was taken to the Jones Funeral Home in Mannington, West Virginia. From there, it went to the home of his brother, Levi Alfred Yost, on Clay Street. Levi had enough sense to know that Ernie would not want a Christian funeral. Heck, even one "God bless" or "Please Lord watch over us" had sent Ernie reeling during life. What would it do in death? Would it prod him to claw his way out of his death box and haunt this innocent town from one corner to the other, from the dusty coal mines to the clearing in Hangman Forest? Would there be another round of spine-tingling terror? Would there be more conjuring, sleight of hand, murders, and bombings? Levi thought it best to have an atheist funeral for his demon-loving brother at 1:30 p.m. on Sunday, April 11 with a burial at Snodgrass cemetery.

Nellie's body had also been transported to the Jones Funeral Home, but when her kin learned she was sharing accommodation with "that cinderblock of evil," they transferred her to the R. Lee Harr Funeral Home in Monongah, West Virginia. Nellie's relatives were not only filled with grief; they were also seething with scorn. They cut Ernie's picture out of every last photo album on every last shelf. Chop. Chop. Chop. There were wedding pictures of Nellie next to a blasted hole. A blasted hole was better. It did not abuse wives. It did not point guns or fill folks with daylight. A blasted hole did not snatch the life from a young filly and feed her flesh to the souls of hell. Nellie's services began an hour after Ernie's—at 2:30 p.m. on April 11 at the First Methodist Church, with Reverend Joseph Van Sickle officiating—and her final resting place was Enterprise Cemetery.

Jal was in his cubicle at the roundhouse with newspapers fanned out all over his workstation. Local reporters had gone hog-wild with this tale about the double-murder suicide and bombings. They were printing piece after piece, angle after angle, and the townsfolk were scarfing it down like a chocolate éclair. Some of the editorials were titled: "Ernie Lee Yost Kills Wife and Tucker Moroose," "Mad Effigy of Mrs. Yost Found at Residence," "Little Dog Averts Weird Plot to Burn House," "Effigy of Wife and Charred Home Survive City's Weirdest Day," "Yost Dead: Lingers 15 Hours After Slaying Wife and Lawyer," and "Blind Spots Yet Remain in Yost Tragedy." In addition, the story made it into papers throughout the nation: from Florida to Delaware and even as far west as Nevada and California. It was big news and was being billed as the most shocking incident in West Virginia since its birth in 1861. A few writers went so far as to call it one of the most disturbing crimes in the history of the nation.

The story was a chocolate éclair to Jal, too. He could not get enough of it. He read the articles over and over, almost memorizing them. They made him feel close to Tucker. The words were like a bridge, a magnet, a spiritual link, a connecting of hearts. Jal was open about this "odd bird" hobby and did not care if Butch or the other supervisors caught him reading during work. He figured the bosses knew he was distraught, and probably had pity. Plus, he was fixing to lose his job anyway. What did it matter if he was goofing off here and there? Would they fire him early? Would they dock his eleventh-hour pay? Would they curse him up and down? Frankly, he did not give a damn. He was down in the dumps without a ladder, and nobody could make him feel any lousier.

In one sense, Jal was not crying in his porridge. He felt lucky he was not in jail. He had squirmed off the hook. His batty-headed antic of waving his gun like a cowboy and scaring the bejesus out of folks at the hospital had not been reported—not to the Fairmont police, nor to the editors of the local paper. Dr. Johnson had always been friendly with Tucker, so decided to give his little brother a break. After all, nobody had been hurt. No real harm had been done, other than a few episodes of anxiety and some red throats from screaming like marmosets. Although Jal thanked Dr. Johnson up, down, and sideways for not turning him over to the cops, he mostly felt obliged to Tucker. His brother had come to his rescue again. Even from the grave, Tucker was a puppet-master and Jal's guardian angel.

Tucker's body was first taken to the Ross Funeral Home and then to the farmhouse on Dewey Street for an open-casket wake. A black curtain was hung over the door, and folks came from all over the state with bouquets, greeting cards, and hankies, prepared to dab their grieving eyes. Guests wore black and a smorgasbord was served alongside a tray of cookies called "Ossa de Mortu" or "Bones of the Dead." Folks had uplifting words for the Moroose family: "Tucker is God's high pillow and Gabriel," "Tucker was the finest person this world has ever known," and "Tucker kicked failure between the eyes and became a rollicking success."

Margaret and Ginger had to be mildly sedated during both the wake and the funeral (which was held at the First Baptist Church on April 10). Jal found himself alternating between holding up his mama and propping up Ginger. The women were like plundered villages. Their emotions were in smithereens. They were no longer their normal feisty selves—they were wobbly and fragile, like butterfly wings or rice paper. Tucker's final resting place was Woodlawn Cemetery, which was a mere three-minute drive from the farmhouse.

After the burial, Tucker was memorialized at a special meeting of the Marion County Bar Association. A committee read a prepared resolution: "On Wednesday, April 7, 1948, without any warning, grim tragedy struck within our association, and by violence removed from our midst one of our beloved members… May Tucker Moroose's memory remain long and be kept green in the love and affections of his family and in the memory of the members of this bar. May his soul rest in peace." The association also gave the Moroose family a plaque, which Margaret kept in a treasured spot on the wall so she could forever remember her favorite son.

Jal was still in the roundhouse and it was getting close to lunch time. He set aside the newspaper articles. He had been a slouch all morning and was adamant about getting a few axels smoothed. Being a ninety-percent slacker was fine, but he had too much self-respect to be a 100-percent or full-throttled one. He donned his goggles and flipped on his sanding machine.

Five minutes later, Butch poked his head into the cubbyhole. "Hey. Switch that thing off."

Jal did what he was told, praying he would not get the boot. He was always a bundle of nerves over "the boot."

"There's somebody here to see you."

Who in hermit's name could be coming to see me? Jal asked himself as he made his way to the visitor section of the building. He found Ginger. Her spirit was thrashed and her heart was in ruin. She was a cloud without sail and lacked any puff.

"Didn't figure on seeing you here." He embraced Ginger and led her outside. "You weren't at the reception."

"I couldn't go. I just couldn't do it anymore."

"I understand. At least you missed the rigmarole. My ma's got all these fluky rules about wearing black for fifteen months and being all solemn. She's got different rituals for heavy mourning, half mourning, and light mourning. Plus, she says we can't mention Tucker's name or it'll draw him back to the earth as a tortured soul."

"That's poppycock. *Not* mentioning his name seems like torture to me. I can't imagine forbidding my daughters to speak about their father. Doesn't seem healthy or right."

"Mom's from the old country. Plus, everybody knows she's full of prunes." Jal chuckled.

"I just came by to let you know… me and the girls… we're moving to Baltimore."

"Baltimore? You don't have to go all the way over there."

"Yes, we do."

"Did you know the fellow who killed Tucker was a devil worshiper?" Jal asked.

"Yeah. I guess that takes some fierce belief. There are too many folks out there with fierce belief… could you say goodbye to the Moroose family for me?"

"Why don't you tell them yourself?"

"Your mother never liked me. After all, I'm not Catholic. And I hear she's still in a bad way. I don't think seeing me would do her any good."

"I'll tell them."

"I found this with Tucker's things, and I think you should

have it." Ginger handed Jal an envelope with black lettering. It read, "Jal's Pharmacy Fund."

Inside was a thick heap of twenty dollar bills. Jal was stunned. Jal was relieved. Jal was a pig in a pasta patch. The joy was coming at him like a "Happy Cow" ice cream truck. He had visions of paying off his thousand-dollar gambling debt, buying a new car, and taking his first vacation to Hawaii. He had always wanted to swing by the state and give surfing the once-over. The moolah had come at exactly the right time. Tucker had saved Jal's bacon once again. The cabbage would tide him over until he found a new job, maybe as a salesman at Hartley's Department Store or as a construction worker. Plus, he could get all current on his rent. His landlord would keel over in a heap of bliss. College and pharmacy school were not an option, of course, because Jal figured he could not make the grade. Some folks were donkeys when it came to book learning, and Jal knew he was a dough-brained mule. Tucker would not want his cabbage wasted on failing grades and no degree. Tucker had been rational above all else. He had been about getting ahead, not dropping further behind.

"Also, I think you should have these." Ginger was clenching something in her fist.

Jal held out his hand, and she gave him Tucker's treasured onyx cufflinks.

Jal swallowed hard, choking down his tears. The black stones glistened in the sunlight. Tucker's soul was not in some box in the cemetery. At that moment, it was right smack-dab in Jal's hand.

As Ginger headed for her car, she turned and said, "When life gives you lemons, Jal… turn it into lemon pie."

Chapter 24

A LEMON PIE IN THE SKY

FOLKS TOLD HER that Baltimore was hipper-dipper, that it was the butterfly's boots, and that it had been the home of Edgar Allen Poe, Frederick Douglass, and Billie Holiday. It was a place Ginger and her young'uns could get a fresh start. Who better to give it to them than a whole bunch of strangers with no link to her sad-sack past? She wished she could follow in Tucker's footsteps by snagging a law degree and becoming a mouth-piece. But Ginger needed a job compatible with raising three children under the age of ten. Plus, the workplace wore a tie, not a skirt and high heels. It was a man's world, and it could shred a woman into bits, sort of like turning her from a mighty carrot into a trifling splash of color in a salad. So Ginger set her sights on getting a master's degree at

Johns Hopkins University and then going to work as a teacher. Finishing up at three p.m. every day seemed like a sunny idea. It was conducive to bringing home the bread, as well as providing a stable family life for Sharon, Sheila, and Shirley.

There was a "for sale" sign in the front yard of the Cleveland house, and the movers were finishing up with their pushing, pulling, and toting. They left the "big dread" for last: the confounded baby grand. They knew they would have to angle this monstrosity onto their truck with precision and secure it well, lest it become a pile of jagged wood by the time they crossed the state line. Then, they got some A1 news.

"You don't need to load the piano," Ginger said.

"What?" The moving company foreman pulled her aside. "Ma'am, if my boys have been complaining or making a fuss..."

"Nobody's been making a fuss," she replied. "They're doing a mighty fine job. I'm just leaving it here. That's all." She started to leave, but then stopped and turned. "On second thought, you take it on home with you. I'm sure your wife will be pleased."

"Really? Why, thank you, ma'am. She'll be keen as mustard. She will."

June, who was in her front yard, waved goodbye to Ginger, the children, and Fido as they climbed into the car.

"Now when we get to Baltimore, girls..." Ginger gazed into the backseat. "We're gonna play a special game."

"What's that, Mommy?" Sharon asked.

"We're not gonna go by the name 'Moroose' anymore."

"What are we gonna be called?"

"Morris. My last name. And you're not gonna tell anyone that your daddy was Italian. It'll be our little secret."

"But why?"

"Because there are a whole lot of folks out there with fierce belief."

While Ginger and the girls were heading to Baltimore, Jal was moseying around downtown Fairmont. He was doing some pondering—or "well thinking" as he had called it as a child. Since being blessed with the golden envelope—which turned out to hold an eye-popping forty-six hundred dollars—he had been doing headstands and mental cartwheels over how to spend the cash. This was a landslide of a decision, and he did not want to be rash or make a wrong turn. Should he get a Buick Roadmaster or a Chevy Fleetmaster? Maybe a Ford or an Oldsmobile would be a better choice. Should he take a trip to Hawaii, Tahiti, or perhaps the Virgin Islands? His brain was knotted up like a shoelace. Should he keep his ratty apartment or spring for a more highfalutin' place? Should he pay off his gambling debt or kick it on down the road? The dough was burning a hole in his trousers. He was itching to take off his thinking cap and spend, spend, spend.

Jal trotted past Shurtleff Shoes, the Ruth Ann Brady shop, Fairmont Florists, and the Rizzo Millinery. He got a sour taste in his mouth when he noticed a restaurant sign that read, "No dogs. No Negroes. No Italians." *What malarkey*, he thought to himself. He was itching to storm across the street to National Auto, grab a crowbar, and whack the guts out of that filthy sign. He might have done it in the dead of night when the flatfoots weren't around, or maybe on a dare with the motor running and a getaway plan. But he had no dog-faced buddy to egg him on, so Jal kept walking.

He passed the Western Union office, Hartley's, Chez Louis, and the bridal shop, where an old lady was plucking a fuchsia dress out of a car. It was Mrs. Neubaum, but Jal did not know her from Adam. To him, she was just a regular Fairmontian doing her regular chores on a regular Saturday.

When Jal came upon the McCrory building, his steps got shallower and his reflecting got deeper. He noticed a shiny gold plate on the structure that listed Tucker's name and suite number. He exhaled, then inhaled, and then exhaled again. Should he go inside and do a once-over of the crime scene? Or should he leave well enough alone? Would checking out the place make him feel closer to his brother? Or would it capsize his spirit, landing him in an apple box of woe? Jal hemmed and hawed, waffled and hedged. He was a tiddlywinks of vacillation. While he was chewing on what to do, a man exited the structure with a strong and pronounced stride. It was Worley, but again, to Jal, this was just a regular Fairmontian doing his regular chores on a regular Saturday.

Worley was curious as to who was peering at the building's plaques. "Howdy. Can I help you, sir?" He spoke with his usual festive conviviality.

"Oh. Hi there... uh... I was thinking of checking out my brother's office."

"Who's your brother?"

"Tucker Moroose."

Worley got all peppy and held out his meat hook for one of his signature handshakes. "Why it's a pleasure to meet you. I'm J. Worley Powell. Tucker worked in my suite."

Worley's shake was a whopper, and Jal felt like his right arm was riding the ocean's waves.

"I'm just sick about what happened," Worley continued. "Just sick. Tucker was a fine lawyer and an even finer gentleman. Also, he was plumb funny!"

"He could tell some good ones." Jal smiled.

"Every damn day, I had to check both of my legs to see which one he was pulling." Worley roared with laughter. "Now, which brother are you?"

"I'm Jal."

"Jal... Jal..." Worley rolled the name around in his head. "Oh, yeah. Jal. You're the kid brother. The young one."

Jal nodded.

"He had nothing but good things to say about you. Let me take you upstairs and give you a tour."

Jal was hesitant, but followed. The men went through the front door and stepped into the elevator.

"Do you know the law firm Rose, Padden and Petty?"

"Nope," Jal replied.

"Well... they aren't handling divorces anymore 'cause of what happened to your fine brother."

"Really?"

"Yep. They changed their whole policy."

The tour was painful for Jal, but necessary. It was like pulling a bad tooth. Jal found that learning the particulars was helpful, much like reading the newspaper articles over and over. It helped patch up the hole in his heart, opening a way for him to heal.

After saying farewell to Worley, Jal continued his ramble down the sidewalk. He passed the Home Savings Bank building, Fort Pitt Shoes, and Roger's Jewelry. He saw children playing ball in a park, two blonde zazz girls exiting Hollywood Ladies' Shop, and a bum on a bench, scarfing down a plate of chow.

When he came upon Crane's Pharmacy, he stared at the front door. He got a thick lump in his tummy. This was his lemon pie in the sky—the treat he knew he could never have. He was itching to bake that beauty and serve her up on a silver platter. *If only I had the aptitude, fortitude, and drive,* Jal said to himself. *If only I was a doer and had stick-to-itiveness. If only I was a little more like Tucker.*

Jal knew it was not wise to gnaw at things that could not be. He needed to be practical and constructive, so he set aside the pie in the sky and continued with his stroll. He passed Sherwood's Barber Shop, Clyde Holt Office Supplies, and Star Restaurant.

And that is when he saw them. He was shocked. He could not believe his baby browns. It was a pair of fancy-schmancy Florsheim ground-grippers. They had a snappy buckle, supple leather, and deep tones of gray. They had modern styling and a ruggedness that promised long wear. Jal knew there was only one fellow in town who wore spiffy and pricey clodhoppers: Mr. Clark! Although he was now a brittle-boned dinosaur of eighty, he was standing there, poring over a newspaper.

"Mr. Clark, I see you still have the same taste in shoes."

"Is that little Jal Amoruso all grown up?"

"Are you still in the Klan, Mr. Clark?"

"That mouth's gonna get you in trouble one of these days. You just might end up dead like Tucker."

With this, Jal came undone and barked, "Don't talk about my brother."

"If Tucker had stuck with the coal mine like a good little Italian, maybe he'd be alive today." Mr. Clark roared with laughter.

Jal ignited, grabbing the Klansman's collar. Then, he drew back his fist, ready to pop him between the eyes. Mr. Clark cowered, bracing himself for a humdinger of a punch and a trip to State Hospital on a stretcher.

But as Jal stood there clenching the shirt, he heard Tucker's words in his head: "A gentleman uses his brain, not his fists." And this became a pivotal moment. Jal realized it was time to grow up. It was time to mature, to sprout into a man. It was time to stop drifting, to put his rudder in the water and find direction in life. He also reckoned he was not alone. Tucker was rooting for him from inside those chipped pearly gates. After all, the two of them were a tag team, siblings with a special bond and with a hankering for success. Tucker had handed him the baton, and Jal needed to win—for the Moroose family and for Italians everywhere. He could not—and would not—let his brother and the others down.

So, Jal took a long, hard look at Mr. Clark and the cotton shirt that was taut around his fist, and for the first time in his life, he could not do it. He could not throw the punch. He could not bonk, whop, slap, thwack, or pummel. He had finally overcome his black shadow. It was no longer his hobble and his hurdle. He felt it lift from his body like a dead layer of skin and fall to the sidewalk in tatters.

Jal released the collar, leaving Mr. Clark feeling confused and even a tad disappointed. The Klansman liked propping up his bias rather than having to disassemble it. He fancied thinking of darkies as troublemakers and thugs.

Mr. Clark's mouth hung open as Jal moseyed away, basking in the warmth of the sunshine. Jal's shackles were gone. They would never plague him again.

Jal was fixing to splurge. It was weeks after his stroll through downtown Fairmont, and he planned to spend his entire cash-filled envelope in one stroke like a mayor cutting a ribbon or a sailor christening a boat. He was raring to plop down the whole wad on a shell game of hope. To his mind, it was a dadgum gamble, like doing surgery in a straightjacket or firing a gun wearing blinders. The whole caper was wobbly and iffy, but Jal did not care. Jal had lost his job at the roundhouse and was in an impetuous mood. He was ready to flirt up a storm with lady luck. He just hoped he could win her over in the end.

It was the first day of his venture, and he was wearing a new suit and Tucker's onyx cufflinks. He parked his banged-up car in front of a brick building with white trim. He felt runty and jittery. He felt clumsy and thick-headed. He felt like an amateur and a small-fry.

He stood behind a rope and long line waiting his turn, moving up one person at a time. He kept tabs on what others did and tried to copy. He did not want to be goopy. He did not want to look like an oaf. He did not want to get booted for being a lame-brain. He hoped Tucker's spirit was in the room. He sure as heck needed a guardian angel.

Finally, it was his turn. He tried to act confident as he sashayed up to a window and plunked down the envelope with the forty-six hundred dollars.

"What's this?" The woman was stumped.

"The money."

"No. I need the forms. Did you fill out the forms?"

"Yes, ma'am." Jal felt like a dodo and pulled the paperwork from his satchel.

While she was reviewing the pages, Jal began to sweat. Had he done it all wrong? Had he made errors? He was twitchy and insecure. The new venture was starting to feel like it had gone comatose at the starting gate.

"Everything seems to be in order." The woman eventually smiled, and Jal was relieved. "You need to mail the fee by no later than the middle of July."

"I can mail it?" Jal was confused about how the process worked.

"Yes, of course. You can send a money order." She grinned real big. "Welcome to the university, Mr. Moroose."

"I'm gonna be a pharmacist!" Jal beamed.

Afterword: The Aftermath

Jal Moroose (my great uncle) – Jal graduated from college, married, had two sons, and worked as a successful pharmacist for forty years until he retired. Today, he is ninety-four years old and still owns the gun that he took to the hospital to shoot Ernie. About his many brushes with death and near-imprisonment, he says, "God saved me. God saved me many times."

Margaret Moroose (my great-grandmother) – Margaret died at age seventy-one due to an allergic reaction to a routine flu shot.

Philip Moroose (Tucker's half-brother) – Philip married, raised a step-child, enjoyed tinkering with cars, and worked in the coal mines until his death in 1983.

Miriam Rose Moroose (my great-aunt) and **Vito**

William "Billy Jack" Giacalone – Rose was Bill's mistress (or moll) for decades. She died at the age of 86.

Bill was feared and ferocious but well-liked. He went to prison on various occasions for weapons possession, racketeering, extortion, tax evasion, and gambling, but never for murder.

The FBI considers Bill a top suspect—if not the prime one—in the 1975 disappearance of Jimmy Hoffa. This unsolved case is considered a huge embarrassment for the Bureau. Despite keeping Bill under constant surveillance, the FBI could never get the goods on him.

Bill gave Rose a padlocked freezer at one point just before he went to prison. She was secretive about it. What was inside? Money? Jewels? Jimmy Hoffa's personal effects? Incriminating paperwork about the Detroit mob? The freezer disappeared from her possession years later (after Bill was released), and the contents remain a mystery to this day.

Bill died in 2012 at age eighty-eight. His son, Jack (Jackie the Kid) Giacalone, is reportedly the new boss of the Detroit mob.

Ginger Morris (my grandmother) – Ginger moved to Baltimore and never saw the Moroose family again. She got a master's degree at John Hopkins University, became a teacher, and went by the last name "Morris." She traveled around the world, became a ballroom dancing instructor, and was awarded "Mother of the Year" by the governor of Maryland in 1980. She gave up the piano after Tucker's death out of guilt, saying, "If I had let him go to the legal conference, he would still be alive." Ginger passed away in 2007 at age ninety-two. She is buried next to Tucker at Woodlawn cemetery in Fairmont.

Sharon Morris/Moroose (my mother) – Sharon is a talented pianist and painter, and worked as a social worker for thirty years. Today, she is retired and lives in Washington, D.C. with her husband.

Sheila and Shirley Morris/Moroose (my aunts) – Shirley got married and had two daughters. She died of colon cancer on June 9, 1997 at age fifty-five. Sheila is married with two children and lives in Maryland.

Chester and Faire Morris (my great-grandparents) – Chester is related to the renowned Robert Morris, who signed the Declaration of Independence, the Articles of Confederation, and the Constitution. Although Chester is described in this story as a physician, he was actually a Renaissance man or a jack-of-all-trades. He was a landlord, had a substantial farming business, and worked periodically as a government advisor. Chester died in 1975 at age ninety. Faire died in 1984 at age ninety-two.

J. Worley Powell – Worley advanced to judicial court judge and passed away in 2001 at the age of ninety-seven. My family is forever grateful to him.

The "Hell's Half Acre" Home – I toured Ernie's house twice: in 2012 and in 2016. It looks much the same as it did in 1948. The burned basement, where the bombs exploded, has never been repaired. Nellie's relatives live there and have the gun that killed Tucker.

There was a fight for ownership of the property in 1948—a case that made it all the way up to the West Virginia Supreme Court in 1949. The judge in the case said he was heartbroken: he had to award the property to Ernie's kin (rather than Nellie's kin) because Nellie had died first. The fact that Ernie had caused Nellie's death was irrelevant. The case is Wright v.

Davis, 53 S.E. 2d 335. Nellie's kin later bought the house from Ernie's daughters.

The "Hells Half Acre" carving on the steps was quite visible in 2012, despite intense efforts over the decades to scratch out the haunting words. In 2016, I found the lettering was much less perceptible.

Nellie's family tore out walls in Ernie's home searching for the seventeen hundred dollars. The money was never recovered. It is believed a policeman or investigator stole it.

There is a rumor—still circulating to this day—that Ernie robbed a bank, but there is no evidence.

There have been odd happenings at Ernie's house. For example: years ago, the thermostat seemed to change on its own.

While researching for this book, I contacted members of the Yost family. Most knew nothing about the double-murder and bombings. They had only been informed of the suicide.

Vivian Yost Andrews (Ernie's oldest daughter) – After the tragedy, she moved into Ernie's house with Tutu and five other rescue dogs. She lived there for six months. Witnesses describe her as a tender-hearted person. She loved Shakespeare and animals, and died in 2002 at age seventy-nine.

Edwina Yost Davis (Ernie's youngest daughter) – She died in 2013.

Herbert (Herb) Arthur Sloane – According to sources, Herb was the first person to organize a specifically Satanic cult. This would make Ernie Yost one of the first practitioners of the religion. Herb's wife was indicted in 1938 for operating a "white slave ring" in violation of the Mann Act (an inter-state prostitution law), although she was later acquitted. Herb was not implicated, but is said to have participated in a sexually risqué lifestyle involving hookers, strippers, and bondage sex. Herb remained obsessed with his life-sized doll, April Belle, until his death in 1975 when he was sixty-nine.

My other great-uncles and great-aunts from the Moroose Family:

Betty Moroose (Tucker's sister) – Betty worked at a glass factory and later for the Marion County Board of Education before getting married and having two children. She enjoyed sewing and gardening and died in 2015 at the age of eighty-nine.

James Moroose (Tucker's brother) – James worked in the coal mine for thirty-eight years. He was married with three children and liked playing craps, although he was a conservative gambler. Black lung contributed to his death in 1993 at the age of eighty.

Louis Moroose (Tucker's brother) – Louis ran a furniture store and liked playing poker and golf. He was married with one child, and died on November 1, 2006. He was eighty-five years old.

Mary Moroose (Tucker's sister) – Mary worked at the Owens-Illinois Bottle Company. She was married with a daughter. She loved baking and gardening and died on September 16, 2000 at age eighty-nine.

Robert Moroose (Tucker's brother) – On the day of the shooting, Robert dropped his plan to follow in Tucker's footsteps and become a lawyer. Instead, he moved to Florida and got a job at Uniroyal Chemical Company. He was married with two daughters and enjoyed sports, especially golf and West Virginia University football. He died in 2010 at the age of eighty-three.

℘hotos

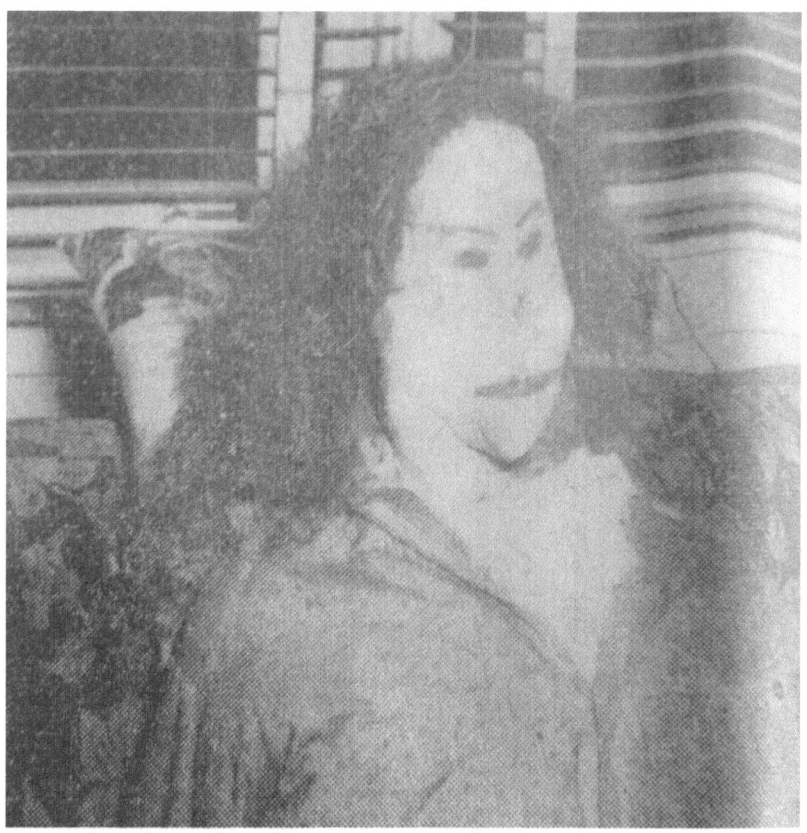

Ernie's satanic doll (or effigy). It appeared on the front page of the April 8, 1948 edition of the local newspaper. Reprinted with permission from the Times West Virginian.

My grandfather, Tucker.

My grandmother, Ginger.

My great-grandmother, Margaret.

My great-grandparents, Chester and Faire.

Carving on the step at Ernie's house. It appeared on the front page of the April 8, 1948 edition of the local newspaper. Reprinted with permission from the Times West Virginian.

2012 photo of Ernie's house and stone steps. "Hell's Half Acre" was carved into the top step, and the eerie words are still vaguely visible.

Tucker and Ginger's daughters. Left to right: Sheila, Sharon (my mother), and Shirley.

The shack on Cleveland Avenue where Ginger and Tucker lived. Photo taken in 2012 after there had been a fire.

Rose Moroose, my great-aunt.

Tutu leaning against the back door of Ernie's burning house. This appeared on the front page of the April 8, 1948 edition of the local newspaper. Reprinted with permission from the Times West Virginian.

WHERE THE PLOT FAILED

Ernie's house on the day of the fire. The top image shows the structure when the police arrived. The bottom photo shows the home after some flames have been extinguished. This appeared on the front page of the April 9, 1948 edition of the local newspaper. Reprinted with permission from the Times West Virginian.

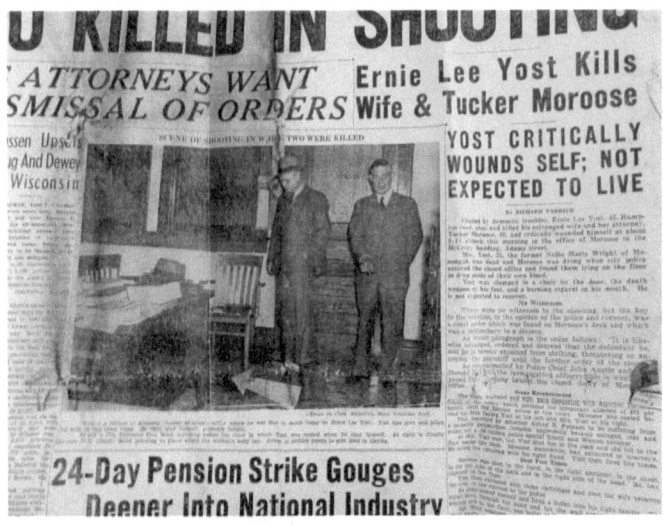

Tucker's law office on the day of the double murder-suicide. Image of Detective Don West (left) standing next to the chair where Ernie shot himself. The arrow points to where the gun was found. On the right is County Coroner D.E. (Dusty) Kidd who is pointing to where Nellie's body was located. This appeared on the front page of the evening edition of the local newspaper on April 7, 1948. Reprinted with permission from the Times West Virginian.

The gun that was used to kill Tucker and Nellie. It is stored at Ernie's house to this day.

*Ernie's actual basement. Photo taken in 2016. The black burn marks
from the explosions have never been repaired.*

For additional photos related to this story, see
www.DevilintheBasement.com

Appendix 1:

NOTE ON FICTIONAL CHARACTERS

Mrs. Neubaum – When interviewing locals in Fairmont, some described an elderly gossip who was convinced that Ernie had robbed a bank. I call her "Mrs. Neubaum." This woman may have resided on Ernie's street or simply in his neighborhood. Had she heard about the missing seventeen hundred dollars or had she been snooping around Ernie's property and peeping through his windows? We may never know.

Mr. Clark – Several interviewees described a Klansman and retired law enforcement official who had confrontations with non-whites in Fairmont. This man, who I have named "Mr. Clark," reportedly participated in the KKK march through town and the well-pub-licized 1920 lynching in Duluth, Minnesota.

Hangman Forest – There was allegedly a clearing in the woods where Klansmen met for private ceremonies. I call this "Hangman Forest."

Detective Frank Ganges – Although the police chief, firemen, coroner, and most of the police officers were real people, I created the character of Detective Frank. This is because it is unknown who stole Ernie's money, and I did not want to pin the theft on an innocent person.

Lastly, some names in this book were changed to protect privacy, or they were invented because actual names are unknown. For example, Laura Smith, Pete Palin, Will Kleeman, Carlo Lorenzo di Francesco, and Jal Moroose are not real names. Other folks with fictitious names include: the New York Republicans, Jal's childhood friends, the rank-and-file members of the satanic cult, and the low-level mobsters who worked under "Billy Jack" Giacalone. Unless a person is dead or I had permission to disclose identity, I took pains to use a fabricated name.

Appendix 11:

AUTHOR BIOGRAPHY

Charlotte Laws has authored a number of books, as well as over a hundred articles in noted publications, such as the *Washington Post*, *Salon*, the *Los Angeles Daily News*, *Huffington Post*, *Gawker*, and *Newsweek*. She starred on the NBC show, *The Filter with Fred Roggin*, and is currently a political pundit on BBC News. Laws has appeared on CNN,

Nightline, Fox News, MSNBC, *The Oprah Winfrey Show*, *The Late Show*, and *Larry King Live*, and has been the subject of articles in the *New York Times*, the *San Francisco Chronicle*, the *New York Post*, the *Guardian*, and the *New Yorker*, to name a few. She was a Los Angeles politician for eight years and has worked with the FBI. Laws penned the award-winning memoir, *Rebel in High Heels*, and was voted one of the "thirty fiercest women in the world" by Buzzfeed. She has a doctorate in social ethics from the University of Southern California, as well as two master's degrees (social ethics and professional writing) and two bachelor's degrees (philosophy and theater). She completed post-doctoral work at Oxford University, England. Laws is a well-known anti-revenge porn activist and animal advocate, and lives in Los Angeles with her husband, her three rescue dogs, and her four rescue chickens.

Twitter: @CharlotteLaws
Facebook: https://www.facebook.com/charlottelawsfans/
Websites: www.CharlotteLaws.com and www.
DevilintheBasement.com

Appendix III:

WHY THE NONFICTION NOVEL

Borders tend to be lawless, bumpy, and chaotic. They can be lonely, unnerving, and peppered with menacing "No trespassing" signs. Those who venture into these rough and uncertain territories do so at their own peril, risking ridicule, emotional lacerations, and failure. The guardians of the status quo police the boundaries with rigor. They lie in wait with a firing squad of questions to which there are rarely satisfactory answers. They are masters of suspicion and push back, and they do not look kindly on intruders.

This book is an intruder.

Devil in the Basement is a "nonfiction novel,"[2] which means it resides on the border. It falls into the no man's land of the publishing world. It wears the

---

2 The "nonfiction novel" is sometimes called "creative nonfiction."

scarlet letter. The "nonfiction novel" is part-fiction and part-fact, or what some people call "faction." It is a mythical creature like Pegasus with the torso of a white stallion and the wings of a dove. It embraces dissonance. It is a string of flowers woven into a maiden's hair or the merger of cookies with cream. It is infinity latching onto zero, for they are better together. The "nonfiction novel" is a brew, a union, an intriguing mélange, a blending of disparate parts.

Literary gatekeepers are disillusioned with this genre.

Some say the disillusionment occurred not long after Truman Capote released his best-selling "nonfiction novel," *In Cold Blood*.[3] Of course, being brash was easier for Capote. He had the clout to be disobedient. He had the clout to stare down naysayers. He had the clout to venture into forbidden terrain and to defy tradition. Capote not only mixed fact with fiction, but he made another bold move: he told his tale from three perspectives, rather than the more customary one.

Devil in the Basement likewise adopts the strategy of multiple viewpoints (and multiple voices). This allows the reader to absorb the story through a variety of characters: the hero and the villain, the aristocratic bearcat and the shifty detective, the Klansman and the mobster's moll. A nonfiction book with a single voice cannot dig down into the gut of a drama and unearth a full range of emotions, a circumference of grit. Instead, it tends to rake over the surface in a dry, calculated, and technical way. It ignores the cauldron that lurks beneath

---

3 Other popular "nonfiction novels" include: *The Armies of the Night* and *Executioner's Song* by Norman Mailer, *Rocket Boys* by Homer H. Hickman, Jr., *A Civil Action* by Jonathan Harr, *Hell's Angels* by Hunter S. Thompson, *Dispatches* by Michael Herr, *In the Time of Butterflies* by Julia Alvarez, *The Electric Kool-Aid Acid Test* by Tom Wolfe, *Hiroshima* by John Hersey, *Schindler's List* by Thomas Keneally, and *The Daughter of Time* by Josephine Tey.

the tearful outbursts, forced smiles, cunning eyes, impassioned embraces, and murderous rampages.

Truth requires a nod to motivations and feelings, even when there are question marks.

An artist who wants to capture reality does not shove some paint palettes under the rug because the exact shade of a blouse is unknown. She selects a hue of blue, for example, that she feels is close, is possible, that enhances the portrait as a whole. The blue—even if the color is a guess—adds to the big picture and is more realistic than leaving the blouse colorless in the first place.

This is also true for a literary work. Although it seems paradoxical, a "true story" is less "true" without at least some focus on the feelings and intent behind actions, even when these variables are unknown. An author may need to lean on conjecture, on hypothesis, on selective invention for the sake of the whole. She must choose bold colors, for to do otherwise would be to write in black and white, to depict a world that is not tangible, full-bodied, or real.

Devil in the Basement strives to create a colorful world while staying true to details regarding the devil-worship rituals, bomb blasts, racist encounters, and murders of 1948. It does not profess to be linguistically accurate to the time period or omniscient about every conversation that happened decades ago. It simply takes evidence—based on interviews, newspaper reports, and historical documents—and then puts a dab here and a gloss there. In the end, it hopes to be breathless, to blossom into a kaleidoscope of drama, to depict a world that is running toward disaster.

It is much like a Hollywood film.

Hollywood produces "movies based on true events"— a category that is not deemed a curiosity, an interloper, or a freak on the fringe. This genre is not an outsider to be shunned, ignored, or relegated to the border, but rather an artform to be embraced, applauded, and revered. It dwells on a pedestal called "Inspiration."

The "movie based on true events" is the silver screen's equivalent to the "nonfiction novel." Feeling is merged with fact. The soft is folded into the hard. Silk is woven into coarse and durable burlap. Scenes and characters are sometimes reimagined so as to reinforce a theme or to elevate the drama. Gaps in the true tale are filled with the fabric of intensity. The end result—or the goal, at least—is an emotional masterpiece that conveys the impact of a shocking crime, a memorable relationship, or a historic event. The knowable and the unknowable sail the ocean together with hopes of gaining insights into human behavior, relationships, life, and the nature of reality.

"Fact" already wades into fictional waters, albeit in the dead of night.

"Pure" nonfiction does not depict pure truth, despite beliefs to the contrary. In other words, this genre is not wholly trustworthy. Authors may unknowingly patch the holes of their "true tales" with the spackle of hope or the veneer of fabrication. This is because facts often come from recollection—the author's own (as in a memoir or autobiography) and the recall of others (as in interviews for biographies and other narrative works). And recollection is notoriously flawed.

Not only are memories faulty, but they are subjective and often infused with a positive spin because it can be painful to recall the unpleasant. Memories are mythmakers and sanddancers, shifting erratically with changes in perspective, interpretation, and meaning. Science affirms this idea; studies show that the witnesses of crimes and major events remember vividly and confidently, but also inaccurately.

Nonfiction's lack of reliability lends respectability to the "nonfiction novel."

Devil in the Basement aims to be respectable while cavorting as a dissident. It aims to reveal truth while painting with vibrant hues. It aims to extract "facts" from both the head and the heart, like a beach coaxing sand dollars away from the sea. It aims to morph into character after character in search of the profound, the stirring, and the authentic. And, all the while, it understands that "truth" is a phantom, a flickering light, a fairy floating in a cloud, and that the reader is the interpreter of this "truth," as well as the final arbiter of all things literary.

Thanks for joining *Devil in the Basement* at the border for some rousing rebellion.

Glossary

Ale, Alfio and Amedo – Jal's childhood friends
Arnie – member of the satanic cult
Barney brothers – guys with a moonshine network
Benito – cop, a snitch
Bessie Yost – Ernie's first wife
Bill (or Billy) Giacalone – Detroit mobster, Rose's boyfriend
Butch – the roundhouse foreman, Jal's supervisor at work
Carlo – young Italian boy who did odd jobs around town
Chester Morris – Ginger's father
Chief Austin – police chief
Mr. Ray Clark – Klansman
Daisy – Ginger's dress
Mr. Deveny – building owner
Don – police detective
Ella or Ella May – Ernie's doll
Ernie Yost – mechanical expert at the coal mine, married to
Bessie and then to Nellie
Eugene – member of the satanic cult
Faire Morris – Ginger's mother
Fido – Tucker and Ginger's dog
Frank Ganges– police detective

Ginger Morris/Moroose – Tucker's wife

Herb Sloane – devil-worshiper and head of first Satanic church

Herbie - Jal's friend at work

Irene – Nellie's sister

Jal Moroose/Amoruso – Tucker's younger brother

Jimmy Dee – clerk and part owner of the general store

Joe - mobster

June – Black woman who lived across street from Ginger and Tucker

Larry Levers – owner of the pool hall

Laura Smith – Rose's friend

Margaret Moroose – Tucker and Jal's mother

Matilda – Ginger's waitress friend

Mildred - Mr. Olden's secretary

Nellie Yost – Ernie's second wife

Mrs. Neubaum – the town gossip, lived across the street from Ernie

Nick – Tucker and Jal's father, no longer alive

Mr. Olden - landlord

Otis Jones – Ernie's friend, devil-worshiper

Pete Palin – Tucker's racist neighbor

Philip Moroose – oldest child in Moroose family, half-brother to his siblings

Roy Palin – Pete's racist fifteen-year-old son

Rose Moroose – Moroose sibling, wild flapper type who later dated Bill

Rudy – police station supervisor

Sam Perkins – supervisor at the coal mine

Salvatore – Jal's childhood friend

Sharon – Tucker and Ginger's oldest daughter

Sheila – Tucker and Ginger's daughter

Shirley – Tucker and Ginger's daughter

Thomas - mobster

Tony G. – cop who is loyal to Margaret and the Moroose family
Tucker Moroose / Amoruso – son of Margaret, favorite son
Tutu – Ernie's dog
Vince - mobster
Vivian Yost – Ernie's oldest daughter
Wanda Corley – Tucker's secretary
Will Kleeman – Ernie's next-door neighbor
Worley Powell – lawyer